Also by Richard Kalich

The Zoo

Praise for Richard Kalich

"Richard Kalich is a successful novelist, one who has succeeded in consistently producing perplexing fictions that fail to categorize themselves and escape the warping influence of authorial intent."
Christopher Leise, *Electronic Book Review*

"He's after what it means to be profoundly out of step with one's culture yet still unwilling to let go of the American dream."
Brian Evenson

"Kalich represents the best in contemporary fiction. He has every chance to become - why not? - a living classicalauthor."
Hooligan Literary Magazine, Moscow

"Speaks with a singular honesty, power and eloquence about our spiritually diminished modern world."
Mid American Review

Praise for *The Nihilesthete*

"One of the most powerfully written books of the decade."
San Francisco Chronicle

"A brilliant, hammer-hitting, lights-out novel."
Los Angeles Times

"A shocking, chilling fable."
Seattle Times

"A tour de force... equals the best work of playwright Sam Shepard."
Columbus Post-Dispatch

"A great black comedy... The names Swift and Kafka are not too lofty to mention here."
Sunday Oklahoman

"As important and original a novel to have been written by an American author in a generation."
Mid-American Review

"A major American writer."
Carlin Romano, *Philadelphia Inquirer*

Praise for *Penthouse F*

"This is an important work that deserves to be read by everyone interested in serious fiction."
Marc Lowe, *The Review of Contemporary Fiction*

"[*Penthouse F*] is akin to the best work of Paul Auster in terms of its readability without sacrificing its intelligence of experiment [...] Kalich delivers a fresh, relevant, and enticingly readable work of metafiction."
American Book Review

"Thrilling and confusing in equal measure, *Penthouse F* is an important book that dismantles the reader, leaving you in fragmented bits and pieces like the barbed clips that make up the novel's structure."
Colin Herd, *3:00AM magazine*

"Ghosts haunt this book from first page to last: Dostoevsky, Mallarmé , Kafka, Mann, Camus, Pessoa, Gombrowicz – and, oh yes, most perniciously of all, "Kalich." For he is a man who tortures himself both with the novels he has written and with those he has not. Let us forgive him even if he will not forgive

himself, recognizing as we do the one truth of this tale that seems to be beyond doubt: 'It was all in his head like everything else about him.'"
Warren Motte, *World Literature Today*

"A marvelous book. It manages to do in a short novel what the great postmodernists like Coover and Barth take five or six hundred pages to do."
Brian Evenson

"If one of the great European intransigents of the last century – say, Franz Kafka or Georges Bataille or Witold Gombrowicz – were around to write a novel about our era of reality TV and the precession of simulacra, the era of Big Brother and The Real World, what would it look like? Well, it might look like Richard Kalich's *Penthouse F.*"
Brian McHale

"In the strange, sometimes frank ways that Robbe-Grillet and Cooper and Acker approach a kind of lurking moral presence in their work, Kalich too creates something somehow both spiritually clouded and passively demanding: what is going on here, in this business of words, and people? The answer, perhaps both political and existential, whether you agree with one side or the other, operates in the way texts I most often enjoy to get wrapped up in invoke: a door that once opened, is opened, and you can't get it all the way back shut, try how you must. This is a book, a body of work, an author, deserving a new unearthing eye."
Blake Butler, *HTML Giant*

Praise for *Charlie P*

"*Charlie P* is energetic, delightfully sardonic, dark without being oppressive, playful and very readable. Richard Kalich

has hit a voice that commands attention and allows the reader to endlessly and wittily process cultural hyperbole and inflated newspeak. Charlie P is the urban everyman, the self-regarding and coreless creature of our times. Kalich has captured him through endless reflections down the tunnel of the facing mirrors. One reads and reads and smiles. *Charlie P* captures the note of our late modern times."
Sven Birkerts

"With his continuous comic exaggeration, Kalich is able to describe, highly uniquely, the overwhelming, vertiginous, risky sensation of being alive."
American Book Review

"Like most good comic novelists, Kalich is adept at teetering on the precipice wherein he might decide to dilute the fun with the grim, creating that suspense where things might get really bad at any moment."
Rain Taxi Review of Books

"[Kalich is] after what it means to be profoundly out of step with one's culture yet still unwilling to let go of the American dream. And this tension between dream and reality makes *Charlie P* a deliciously painful book."
Bookforum

"I would rather that the familiar be embraced and the novel resonate beyond itself and intone the spheres of Plato and Beckett. *Charlie P* resonates."
Review of Contemporary Fiction

Central Park West Trilogy

The Nihilesthete

Penthouse F

Charlie P

RICHARD KALICH

BETIMES BOOKS

The *Nihilesthete* was first published in the United States of America by The
Permanent Press 1987
Charlie P was first published in the United States of America by
Green Integer 2005
Penthouse F was first published in the United States of America by
Green Integer 2010

Central Park West Trilogy

This edition with three works in one volume published by agreement with
Richard Kalich by Betimes Books 2014

Cover image © Bernard Piga

Cover design by JT Lindroos

ISBN 13: 978-0-9926552-7-3

CONTENTS

Central Park West Trilogy is destined to become a cult classic, pressed into the hands of friends with a promise, "You've never read anything like this before."

To read Richard Kalich is to be plunged into an uncompromising world, to be exposed to dark deeds and strange thoughts, to be challenged.

The novels collected here tug at our concepts of civility, identity, truth and art. They are postmodern fables; dark, shocking, funny, astute, and compulsively readable.

They share a ferocious energy and break down standard notions of plot and character to form a body of work that is distinctive.

They are unsettling books, relentless in their demands on the reader – who must pay attention, question the narrator, and stare unflinching at the nightmarish visions unfolding before him or her. The works are written to provoke; the reader may want to recoil and turn away, and yet find themselves caught up in the galloping pace of the plot.

But there is also room for laughter, to find humour in the outlandish adventures of Charlie P in particular. Unsurprisingly, the humour is often a perverse, provocative kind. Kalich doesn't want his readers getting too comfortable. As he would surely say, what is the value of a book that doesn't question cosy notions of what it is to be human, to be civilised, to be cultured?

Instead of answers, we are given shattered fragments, from which we must try to piece together the whole. Kalich experiments with narrative form and characters, pulling us into a murky place where we are left to wonder: what is the difference between Kalich the author, Kalich the character and Kalich the man? Can we ever know what is going on inside the head of another human being?

The Publisher

The Nihilesthete

RICHARD KALICH

For my brother, Robert Kalich

Case Record of
Robert Haberman, Caseworker

APOLOGIA

I write these notes for what they are worth . . . for me. Under no circumstances, in any shape, manner or form, were they intended . . . for you. They were written and kept solely for the singular joy I received from them; and—the most important reason—for what they added to my original experience and thought.

In no way should they be considered true indicia of what they depict. For what they depict is me. My life's blood is the ink . . . these pages merely frame, place and perhaps help circulate the words. If, perchance, these pages do fall into your hands, please do not be so quick to judge. Not my words, MY LIFE! That is the important thing. The rest, these futile scribblings, they are mere artifice. Despite all my efforts, it would be folly to think I could ever capture the fecundity of my moods with words.

It's time I changed my life again . . . but HOW!?!

Something interesting happened to me today. As I was walking home from the subway after work, I stopped to watch an artist draw a picture of Christ on the sidewalk in front of the Maine Monument. There was a crowd surrounding the artist, but one area was left open purposefully. This visual corridor was to accommodate a limbless figure in a wheelchair who was also watching the event. It wasn't long before the wheelchair-bound figure came to dominate my attention.

It was immediately evident that he was some sort of retard, a freak of the kind I had seen just a few nights earlier on a TV expose program. He certainly didn't have the slightest idea what was going on around him. I could tell this by the fact that he didn't adjust himself in any way to the dogs, pigeons, squirrels, even the kids romping about. One child nearly landed in his lap (if he had a lap) when his Frisbee knocked into the retard's chest. Nothing seemed to disturb him or penetrate his consciousness. Except The Artist and her Drawing!

When I accidentally moved into his path just before leaving, I could swear I noticed a pained expression come over his face, or a grimace of defiance. And also, I think—I couldn't be sure at the time—I heard him make a mewing sound like a cat's cry.

As I continued on home I persuaded myself it was just an idiot's reaction and was prepared to forget it. I had even begun to warm my supper up and was, as usual, watching the 6 o'clock news, when I realized I couldn't. The image of the retard's face kept flickering before my eyes, intruding itself on the TV screen. And so despite my weariness, and customary unbending attitude to changing my regimen, I decided to return to the Maine Monument. While getting dressed and walking there, I remember being unable to shake the feeling of being a criminal returning to the scene of the crime.

As fate would have it, the retard was still there when I arrived. The crowd had dispersed, and the artist had just finished collecting the last of her art supplies and was now busily engaged in tallying up her earnings for the day. I waited patiently for her to finish and strode briskly up to her sketch at the precise moment she was taking her leave. Strangely, or maybe not so strangely, the retard lapsed into silence the second he saw me. No more mewing sounds came from his direction. And though I gave every appearance of doing no more than admiring the artist's drawing, even positioning myself in such a way so as not to interfere with his line of vision, in reality I never took my eyes off the freak.

Likewise, I could feel his boring into me.

Almost immediately I came upon a plan of action. Why or what motivated me I can't really say. Call it premonition . . . some blind instinct . . . but in my own way I knew what I was doing. I stepped on the drawing. As it was done in chalk,

I was fully cognizant of the effect my shoe would have on the creation. AND SO WAS HE!!! It was just as I expected—the moment the sole of my shoe touched the sketch, the same pained expression appeared on the retard's face. And he made the same mewing sound. It was evident he was RESPOND-ING! We were like two implacable enemies on opposite sides of the arena, each making ready to do battle over his most prized and precious turf. Each recognizing the other for what he was. I was about to go over to the man and take a closer look when a woman emerged as if from nowhere and whisked him away. By the time I regrouped from my moment's hesitation, they were gone.

That evening I tossed and turned in my sleep.
Needless to say something was brewing inside me.
I promised myself I would try again the next day.

He was not there the next day nor the next day nor the next. I am in the doldrums. I have nothing but my job and my apartment. They are not enough. I go on looking.

NEW YORK MEDICAL CENTER
Institute of Rehabilitation Medicine
800 East 34th Street, New York, N.Y.
Area (212) 679-0000
Cable Address: NYU MEDIC

<table>
<tr><td></td><td>Nov. 28, 1985</td></tr>
<tr><td>Director, Dept. of Social Services</td><td>RE: BRODSKI</td></tr>
<tr><td>Dept. 29</td><td>d.o.b.</td></tr>
<tr><td>765 East 126th St.</td><td>3/18/61</td></tr>
<tr><td>New York, New York</td><td>IPM Chart</td></tr>
<tr><td></td><td>#29205</td></tr>
</table>

Dear Sir:

We are referring the case of BRODSKI, (no known first name), a
24 year-old single unattached male, to your agency for possible service. Brodski has been cared for all his life by Mrs. Maria Rivera, a
woman who refers to herself as his mother. Actually she is not blood

related but only assumed responsibility when his actual mother (unknown) abandoned him at birth. Mrs. Rivera is 68 years of age and her health is deteriorating rapidly. She suffers from bursitis, arthritis, and C.V.A. Still, she is reluctant to have anyone but herself care for him and only because of his recent hospitalization has this case been brought to our attention. If it were up to Mrs. Rivera, Brodski would remain in her care and no outside help would be requested from any agencies. It must be admitted that she has done an excellent job. When born, Brodski's life span was short and only through extraordinary mothering care has he been able to reach his present age. That is our medical staff's opinion.

The family resides in a two-room apartment with self-service elevator which gives easy access for his wheelchair.

Mrs. Rivera has been in receipt of social security since Brodski's birth and he receives SSI.

Brodski is a low grade idiot; additionally born with a rare condition: Cri du Chat syndrome. (This diagnosis is inexact or partial; our medical staff is still unclear about some aspects of his disease.) He has vestigial arms and legs. At birth he had a high-pitched, unnerving cry, closely resembling the cry of a cat, therefore the diagnosis. He is totally dependent in self-care activities. He should be turned at least twice during the night to prevent skin breakdown. He is in adult diapers and is transported by wheel chair. We feel placement in a facility would bring about a rapid death. He now only responds to one person, Maria Rivera, but for his own good must be made receptive to others. We have explained this necessity to Mrs. Rivera. However, as suggested, she is a proud woman and fretful of having anyone come into her home and upset the relationship she has with her stepson. Understandably, she is overly protective. Whatever your agency decides, if possible, we would recommend that Mrs. Rivera remain with Brodski and continue to assume those responsibilities that her health permits.

It should be reiterated that it is just Mrs. Rivera's attitude regarding outside help that remains this case's greatest problem. Because of this, all outside agencies over the years have refused to get involved and the case has remained isolated. However, perhaps now, because of her own increasing years and the infirmities of age, as well as Brodksi's recent need for hospitalization, she might be more receptive to outside help. At least I hope so. In any case your agency should handle the matter most discreetly no matter what course of action you take.

There are no relatives, friends; no one to contact in case of emergency.

Our request is that you go in and do what you can, perhaps a part-time Home Attendant at first. In the meantime, Brodski will continue to receive Home Care visits from this hospital. Please let us know of your findings and assessment of the case as soon as possible.

We thank you kindly for your cooperation. If further information is needed, please do not hesitate to call me at 679-0000, extension 2372.

Sincerely Yours,

Thea Goldstein
Senior Social Worker

Gerald Umano, MD
Director, Out Patient Services

GU: ime

It's him! It's him! Who else can it be? "Lowgrade idiot, limbless . . . Cri du Chat." What luck. What coincidence. For two weeks now I've hunted all over for him in vain and now he shows up on my desk. What could be better? Though everything in me pines to rush out to him at once, I shall wait. The waiting will do me good. It will calm my anticipation and heighten it at the same time. Yes. Before visiting him I shall first have a good long lunch.

Meanwhile, I will perform my office duties as usual. Especially . . . as usual.

Ahhhh, for the first time in God knows how long, I feel good. Good! Lunch will be delectable. I shall savor every morsel.

I did not go into his room. I refused to see him. Though refused is too strong a word. Naturally I made proper apologies to "Mother." I explained that it was already late, that I was in a rush, having many more field visits scheduled for the afternoon. That tomorrow would be soon enough for meeting him. Today I merely wanted to meet her. To introduce myself. My agency's services.

What was that, Mother? You don't need services. Just more money. You can hardly pay the rent with the income you now have. Food prices are up and going even higher. No, no, it's not a joking matter. But why do you laugh so, then? A nervous giggle? And the way your ears perked when I mentioned that you could be getting paid for being his Home Attendant. I shall never forget that look. It's recorded indelibly, like everything else.

But enough. To be sure, I said I've intruded enough for one day. I must be off.

If only she knew how much I mean to intrude.

And, lo and behold, tomorrow is Saturday. It's not a working day. I have the entire weekend to plan my approach. Did the Almighty need more when He created the world?

For the first time in the longest, my weekend will be full.

Nothing is more difficult than the weekend. Television can take us so far, the telephone never rings, and one can manage just so many trips to the refrigerator. It is not being alone but being with ourselves that is the killer. An entire metaphysic of distraction has evolved to stave off this terminal disease. We jog, we eat, we watch television, we read the tabloids, we fornicate, we go to the movies, opera, bars, ballet, we rush to and fro, hither and yon, to the neighbors, the beaches, boutiques, discos, friends, brunch, bar b-que, the window, anything . . . just to get away from ourselves. By the time Monday morning comes around, and the grunts and groans of pleasure have subsided, though no one would ever admit it ("Yes, Harriet, I had a wonderful weekend"), we are truly grateful to return to our daily hells. Anything is better than being with ourselves.

But this weekend was different. I had Brodski. We were as close as two lovers pawing each other through the night, sweat pouring profusely from our maddening embrace. For forty-eight hours I was with you, my sweet. I was as content as a scientist peering through his microscope. Indeed I am developing my own special kind of myopia. Brodski is on my slide. He is my cubic unit of measurement. Though I shall give him wings, he shall never fly. Poor thing, he shall never fly.

What are his weaknesses? More importantly, what are his strengths? His passions? Is he capable of perception? Recognition? Of forming a bond? Of extending trust? Of having a r-e-l-a-t-i-o-n-s-h-i-p? If not, can he be made to do so? Of course he can. And I will make him. This idiot who responded to the artist's drawing and to nothing else . . . but me. This idiot . . . that look . . . that gesture of defiance. Yes. There is life here. A glimmer. Something to work with. To harvest and bear fruit.

Oh, my work is cut out for me. It won't be easy. It never is. But it shall be done. There is none better at it than I.

I visited my pending case first thing Monday morning. My stratagem was simple: to catch the old lady off guard. Friday I left early, exhibiting, despite my apologies, just the slightest hint of indifference. It wasn't. When I declined my opportunity for seeing Brodski, I knew what I was doing. I always know what I am doing. This morning I am all eyes and ears. Everything about him is of interest to me. I am deeply concerned. Nothing is irrelevant or takes too long to listen to. I want to see all, learn all, know all. The old lady doesn't know what to make of me. She is startled, baffled, confused. She is just where I want her. By being unsettled, she fixes her idea of me all the more firmly. In narrowing her perception of me, she opens me up. She believes anything is possible of me. What a strange man, she giggles to herself. Nothing could be better. Strange man, laughter. This is a good place to start . . . a relationship.

When I perused Mother's room Friday I was not impressed. All the usual welfare recipent's accoutrements were there—a hodgepodge of Woolworth's, Salvation Army junk stores, neighborhood furniture stores (selling everything on credit) and family memorabilia. Start with the prerequisite TV set (16 inches) and the mandatory photos of the Kennedy's and Martin Luther King atop the mantel. Then another photo in grainy brownwhite standing in arrears. Every item seen a thousand times in a thousand households on a thousand field visits by this caseworker. Plastic covers on the sofa and chair, smoked mirrors, furniture simulating some original design "downtown." And lest I forget: the obligatory crucifix and reassuring pious declarations ("In this house God dwells") and other hanging atrocities preaching the gospel of universal love. And a bureau with gilt-edged glass doors behind which huddled a bunched-up community of bric-a-brac, each relic perpetuating some ancient family tale. In sum, everything cheap, tasteless, functional, without style or elegance—unless, of course, you think the maxim "Cleanliness is next to godliness" still holds some semblance of value in today's world. Needless to say, I don't, but she does. Mother does. Good. Men like me thrive on simple souls like her. It makes our job easier.

When I arrived; Brodski was in the bath. Mother was giving her son his daily baptism. "Wonderful. Don't let me interrupt you," I said, making sure to avoid her dripping hand. "Go right on with what you're doing, Mrs. Rivera. I'll only take a peek. No, not at Brodski. At his room. After all, he still has some rights, doesn't he? Modesty is fundamental to all human beings, is it not? And he is human, isn't he? Even if he is a . . . Yes, yes. I'll wait till you bring him out all fresh and clean. Puffed up and crinkly pink like freshly starched linen.

No one wants to be seen in soiled clothes, you know. Least of all a man without arms and legs."

Mother smiles tenuously and continues about her business. Though seemingly happy and content, she doesn't know what to make of me. Or does she? When we are utterly confused, only the extreme reactions are possible. Either we set up massive security blocks or we give in altogether. The Jews in concentration camps proved that, among other things. Auschwitz was the breeding ground of mind-boggling feats of heroism and survival, and of succumbing to fate without so much as a whimper. Personally I prefer a good battle. There's no real victory without it.

Brodski's room: It couldn't have been more interesting. I must admit I was caught completely unawares. In my wildest dreams I couldn't have imagined this paragon of style, proportion, form, taste, loveliness. Everything as it should be (or nearly). Brick walls, simulated antiques, fine reproductions of old paintings wonderfully selected, correctly placed, handsomely framed. Decorum, taste, subtlety, all are here. I don't know how to explain the contrast to Mother's room. After all, they live under the same roof, have the same decorator, have they not? But that's it. They don't! It's the only explanation possible. Brodski has decorated his own room. Somehow he has managed this. But how? I must find out. That among other things.

Before leaving his room I roll up his bamboo shade and take a quick look outside. Just as I suspected. The little devil saved the best view for himself. A marvelous vista. I'll wager that without having to be propped up one extra inch he can see across the river to Queens. Before returning to Mother's room to await Brodski, I snap the shade exactly back to place.

I seat myself on the old woman's sofa. At one time it might have served as a love seat, I think to myself. All in me is taut and tense. I am filled with the only excitement I know. I await Brodski.

How shall I appear? What should I say? All kinds of possibilities are open to me. Some have already been worked out, tested in earlier experiences. I am not unused to such things. Still, each time is different. Each time is new. The unknown is always there. The unpredictable. That is the challenge. The reason I am here.

Mother enters cradling her son in her arms. He is in some kind of homemade crib or casket, swathed in adult diapers. My first impression is of Pharoh's daughter carrying Moses from the river bed. Indeed, he is her Moses.

Brodski's head is small, maybe half that of a normal man, or a third, it's hard to say. Conical in shape. His features are either not there or swollen and distended from where they should be. Nothing is as it should be. At least not according to normal expectations. His ears are low set, not precisely even or paralleling each other. His mouth is that of a tiny bird. His nose is full, fleshy and much too large; it looks as if it was pressed on his face by a giant hand. His eyes are . . . his eyes are dead. They do not see. There is nothing behind them. Or at least so it seems to me . . . now. His hair line, as his chin, recedes. In fact, there is no chin. Just a little point protruding from his face. Certainly there is nothing you could describe as a jaw. His neck is also missing—rotund masses of skin webbing appear in its place. Altogether his face lacks harmony, the features are dissonant. Someone or something just threw them together for the fun of it. And he missed. But did he? Who's to say?

My first reaction is one of extreme joy and at the same time disappointment. Yes, disappointment. Because he does not recognize me. But then, he does not perceive me. He does not perceive anything. He is still too happy savoring the afterglow of his good warm bath. His little libidinal pleasures. "It always takes him a few minutes to get back to normal after a bath, Mr. Haberman," Mother says. "He loves it when I bathe him. The warm water, the sponge, the suds."

"And when you touch him, Mother?" I querry straight-faced.

Again she is caught off guard and smiles embarrassedly.

I register each word and reaction well. They will serve me in good stead later on. One never knows enough, I say to myself. That is a maxim of mine. (One of many).

The first sound I hear from Brodski is the familiar cat's cry I heard at the park in front of the Maine Monument and have not been able to forget. His mewing does not surprise me now. I respond to it by offering up my warmest smile and laying hands on him. After this gesture, Mother breaks free from her reticence and invites me to join her for coffee. I agree, making sure first to fondle her son once more. Mother places Brodski gently, ever so gently, in his bed. A sort of hospital bed cut to crib's size. And I notice his size. For the first time I take measure of him. He is diminutive. I could carry him with one arm. Despite the absence of limbs, I realize now I had expected more. But there isn't more. This shrunken and misshapen torso is all there is. Not much . . . but it will have to do. Of course one can never measure a man by his size. Never will this aphorism prove truer than with Brodski.

Over steaming hot coffee I tell Mrs. Rivera how I can help improve her financial situation. How she is entitled to SSI benefits to supplement her meager social security income, and also how I can help initiate an application for food stamps. "With SSI supplementing your income, Mother dear, and food stamps, you'll be more than able to pay your rent. You'll be able to live in absolute luxury."

Mother smiles gratefully. She clasps my hand. It is evident that she is a warm, loving person. A humanist from an earlier age. And I have won her trust. Despite any previous report from the hospital it is easy with these types. I have never lost one yet.

I turn my attention to another subject. My inquiries concern her son's room. If I can learn no more than this, this morning, my day will be complete. It is. Everything falls into place. It could not be better. In almost conspiratorial tones Mother tells me how they have worked out their own special system of communication. Not based on words, but smiles and mewing sounds and gestures. The language is one of contortion and dissonance. Each time Brodski contorts his face or smiles in his special way, the old lady knows what he is thinking. How he is reacting. He has a thousand faces, she says with maternal pride. Thus she was able to create his room. Piece by piece, trial and error, each tidbit, momento, brick in place, is really Brodski's by design. The result of an enigmatic smile or a mewing sound only she could decipher. "It wasn't easy," she says. "Sometimes he can become very difficult. He's . . . how you say . . . a perfectionist. Everything has to be exactly right, otherwise he won't permit it. He's definitely a tyrant, my little one." I smile as I think to myself: Were Pharoh's pyramids built so differently? If only I know this much about him, it is enough. For one day's work, it is enough.

"I must be going," I say. "I have many things to do. Besides, perhaps I have already overstayed my welcome," I add demurely, searching the old lady's gaze for a reaction. It is just as I expected. "No, no," she exclaims anxiously. "Please stay. Here, have another coffee and some cake."

"Oh, well, just one more peek at Brodski then." I tiptoe into his room. Why tiptoe? To show concern, of course. Brodski lies in bed, a quaint infantile pout on his lips, his eyes directed towards mine. Whether he can see me or not is a matter of conjecture. I walk toward the window and pull the shade. Sunlight infiltrates the room. Brodski lets out a soft purring sound. He smiles. He can . . . he can see me. Or was he just responding to the light? Food for thought, but a good place to take my departure. Either way I leave with a good impression. The old lady will tell him of me if he doesn't already know.

Back at the office my Supervisor asks me about the pending case. What am I going to do with it? Accept or NA. (Not accept)? "Why, accept, of course, Mrs. Knox. Protective services. Both Mrs. Rivera and the cri du chat need all the help we can give them. Maybe later we'll put in a part-time Home Attendant. Right now the old woman's not ready for it. She'd never let a stranger come into her home. I think its enough for now if we just keep an eye on them."

Mrs. Knox and I have worked together for fifteen years, ever since I was first assigned to the Harlem Center. Not once has she called me by my first name. It is always "Mr. Haberman." I am, of course, no exception. She is that way with everyone. Her excessively formal approach is not that unusual at the Department. It blends in with the office decor. Anonymous, drab, impersonal, the same gray office furniture you find from Harlem to Wall Street. Sometimes when I speak to her I call her "Marilyn Knox" in an aggressively facetious tone. Not once in fifteen years have I ever called her just "Marilyn," though. Our mode of communication is as fixed and limited as Brodski's. Maybe more so, I think. Maybe more so.

While scribbling these notes about my Supervisor I am reminded of an incident that happened some thirty-three years ago. I had just graduated from college and started working for the Department at a downtown office. Even then, after only a few months on the job, I knew I hated it. And every day if I could manage it I would rush to the field. I thought I had someplace to go in those days. Youth always has someplace to go—even if it's only to dream. I even had some vague notion of getting involved in one way or another with the arts. As luck would have it, Mr. Burke, a civil service lifer, was returning to the office from lunch at the exact moment I was making my exit. And we bumped into each other accidently—he coming in, I going out of the elevator. Some words were exchanged, leading to more words. And then, I shall never forget his face—a strange mixture of undisguised contempt, hostility and irony—when he said, "If you're not out of here by thirty, you'll never get out. You're stuck here all your life."

"That will never happen to me," I parried smartly.

"You want to bet?" came his quick retort.

"I'll bet my life on it," I said just as quickly.

When I reached forty,—I not only remembered the wager I had made, I realized I had lost it.

FORTY YEARS OLD! The year of my turnaround. What was I like at forty? I can hardly recall.

I think the most important thing about me then was that all the normal human responses had left me. Friendship, for example, held no further promise. I had gone as far as I could with it. There were only so many conversations one could have in a lifetime, and I had had them all. Intellect, too, I had stretched to its limits. I knew how far it had taken me. Not very. Work—I won't go into that now. And love. Ahh yes, L-O-V-E. And all its accoutrements . . . Passion, lust, sex . . . that alone could save me. Hardly. I had been there once, but now it was nothing more than a diversion, an exercise. No, not even that. More like a repeat performance. One I had tired of and bought my last ticket for long ago. Whenever I pictured two people making love (and that was rare), it always struck me as something strange. It reminded me of one of those modern metallic sculptures with pieces scrambled together in interlocking fusion. But what brought people together in the first place? And what metallic paste or glue could hold them together and make them stick? . . . I didn't know.

People, in short, had nothing to offer me. I couldn't go anywhere without being vexed by them. If they came too close to me, I would virtually break out in a rash, and rather than scratch myself (which did no good anyway), I simply avoided them at every turn. Rush-hour crowds, rallies, gatherings were anathema. Invariably I would take the rear seat in a bus (which I never rode during rush hour), or seat myself in the first row of an empty movie house on the extreme left. Even a blind man tapping his stick and waiting for help was enough to prompt me to make a stealthy retreat in the opposite direction. Not because I was against helping him, but rather because the very idea of getting so close to him was repugnant to me. Similarly with elevators. I would gallop like a madman or wait thirty minutes before sharing it with a fellow passenger.

And so, alone in my apartment, sitting, standing, pacing to and fro, eating chicken, drinking tea, walking to the corner and back at regular intervals, twice for newspapers, and three times or more merely to get out, pacing up and down the lobby corridor for the mailman who never delivered anything but bills to me, watching TV, listening to the radio, going to a movie, reading a book, waiting for the telephone which never rang, taking more tea, eating more chicken, waiting for the next news report, the next weather report, the next TV program, the next radio broadcast, scanning the movie clock for the next movie to be seen, searching my library shelves for the next book to be read even before I had finished the last one, I filled up every hour of every day of my life. All of it—the sitting, watching, listening, eating, reading, waiting— done without hope, without expectations, without the slightest delusion that anything would change. As my father had gotten into the habit of saying several years before his death, "life was just so much more chicken to eat every day."

Weekends were just as bad. After leaving work Friday at noon (and cashing my check at the bank every other week), I would march straight home and stay there till Saturday night. Then, more to break up the routine than to relieve the boredom, I would head over to a neighborhood tavern where I would remain until the murky dawn, when I would reel and stagger to my apartment to sleep. When I awoke on Sunday afternoon, I was already dreading Monday morning when I would have to return to work. Monday morning: only seventeen hours away.

And then something happened. No, *IT* happened! A small incident, seemingly meaningless, I almost can't remember it. But yes, it changed my life!

It had rained all week. The black asphalt gutters were slick and gleaming. There was a cleansing fragrance in the air. I was seated in an outside cafe in Greenwich Village. People, getting out for the first time all week, sat clustered in bunches before me. The nearest table, though more than several yards away, was still within hearing distance. As was my habit, I observed without being seen: Men and women, friends, groups of threes and fours and more; people speaking and telling each other what they must have said one thousand times before. My wife, my mistress, my girlfriend. My husband, my lover, my boyfriend. Do you know of a job for me? I'd give anything for a . . . How do you differentiate between love and sex? My mother has cancer of the bladder. Really? My father had a colostomy last month. I'm thirty years old. Do you believe it? I'm thirty years old! Why does it have to be this way? So you mean there's no answer!? People repeating the same conversations as if for the first time. Each time. The miracle of humanity: forgetfulness.

And all I could do was look, listen, spy and smell the air, so clean, the black asphalt gutters slick and gleaming. I asked myself what was strange about them. Different from myself. Was it the way they looked? But they all looked the same. We all looked the same. Except for our piecemeal features, there was no difference. It was the way they were *together*. The way they spoke, forgetting themselves in conversation. I had never talked like that. *They were leaping out of themselves and landing on the other shore.* I had never taken that leap. Never landed on the other shore. Gulping down a vodka tonic, I called a young waiter over. He possessed a naive innocence mixed with insatiable hunger. From an earlier talk I had ascertained that he was an actor. From out of town. In the big city to make good. He was looking forward to the day he would become eligible for unemployment benefits and be able to devote himself full time to making the audition rounds. Now, hardly knowing why, I told him I was a producer and he was right for a part in a play I was currently developing for Broadway. His eyes opened wide. The charm of youth, the gaiety, the smile, oh, what a smile, he could captivate anybody with that smile—or so he thought. Putting on my most impressive air, I continued, "You couldn't be better. The more I look at you and hear you speak, the more certain I am. And to think, meeting you like this. Purely by chance. It must be fate. Now, let's see. Today is Friday. I'll be out of town for the weekend. Call me Monday morning. Here, take my card. Opps, forgot it. Do you have something to write on? Don't forget now . . . Monday, 9:00 a.m. sharp. By the way, what did you say your name was?"

When I arrived Monday morning at the office the phone was already ringing. It was him. Not mincing words, I told him there must be a mistake, that he had dialed the wrong number, that this was the Welfare Center, not some theatrical producer's office. Sensing that he was about to hang up, I said, "Don't be so quick to go. From what I know of you actors, you might need public assistance more than you need any starryeyed audition. They always pan out badly anyway. Especially if you're not eligible for unemployment benefits."

Again: "No. I told you already. This is a Welfare Center."

He called back four times. Each time there was a little more disappointment in his voice . . . except on the last call. When I answered the last call, all I heard was a lingering silence, followed by a clicking.

I KNEW I HAD FOUND MY WAY!!!

One month later, when by coincidence I came upon him again, this time waiting on tables at a different restaurant, I asked him, "What happened? Why didn't you call? . . . You did? You must have taken down the wrong number. What a shame. We cast the part yesterday. But. . . but you really were perfect."

After walking several blocks on my way to the bus this morning I noticed an elderly couple smiling at me. Looking down, I discovered my fly was open. I wondered why the man at least hadn't stopped to tell me. My momentary rage at the passengers in the front of the bus who wouldn't make way for me was dispelled when I realized that I had not been the slightest bit embarrassed.

It is time for reflection, to call back the troops, to reconnoiter. First impressions are important but not everything. Mostly they are terribly deceiving. We bring ourselves into them without half-realizing it. But that is not my problem. I never bring myself into anything. Besides, I am not a moralist. One quick look and here's what's wrong. Nor am I a charlatan selling saran-wrapped panaceas to the world. I have no easy answers. Snap judgements are not part of my repertory. Many a medical man has lost his patient with just such a premature diagnosis. But not I. I never lose a patient once I set my sights on him. They are too few and far between to treat so shabbily. That would be immoral. If anything, my examinations are thorough, my laboratory spotless. Perhaps I am a moralist.

This is what I have decided: I will send Mrs. Rivera a form letter advising her we have accepted Brodski's case. She will receive it tomorrow, or at the latest Wednesday. In the meantime I won't call her. Or visit.

No braggadocio intended but I have an absolute genius for w-a-i-t-i-n-g.

I was seated in a coffee shop in the Lincoln Center area this Sunday having brunch. Pancakes molten with butter and syrup and a generous portion of fruit salad on top. Four black people were sitting at the table to my left. The waitress passed a comment about one of the black people's weight when she surmised on the basis of the order that he was on a diet. The man and his three friends—another man and two women—all laughed uproariously. Evidently the waitress had hit on a sore spot of the dieting man. One of the women asked the waitress for her name. "Eloise," she answered, still bubbling over with laughter. And then a strange thing happened. All four blacks promptly introduced themselves. "Willis, James, Edna, Martha." They were so happy to enter . . . "human relations."

Are you so childlike, my darling?

Do you, too, crave Big Daddy?

Of course, the blacks weren't young. With young people today it is a whole different matter. But Brodski, considering his condition, is *OLD* at twenty-four.

Hallelujah! Mother called. Round one is mine. The most important round. It sets the tone for all the rounds to follow.

"When will we see you?" she said.

"Soon, Mother dear, soon."

She called at 3:30 in the afternoon. I was there at four. I had a choice. To respond or not to. I decided to respond at once.

I responded this way for several reasons:

First, I could hardly restrain myself any longer. It was Thursday already. And I am only human.

Second, I thought I detected an urgency in her voice. She made mention of Brodski being upset, possibly even ill. Could it have been my visit? Did he sense something? I don't know but I must find out.

Besides, last time, I disappointed her by leaving too soon. This time I shall make her happy by arriving before I'm expected. This way I keep my advantage. She (or he) beckons and I appear.

Of course, next time might be different. And there will be plenty of "next times."

Third, and most important, I bear glad tidings. A little gift. It is my way of finding out what I need to know. My special Rorschach test. I deliberated long and hard on what it should be. Finally I came upon just the right item. I am good at such things. Like all expert psychologists, I design my projective tests to catch my subjects off guard.

My little shopping spree was not without difficulties. I couldn't purchase my present ready-made at a store. I had to improvise. I had to purchase a costly art book first and cut out the print reproduction I wanted and then have it enlarged to poster size. After that was accomplished, I had it framed, a plain silver boarder, (quite expensive), and finally I had it gift wrapped. So much trouble for my little one. If only he knew: he is no trouble at all.

You should have seen his reaction. And it was genuine. I'm sure of that. Or should I say I made sure? Not only does this psychologist have his inkblots, but he has his placebo as well. Such things are mandatory in my work. Before giving Brodski his gift, I opened the other. Though it wasn't actually for him, at the time he couldn't know that. Mrs. Regina Douglas, our medical social worker, advised me what to get. She said a person suffering from his condition, a cri du chat, would most likely be attracted to the same things as an infant. Something glittering and shiny, preferably an object that moves. I purchased a shiny new egg beater for Mrs. Rivera. And waved it in front of her eyes. The old lady was absolutely gaga at my kindness. But Brodski wasn't. He showed no response.

His eyes were dead. Then I unwrapped his present. A framed poster-size print of Edvard Munch's The Scream. Within seconds his face lit up. His eyes opened wide. So wide he looked ridiculous. It was as if at this moment he was seeing the whole world. The room absolutely resounded with mewing sounds. He passed his test with flying colors.

Even Mrs. Rivera was impressed. "I have never see him respond like that," she said.

To this woman I am fast becoming a benefactor. To Brodski, a philanthropist of the arts. And really, I have no interest in the arts. In anything, "make-believe." Of all the riddles in the world, man's need for beauty baffles me most. But then, why has it preserved so long? Longer and more durable than governments, dynasties, moralities, civilizations, even religions.

Could I be wrong?

No. Never!

I have one more little thing to do. My investment, if I calculate correctly, shouldn't cost me more than a few minutes. It's my way of following up the previous day's work. Like any good researcher, I have to validate my findings.

I visited them on Friday at noon. Almost at once my investment showed a handsome dividend. Mother was feeding her child. Brodski was slurping his food—soft-boiled eggs, the yellow ooze dribbling like a melting icicle from cheek to chin. He was refusing to take another swallow when she uttered, half to herself, "He has no appetite."

I replied quite harmlessly, "What does he live on, air?"

She looked at me with solemnity and sadness, her voice giving vent to the most ancient of maternal grievances. "Not air, Mr. Haberman, but that." And she pointed to his room filled with paintings, various art objects and an old RCA windup victrola.

Immediately the blood began to course madly through my veins. I stood up from my chair and headed for the door. My last words before leaving their humble abode were, "Bon appetite."

SO BRODSKI'S AN AESTHETE! A lover of beauty. Well, well, it is just as I have surmised all along. My little ugly duckling is really a swan.

All right, little one, we shall travel to Parnassus together. On Mt. Olympus you will stand and see the Seven Wonders of the World. Did I say you will stand? My error. I will stand and upon my shoulders you will see. Just as Atlas bore the weight of the world on his shoulders, I shall bear you on mine . . . To see.

An aesthete? Yes: I have found my Road to Damascus.

From now on I pledge all my time to Brodski. Is he worthy of it? That is entirely up to me. Social Counselors tell us that we get from a relationship what we put into it. I shall put myself into Brodski. For sheer effort and single-mindedness of purpose, no one shall ever have given more.

Over the next several weeks not a day goes by that I don't visit Brodski. Always I bring him gifts. Not necessarily those you can purchase in a store. One day I might adjust a painting that is hanging lopsided or is off center by a fraction, another day I might tilt his head to make it a trifle easier for him to observe his marvelous view. All in all the household begins to take on a different feel. My own.

My greatest gift, however, is that I offer Brodski what he cannot receive from anyone else. A mirror to see himself in.

Not what he looks like, but what he is like. In every one of my acts, gestures, smiles, faces, there is only one motive. To make his room, his world, his sanctuary a little more beautiful. To make the outside correspond to what is within.

For the first day and part of the second, Brodski wouldn't let me enter his room. Mother had to stay as chaperon until I won his trust. I did not take offense at this slight. On the contrary, I would have been disappointed if he had acted otherwise. After all, what else does the little fellow have but this? For him, to as much as twitch a muscle requires a prodigious effort. He lies on one side of his torso, then, thanks to Mother's gentle nudging, he lies on the other. This room is more than his home. It is his temple, his shrine. A place for him to pray. It comprises all he has and what he is. Thus I gather all my forces. It is the first place I invade.

The thought occurs to me that in all of Brodski's household there is not the smallest space for a game room. I must make one. Indoor sports in the usual sense are not my forte. Sex has never been my game. Whatever modicum of interest I had waned years ago. But there are other indoor sports far more interesting than sex. And one doesn't even have to work up a sweat to play.

For the past few days Brodski has not taken his eyes off me when I visit. Each time I move, I bring a ray of beauty into his home. If I have not created the apartment, I have certainly brought out its best features. Thanks to me, his world finally receives the attention it deserves. It is not that I have impeccable taste or am so gifted a decorator. It is just that I know how much he needs *BEAUTY*. It is my job to accommodate myself to his need. Like a good curator who enhances the paintings in his museum by ensuring their proper placement and location, I enhance the *objets d'art* in Brodski's room. To begin with, his prints are brought into line. If I can help it, they are never off by so much as a fraction of an inch. The light, thanks to my chiarascuro lighting, shines on them perfectly. At any time of day he can see each to best advantage. Of course, I don't teach Mother the workings of the dimmer lighting system I have installed. Thus when evening comes, by the very loss of beauty, he knows I'm not there. Brodski's tiny sculptured pieces and figurines are also arranged to best advantage. In the way they face each other, where they stand, on what dresser, night table, desk, each becomes in its own way a singular work of art.

My efforts are not limited to Brodski's room, I also make my talents felt in Mother's. Why not? Beauty knows no limits. Why should Brodski's world be restricted to one room? My efforts do not go unappreciated by Mother. Though she doesn't fully comprehend why I am doing what I am doing, she approves wholeheartedly. She can see the improvement, maybe not in the aesthetic sense, but more importantly, in the way her son responds. The hideous smoked mirrors (Brodski could never bear to look at himself) go first. Next, the plastic covers. Then the horrid photos of the Kennedys and King. (She argued here, I admit). And also, those absurdly grotesque religious articles and savings. (She argued here, also). With a little effort, hiding one thing, accentuating another, even the most unattractive women can be made attractive. There is no such thing as an ugly woman. I am fast coming to the opinion that there is no such thing as a tasteless room.

Without doubt all those hours I wracked my brains studying lighting techniques were not in vain. The way Brodski never closes his eyes lately tells me that. On earlier visits I noticed that whenever he was exposed to the unsightliness of Mother's room, he would go into that vegetal stare of his. Now he doesn't.

So now he has two rooms. Thanks to me, his world has grown twice as large.

Does Brodski appreciate me? Let us see. One day I remove the shade from his lamp and insert two five-hundred-watt bulbs. The strongest voltage possible for that particular lamp. With the bare bulbs shining on the off-white walls, the room is illuminated to such an extent that the infamous cat's cry not heard in recent days now reappears, reaching startling crescendoes. I respond by lowering the lights, dimming them just a little, not enough. Brodski continues to wail. I continue to dim the lights, knowingly passing the point where his cries or lack of same tells me to stop. He does not understand. He has built up such confidence in me. Hard won confidence. I continue to diminish the light to the point where I doubt he can see his precious prints, much less appreciate them. I watch the little darling closely as he strains his eyes. He lets out a shriek for help, but Mother is out and only I am here. Only I can resolve his plight. He cannot comprehend why I am so off in my aesthetic judgement. My taste before has always proved impeccable. At last I pass him a befuddled look. What do you want of me? it says. Finally, just at the moment when insight occurs, "Aha!" I shout. I transpose the bulb, put on the lamp shade, and all is well. Poor darling, what a time he had of it. And you ask: Does he appreciate me?

Of course, I want to be much more than merely appreciated. To this end I have devised a game. A game in which the participant cannot lose. It is simple enough. One needs only a theatrical spotlight, a tray, a stopwatch, a picture that has some special value to one participant, and a dozen or so other art objects, so differing in quality and aesthetic worth from one to another that their variance can be perceived by any fairly refined eye.

Brodski has such an eye. He also has a favored picture (his poster print of Munch's The Scream). Therefore I had only to provide a spotlight, a stopwatch, a tray, and several dozen objects possessing varying degrees of aesthetic worth. Though some of the materials for my games are quite costly, I have accumulated quite a tardy contingency fund for just such purposes. The country spends billions on its pleasures; should I quibble about the cost of mine. If anything, I am a man of the times. Now to the game:

I focus the spotlight on Brodski's favorite painting. With a click from the extension cord switcher I can illuminate the print any time I want. Then I place the aesthetic objects in a tray upon the dresser directly in front of Brodski's bed. Two at a time. He could not see them more clearly; he does not even have to crane his neck (if he had a neck) an inch. His task is to differentiate between each pair, to select the more preposessingly beautiful object. He can accomplish this easily; a purr, a nod or a smile is all that is needed. Each time he does so I reward him by putting the spotlight on Munch's The Scream. Depending upon the time it takes him to decide and the difficulty of the choice, his favorite picture will remain center stage. Since I learn quickly that Brodski can hold his gaze unstintingly for long stretches of time, I vary my reward anywhere from 10 seconds to perhaps as much as a minute or two. Because of the way I have constructed the game and his infallible eye, his reward has been cut short to 10 seconds only once. And in all honesty that was due to no failing of his, but rather of mine. Once, purely by accident, I miscalculated.

Perhaps it wasn't an accident. The fact that without exception Brodski had been selecting the correct object instantaneously (not once did I even have a chance to use my stopwatch) might have had something to do with it.

In any event, in all future games resembling this one, the gradient scale of difference between one object and another will be less. A great deal less.

ASSHOLES!!! They want to take Brodski away from me. Before I've even started. Before I've even insinuated myself in his soul. Some fool comedian from downtown came up with the bright idea of calling for a realignment in the East Harlem area: Procedure 2-387. Effective immediately. We are to transfer all cases north of 116th street to Units F through K.

I rush to my Supervisor's desk. Mrs. Knox bids me wait. "Can't you see I'm busy talking to Mrs. Sampson, Mr. Haberman? Please wait your turn." Mrs. Knox is absolutely religious about office protocol. She knows every procedure and memorandum by heart. She follows every regulation to the letter. Procedure 3-679 says this; Memorandum 5-354 says that. In the afternoons, when the office empties out, she keeps herself busy by studying procedures and memorandums over and over until she has them memorized like some apple-a-day schoolgirl in Sunday school class. "I'm sorry, Mr. Haberman," she says, "but no matter what you say, it's still against departmental policy. We can't allow it. It's procedure!"

"But my client will die without me as his caseworker, Mrs. Knox. I speak to Mrs. Rivera at least once a day. Often more. It's a special case. A special situation. I've only had this case for a short time now, but already I've made fantastic progress. If you let me, I can perform miracles with this client."

"Well, then, Mr. Haberman, you'll just have to perform miracles on some other client."

"But Brodski's used to me. And besides, Mrs. Rivera won't let anyone else in the apartment but me. Mrs. Knox, I'll even keep this case if you don't give me credit for it. You don't have to count it on my caseload. That's right. You heard me. My caseload will be one case larger than anyone else's in our unit."

This last comment registers. Parity is the law of the land in civil service. No caseworker in Unit B, in the entire Department, does anything without getting credit for it. Statistics keep everybody doing the same job . . . statistically. Everybody is insured the same amount of work . . . statistically. No more can a conscientious caseworker ask. Two (2) pending cases per worker a week; one hundred (100) cases per worker in all. Not one iota more or different from the rest. The civil service snail marches on in perpetuity.

Mrs. Knox's reaction is one of great puzzlement. In fifteen (15) years she has not heard me say anything so strange. I can hear her civil servant's computer clickety click: What could he be up to? Is this an easy case for him? Probably doesn't even have to visit. Must have worked out some sort of system with the client to make it easy on himself. Despite our fifteen years together in Harlem, Mrs. Knox doesn't know me at all.

Suddenly the computer flashes into synch.

"My, my, Mr. Haberman, you really feel strongly about this case."

"And it's only an inter-office transfer, Mrs. Knox. We aren't even being asked to transfer the cases to another center or downtown to C.O." (Central office).

"I'm sorry, Mr. Haberman, but no matter how extenuating you say the circumstances are, this has to be my final decision. Not mine, you understand . . . but Procedure 2-387."

I take a chance. Overstepping Mrs. Knox, and bypassing all that's holy in office hierarchy, I head straight for the Director's office. Tom Sanders, born black but truly green, a plant lover par excellence, holds that estimable position. His office rivals the Botanical Gardens. On every ledge and border, in every nook and cranny, corner and crevice, his green thumb has given birth. Never between the hours of 9 and 5 p.m. can anyone disturb this man from his chaparral habitat. In past office visits I have learned more in an hour from Tom Sanders about plants and flowers than thirty-three years with the Department has ever taught me about casework. This time I don't even make an effort to wade through his jungle defenses. Rather I mention something about a hundred-year-old bonsai tree. His ears perk up. His green thumb stops watering a cabbage plant in midstream. A hundred year-old-bonsai tree is a real coup. Anything much older is a national treasure in Japan. And I know where to get it for him. After discussing terms—where, when, how much—I barter for my favor. "Despite the new procedure on transferring cases, Tom," I say, "there's a certain case I'd like to keep. You see . . ."

He interrupts me. "No time to discuss it now, Haberman. You've been here long enough. Do what you think best."

"But Mrs. Knox . . ."

"Never mind Mrs. Knox. I'm the Director of this center, am I not? Now when did you say you can get me that bonsai . . ."

Even before I close the door behind me I can hear the familiar water spray jet out from his plant jug. And seconds later, if I strain my ears hard enough, I can also hear him on the phone with Mrs. Knox. "Now what kind of new procedure was that caseworker talking about?"

As I return to my desk, I notice Mrs. Knox's eyes averting mine. All her attention is seemingly focused on a case record she is reading. I think: Yes, Mrs. Knox, what the hell kind of procedure were you talking about!"

I just realized that up to this point, I've neglected to comment on my fellow workers other than my Director and my Supervisor, Mrs. Knox. Those worthies who make up Unit B. That's what we're called here. I'm B-24. Someone else is B-23; B-22; B-21. And so here follows Unit B:

To begin with, there's Richard Gould, B-23. Married, two children, smokes a pipe, and lately reads a lot. Hates this job but states he would hate any other job even more. Richard Gould would never put himself in a position where he could fail. Be threatened. Have to compete. For that reason he is important to me. Except for his habit of flinging the phone at me on occasion, I find I can bully him all I want to with small fear of retaliation. And I do. Oh, he has all the defenses: the entire gamut from indifference to moral lethargy. "What's the difference anyway" is his daily recitativo. But underneath. What denial. What self-betrayal. He can't fool me. Every now and then when I need a whipping boy, he's perfect. Of course I try not to take undo advantage of him. That would be unfair and tantamount to self-destruction. For if I did, I couldn't stretch out my good fortune. Besides, I would never give myself away. If you know that about me, you know a lot. Have I said that before? Even if I have, it's worth repeating: I never give myself away.

Then there's John P. Nolan, B-22. Rodent Face, thirty-ish, and a devout Catholic. Once studied for the priesthood. He missed his calling. He should have stayed there. He's a born saint. Martyrdom as pure as his (he volunteers daily to make my field visits; those of others in the unit, too) I find laughable. To give you an indication of the laughability of his condition, he admires Mr. Gould. I quote: *He's made a contribution. He's got a wife and kids. I don't have that. They're part of him. I think that's wonderful. If I didn't love anyone. . .* his squeaky mouse voice fades here before continuing . . . *if I die I won't have anyone to remember me.* I ask you. Who can top that? Is it any wonder the Pope is against the pill? With devotees like Rodent Face around, what smart politician wouldn't want to increase the electorate? And if anything, the Church is political. As if you didn't know.

Next follows B-21: Arlene Sampson. A black woman fifty-five years of age with an ego grounded in Mother Earth. And she is Mother Earth. Not a day goes by that I don't hear "Big Daddy" (her husband) and "Mother" (her mother) and "the kids" (her children) pass from her lips. After working all day at the office she goes home to cook for the entire family. But especially "Big Daddy." When she returns to the office the next morning she always has something "bad" to say about him. How unappreciative he is. How cheap. How he's always complaining about something. How he's never satisfied. "The kids" are eighteen-year old Darcie (her "baby") and twenty-four-year-old Donnie (her "big boy"). They call her at the office once a day, every day, to receive instructions on how to live their lives. To be so connected to the world, to know your place so well, to have a place . . . it is any wonder I need Brodski?

The games continue:

As I have been doing pretty much right along, I continue to make it easy for Brodski. The more I indulge him today, the harder it will be for him tomorrow. I remember as a child wanting to sleep late in the morning and my father coming into my room and cruelly awakening me. "Wake up . . . get out of bed." I have never forgotten my mother's reaction on one special occasion. "Let him sleep, Abe, he'll have to get up early the rest of his life, now for school, and later for work."

So I allow Brodski to sleep late. He, too, will have to rise early the rest of his life. And like my father, I will be the one to wake him.

This afternoon, unbeknownst to Brodski, I place a miniature portable radio on his window ledge. Disco sounds blare away in his room. Brodski's wince is my command. Immediately I speed into action. First I shut the window, slipping the radio behind my back and into my right rear pocket. Next, in easy sight of Brodski's hawking eye, I hurry to his RCA windup victrola. Seconds later the soothing strains of a Haydn concerto stretch languidly across his room. Brodski's purr tells me I am right. His taste is classical. His smile thanks me for transporting him to a calmer age.

Upon entering Mt. Sinai Hospital a little past noontime today on my way to a pending case, I noticed a group of children congregated around a telephone booth in the lobby. One little boy looked like me when I was his age. He'll look like me when he's my age. What will I look like . . . then? Suppressing an anxious feeling in the pit of my stomach, I decided not to make the visit and rushed over to Brodski instead.

Not all my games require so much of me. Sometimes (far too rarely) my best ideas come from completely unexpected sources. It is just a matter of keeping one's eyes and ears open. Just as a lover sees all the world's objects as treasure for his beloved, I see everything for Brodski.

For the past several weeks there has been a recurring problem in the Brodski household. A newly arrived tenant is the cause. It is this denizen's habit to fill his skull each morning, noon and night with the same disco sounds. Closing the windows is not a real defense against these mind-obliterating waves of sound. Neither is turning up Brodski's RCA victrola. Even if it were possible to increase the decibels of this ancient machine, which it isn't, it would do little good as Brodski's own music would only have to compete against his neighbor's hi-fi. The sonorant sounds of the cry of the cat have been on the increase ever since the disco-loving neighbor moved in.

But I have solved the problem. What I did was really quite simple. It only required a pair of headphones and a tape player. When I placed the headphones around Brodski's head, permitting him for the first time in what must have seemed like forever to hear his precious music undisturbed, his eyes shone with such an eerie glitter that it gave me chills. There was no telling where he was transported this time. But I know one thing: he was no longer with us. It is quite conceivable that wherever he was, he learned the meaning of the expression: I GIVE THANKS TO THE GODS. Yes: I am fast becoming a God to Brodski. A God that doesn't even ask for thanks.

What I said a few pages back about art deserves further comment. I ask myself why, if I feel the way I do, do I allow art to take up such a large sphere of my life? Certainly Brodski is not the first beauty-lover I have chosen to play my games with.

Am I nothing more than a Freudian footnote repelled by the very thing I love?

Love Brodski? No. Never!

I've gotten in the habit of visiting Brodski every morning. Or rather I make it my business to visit him. I want the little fellow to start the day off right. Mother has told me more than once how Brodski always has trouble with his breakfast. "He can't hold a mouthful," she says, "or if he does, he'll hold it for hours at a time without swallowing. He'll get sick if he don't eat, Mr. Haberman," she bellows in panic. "He'll die. He's so stubborn . . ."

I have found a way to whet Brodski's appetite. Every morning I bring him something that makes his tiny bird's mouth water. Not caviar or chocolate mousse. Not even that wholesome and nutritious baby formula I have taken the pains to persuade Ms. Gonzalez, assistant to the Chief Nutritionist at Mt. Sinai Hospital, to make up for him specially. That goodie I've presented to Mrs. Rivera already. What I bring now is for Brodski alone. I bring him BEAUTY. One day it might be a tray emblazoned with a Modigliani face; another day a saucer or cup with a Picasso or Matisse imprint. Each morning I visit he eats his special baby formula to the accompaniment of the soothing strands of Haydn or, for variation, Chopin, the headphones I gave him enveloping his little head. I place my art-treasure before him, and only when he swallows his mouthfuls like a good little child does Daddy give him his reward.

For the rest of the morning I can rest secure. Breakfast is the most important meal of the day and I know my darling has had his. It shall hold him in good stead until I return later for lunch. Indeed, he can't wait for my return. I can just hear his little tummy churning with anticipation. And why not? Is there another parent in all the world who feeds his babe quite like me?

This daily breakfast visit is accomplished not before clocking in at the Center, but after. Generally, I'm clocked in by

8:00 a.m. and on my way to Brodski's only minutes later. Luckily for me, Brodski resides only a few short blocks from the office. When I return to the office late, my time card covers me. Regardless of how my time card reads, though, and despite the fact that I deliver the Daily News to Mrs. Knox's bin religiously every morning before I take off for Brodski's— once, when all the usual newspaper stands were closed because of a crushing snowstorm, I walked eighteen blocks out of my way to assure such delivery—Mrs. Knox still applies her rules mercilessly. If I'm not sitting at my desk at precisely 9:00 a.m. ready for work, I'm late.

"Where have you been, Mr. Haberman? On a coffee break already?"

"No, Mrs. Knox," I improvise, "to the field. I've even posted it on my W712." (Field record form).

(I would if she'd let me).

(She doesn't).

"Mr. Haberman, you know very well workers aren't allowed to go to the field anymore directly from their homes. Clearly Memorandum 6-873 forbids that *clearly.* Workers first have to clock in at the office. And then, only if it's an emergency, and they obtain special permission from their Supervisor, can they leave for the field. But *never* under any circumstances before 9:15 a.m. Mr. Haberman, Memorandum 6-873 has been in effect for nearly two years now."

"But . . ."

"There are no buts about it, Mr. Haberman. From now on you'll either be seated at your desk promptly at 9:00 a.m. like your co-workers, or else I'll have to report you to your Director."

Mrs. Knox's eyes rise above mine and search out the other workers.

"Oh, by the way, Unit B, thanks to Mr. Haberman, I'm going to have to keep a time sheet on my desk for you to sign in on every morning. No, Mr. Nolan, it's not enough that you clock in officially downstairs. I have to know who's doing an honest day's work around here and who's not."

"Why? Because your Supervisor says so, that's why!"

NOTE TO MYSELF

From here on, Brodski's daily morning breakfast visits will be made one half hour earlier. He *must finish* his breakfast by 8:45 a.m.

Mrs. Knox and the other workers notice other changes about me. Most evident is my new found panache. Every day now I come into the Center dressed to the hilt. Accustomed to my pre-Brodski days of disheveled bachelorhood, they must now see me as something of a dandy. In my entire worka-day life no one in the Department has ever seen me so made up. "Could he have a lady friend?" says John P. Nolan. "No, never," comes the quick retort from Mother Earth. "Everyone knows Haberman's attitude toward women. He hates them."

"If so, she must really be some dish," continues Rodent Face, "to get old Haberman dressed up and polished like this. He looks like a veritable peacock the way he's preened. What's that: pomade on his hair? He even smells pretty."

Mother Earth, who combines with her absolute certainty an amnesiac's memory bank, hones in on who.

"I bet it's someone in the office," she says. "Or at least up here in Harlem. Why else would he dress this way unless he was going to be with her every day?"

"Or could it be a client?" querries Richard Gould, our guilt-laden jew, who always thinks (and says) the worst.

Every day is a maddening rush to get out of the office. I do eight hours' work in three. Exhausted but exhilarated after I finish my paper work, I'm ready to leave for the field. No, not for the field . . . for Brodski.

My fellow workers stare at me in narrow-eyed hate. Why do I rush so? How do I get my work done so quickly? It's been established that I don't have a female friend.

"At this rate he'll do a full month's work in a week," complains Mother Earth to Rodent Face.

The look on Rodent Face is the same look every fledgling priest must have the first time a member of his flock asks the great question.

One morning Mrs. Knox calls me to her desk for a conference. Her face wears an expression I've seen only once before in fifteen years. That was the time someone in the office stole her binful of memos and procedures. Since then she padlocks her desk cell. "It will never happen again!" she shrieked in hysterical frenzy. Though she never actually accused me of the crime, it was evident from the way she acted towards me for the next several months that she held me to blame.

Now she has the same expression on her face. "Mr. Haberman," she says, "your W712 is highly irregular this month. It seems you've posted ten visits on your Brodski case in addition to the basic statutory visit. Mr. Haberman, it's impossible for you to spend so much time with one client and not do a disservice to all your others. If you continue this way, you'll neglect your entire caseload."

"But Mrs. Knox," I interrupt, "that's not true. Just look at my case record on Brodski. Every visit was necessary, and I've visited all my other cases due this month too."

"Please don't interrupt me till I'm finished, Mr. Haberman. I've already read your case records. We both know a worker can enter anything he wants to in his case record entries. I'm talking *statistics*. Downtown doesn't come here or call us and ask how many clients did you help at the end of the month. Do this or do that. No. They just want us to keep our controls up to date. My job has turned me into a statistical clerk. That's all any of us really are, Mr. Haberman. But with one big difference. I'm the one that has to make out the monthly reports that go downtown. Now tell me, how am I going to explain these numbers? Tell them you visit ninety-nine cases once every three months for ten minutes each, and another for four weeks straight without a letup? Mr. Haberman, it's downtown who won't stand for it. Not me. If it were up to me, you could enter anything you want to in your case records. I wouldn't even read them." She pauses here, pawing the ground before the kill. "Now, Mr. Haberman, as I was saying, if you don't change your work habits regarding this case, I'm going to have to transfer it to another worker like it should have been transferred in the first place."

From that day on I don't post one visit more than I'm statistically allotted on my W712 for case SSI 6718798 aka Brodski.

Moreover, I furnish newspaper delivery service to my Supervisor every morning free of charge.

"Oh, keep your money, Mrs. Knox. It's on me!"

The way they spoke about it in the office this morning. On the trains. In the streets. Tears trickling down their silly faces. Their voices cracked with pain Why would anyone want to kill him? An artist. A music maker. A pure soul like him. The killer must be crazed ! Sick! Nuts! Why? Why? Why? They're so dumb. So blind. I wanted to tell them why. Everything inside me ached to tell them why. But I didn't. Why should I? They wouldn't understand anyway. They dare not understand. They're happy to live their lives through other people. They know everything there is to know about other people. Celebrities: This one and that one. Where he was born. When she died. When they were married. Divorced. Who she's having an affair with. Had an affair with. Where she had her children. When. And with whom. Her abortion. Abortions. They have a celebrity-scrapbook programmed in their minds indelibly recording their favorite's first hit. First success. First break. First! First! First! When was my first break? When does my career start? Change? Turn? Never. That's when. That's why he was killed. Because HE HAD CELEBRITY! Because HE DID SUCCEED! Because HE IS A HOUSEHOLD NAME!

Why him? Why not me? Why should he have everything and me nothing? Why should I have to be here every day doing a job I detest; in my room alone every night watching his ugly face on TV; listening to his songs on the radio? They're not my songs. It's not me gaining acclaim. He told us lies. All artists tell us lies. Turn our heads from the truth. From reality and experience. *Our Experience!* All artists would have us believe that everything is possible. Sure. For him it was possible. He made it! But what about me?! Who's knocking my door down? Where's my chauffeur-driven limousine? When was the last time I received the plaudits of the crowd? A standing ovation? A single compliment? If I died today, who would care? I hate all artists. I hate anyone who wants to be different. Exceptional. I hate anyone who wants special attention. Who gets preferential treatment. I hate anyone who tries to ensnare us in his net of artistic grandiosity. Who does and makes and creates and gives birth to. Who aspires to become more than he is. I hate anyone who believes in life! It's not true. They're not alive. They're all fixed, immutable, dead inside. This office and that chair and these case records on my desk and the four walls in my apartment and chicken dinner every night. That's it! Once and for all! For a lifetime!

I'll tell you something. A little secret I've known ever since that first time in the Village with the actor. I'll tell you when we're not dead. When we do come to life. The killer knows. The one that did away with your music maker. He knows. That's why he murdered him. The moment he saw him lying there on the ground in a crumpled heap . . . he knew. Ask him. He'll tell you. Only when something is dead can we possess it. Only when it's dead can we really control it. Conquer it. Make it our own. Until then it's transient, free. It can come and go. Only when something is reduced to its final state;

when we've made it a thing, an object, fleshlike and carnal, is it ours completely. That's when God must have known he was God. Not when he made the world but when he destroyed it. Massacred it. When he told us we were going to die. When he made us conscious of that. That's why he kills us in the end. He becomes immortal when we die. He lives forever only when we cease to be. If it were up to me, I'd exterminate all the artists in the world. All the believers. I tell you I'm glad. Glad I tell you . . . Glad . . .

NOTES TO MYSELF

Somehow I've managed to either lose or misplace (not like me) the detailed entries I've made on various games I've recently played with Brodski. Rather than attempt to recount them here, it is enough to say they proved extremely successful.

Brodski is progressing—if I may use the expression—by leaps and bounds.

NOTES TO MYSELF

The little fellow is getting oh so bold. He has delusions of grandeur. He thinks he can stand on his own two feet without me to support him. Good. Let him think so. When it is time for him to fall, the incline will be all the steeper. And he will FALL.

NOTES TO MYSELF

Things are going along much too smoothly. Beyond all expectations, progress is being made. I must put a slight halt

on such proceedings. I don't want to spoil Brodski. Not true.
I don't want to spoil myself.

I ask myself: If I had no arms and legs and my world consisted of no more than the smallest-size mattress of a hospital
crib-bed, what would I want most in the world?

The answer: I know the answer.

All the signs are there. Brodski is ready for the next stage. Previously, when I visited him, if I was a bit tardy or off schedule for noonday lunch, he would become irritable or not touch a bite. Now, even if I don't join him, his appetite couldn't be better. I can remember when his gaze followed my every move. When I was the hub and center of his attention. But no longer. In fact, this afternoon when I appeared, he hardly raised his eyes. But don't get the idea that his indifference is repugnance. No. Quite the opposite. It is rather that I have become like a member of the family to him. As an old beat-up piece of furniture no one notices. These are the surest signs of love and trust I know. Of course this change didn't come all at once, but gradually, over a prolonged period of time. Naturally I had something to do with it.

Nor does he lose himself in my games as he once did. I have only to compare his earlier results (which, of course, I keep) to more recent findings to realize that his average mean time for staring at his favorite painting, Munch's The Scream, has lessened considerably. In the early days he could hold his gaze for hours at a time, once even achieving the impressive total of three and a half. Now the best he can manage, no matter what tricks of contrast and shading I employ, is a scant ten minutes. And his intensity is gone. No longer does he whine and shriek if I take the print away, or illuminate it poorly, or even as I did in one special instance, deny it to him altogether. Indeed, as with everything else in this four-walled enclosure, (if I might paraphrase) he has grown accustomed to its face. This is as good a barometer as there is that he has outgrown our first phase and is ready for the second.

Of course, as I intimated earlier, none of these changes merely happened by themselves. They needed a helping hand. But my fingers have always been long and dextrous; "piano fingers," my mother called them. Thus for a period spanning several weeks now I have exhibited no real talent for creating games worthy of inspiring his attention. They are all pale imitations of what used to be, lacking in originality and power—and what is more crucial here, far too similar and repetitive. It is only a tribute to Brodski's extraordinary aesthetic need that his interest did not completely wane long ago.

I have helped him reach this second stage in other ways too. For example, by propping his little head and torso against a pillow, I have made it possible for him to (in effect) sit at a window for hours at a time and gaze at his wonderful view. Even when I'm not there he can maintain this position and usually does. And once even, when Mother went shopping, I carried him to the rooftop so he was able to see the four-cornered vista of the city. If anything can inspire a man to spread his wings, I have always maintained, it is a lovely view. From the look on Brodski's face I'm not that far wrong. If he wasn't ready to fly, I daresay he did stretch his wings. Or at least those vestigial excrescences we call as much.

And this is just what I want. This is the Second Phase. To stretch Brodski's wings. To prepare him to fly. No longer must he be content with or limited to the four-walled environ of his home. He must be allowed to reach whatever aesthetic heights he can. To achieve this, I will have to take him out into the world. He will have to see the world. Only then will he be able to grow in proportion to what he can absorb. This, then, is what I have been preparing Brodski for. To yearn for the world. To want to see, touch and feel the world. Yes: The world for Brodski will come into focus, but I will adjust the lens.

Damn it! Nothing comes easy! Nothing happens quite the way one expects it. Here I was indulging myself in idle thoughts on how well Brodski was progressing and what happens? A real problem occurs. Mrs. Rivera objects to my taking her son outdoors. Oh, I expected some of the usual arguments passed down from time immemorial by mothers protecting their children. In this case, more understandable than most. The world is crazy today. On every street corner and in every unguarded building lurks danger. People are tossing absolute strangers in front of subway cars. But she is more adament than I could have imagined. I only need listen to her words and observe her face to know it will be no easy task to sway her. "Mr. Haberman," she exclaims, "that is the one thing I cannot allow. I did once but never again."

"You mean he's only been outside once in his entire life, Mother? Is that what you said?"

"Once, Mr. Haberman, and I shall never forgive myself for it. It was the day I had a doctor's appointment due to my arthritis and I had to leave him with my girlfriend. How was I to know she would take him out? I gave her strict instructions.

Mr. Haberman, he saw something that day. Something happened to him that day. I don't know what, but I swore to myself I would never let it happen again."

"When? Where?" I query, already knowing the answer.

"It was at the Maine Monument, Mr. Haberman, last fall. No, it wasn't the children playing that annoyed him, or the odd looks he got. My friend insists it wasn't that at all. It was something far worse . . ." She pauses. "Only no one knows what."

"No one, Mother?" I say, feigning incredulity.

"No one, Mr. Haberman," she continues, shaking her head for emphasis. "For a whole week he couldn't eat. He just laid there like a corpse. Not a cry, not a sound out of him. The poor child. That's when I brought him to the hospital. And when he was discharged, the social worker there referred us to your agency. That's how we met you. Don't you remember?"

"But I never knew what caused his illness, Mother. I just took it for granted it had something to do with his general condition. Are you absolutely positive it doesn't? How can you be so certain about something like that? That it was something outside!?!

"Mr. Haberman," she answers, "ask me anything but don't ask me to let my little one go outside again. The world," she stammers, "the world is not a kind place for the likes of him." Her face turns deathly serious. "Mr. Haberman, he has absolutely nothing to defend himself with against the world."

The discussion goes on and on. I let her make all her points, hoping to hear a flaw in her argument, hoping to find something against which I can mount a counterattack. But nothing emerges. The only thing to my benefit is that Brodski, I notice, is listening too. Just look at his face. He knows what I want. He wants the same thing. The little darling is upset with Mother for preventing him from going outdoors. That is good. I will go home now and plan my counterattack. Brodski's last grimace has brought my beachhead into view.

NOTES TO MYSELF

One thing I must never do. I must never depart from my battle plan. I must never forsake what I know. No general likes to conquer a barren land. Better to fill it with the world's treasure. Only then does it become worthy of conquest. Only then does the enemy have something to lose. Any butcher at the slaughterhouse knows as much. . . . So I must fatten Brodski up with the world's treasure. There is no departing from that. In addition to Brodski, *Mother will have to lose.*

One day after Mother's affront I withdraw my services from the Brodski household. Days go by and I don't call or visit. Nor do I answer Mrs. Rivera's telephone calls. I have instructed my unit clerk and co-workers to inform Mrs. Rivera when she calls that I am too busy to talk, or in conference, or out in the field. My co-workers are only too happy to oblige. One of the Department's most trying problems is client telephone calls. Actually these calls serve as a kind of safety valve. Overtaxed, daily enraged by the monotony of their jobs, the caseworkers vent their frustrations on the clients. The clients can't fight back. They can hardly afford the telephone calls. Thus every time a telephone rings in the office the caller is bombarded by a series of barks, growls, and slam-downs. How do these good samaritans rationalize their behavior? They don't. Oh, there is always someone who has to be different. Mrs. Abigail Hill, for instance, better known as "Dear Abbie," daughter of a Baptist minister from the Deep South. She insists in her slow-minded drawl that it is for the client's own good. "They can become too dependent upon us caseworkers, you know. Why, if we let them, they'd call every day. More than once!"

It goes without saying that I am no exception to this Telephone Answering Rule. But, as with everything else, I've put my own stamp on it. A favorite ploy of mine involves "Spanish-speaking only" clients. When these leather-skinned Latinos call, such vituperation and curse words spew from my lips that sometimes it takes the better part of the morning to get it all out. And why not? Not only don't they fully realize that I'm cursing them, they can't report me, certainly not to—and this is critical—Mrs. Knox. What could they say? "No hablo ingles"; "No comprendo."

Come to think of it, ever since meeting Brodski my telephone etiquette has improved considerably. Well, as they say, for every winner there's a loser.

Mrs. Knox has proved pliant in solving this problem. As usual, she merely invokes her own set of rules. "From now on," she said one fine morning, "Group B will not accept telephone calls from clients after noontime unless it's an emergency. I've no patience to sit here bouncing like a rubber ball answering phone calls in the afternoon when you workers go to the field and I'm left here all alone at my desk."

"What about Mrs. Ramsey, our unit clerk?" queries B-23. And the emergency worker. . ."

Mrs. Knox turns to face the offender abruptly. "I've no time to discuss the matter further, Mr. Gould," she says through clenched teeth while removing the receiver from the phone. "I've got to make a personal call."

Three days pass before a message from Mrs. Rivera breaks through the lines: Brodski is ill. It's an emergency. His mother says he needs you. My immediate thought: We shall see how much.

One day turns into two. Monday turns into Friday. A second week begins. Still I don't call or visit Brodski. Each morning the first thing I do when I arrive at the office, after signing Mrs. Knox's time sheet and delivering the paper, is empty my mail folder. After separating Mrs. Rivera's messages left the proceeding day from the other contents, I add them to an already impressive stack on my desk. I have let Mother's messages pile up. They give me great satisfaction. They assure me that my battle plan is working. Finally, after several heart-warming message-laden days more, something unexpected happens. Something I had hoped for but couldn't count on. Something only my great wealth of experience had led me to believe would occur.

The breakthrough comes in the form of a telephone call from Mrs. Thea Goldstein, Brodski's social worker at the Institute of Rehabilitation. She says that it will be necessary for Brodski to come into the hospital to have some special tests made on him. These tests cannot be given at home. Special equipment will have to be used. Will I be good enough to double-check with (and exert pressure on) Mrs. Rivera, she asks, so that no foul-up on the appointment date occurs. I answer: "I'll be only too happy to." There is more than satisfaction in my voice. There is gratitude.

On the day of Brodski's hospital appointment I visit his home. What a shame he is not there. Writing hurriedly I jot down in pencil a note for Mother on my Form W-26 and slip it under the door. In addition to my name and telephone number, the note indicates an urgent request for Mrs. Rivera to call me the next day. "We have something important to discuss," is the exact wording.

Promptly at 9:00 a. m. the following morning Mother calls. I tell her that if I can, I will visit her that afternoon. She replies anxiously, "Please, Mr. Haberman, please do." I answer, Why, of course, Mother dear, if there's any way possible for me to get out there, I will."

The appointment was made for 2:30 p.m.; I arrive at 4:00. Mother is haggard, pale, anxious. There is a suggestion of fear in her eyes. Brodski is glad to see me. If he could have, I could tell, he would have leaped for joy. Brusquely bypassing Mother, I enter his room. A present is in order. This time I have brought him a real prize. It is enough to make up for the long weeks of privation and pain he has had to endure through no fault of his own, but because of Mother. It is a projecting camera, screen and art slides of some of the world's most beautiful sites. The Pantheon, St. Paul's Cathedral, London, Grecian Ruins. Each slide has been handpicked by me. Specially chosen for its unique beauty. I want only the best for my darling on this occasion. The result is a veritable panapoly of the Seven Wonders of the World. Hadn't I promised as much earlier? With Mother waiting in her room, I spend hours with Brodski. I didn't even have to ask her to allow us to be alone. She consented of her own accord. Voluntarily. She understands these moments between the little one and me should be private. Hours go by. Not a word or sound passes between us. Not even the soft purring sound I have become accustomed to hearing when he is happy. Only the barely audible hum of the camera projector. The room is pitch dark. With each new slide I can sense Brodski becoming more and more enthralled. He devours them as a fat man does sweets. It is so easy to please him, I think. All you need to do is expose him to beauty. And the world has so much.

Each slide I have chosen is a superb work, the subject wonderfully captured by a photographic genius. Thus for a period covering more than four hours he shuttles from the ruins of ancient Greece to a modern glass-sheathed skyscraper; from the Cathedral de Notre Dame to the palatial villas of Uruguay. He sees these vistas as few others have seen them. Or at least have appreciated them. His gaze of religious wonder is only broken when he marvels at my dextrous fingers clicking the machine on and off or bringing each slide into perfect focus. It must seem something of a miracle to him. Don't forget, in his entire life he has never been to a movie. Or even watched TV. Mother won't permit him. No good for his eyes, I recollect her once telling me. Finally I deem it time to have my talk with Mother. I leave Brodski to observe Giotto's The Flight into Egypt and I enter her room.

My face projects a stern demeanor, even fierce, as I ask her to join me. "Here, sit beside me, darling, on this sofa. I have something important to discuss with you." And so, seated together on her sofa which in earlier days might have been a love seat, I sow the first seeds that will eventually decide the old lady's doom. Without explaining my behavior or the reasons for my withdrawal these last several weeks, I tell her *"THEY'VE"* decided to place a Home Attendant in her home to help care for Brodski. "They" feel this is an absolute necessity because of the medical reports "they" received only recently from the hospital.

Mother objects. The last thing she wants is a stranger coming into her home and caring for her child. Her reaction is precisely what I expected. I press my advantage at once. "The only alternative, Mother, would be for you to become Brodski's Home Attendant. I don't know if they will permit it, *but if you want me to,* I'll make the recommendation. Of course, it won't be easy. There's a real problem here. Relatives living with clients aren't generally allowed to serve as Home Attendant.

The Department has strict rules on that. But maybe if I can explain the extenuating circumstances and submit a special approval memo . . . well, maybe, just maybe. Of course, we won't tell anybody of your real relationship to Brodski. I mean that you're not even blood related. If they knew that, they just might decide to take him away from you altogether. Oh, don't worry. I won't tell. And I think I can pull this other thing off too. Anyway, It's certainly worth a try. Now, what do you say, Mother? Will you have a go at it?

The old lady looks at me askance. She hardly comprehends what I am saying. Probably the only words that do register are that "they" want to put a stranger in her home, and even worse, that "they" can take her child away from her.

"I don't want to get you into trouble, you understand, Mr. Haberman, but if you would be so kind to do what you say, I'd be very grateful."

The tone of her voice is meek, confused, pitiable. Her eyes moistened long ago. Hearing her speak and observing her now, naked as I do, on the love seat, an image flashes before me of a lovesick suitor begging for his beloved's hand. Nothing is more revolting. My voice gains strength as I respond.

"Why, of course, Mother darling. No trouble at all. I only hope I can gain approval for you. I'm convinced you'd be an excellent Home Attendant. And you know something—there's a good deal of extra money in it for you. Home Attendant's make $3.35 an hour, and you'll be working full time. Twenty-four hours per day. Though you'll only get paid for twelve. Can't help that. That's the policy. But then, you'll be getting meal allowance and carfare."

By her reaction it is apparent that Mother isn't interested in the money. But is that really true? Though she shook her head doggedly, indicating fierce disapproval I thought I detected just a hint of disappointment when she heard me say that Home Attendant's don't get paid for more than a twelve-hour work day even if they work twenty-four hours. Or am I imagining things?

Taking her by the arm I lead her to my next point.

"Here, now Mother, before I go, let me teach you how to work this photo machine so you can show Brodski the same beautiful pictures when I'm gone. After all, I can't be here all the time and you know how the little one just loves to look at them."

Together we enter his room. Brodski is still gazing devoutly at the slide of The Flight into Egypt, as he was when I left him at least thirty minutes earlier. His expression is a fusion of ecstasy, wonder and awe. He seems hypnotized. Mother turns soft looking down at him. She smiles. All will be well are the words etched across her face. I demonstrate to her how to work the machine. After supper that evening she promise me (and him) that she will again show Brodski my slides.

Before leaving, I collect the slides I have shown to Brodski and replace them with a different set. These are not so pretty. Some are the same slides I have already exhibited with a defect in them—perhaps they are slightly darkened due to a lack of light when shot or a different exposure, or less distinct because the camera had moved when shooting. Also I have included a few slides haphazardly that are worth no more attention than an everyday Brownie snapshot.

I have to call upon all my strength to go, realizing only too well what I am going to miss later than evening. The exquisite expressions on Brodski's face (and Mother's in response to his) when he views these horrors; the squeals and cat cries that will dominate the room when Mother in utter futility makes every effort to bring these slides into sharper focus.

Poor thing: Only I can bring joy to Brodski's household. Only I can bear Brodski beauty. Mother, it seems, can cause only pain. What will Brodski be thinking? For that matter, what will Mother? She doesn't have any idea I exchanged the slides. And even if her son knew, which he doesn't, he couldn't tell her.

The amazing thing is not how much we expect when we're young—when we're starting out—but how little we end up with as adults. And yet it's enough. We adjust. We make the best of it. We live our lives! . . . Do we?

*Xerox copy placed in manuscript; original word union made by Haberman:

ni-hil-ism (ni'e lis'em, ne'-), n. 1. total rejection of established laws and institutions. 2. Philos, a. an extreme form of skepticism: the denial of all real existence or the possibility of an objective basis for truth. b. nothingness or nonexistence, c. See ethical nihilism. 3. (sometimes cap.) the principles of a Russian revolutionary group, active in the latter half of the 19th century, holding that existing social and political institutions must be destroyed in order to clear the way for a new state of society and employing extreme measures, including terrorism, and assassination. 4. anarchy, terrorism, or other revolutionary activity. 5. annihilation of the self, or the individual consciousness, esp. as an aspect of mystical experience. 6. total and absolute destructiveness, esp. toward the world at large and including oneself: the power-mad nihilism that so strongly marked Hitler's last years. (Nihil + -ism) -ni'hil-ist, n., adj. -ni'hil-is'tic, adj.

Aes-thete (es'thet or, esp. Brit., es-) n. 1. one who has or professes to have a high degree of sensitivity toward the beauties of art or nature. 2. one who affects great love of art, music, poetry, etc, and indifference to practical matters. Also, esthete. Gk aisthetes, one who perceives, equiv. to aisthe- (var. s. of aisthanesthai to perceive) + tes n. suffix denoting agent) -Syn. 1. connoisseur. 2. dillettante.

N-I-H-I-L-E-S-T-H-E-T-E

At the office the next day Mrs. Knox is vehemently against allowing Brodski's mother to be made Home Attendant. "Clearly the Department's policy regarding relatives being made Home Attendants couldn't be more *clear*. Especially those relatives already living with the clients and performing the functions free."

"But Mrs. Rivera's not really a relative, Mrs. Knox. Just a sort of volunteer foster mother. And we both know it's an unusual case. A special situation."

My "buts" continue well into the morning. Finally, after what must seem like psychopathic persistence on my part, she relents.

"If you want to take the time to write"—she grits her teeth—"an Exception to Policy Memo, Mr. Haberman, requesting special approval for this client, I won't stand in your way. But remember one thing, Mr. Haberman. You'll have to type the memo yourself. I'm not going to ask Tonita to type it. I wouldn't dare think of wasting our office typist's time on something like this."

"Thank you, Mrs. Knox." (Thank you very much).

This much going to task for a client is nonexistent in the Department. Not only does it require a great deal of extra work in the actual drafting of the memo, gathering of facts and details, careful choice of words, and adherence to precise instructions regarding memo form and structure (Procedure 2-587), but Exception to Policy Memos are rarely, if ever, approved by case consultation anyway. And why should they be? Every time the Department puts its stamp of approval on anything it costs the city money. So departmental policy is to unequivocally say *no* to everything. (The unwritten but all-encompassing law of Civil Service Land). But I can manage it, I think to myself. All I need is a strong letter from Dr. Umano at the Institute of Rehab—Thea Goldstein can manage that. And certainly soliciting the support of the Director won't hurt either. He just L-O-V-E-S the bonsai tree I got him. I am a Field General, Foot Soldier, and Specialist in Intelligence . . . but my true place in the army is in executing "maneuvers."

Three weeks later, after a barrage of phone calls from case consultation requesting followup memos and information, after overcoming bureaucratic red tape ad infinitum, Special Approval is granted for Maria Rivera to become Home Attendant.

I don't ask Mother's permission to take Brodski outdoors yet. Instead I wait for her to receive her first Home Attendant check. This is part of my strategy. Perhaps the most important part of my battleplan.

One hour after she cashed the check (I followed her to the bank; our IBM printout sheet on check rolls told me when the check would be delivered) I visited her at home. She was busy preparing the evening meal. What is this: a new set of dishes, Mother? And a matching pair of aprons for you and your son? My, my, Mother, if you're not a big spender, you're certainly a fast one. Oh, well, as they say, "easy come, easy go."

Almost before I enter her apartment, she senses something is wrong. I appear frantic as the words pour from my mouth.

"Mother, Mother, we made a terrible mistake," I lie. "I just learned that "they" can take your son away from you if you do something illegal such as become Home Attendant. I had no idea the rules and regulations were that punitive, but they are. You must not for a moment serve in this household as a Home Attendant. Nor cash one single Home Attendant check. If you do, I don't know what they'll do to you. Yes, I do! *THEY'LL TAKE YOUR CHILD AWAY FROM YOU!*"

Mother peers at me incredulously. Some sort of pre-reflective survival mechanism pushes ordered sentences from her mouth even though her face is a miasma of confusion.

"But you said it would be all right, Mr. Haberman. You said you would take care of everything. Now what should I do?"

"But I will, Mother, and I have. All you have to do is resign your post as Home Attendant. I'll tell them I spoke to you and you reconsidered. Realizing your error, you decided you didn't want to take one dollar from the Department. And you haven't."

"Haven't what, Mr. Haberman?"

"Haven't stolen one dollar, Mother. After all, you haven't yet cashed a single check, have you?"

Her face turns ashen. Her jaw slackens. She seems about to faint. I seize the opportunity to let my eyes wander about the apartment.

"Mother! What's this? I don't remember ever seeing these dishes before. And these aprons, Mother! Where and when did you get them?"

She does faint. Ka-plomp. In a large, heavy wooden kitchen chair. Her voice, too, goes limp.

"Just an hour or so ago, Mr. Haberman. In the . . . in the G & S General Store on Lexington Avenue and 116th Street. I . . . I cashed the check I received this morning and then I went to the store and I purchased . . ."

"YOU WHAT!?!"

My words grip her like a vice. She opens her mouth to say something but she can't. She is like a mute groping for sound. Only the effort is there.

The look on my face tells her what she already knows. That she has done the worst.

"Oh, Mother," I yell, "how can I save you now? You cashed the check. You committed a crime. We can't even return it. And you . . . you even spent the money. *They'll definitely take your child!!!*"

I tear the apron from her middle and crumple it in my hands. Tears stream from her eyes. A soul-searing cry vocally the equivalent of Munch's anguished vision issues from her lips. She collapses in my arms.

It took me almost two hours to apease her. I had to call upon my cumulative years of experience and not inconsiderable powers of persuasion to do so. My biggest fear was that I wouldn't be able to dissuade her from using her own money to pay the Department back. I had to convince her that the Department would look upon that act only as a mere gesture, and never agree to accept her money as restitution. A crumbled, dog-eared newspaper clipping I just happen to have had with me illustrating a situation in which a recipient attempted to make up stolen funds with her own meager savings was all the proof I needed. "No, Mother," I said with just the right tone of emphasis, "the Department is neither lenient nor understanding in these situations. And understandably so. They've been burnt too many times in the past by real criminals. Why, it's been documented that just last year millions of dollars were stolen by clients alone."

From that point on it was easy. As Mother sat in a fetal position in her wooden chair, convulsed with sobs, I explained over and over how I wouldn't tell anybody what she had done. How fortunate she was I was her caseworker. How if we stuck together on this, we could beat the Department, the cruel system. "No, Mother. Nobody's going to take your son away from you. Not as long as I'm your caseworker, they won't. You have my solemn word on that. *I promise!*"

That evening I stayed with Brodski for the first time till well into the night. Mother went to the movies with a friend. Why not? She has the money now and *I insisted!*

Bundled in a warm, brown woolen army blanket and strapped to his wheelchair, the little fellow has been outside each afternoon for the past several weeks. As I expected, the more he gets to see of the world, the more of himself he begins to discover. And the closer I get to discovering him. Brodski never seems to tire of this interchange. Nor do I. There are but two unvarying rules to our daily excursions. One is: He sees only the beautiful. If I see a doddering old lady, humped over in a crab crawl on the other side of the street, or a man with an enlarged goiter, or even a dog raising its hind leg or squatting on its haunches, or worse, its master shoveling up its leftovers, I whisk Brodski away as if he were a Jew in Germany, the year '39, and the Gestapo coming. For Brodski, the world must seem like Marco Polo's Venetia, and I like Marco Polo. On each trip I bestow on him untold riches to behold. Second rule: He must know I am solely responsible for his daily joys. Mother is not and never has been. Each turn of his wheelchair reminds him of this rule. By the way I push it, at which angle I hold it, move it forward or don't move it forward, do an about-face, come to an abrupt halt, Brodski comes to realize that if he is on wheels, I am the driver. The starter, steering wheel and brakes are mine to control.

With such power at my disposal it sometimes takes great restraint to stop myself from denying Brodski. Like when we were at the museum last week. He had just spent two hours meticulously scrutinizing an exhibition of thirteenth century Columbian handiwork, and then, when I ushered him upstairs to see Picasso's Guernica, I could swear the little fellow had an orgasm. One slight twist or turn to the right or to the left and his world would have grown dark. Literally disappeared. But I don't succumb to temptation. I have few virtues but one of them is self-discipline. Without that, nothing.

That doesn't mean I'm not subject to human error. Accidents will happen. For example, after allowing Brodski so many minutes to see Guernica, was it my fault I tripped and sustained an ankle sprain? That we had to leave prematurely? Surely, he couldn't blame me for that. Nor could he hold a grudge. Not when early the next morning—it was Saturday and I had no work—I returned with him to the museum to view his precious painting. It was the first time I ever spent the weekend (or part of it) with Brodski. He learned several very important lessons that day. Once again, he learned who is master, who controls his fate. And he also learned of my benevolence and the fact that he can count on my word. For I had assured him the previous night that we would return.

Have you ever noticed how an absolute stranger standing in an elevator will find it impossible to prevent himself from laying hands on a beautiful child? The need to caress the child's cheek is overwhelming. It seems the most natural thing in the world. Such is the power of beauty. This is the way Brodski sees the world. Everywhere we go he sees beautiful children. If only he had hands to caress them.

Not for the first time (that was something special, just for Brodski and myself) but the second, or perhaps the third time out, I allowed Mother to join us. I knew she was curious about our little trips and felt left out, and who was I to say no? On that occasion Brodski was not so fortunate. His aesthetic expectations did not fare so well. No museum, city landmark, or Manhattan skyline did he see that day. Poor fellow. Who could foretell Mother's idea of "fun" would be to take him for a walk on Fifth Avenue? In Harlem! From 118th Street all the way up to . . . Brodski was positively ruined by the time he returned home that evening. He lay crumpled in his crib, shattered and mute. I never thought he'd recover or go out again. The filth, the stench, the poverty of Harlem, Mother did not miss a thing. The cries of the cat cascaded that afternoon in Harlem with as much force as a tidal wave. Every resident for blocks around stuck his beady-eyed black head out the window. They knew we were there. How could they not know? In addition to the startling range of Brodski's vocal cords, his tears in sheer volume must have equaled a record N.Y.C. downpour.

The trip didn't do Mother much good either. Since that time she hasn't asked to join us again. Not that Brodski misses her. Now, whenever I come to take him out, he gives her such a peculiar look it could only mean one thing: Stay home! And I quote him correctly. You can bet the little tyrant never says please. I am, of course, not so impolite. Knowing the way Mother feels, I would never suggest a repeat performance, though. Besides being unnecessary, it would be in bad taste to dupe her again so soon.

Mother's itinerary of Harlem would have had a similar effect on anybody, not only one as sensitive as Brodski. I, for instance, when making my field visits always walk with my nose buried in a newspaper or book so I won't have to witness some junkie reeling in his stupor, or a wino slobbering at the mouth, or some other irredeemable social unfortunate making ready to mug me or put a shiv in my gut. If he does, he does! There's little I or anybody else can do about it. Thats the way it is. Today! So far, I count my blessings. Ever since I've worked for the Department, I've only been accosted in the field three times. (Four if you want to include an argument that led to fisticuffs which I really was more responsible for than not). In any event, I know of no better way to show my contempt for the residents of Harlem than not to notice them. One thing blacks have in common with all disenfranchised groups is that they have to be recognized. Have a name. Ask any cop on the beat what happens if he doesn't refer to them by name. The appellation "Hey you!" is enough to start a race riot. I guess they've been invisible too long. My own problems of anonymity is of an entirely different origin.

Seeing the way Brodski responds to the world, I am reminded of my father when he went to Paris after many years of saving and prodding by my mother. I shall never forget his grandiloquent summation when he returned.

"So what do you think, Abe?" asked Uncle Tom. How did you like Paris?"

"Paris! Who needs Paris," was his reply. "I had to travel two thousand miles in discomfort and spend all that money to see a lousy river. Tell me, Tom, what's the difference between the Seine and the Hudson? . . . I'll tell you. There is none!"

Only Brodski is not my father. Rather he is like a newborn infant. He sees everything as if for the first time. He marvels at positively everything. There is nowhere I can take him that is better than another. That is not to say that he does not discriminate. He still continues to dismiss the ordinary and the commonplace with disdain. I still have to shield him from unpleasant sights. It is just that with his new found exposure to the outside world he has grown to the point where he can find something of value everywhere. Each place and sight has its own special worth to him. Its own miracle. But it is all so ill-defined. Just how ill-defined came as a surprise even to me.

I was rolling Brodski up the ramp to the museum the other day for the umpteenth time when he let out a soft whimper. I hardly noticed at first and continued to climb, when to my surprise I heard him again. Looking down at him, I realized that his utterance was really a cry of protest. The little fellow was objecting to going into the museum. Something else had caught his eye. What? Impelled by a sense of urgency, I turned around. Maybe I could learn something from this. It was midafternoon and the area was only sparsely populated with what seemed to me a few inconsequential pedestrians walking the streets. I continued to gaze around, half hoping, half knowing, that this incident might be the first real turn of events since I had begun taking him outdoors more than a month ago. So far nothing out of the ordinary had happened. So far I had only learned from him pretty much what I already knew. With this in mind I searched the streets eagerly but nothing appeared. Nothing showed itself. So what was it that drew his attention? Finally it dawned upon me. Sitting on the other side of the street in front of an old brownstone, slightly obstructed by a large tree, was an ancient lady in a wheel chair with her Home Attendant standing erect by her side. The ancient lady wore a wide-brimmed straw hat and was wrapped in a multicolored patchwork quilt, and the Home Attendant was shading her from the sun by holding a parasol over her. The ancient lady had bony, stooped shoulders, a face so old it was young, ghostly white, heavily veined papyrus hands, and legs, exposed from the knees down, made of the same or similar material: lacking musculature and tone, seemingly held together by varicose veins and layers of stretched rubbery skin. Not a pretty sight. So what could have captured Brodski's attention? At first I thought it was simply the fact that he identified with her. That she was a wheelchair victim like himself with a woman (Mother) caring for her.

But it wasn't that. Only the day before I had to rush him away from another person in a wheelchair, also old, also accompanied by a female Home Attendant, because he reacted so badly upon seeing her.

My second guess seemed closer to the mark. Perhaps he found the old lady's patchwork quilt especially beautiful, and it was. More like a tapestry. Even I thought it a waste to use as a mere blanket. But it wasn't that either. With the midday sun strongly beating down on the old woman, the Home Attendant had occasion to remove the quilt from her lap; but Brodski continued to stare! Now I was really baffled. If it wasn't that, what was it? I must have asked myself that question a hundred times in those few minutes, each time becoming more puzzled and confused, each time feeling that the answer to my question was vitally important if I was to gain a more complete understanding of Brodski.

At last I realized what it was. Brodski was seeing a picture. A beautiful quintessentially self-contained frame of: Servant Holding a Parasol Over Her Mistress. The painting (if painted) could have been from another century. It was worthy of Renoir or any of the great French Impressionists. Brodski, the little darling, had seen a picture in real life. Not one already made by an artist, but one that might have inspired the artist in the first place. His wonderfully sensitive eye had caught something neither mine nor anybody else's—other than an artist's—would have seen.

From that point on I was no good either to Brodski or myself. Through our entire tour of the museum only one thought raced through my mind. I couldn't wait to return home to decipher the meaning of what had just been revealed to me, to study how I could take advantage of it. Exploit it. Render it useful. I paid Brodski little or no attention the rest of the day. I did not anticipate his whimpers of protestation. Only after some delay did I respond to his directives to make a left or right turn, to stand still or go forward. Brodski looked at me strangely more than once.

When Mother called me late that evening and alluded to his bad mood I thought I was the cause for his distemper.

It was still some time before I found out how wrong I was.

After much deliberation I have decided on a new course of action. No longer will I expose Brodski to beautiful sites alone. Museums, skylines, landmarks, art exhibitions, will no longer be our exclusive domain. From here on I will not take Brodski anywhere. He will take me. I will walk along the streets of New York like a hunter trailing his hound dog and he will tell me where to stop, what to see, what is of consequence and what is not. This is the best way, I have decided, if I am ever to truly discover who Brodski is. As always: I am on the hunt for Brodski.

Nothing he sees can he give a name. He has never learned words to describe anything. Objects are not representations or even symbols assigned to linguistic conventions to him. They are only pure images. Oh, if only he could tell me what he sees.

But he will.

It is my job to make him.

Strange: Now that I have given him leeway in leading me around I have at the same time tightened my hold on the reins. Maybe it isn't so strange. I don't want Brodski to miss a thing. And I don't want to miss Brodski.

Is not all art made of the same two opposing tensions? Absolute freedom and classical restraint?

If I am an artist . . . my art is Brodski.

So I have taken Brodski out of his wheelchair and carry him now in a papoose. I got the idea from observing a young mother carrying her child in just this way. With Brodski snugly fitted in this satchel, a kind of marsupial pouch, it's easier for me to follow his movements. Or for him to control mine. He's truly now an extension of me, as I am a part of him. If he as much as quivers, my entire system quakes. We are what I always hoped we would be: One.

If I cannot discover the mystery of who he is now, I never will. Come darling, show me who you are. Only then can the real game begin.

Guess where he takes me. Of all the places in the city we always end up at the same site. The Maine Monument! Once there, all cries, purrs, mewing sounds, even scarcely perceptible squirmings of his body cease. He goes into a trance. The only thing that exists for him then is the artist who does her sketches in chalk. By now she is quite accomplished. Her chalk arabesques of Christ and other holy figures reflect a certain felicity of style along with a rigid adherence to technique. The Chalk Artist always has a large crowd surrounding her and her rumpled brown paper bag is always filled to the edge with money. But Brodski pays little heed to the crowd or to the money. He is held spellbound by the artist at her work. He can lose himself for hours at a time watching her, and does (he refuses to go home with me until she is done) oblivious of all else: time, people, children gamboling about, the elements, have no effect on him. I'm convinced I have never seen him happier than at those moments.

Why, then, when we return home does his mood change so drastically? I am almost afraid to leave him alone with Mother and more often than not do not. It starts when we leave the artist, and by the time we're home, he's bleak, wan, dissolute, uncontrollably temperamental. There is no talking to him. Nothing I say or do affects him.

Mother feels equally helpless at theses times and is actually grateful when I stay on. Still, she takes these opportunities to wag her finger at me. "I knew no good would come of your taking him outside, Mr. Haberman," she moans. I can only respond by telling her the truth. "On the contrary, Mother dear, this afternoon he was fine. Up until the moment we left for home he was perfectly happy. In fact, to be perfectly honest, I have never seen him so happy. It's quite evident his dark moods must have something to do with his returning home. Both of us should admit that much."

But I know this is not the whole truth, either. There is a clue here, a symptom; but what is it? Something profound is disturbing him. The artist? The trip back home? Figures of Christ? What is it?

I must find out.

One evening I send Mother off to play bingo with her friend at a church function. She goes out quite frequently now. Maybe two or three times a week. Brodski and I spend these nights together until she returns. This evening I have decided to try something. My aim is to determine whether it is the artist's pictures or the creative process itself that fascinates Brodski. For that reason I have purchased one of those Paint-Yourself-by-the-Numbers kits. As the instructions are easy to follow, and the colors furnished quite eyecatching, I am flattered by the result. My drawing (I won't say creation) of a pastoral landscape is really quite good. Brodski is not as impressed as I. His mood is just as sullen now when I have finished as it was earlier when I began. There is even a hint of mocking disdain on his little bird's face.

Well, then, at least I have learned this much: his mood changes have something to do with the artistic process, the mystery of creation. How else could you explain his utter contempt for my drawing, which in all fairness is at least as pleasing to the eye as some of the Chalk Artist's lesser efforts, except that the little devil knew I was cheating? I am satisfied. I have trod another step on my Road to Damascus.

That night I fall asleep muttering the words: "But what does it mean?"

Doesn't it always happen this way? Purely by accident, when least expected. Once a week someone in the unit is designated "E" worker and cannot leave the office under any circumstances *all day.* Mrs. Knox never deviates from her schedule. You could have a real "E"-mergency in your home. Your father, mother, brother, sister, wife, child, could be sick, mugged, raped, dying, dead, but on "E" day you don't leave the office. Mrs. Knox won't allow you to. As luck would have it, today was my day to be "Emergency Worker." Of course, if it didn't happen this way, it would have happened another. Brodski already had planted the seeds. They were germinating inside me just waiting to sprout. It was just a matter of when the plant would grow, the flowers bloom.

And after lunch time today they did!

As always, it started with Mother. It seems the more time I spend with Broadki, the more greedy for money she becomes for doing less work. Lately, in addition to doing my usual housekeeping chores, cleaning the apartment, adjusting and focusing the lights on his paintings, centering them, dusting and even doing the ironing, laundry and some cooking, I've also assumed a good portion of her Home Attendant duties. And she knows it. In the evenings, even when she is there, it's I who bathes the little fellow and then puts him to bed. Of course I use these hours to good advantage. For instance, I have learned that when in the bath, he doesn't respond any more to a Ruben's nude than he does to a *Penthouse* centerfold; the erotic imagination is really quite lacking in him. But the way he responds to touch is something else. When I fondle his privates and watch his member grow to a size it's impossible beforehand to imagine; or the way he screws up his face and shuts his eyes and squeals for joy with his whole body seeming to knot up in a ball of concentrated delight, it never fails to get me laughing nearly as loudly as he wails. Also the warm water and suds, (the soapier the better), the touch of my hands on his body—these are the things he loves. If he lacks erotic imagination, there's no doubt he's tactile. Perhaps he just doesn't know how to associate pictures with actual sex. After all, he hasn't had any experience. My touch (and Mother's) are the only sexual pleasures he knows. I must admit when I stroke him, I, too, realize some pleasure. Though it would be remiss to call it sexual. I get the same feeling, though not as intense, when holding a butterfly by the wing before letting it go, or crushing it between my fingers, depending upon my whim.

When Mother came into my office this afternoon complaining of not having received her Home Attendant check, I was surprised because she brought Brodski with her. She could have taken him first to a friend, but the moment her mailman told her "No check," she couldn't wait to get to the center. It just goes to show how far greed has taken her; and dissatisfaction. Only two short months ago she was on her knees begging me not to take him outside. And now this. For a few paltry dollars, she exposes him to the riffraff of a welfare center. I didn't remonstrate or lecture her, though. That's not my way. There's nothing to be gained by that. Instead I took hold of a handle on Brodski's wheelchair with one hand, and Mother's arm with my other, and steered them both away from the reception area to my desk, all the while assuring her that everything would be all right. At my desk I introduced her to Mrs. Knox. It was the first time my Supervisor (and the rest of my unit, who just sat gawking. Even when it's not their "E" day they don't take advantage of fieldtime) met Mrs. Rivera and Brodski, and even she was a bit ruffled. Some primordial human spark ignited eons back now flickered in her.

Addressing Mrs. Knox, but making certain to speak loudly enough for all concerned to hear, I say, "Look at this, Mrs. Knox. Isn't this typical of the Department. Here's a woman who works harder than anybody else and the Department doesn't even pay her."

Mrs. Knox rises from her desk, walks over to mine and bids me go fetch the replacement-of-lost-check forms while she picks up where I left off in comforting my client. As I take my leave I can hear her say, "Don't you worry now, Mrs. Rivera. All we need is for you to sign the lost-check forms and have our notary witness your signature. Once you do that, Mr. Haberman will be able to replace your check in no time."

After returning to my desk with the proper forms, I leave Brodski and escort Mrs. Rivera to another floor to seek out a notary. On the elevator I continue to put her at ease, spelling out what I know she needs to hear. "No, Mother," I say, "I don't blame you one iota for thinking the way you do. For wanting money. The finer things in life. In fact, I admire you for it. A parent has got to be crazy to make her children her entire life in today's world. There's no reward in that. Not with kids the way they are today. When they grow up, they leave you. They don't even look back. Why, just look at your own. He's no exception. And to think, all the love and care you frittered away on that ingrate. All the years of sacrifice you spent on him. I'm telling you, Mother, the best thing you can do for yourself is to enjoy the few years you have left. Don't worry about Brodski. He can take care of himself. Or better yet, he's got a softie like me to do it for him. And to think, only a few short months ago he didn't even know I existed."

After another hour Brodski and Mother (check safely deposited in her purse) were ready to leave the office, when those aforementioned wholly unexpected things began to happen.

To begin with, Mrs. Knox transcended her rigid strictures by going against departmental policy and recommending that we issue carfare allowance to Mrs. Rivera and Brodski. "But Mrs. Knox," I exclaimed in utter disbelief, "you know my clients live within walking distance of the center. We're forbidden to give them any money for transportation."

"Show a little understanding, Mr. Haberman," Mrs. Knox responded in an indignant tone. "It's already late. In a short while it will be dark out. Besides, you can't really expect a senior citizen like Mrs. Rivera to walk your client home in a wheelchair." She paused. Second thoughts? Hedging the bet? "I'll tell you what, Mr. Haberman. Go speak to your Office

Liason. Tell Mr. Becker that if it's all right with him, it's all right with me."

Surprised? I was too shocked to be surprised. Besides who was I, a lowly caseworker, to argue with my Supervisor?

Hans Becker is a European Jew out of a concentration camp with the blue numbers on his arm to prove it. From Austrian Aristocracy to Auschwitz. A complete reversal of life-styles. After he saw the Old World die, he dedicated every nerve ending of feeling he had left to helping to build the new. Residents of Harlem stand to profit from this historical synaptical connection.

He once held the lofty position of Director, but has long since been demoted to low man on the totem pole: Office Laison. His greatest crime was that he said "yes" to everything. Each time a member of his staff asked, "Can I give Mrs. Smith a grant for household replacements?" Yes. "Moving expenses?" Yes. "Winter clothing?" Yes. "Summer camp?" Yes. "Three months' rent in advance, security deposit and brokers fee?" Yes.

The downtown financial analysts felt shivers run up and down their collective spines. After auditing Hans' welfare center's monthly grant total for eight months straight and comparing it to all other centers throughout the city, one even went so far as to send a memo to the Mayor's office claiming that Hans was the single biggest reason why the city of New York was chronically in the red. That was Hans' downfall. Now the only thing they let him say yes to is requests for transportation allowance. He can approve no more than a token or two.

However, that's not the way Hans perceives his position. He figures his change-of-work life was a blessing in disguise. With such a reduction in his work responsibility, he can now devote himself exclusively to his extracurricular ("shady," to quote recent memos from downtown) activities. In short, he can help "the people" full time. Despite all his love and care for his black brothers and sisters, though, our Office Liaison has massive attacks of fear. Hans Becker never leaves the office at 5 p.m. alone. He's terrified to do so. He'll stay three hours overtime without pay waiting for the night watchman to walk him to the subway station, or even better, a fellow worker to drive him home. The blue marks are printed in more ways than one.

After interrupting our Office Liaison from what seemed like one of his shadier projects (he was conversing with a large man with a flaming red beard and black beret—judging from his words, an artist—about joining him in his battle to create an art exhibition here in Harlem) and telling him (actually I demonstrated it; Brodski and Mother accompanied me into his office) of my request for transportation, he grabbed me jubilantly in a bear hug and kissed my forehead. "You surprise me, Robert. I always knew you were a good caseworker, but this . . . we should all give such love to our clients. I was just telling Leo here, we need more men like him (and you) in Harlem. Not like those robots downtown. They've no love in them. They're not human beings. They won't even let me use my regular office hours to set up an art show with Leo. Of course"—he smiles, returning to his desk—"I don't have to listen to them."

In such a way I received carfare allowance for Mother and Brodski. Unplanned? Wholly unexpected? To be sure. But now for the real kicker. The *coup de grace*. Not wanting to detain my Office Liason and his artist friend any longer, (not only are we interrupting Becker's meeting but it seems from a few words muttered by the artist that he's looking forward to a belated lunch), I turn towards the door. Mrs. Rivera has already stashed the two tokens in her change purse and there is no further reason to stay. Our business is over. But Brodski won't leave. Once again, something has caught his eye. He is staring fixedly at the Office Liaison's desk. What is it this time? The Office Liaison's desk is no different from any other; just an ordinary gray metallic office desk, the kind you see in every office. Notes, paper, case records piled on top. Two bins, one for incoming material, the other for out going. Nothing out of the ordinary. So what has captured his attention this time? There is no artist at work here, no creative process being unfolded, nothing beautiful to see. So what now?

More than ever I am baffled, and embarrassed too. I'm holding Becker and his friend up and I feel a slow burn beginning to smolder on my neck. Putting my full weight against Brodski's wheelchair, I commence to forcefully push him out the door. But he lets out such a shrill cry that the entire fifth floor reverberates with sound. And even though we are halfway out the door, by some peculiar arrangement of neck vertebrae that enables him to turn his head at a 270-degree angle, he turns around and continues to gawk in the direction of the Office Liaison's desk. I am peering at him dumbfounded when the Office Liaison rises from his desk chair, strides over to Brodski, squats down, and attempts to line up his sightline with whatever seems to be holding his attention. Then, bouncing up jauntily, and half muttering to himself, Becker announces, "The poor boy must be hungry." He hastily retreats to his desk, and after hesitating for a fraction, removes a banana lying between an apple and a plum, and begins peeling away its skin. He then offers it to Brodski holding it up temptingly just a few inches in front of his face.

Alas, Brodski's plaintive wailing only grows worse. He stretches and twists his neck to what appears to be several inches beyond its limit in an obvious effort not to lose eye contact with what continues to hold his gaze. Pivoting on his heels to face his artist friend, the Office Liaison says, "So what do you think, Leo? You've got the artistic eye. There's something about my desk upsetting him. What is it?"

Artist not saint, Leo Byron, laughs in malicious glee. "I don't know about the retard, Hans, but I'll tell you what all his shrieking and crying has drawn my eye to. That damn chicken leg I brought over wrapped in aluminum foil heating up on the radiator. It's a perfect still life. Oh, sure, for a few seconds I thought it was the apple, plum and banana lying on your desk. To tell you the truth, I was even thinking of doing a repeat of a Cézanne still life with them. But no more. That damn chicken leg's not only given me an original subject, but opened me up to a whole new way of looking at things. A new form. I've even got a name for it. 'Civil Service Lunch.' But seeing it's only one thing. Damn, I've got to paint it! My God, if I can put this on canvas," he continues while walking over to the radiator and taking the chicken leg gingerly in his huge hands, "I could not only surpass anything ever done by Cezanne, but by anyone else, right on up to Picasso. But I guess only an artist sees things this way. I'll be damned if I know what got into that freak of yours."

But I do!!!

From the moment I hear his words, "But seeing it's only one thing. Damn, I've got to paint it," they ring in my ears like a litany. And when he lifts the chicken leg from the radiator and Brodski quiets down, my head begins to reel from the shock of discovery. I can't wait for the day to end, to visit Brodski at home, to spend time with Brodski alone and luxuriate in my joy. Now it is the Office Liaison who is detaining me. I hear him calling my name as if from a distance. "Oh, Robert," he says, "today's your "E" day, isn't it? Will you be kind enough to walk me to the subway after work?"

"I'm sorry, Mr. Becker," I answer, my head still spinning, but I was planning to visit Brodski later."

"But that would be after five o'clock, Robert. What are you going to do, work overtime?"

"Not actually paid overtime, Mr. Becker. But as you can see, Brodski requires all the attention I can give him."

"Shall I wait for you to return to the office then, Robert?" he pursues me. His voice betrays him. It's got an anxious lilt to it. "Will your visit be long?"

I do an about-face and confront the Office Liason squarely in the eyes. "The answer to your first question is no, Becker. And to your second, yes."

S O BRODSKI'S AN ARTIST! He must have told me in a thousand ways already, only I've been too stupid or too blind to see it. What else could he be? What else could all his mood changes and inner transports have meant? And his artist's eye. He sees the world only in images. My God, what pain and frustration he must have endured each time he saw a thing of beauty and wasn't able to express his own. But I shall remedy that, little one. All you need are the tools to create. And I will give them to you. Arms, and more importantly, hands, shall be yours.

Now where shall I find them?

How could I have been so blind?

It is Regina Dailey, our Medical Social Worker, who came to the rescue. I had wasted the better part of a week in the medical libraries and with a half dozen physical therapists and rehabilitation specialists who either were remiss in keeping appointments or begrudged me their time. Besides, they know less than I do, and the medical libraries are for students, scholars and theoreticians, not men of practical interests like myself. But Regina Dailey leads me right to the source. Before the words are half out of my mouth she removes from the bottom drawer of her desk the *Abbey Medical Rehabilitation Equipment Catalog,* and lays it before me. Leafing through the pages,, I feel a thrill shoot through me from sole to soul. It is just what I need. "Where can I get it?" I ask her excitedly. "No need," she says. "Take mine. You can borrow mine for as long as you need it. You're the first caseworker who's shown a genuine interest in his client in my three and a half years here. If you can help one client, I'd gladly handprint a dozen more."

I don't need more. One is enough. For me this equipment catalog is a more priceless treasure than all of Shakespeare's sonnets, science's monographs, and the world's great literature combined. That evening I study the book anxiously. There is more here than I ever thought I'd need to know. All kinds of aids besides arms and hands to help Brodski realize his fate. Before going to sleep I think myself fortunate to live in an age where the human body and virtually all its parts can be so easily replaced. Only the soul cannot be. And that is my province. Not sciences'. I don't require help there.

There are advantages to everything. Even working for the Department. The most obvious is field time. A five-minute telephone contact with a client can furnish me with sufficient information to justify an hour's field visit. Often, all I need to know is that the client is alive (even I cannot visit a deceased client and get away with it . . . Mrs. Knox keeps statistics on expiration dates too). If alive, the client rates a visit, and I record one on my W712. Allowing time for travel, not-at-home visits (that's when no one's at home; at least I say no one was) and innovative collaterals (interviews with a nonexistent super, nameless neighbor, a phantom hospital social worker, a man on the door step), I can account for a full afternoon's work with maybe thirty minutes' worth of phone calls. In thirty-four years, I'd say I never made more than ten to twenty per cent of the field visits I've been credited for. My full forty-hour work week cost me less than twenty.

Of course, not all caseworkers are as bold as me. Richard Gould, for example, would never do anything "so dishonest" as to fabricate a field contact. "I could get caught! Anyway, I like visiting my clients." He spends half the day asking me for advice on how to record the visits he does make. "If I leave at 12 'clock, Haberman, how many visits do I have to make?" or one 'clock? Or two? three? four? Another of his daily queries concerns the advantages of eating lunch before or after he leaves for the field. No matter how many times I tell him he can eat first and still record it on his time card when he does leave for the field as L & F (Lunch and Field) and that no one will know the difference, he never does. His greatest dilemma comes on payday. "I'm going to the field before I get my check," he says. "I don't like walking around with it."

"So why go to the field?" I reply. "Go home. Or better yet, treat yourself. It's payday. Go to the movies."

He doesn't even answer.

Every morning he gets on the phone with a client and says "Good morning, Mrs. Riddick. I'm just calling to make sure you'll be home this afternoon. I'd like to visit you some time after lunch, say around . . ." the words grate on my mind like chalk on slate. But I don't let it bother me. The world is full of Richard Goulds. I'm not like them and never would be. The only tragedy of my life is that I have so few ways to exhibit my talents other than robbing the Department of field time. But I make up for it in other ways. At least I try.

Another advantage of working for the Department is . . . well, I found Brodski, didn't I? If not for that pending referral, who knows where I'd be now . . . and he (though he's not the first playmate to come my way directly through office channels). But who would have thought when we started that the Department would protect me from spending my own money on him? It's not that I'm scrimping and saving here. As far as I'm concerned, there's no better way to spend my money. Oh, I admit I live my life prudently. I have no vices, no excesses, and I ravenously accumulate savings in my contingency fund. But there are limits. If I buy all the equipment I need to do him justice I'd have to be prepared for an outlay of thousands of dollars. This amount exceeds anything my contingency fund would permit by far. Luckily, (luck has little to do with it) I have calculated a way for the Department to assume the entire cost. It's really quite simple. And the money I save now will be put to good use later on. Either on Brodski or on someone like him. All that is necessary is to get Regina Dailey to order the equipment I need. A simple medical request form, W401, emanating from her office to the New York State Department of Health Systerns and Management, and in a matter of weeks Brodski should have everything he needs.

Naturally I can't have her order all the equipment I need for a single client only. So I'll vary it. I'll have her order a utensil holder, which will allow Brodski to hold a paintbrush, pen or pencil (or all three at the same time), for Salvatore Domingo, a client of mine who by coincidence uses a similar contraption. No one will know that Domingo's own holder wasn't really lost. His caseworker says it was. That's enough. For another client, Antonio Morales, a spastic quadriplegic, I'll have her order a workplace desk or adjustable work table, which will serve as Brodski's easel. Even though his past medical history doesn't show any prior need for such equipment, Antonio is now ("miraculously") attending night school and studying computer training. He's the pride of my caseload. A letter from me, plus letters from his school administrator, a social worker at the Institute of Rehabilitation, and our own MSW, all testifying that his long hours of nightly study will be greatly facilitated by having such equipment, will be all that is necessary to establish this need. Even Mrs. Knox won't complain. Not when it's essential to the Department's long-range goal of making Antonio self-sufficient.

When the supplies arrive, I can pick them up at Antonio's home. We have an excellent working relationship. I've known him since he was a child and have never reported to the Social Security Administration that he's earning ("miraculously") extra money by working at his school in a part-time capacity. Also he selects his own Home Attendants (in certain situations clients are allowed to do this) and makes his own financial arrangements with them, which I've never interfered with. On the contrary, I've encouraged him; it does me good to witness such entrepreneurial spirit. I've even helped him along by documenting that the Home Attendants work for more hours than they do, thus increasing their paycheck. I do what I can to help. Sometimes one doesn't have to profit tangibly. To be thought of as a God, or even a benevolent despot, is enough.

Some items won't be so easy to procure. They'll require hours, perhaps days, of research on my part. There's not one client on my caseload, for instance, who I can honestly say has a need for a plate positioner (not for food but as a palette to hold paints and tubes for); or a safety bar kit, which will prevent Brodski from falling out of his chair. Thus I'll have to scrutinize my entire unit's cases as well as those of other co-workers on the floor. What I'll do is stay late in the office several nights and go through all the case records. Especially those referred to the Department by the Institute of Rehabilitation and Hospital for Special Surgery.

Also, I'll keep my ears open. B-25 this very morning mentioned that he has a client who uses a relaxation chair with nineteen different seating positions and seventy more for adjusting the upper body, and what's-his-name across the hallway in Unit K stated something about a youngster on his caseload using a magnetic wrist hold-down. I have never before appreciated just how fortunate I am that at least ninety percent of the cases here at Dept. 29 are composed of the elderly and infirm, or are referrals from SSI and Aid to the Disabled. In my unit alone there are half a dozen amputees who use artificial limbs. After I track down these clients, it'll just be a simple matter of going through the same procedure as before, with perhaps one or two minor variations. The actual caseworker doesn't even have to know. I can forge his signature as well as the client's on any necessary form. Even Regina Dailey is superfluous. I can forge her signature as well. And there's little risk in filling out the W401 form and submitting it in a brown manilla inter-office envelope either. I have all the forms and letterheads at my disposal, and given that, there's no limit to what a man of my imagination and resourcefulness can do. When the equipment is ready for delivery—and I'll know the date—I'll just call the client and say a mistake has been made, please accept the merchandise, and we'll have a man over to your house later this afternoon to cart it away.

Everything considered, I should have all of Brodski's special equipment within six to eight weeks. The arm and hand prosthesis I will order through the Institute of Rehabilitation with the aid of Mrs. Thea Goldstein.

. . ."Why, Mr. Haberman, I think that's a wonderful idea. But why did you say we don't have to order leg prosthesis too?"

While I was waiting for the bus this morning the temperature dipped below five degrees. The wind was so fierce that neither fur, cloth, nor skin could shield against its unrelenting shivers. People on the way to the bus shelter were slipping and sliding on the frozen ice, and those who had already safely reached their destination were shrouded in their own solitary system of survival. Naturally, on this morning, the bus was late. Thirty minutes of refrigeration at the crosstown 66th Street bus stop. When the bus finally arrived, I alone was able to withstand temptation. While all the other men and women hastened to position themselves in place to gain entry, I stepped discreetly aside, and even went so far as to hold the pneumatic door with its hard rubber edge, while helping a woman with child aboard. I was all smiles; the perfect gentlemen. By imposing such discipline on myself now, I will be all the more ready to unleash myself on Brodski later.

Mother has gone away for the weekend of her own accord. I didn't even have to suggest her visiting her sister's home in Massachusetts twice. I did go "halfsies" with her. Though she paid for her friend, I paid for Mother. They left Friday afternoon. I started for home with Brodski (the first time he has stayed at my place for an entire weekend) the moment the checker cab took off. The last I saw of them they had turned in the direction of FDR Drive.

My studio apartment has all the features of an artist's garret now. Everything careless, lackadaisical and purposefully strewn about. The only thing missing is the proverbial skylight, but I do have bay windows and a park view. Still, Montparnasse it's not. There are canvases everywhere: rolls of canvas, stretched canvas, some stretched and mounted on canvas boards. Also a dozen paint-brushes, round and flat and long, and even more tubes of paint in all colors; Payne's gray, burnt sienna, burnt umber, viridian, sepia, zinc white, Naples yellow, cobalt blue, yellow ochre, thalo green, Venetian red. And an artist's smock and easel, and roto tray, and turntable, and palette. Everything and anything that goes into an artist's studio is here, plus all of Brodski's own special equipment.

The little fellow doesn't know what to make of it. He peers open-mouthed as I strap him to his artist's chair—the relaxation chair with nineteen different seating positions and seventy more for the upper body—and commence attaching his arm and hand prosthesis. The occupational therapist I employed has taught me well and I know how to use each piece of equipment as well as how to staple the stretched canvas tightly to the canvas board so it won't ripple. When he is seated at his workplace (easel) with the canvas before him and rivulets of paint already squeezed out on his plate positioner (palette), I say: *PAINT.*

He looks at me, at the canvas, at his surrounding, dumbfounded. Not paralyzed, but stricken in another way. As if in limbo. As if groping to understand, to come to terms with what lies before him. I am tempted to help him. It would be such a simple matter for me to demonstrate how to "finger" the paintbrush with his table writer, or, for more exact control, his pencil holder; how to, with what for him would amount to a Promethean effort, touch the canvas with his brush. But I do not. It wouldn't be fair. The rules of the game do not permit it. The first stroke must be done by him. The discovery has to be his. The miracle must come from him alone. To be godlike, one has to create his own world. It is enough for me (now) to show him the way.

We sit there five, ten, twenty minutes; an hour passes, two. I do not say anything. Do not coax him on. Not so much as a word or hint passes from my lips. Absolute silence pervades the room. Then: he begins to move. Slowly at first, with imperceptible little stirrings of his body, followed by epileptic twitchings and wriggling of his arms and hands. What's this? He's stretching-reaching-picking up the paintbrush lying on the plate positioner in a glass cup, just begging for his use.

He's dipping it in a glob of paint. He's . . . He's . . . HE'S PAINTING!!! His first stroke is slow, halting, tenuous, as if a spanked child were reaching out for the object that caused him harm. He looks enthralled—no, terrified. After his first stroke he jerks back; his paint brush drops from his utensil holder against the glass cup and pan holding the other brushes and tubes of paint, and the entire collection as well as the roto tray spills to the floor. He doesn't even notice. Awestruck, he just continues to stare at the canvas. At a gashed slightly less than linear violet smudge: HE MADE!

A tiny wet spot wells up in his eye. A soft voluptuous half sigh, half groan, and then more tears, a sound that emanates from deep inside him, an indistinct murmur, a shriek, an ecstatic outcry, a crescendo of uncontrollable and involuntary body-racking shakes and sobs. He is crying. Really crying! Not his usual "cri du chat"; but crying like us. Like we humans do.

A half hour passes before he is able to start up again. This time by trial and error, each dip and dab of his brush reminiscent of a naked hand in a fire struggling to save a beloved object. After each new impression, he stops haltingly to examine it. Not for aesthetic reasons. He has no concern for that now. But for the sheer effect of it. The impression he is making on the canvas. ON THE WORLD! It is the first time he has ever been able to affect the world. Make his mark. HE IS PUTTING HIS STAMP ON THE WORLD!!!

After maybe another minute or two he falls back exhausted. I push his chair away from the canvas and together we look upon his creation. Grazing my hand ever so slightly on his utensil holder, as if touching the finger of God, I begin to cry. We begin to laugh and cry together. We stay there in tableau like that, both crying and laughing, the rest of the night.

. . . . I was in a bar having a drink to celebrate my recent victory. On the TV screen in the front were two fighters having a go at each other in the manly art of self-defense. The gladiators were drenched in blood; the grunts and groans of their pummeling efforts magnified a thousand decibels by the microphones the TV people had placed ringside. No one in the audience of tens of millions—not myself, the men loitering under the opalescent light of the bar, or even the acknowledged media experts—could detect where one man had the slightest advantage over the other. There was nothing to separate them. They were both equal. A man standing next to me, guzzling beer, by all appearances an ex-pug, said, "I don't know which one of these guys is ahead now or going to win it, but those guys in center ring know. One guy says, I got it. I'm going to win. The other guy knows he's a loser. It's a matter of will. Nothing visible, nothing tangible, but it's there just the same. It happens every time."

The time is coming to bend Brodski's will. Submit it to mine. Up to now I've treated him with kid gloves. Partly because it was necessary to win his confidence. Partly to see what he could do. How high he could climb. But now he will have to be brought down from his pedestal. Yes: The time is fast approaching for Brodski to *FALL*.

In looking over these notes I find for the most part I have been referring to my encounters with Brodski as games up to now. And in a certain sense they are games to me. But my encounters will grow increasingly more serious from now on. Indeed, the further we go, the closer to the real thing they become. No longer are we playing games. Fun has ceased to be the sole means of keeping score.

One thing still bothered me: Was his artistic talent commensurate with his desire to paint? Any apprehension I had was soon overcome. Once he got used to the equipment and was able to accommodate himself to the necessary adjustment, he began painting in a frenzy. I witnessed such a gushing forth of creative energy I can only compare it to what I've heard tell and read of the great masters. It was as if he were making up for a lifetime's privation with each brush stroke. Everything he's seen and sees turns into a painting. Every part of him seems to create. He shows no preference for right or left artificial limb. Ambidextrous, he paints with both hands. Or more accurately, he paints with his soul. His entire being comes into play: body, mind, soul participate equally. All he is and has he gives to his work. On the average he paints two, three, maybe as many as four canvases a day, although sometimes he takes a week or longer to finish a larger, more ambitious project. I have seen him spend as much as a month on one painting; an entire day on a single feature of his composition. His concentration, like his energy level, is immense. He stays with a work in progress until it is right.

At first I thought he knew where he was going with each new work, but not really. Many times he'll just sit for hours staring with lusterless eyes at his canvas, and then, AHA! he perks up and starts again.

Nothing can detract him from his work. Chopin's military mazurka in F Minor can be playing, or I can allow the cacophony of vulgar street sounds to enter our studio by leaving the window open, but he goes on unperturbed. Even his heretofore favorite painting, a slide of Munch's The Scream, cannot deter him from his mission. When creating, his appreciation and interest in other men's work is null and void. He is like a writer who finds all the other books in the world a distraction when he is working on his own manuscript. Often he even paints with the lights out. In fact, he seems to prefer it that way. Closer to his imagination, I guess. Nor does he eat anything but the most meager breakfast all day. First, because he so eagerly awaits my arrival to take him to the studio (Mother still thinks we go for walks outside), and then, when he's there, because there's no stopping him: he can't wait to get at his own canvas. He attacks it voraciously. He has no need of anything except to paint. Nothing else exists for him.

In such a way are masterpieces made?

I spend each afternoon observing him. He is as indifferent to me as to everything else. Once he begins to paint, he goes into a trance, curling his white-coated tongue over his chinless chin. He is happy, I'm certain. Who has ever been so happy? So full, rich and complete? I envy him during these hours. I hate him. The more he becomes one with his art, the more I come to realize what real work might have meant in my life. Each new inspiration of his only further widens the chasm between me and my own tawdry, humdrum work. I gaze in unblinking awe at each stroke of his brush as if he were a great master and I his student and to miss one would be the same as to miss life's most important lesson.

In fact, so taken am I by Brodski that ever since meeting him, and especially since discovering he's an artist, I have been regularly spending ten to twenty hours a week in the public library doing homework on him. Reading books on art history and method, the question of talent vs. genius, the cat cry syndrome, and on the aforementioned so-called Great Masters. Of course, I read this material in my own way. You won't find any respect bordering on reverence inside of me. The experience of art is not like entering a cathedral for me. Nor do I have any naive expectation that art can effect a profound change within me. Even if I did all the research in the world, would it enable me to paint one good picture? Create a single masterpiece? Nor is cultivation my goal; nor appreciation; nor love of knowledge. Maybe least of all love of knowledge. Nor do I have a college boy's inclination to indulge myself in idle theories on aesthetics, or wild masturbatory speculations on art. And even if I did, with whom would I do so? Mrs. Knox? Brodski? No. My purposes today (always) are pragmatic. Utilitarian. "Be prepared" is my motto. "Know who the enemy is." And so like a West Point cadet who fancies himself a future general, I consume these pages like the battle plans and stratagems and stockpile of military information they really are.

But even with all this knowledge and assiduous preparation I don't delude myself for a second that I will ever be able to enter Brodski's head completely. When all is said and done, I am as alone as he is. Perhaps the best I can hope for is for us to be alone together. For that I must be able to make educated guesses as to what his paintings mean. With this intent and purpose I have begun naming them; labeling them; or, should I say, reducing them to size? It is quite apparent to me that the more I use my own words and vocabulary to interpret his work, the more I might be straying from their original meaning. But what else can I do? He won't tell me any more than I already know, and at least this way I can make some sense out of them for *My Own Purposes.*

And even if his work does remain beyond my grasp, describing his different techniques is well within reach. And although his approach altogether might be called Abstract Impressionism, one technique in particular—his Primitive Minimalist technique—deserves special mention. He starts out flushing all the color and oil on the canvas he can. Satu-

rating its surface to excess. Then instead of adding, he sub-
tracts. From the luscious thick oil of his initial outpouring,
his surface gets progressively thinner as the subject he works
on becomes more and more precise. With time there comes
a certain austerity. By amputating those features of his composition that seem to him superfluous (and to us, essential)
he attains his vision of reality. A vision so pure you can see
it all at once. His paintings at the end strike me as luminous, fundamental. By their very scarcity and lack are they
complete and whole. Knowing the world as it is today and
looking at his paintings—and at him—I ask myself: Could
he be right? Is less more?

He looks as if he has more fun than other artists if only
because he is more preoccupied with taking away than adding to. On his face he wears an absurd, silly glued-on smile. In
spite of the abstract quality and sparseness of his canvas there
are always a few things sprinkled throughout that strike me as
social comment. They are the key; they unravel the mystery
for me. Usually his images are taken from real life. A particular
favorite of mine is his version of Mother and Child. At least,
I call it that. The way I see it, he has the mother typically cradling the babe in her arms with the child's lips outstretched and
groping for the nipple. But he cannot reach it. The mother is
turned away, immersed in another task. It leaves you with the
succinct impression: Will the babe ever reach his goal?

All in all, he plays no favorites. All the great subjects—
good, evil, God, love, right, wrong, sin, guilt—draw his attention equally. There is no doubt his work has merit. Forget all
the books. One glance at any of his final compositions tells
you that.

By the end of the day he has nothing left. He collapses
in his chair, having used up his last drop of energy with the

last stroke of his brush. He is literally in a daze as I carry him home. Only then will he eat and allow his other needs to be attended to. Following supper, for example, he delights in a warm bath. Having soaked for an hour, reveling in his joy, he is ready to sleep with the angels. And, wrinkled as a fetus, I put him to bed. Oh yes, one last thing. His erections are stronger than ever now. Eros, I concur with the Neo-Freudians, definitely has something to do with more than one kind of creation.

After leaving him, I prefer to walk home rather than take a bus or subway. It gives me a chance to unwind for the day. During these brisk wintry night walks my mind conjures up images of the next phase of our relationship. The last phase. Like Brodski, I have things to look forward to, though I don't sleep as well as he does these nights. My obsessions won't let me.

THE FALL BEGINS: Laden with gifts, I rushed into Brodski's apartment at noontime today. Mother and son had not seen me in such a tether for a long time. Mother had already bundled Brodski up and he was ready to leave for the studio to paint. But we never left. Instead I hurried into his room, unwrapped my lavishly giftwrapped presents, and took down from the wall three of his favorite prints. In their place I hung three paintings of his own. They were simply but elegantly framed; each frame wonderfully suited to the particular painting. Then I centered them and adjusted the dimmer lights. When I finished, Mother exclaimed that these "pictures" were even more beautiful than the ones that previously hung there. Bordski didn't utter a word. At first he seemed confused, then happy. My guess is that it was not only seeing his beautiful paintings that made him happy. His happiness had more to do with the only real interest an artist can have in such things: the pride and joy of having *made* them. As he continued to gaze upon his paintings, I slipped out the door undetected by him, signaling Mother to join me. I asked her to care for Brodski that afternoon because I could not. "I have something more important to do."

Her ambivalence manifested itself at once. That the prospect of spending an entire afternoon with her son once again had a certain appeal there was no denying; but she had purchased a week ago two tickets for a Latin music festival to attend with her friend at Madison Square Garden that very day, and that prospect also had a certain hold. So she stood betwixt and between, unable to decide. There was no doubt in my mind that it was up to me to help her. And I did. After rummaging through my suit pockets, I calmly removed two tickets for the same concert for the following Wednesday afternoon and I gave them to her gratis. To make my offer even more attractive, I volunteered to reimburse her for her own two tickets, which were nonreturnable because she had bought them at a special discount price. The fact that my tickets were floor level and hers balcony, I must confess, came as a complete surprise to me, although, of course, it didn't hurt my bargaining position any. Still, in all fairness to Mother, I think that at this particular moment she was more interested in being with her son again than in any fiduciary gain. In any event, my negotiations successfully completed, I left at once.

Now, only when I'm gone, will Brodski come to understand that he won't paint today. It is good that the discovery comes while I'm not there. It will be all the more poignant and telling that way. The last he saw of me I bore presents and was scrupulously hanging his paintings to the exact centimeter required. Now a thousand contradictory thoughts enter his head, and some painful doubts. He doesn't know what to make of me. In the most important way I have let him down. He has only Mother and his paintings to spend the afternoon with. How could I do this to him? Be so insensitive? Not know that they are not enough? Not realize that a finished work, even his own, can never compare to one in progress or yet to be made? It is only the next work, the new creation, that is of real value to the artist: I, of all people, must know that. The ones already finished, hanging on the walls like dead things, are just that: dead. After a half hour he will hardly be able to bear looking at them any longer. He will want to paint. Mother won't have the faintest idea what's bothering him. "You have your new paintings, darling, the ones Mr. Haberman was kind enough to bring over for you. Why are you. . . ?" And a half hour later: "For this I had to stay home and miss my con . . . Spoiled brat! Selfish!" THE FALL HAS BEGUN!!!

"It's not fair!" says Mother Earth.

"Why should our Department be picked on!" says Rodent Face.

"Why not the policemen! The hospital workers! The transit workers! The teachers! The firemen! The clerical workers! say A-21, B-22, C-25, D-24, E-26, and F-23.

The Secretary-treasurer of local 371—an oral fixed type if ever there was one, he can speak for interminable stretches of time about nothing—has just completed his warning speech on *City layoffs!* "No use kidding ourselves," he said. "The rumors are true. Be prepared for it. We're next. You know how the Mayor has always hated this Department. The cops and the firemen are his favorites. Even the garbagemen rank ahead of us in his opinion." Now is the time for questions and answers. And the workers don't disappoint him. They attack in full fury . . . The very same people who only days before were voicing their displeasure with *"How much I hate this job . . . I'll never stay . . . First chance I get, I'm leaving. . . Gone!* now vocalize with the same fervor their indignation about being sacrificial lambs at the mercy of the Mayor! City Hall! Downtown! City, state and federal purse strings! Corrupt city officials! Previous administrations! Etc., etc. The Secretary-treasurer's insatiable need for oral gratification is satisfied beyond all expectations.

His meeting scheduled for the waking hours of the morning, between 9:30 a.m. and 11:00 a.m. continued on until 3:45 in the afternoon. Worthy civil servants, many coming from as far off as Brooklyn, the Bronx and Queens to hear their mighty union oracle, populate our fifth-floor office, which is now filled to brimming with more faces than I've ever seen here. One of the great staples of the world, lunch, is dispensed with. No one has the stomach for it. Not even Mother Earth (fried chicken and chocolate cake) and Rodent Face (liverwurst on rye), whose lunch habits heretofore have always been as constant as Mrs. Knox's clarion call for statistics at the end of the month. Everyone is absolutely aghast at the great oracle's prophecy. And why shouldn't they be? Their entire civil service life-plan freighted with all those wonderful benefits—pension plan, hospital plan, medical plan, annual leave, sick leave, coffee break, and no one harassing them, competing against them for their job, their money, their raises—all those hard-won freebies and fringe benefits will be so much water under the bridge now if they're laid off.

Even I stayed to listen. Not so much because I was interested in what the union delegate had to say (deep down I don't feel anything pertaining to the job has anything to do with me): it was just that I felt it an excellent opportunity to pique my colleagues. When people are at their lowest, I seem to rise to the occasion. I'm at my best in those dour moments and can often, without hardly trying, display a satirist's gift for wit and humor. And from the moment the Secretary-treasurer opened his mouth that morning, I knew the opportunity was there to outdo myself:

"Colleagues and co-workers, our Secretary-treasurer is right. If we have any legitimate grievances, let's form a committee, organize our thoughts, write them on paper, and submit them per procedure 18-787 to his office at once."

"The hell with procedures! We want our jobs!!!"

"Fellow workers, when you signed up with the Department and attained civil service status you attained more than words. You attained a lifelong contract with the City of New York, and I quote: *'You are insured a job for life.'* Could we ask for anything more from this great city of ours?!"

"But I have the least seniority of the whole staff here. If the layoffs come, I'll be the first to go."

"Only so a favored city official downtown can support his mistress in the style she is accustomed to, my man."

"And what about my wife and kids? She's sickly, needs some kind of female operation, and those darn kids all got buck teeth. Who's going to pay for their braces?"

"My dear man, ugliness builds character. We all know that. And as for your wife, women can survive anything. They're the stronger sex. Just ask them. Besides, in today's world, who honors contracts? And even if you are civil service and your job is for life, that doesn't mean they can't take it away from you. In fact, this only proves they can!"

And so I heckled, incited, rabble-roused not merely my colleagues in Unit B and from the other units, but my peers and cohorts who joined us from the other four boroughs as well. I doubt sincerely if even Brodski could have brought me such unadulterated joy. It made up for a goodly portion of my thirty-four years' association with the Department.

It goes without saying that my missed visits with Brodski didn't do any harm either. Why should he be exempt from life's vicissitudes? On the contrary, it fits right in with all the plans I have in store for him in the weeks and months ahead.

Since that day two weeks ago when the Secretary-treasurer spoke to us about the inevitability of layoffs much has happened in the Department. Tonita, our two-hundred-and-fifty pound clerk-typist hippo, has gone off her rocker and called in the police. Something about the Director spying on her. Bugging her telephone calls. A simple case of too much pressure. Perhaps she shouldn't have written on the grievance sheet submitted to the union delegate's office in triplicate, per procedure 18-787, that the Director's horticultural interests were the main reason why the Mayor hates our Department so. She was suspended this past Monday.

And Richard Gould has become fanatical about his W712 field-visit recording form. He goes over it after work every day now. Why after work? Because he doesn't have time during normal working hours. He's too busy racing around in the field or filling out other forms in the office. Of course, he's going back to when he first joined our unit. Not an easy task when you consider that takes in two and one-half years. That's a lot of field time to go over. Especially for a man who has never missed making a visit in his life.

As for our Office Liason, Hans Becker, nothing bothers him. He's been down this route before. But then, why did he cancel his art show . . . voluntarily?

Mrs. Knox? Merely more grist for her statistical mill. "Now everybody will tow the line," she says, "or else!" As her first priority she called for a complete review of all case record entries. "Some are illegible, others merely not written neatly enough. They will have to be written over."

"All of them, Mrs. Knox?" I ask. "Some of my caseload dates back years."

"All of them, Mr. Haberman, and yours in particular. Your handwriting is atrocious. I'm probably the only person in the entire office who can make it out."

"He probably wants it that way," mumbles Richard Gould. "He makes up all his visits. If you can't read them, how are you going to verify anything he says or whether he's been there or not?"

I don't argue with my Supervisor. (Or Richard Gould). The fact is, I agree with her. Downtown means business. For the next several weeks and more, much more, I plan on staying in the office the better part of the afternoon to review and, if necessary, rewrite each and every one of my case record entries. Despite my bold words, and even if I do have seniority, one can never be too safe in times like these. I have enemies in the Department. Mrs. Knox, for example, after fifteen years would like nothing better than to get rid of me. And then, the other workers will take more kindly to me, seeing me work so hard. Besides, my handwriting is atrocious.

There are other things I can do to ingratiate myself with Mrs. Knox and the others. From now on when Mrs. Knox's daughter calls I'll make a special effort to be cordial with her. To take her messages courteously. That's not as easy as it sounds when you consider she's a duplicate of her mother. And in the mornings when my supervisor and colleagues babble on about office gossip, or what they ate last night or watched on TV, or the day's headlines, or some celebrity who's caught their fancy for an hour, I'll listen politely. No longer will I exhibit smug aloofness. In fact, I'll join in. I'll respond with blandishments. Again it won't be easy . . . but it shouldn't be too difficult. These sessions only last ten to fifteen minutes. By 9:15 things are back to normal: The workers are buried in their death routine, the hate has surfaced, the day has begun.

I thank Providence that Brodski is in his final phase. This enforced unresponsiveness to his creative needs happens to coincide with my plans for him. One must always look for the good things, I repeat to myself over and over as I rewrite my past case record entries one at a time.

"Staying in late again, Mr. Haberman?"

"Yes, Mrs. Sampson. It seems these days I can't get enough of you."

. . . Coming home from work today on the subway, between the 96th Street and the 72nd Street stop, I saw a beautiful young woman. Besides makeup (an excessive amount), teased hair and a faraway look (she refused to acknowledge my stare), she had a withered left arm. It was more like a fin than a normal arm. Two forked fingers jutted out from a paper-thin stem that was adorned by a thin gold bracelet.

Before getting off, I pushed past several other passengers to ask her where she bought the bracelet.

I have been going over these case record entries for what seems like forever now; two weeks straight, till 5:00p.m. each day; over and over and over again. My head feels as if it's wedged between a case record vise. I have what must be writer's cramp in my hand. If I never look at another case record again the rest of my life, it will be too soon. Going to sleep at night, all I see are case record W2 entry sheets with their marginal headings: Problem. Family Composition. Eligibility for Services. Health. Relatives. Living Conditions. Service Plan. Recommendation. On and on and on. Again and again and again. Every marginal heading means another rewrite and another and another. Whenever I take a break for five minutes, not leaving my desk, just looking around the office at my fellow workers expending pretty much the same nose-to-the-grindstone energies on similar efforts, one thing alone sustains me: Brodski. The little fellow has not touched a brush now for an even longer period of time than I have been writing these !?*%$! case record entries. He must be as famished for creation as a starving man is hungry for food. Good. That is the way I want him. When I get out, and I will, he will . . . That is the day we both await.

In the meantime, enough frivolous talk, wishful thinking. Back to work. Marginal heading: Problem. Family Composition. Eligibility for Services. Health. Relatives. Living Conditions. Service Plan. Recommendation. On and on and on. Again and again and again.

Pardon my broken record, but that's just the way I feel. I'm tipsy from overwork, boredom, physical and mental fatigue. I hate this job, myself, Brodski. I will get out. He will . . .

It was difficult for me to interpret his reaction when seeing him for the first time in so long. Perhaps it is enough to describe him. He was haggard, drawn; a benign grey beard sprouted straggly on his chin; he smelled badly. Mother had ignored him for the most part, begrudging him her maternal labors, and understandably so. No matter what she did for him, she said, no matter how hard she tried, his mood never changed. He remained dismal and glum "when you aren't here." And now that I am—is he happy? Does he envision at least a faint hope on the horizon? I think so. But even I cannot be certain. What I do know is that his dull gaze and absence of zeal left him the moment I arrived. And when I shaved him and scrubbed him spotless he was restless as if he wanted to go somewhere. To the studio? Then say so, darling. You know the word. S-T-U-D-I-O. Here, after me, like this. S-T-U-D-I-O.

To add to his frustration, I insisted he eat breakfast before we departed. Mother said he hadn't touched a bite (and she's not one to exaggerate) since that last day I called informing her about the emergency in the office that would prevent me from taking him out on our daily strolls for the next several weeks. Only after he had gulped down his last mouthful and I was satisfied that he had something substantial in his tummy did I rush him off to the studio to paint.

It is a good day for creation. The season is changing from winter to spring. There are colors burgeoning about everywhere. A patch of blue in the sky; a mat of green in the park. There, look! A young woman bedecked in a coat of many colors across the street. (He didn't notice). Colors to paint with, my dear. To liven up the old bloodstream. You are alive once again.

Once at the studio, in his chair, with his arm and hand prostheses attached and his easel and canvas before him, he burst into tears. But these are easy tears to interpret. They are happy tears. He is happy. After every few strokes he makes, I adjust the angle on his relaxation chair; because there are so many different positions for seating, and even more for moving the upper body, I have what is almost an infinity of combinations and permutations to play with. At first Brodski hardly noticed. He was so happy to once again be at his labor of love that he probably thought I was only trying to make him more comfortable so he could paint better. After a while, though, when I changed the angles more sharply and it became increasingly evident that I wasn't out to help him—on the contrary, quite the reverse—I heard an occasional cry or muffled whimper come from him. But they were restrained, as though he was afraid to express what he really had in mind. By the end of the hour the angles I was experimenting with were so acute that no matter how he adjusted his magnetic wrist hold-down, or manipulated his universally adjustable hand-splint, he could barely reach the canvas with his brush.

All his plaintive grievances, which had increased considerably, were to no avail. I continued to change the positions each time I thought he was making the least bit of progress in adapting to them. After a certain point—precisely two and one half hours from the time we started, on his twelfth seating position, to be exact (I, too, keep records), and his thirty-ninth for the upper body—his fits and tantrums stopped and not another sound was heard from him. It was as if he had decided to brave it from that time on. Artists have endured more for the sake of their art, so why not he? Besides, it's better than being at home having to listen to Mother's chronic laments, isn't it, little one? At least here there's something to be gained. A worthy cause. Compared to Mother, these little orbital spins of mine must seem as exciting as soaring in space—upside down, topsy turvy, at a 180-degree angle lying flat on his tummy suspended in midair like Cupid aiming his arrow.

Nothing stops him from painting though. As difficult as it was for the little fellow, one thing I'll grant him. He never compromised a stroke. He never shirked his duty. If he didn't hit it right the first time, or the second, or the eighteenth, he just started again. He'd dab his brush in the paint-remover varnish—this was a painstaking procedure for him—and go on from there. He endured all my space-spinning explorations as if they were just so many penances he had to pay to be a member of his holy artistic order.

Was it worth it? As they say, depends on how you look at it . . . or who looks at it. When I took him home at the end of the day he was so dispirited he couldn't even eat or avail himself of his nice warm bath and accompanying genital message (first time he ever missed that). But I'm certain that because of the difficulties I put him through which made him exercise his concentration to the fullest, he did produce good work.

Very different from my own work progress I'm sure. No matter how many times I write and rewrite this dribble, Mrs. Knox still finds something wrong. My handwriting is still atrocious. And she's right. That's not to say I don't suffer as much as Brodski in my work. I do. But evidently suffering isn't the only prerequisite for producing good work. Perhaps one must suffer in a special way.

What way?

I expect that Brodski will show me.

I have cast Mother aside for good. From now on Brodski stays with me and Mother will be permitted to visit my modest bachelor quarters only by appointment. Little did she understand the ramifications of my offer last week to treat her for the Easter vacation to a fully paid return trip to "her country," Puerto Rico. I just gave her the Eastern Airline tickets, Flight number 179 ($197.20), as well as spending money, three hours ago. Away with you! Begone! May you have the worst flight possible and I read about you in the morning headlines: Eastern Airline DC-10 Jet Liner Crashes Killing . . . As usual, Mother took her friend with her, though this time I had to pay her way too. Mother refused to treat her and the woman had already expended almost her entire life savings on making a down payment for a home in her native land. It seems both women came from the same little village, Old San

Juan, and shared the same dream to return to it at some time in their lives together before it was too late. But, of course, they never did. It took me to make it happen. When it comes right down to it—money!—Mother is as tight fisted as any of us. The more she has, the more she wants. She hardly parts with a nickel nowadays if she can help it. And why should she? Did we not come to a tacit agreement over a month ago that I would act as her rich uncle in return for certain favors?

Now I have Brodski all to myself. The arrangements I made with Mother were "temporary," until she gets back from her Easter vacation; when, she thinks, I also have to return to work. But I know better, don't I? At that time I'll tell her I've taken a leave of absence from my job and Brodski simply doesn't want to go home with her. One look at him then and she'll have to agree. And the truth is he never will go back to her now regardless of how I treat him; not when he's actually within "sitting distance" of his beloved canvas, and when his painting is dependent upon pleasing me. Mother's ambivalence and ensuing guilt will be easy to appease. Her greed and cumulative months of frustration with Brodski will far outweigh any tender feelings she still might have for him. Also, per our tacit alliance, a few more dollars in the till won't hurt either. And she won't have to drink alone at night. Oh, didn't I mention it? Mother has taken to sousing it up lately. The negative influence of her friend, a rummy, as well as, perhaps, some deeper, more personal problems.

I've made arrangements with Caesar Rosario, my client, Antonio Morales' Home Attendant, to care for Brodski during my working hours. I told him that after he leaves Antonio's house at 8:00 in the morning (that's when Antonio leaves for school) he can just as well come over to my apartment for his morning nap. Brodski will have already been cleaned, talcumed, diapered, and eaten his breakfast by that time, and other than changing his bed position once or twice, Caesar shouldn't have anything to do until I return home at noontime to care for him the rest of the day.

"Yes, Caesar, the Department doesn't have to know anything about the money you earn. In fact, I prefer it that way. That's why I'll be paying you cash on the line personally. What do you mean can you trust me? Who do you think's been Antonio's caseworker all these years!? . . . Oh, Caesar before you leave, one last thing. My art studio. . . . Yes, Caesar, I do a lot of painting. Painting's the love of my life. You're not into it. Into women. Well, each to his own, as they say. Anyway, no matter. Just make certain you don't touch a thing."

Mother put up more of a fight than I had anticipated. Apparently mixing with the natives regenerated her ancient maternal instinct. And learning that I had transplanted all of Brodski's belongings during her absence—dresser, crib-bed, art objects, prints, everything; his room here is a virtual replica of his room at Mother's apartment, only the view is different, and in some respects better—I imagine didn't do her any good either. But as I thought he would be all along, Brodski was the clincher. The little fellow would have nothing to do with her when she came to visit us this afternoon upon her return from the hinterlands. One look from me when she tried to remove one of his figurines from the dresser and he let out such a shriek of protest that he literally drove her home in tears. I can just see Mother taking a few extra quaffs this evening with her friend.

Maybe I ought to send them a bottle of champagne.

On second thought, I'd better not. My contingency fund's not all it used to be and there's really no sense overdoing it.

How can I say what it's like having Brodski as my roommate? I can do anything I want with him. He no longer has Mother to protect him. Not that she did such a good job of it or ever interfered with me, but just her mere presence was sufficient to dampen my spirits. She could be sitting silently staring vacantly at the four walls (a favorite pastime of hers) and I took it as the foulest intrusion. Ask any unhappily married man what I mean: "My wife doesn't have to say a thing, just her being there, in the next room, is enough to spoil everything. Once we set up house it was all over. I could no longer be one of the boys, much less myself."

Once again I have absolute dominion over my life and what is the same thing: over Brodski. Morning, noon, afternoon and night I can give my wildest impulses free rein. I can take his favorite painting, Munch's The Scream, off the wall, mark it up, cut it up, in front of his eyes, and what can he do to stop me? I can do the same thing with any of his other prints or objets d'art, or even his own paintings. Whatever whim comes to me at the moment, no matter how fickle, I can translate into action. I can toss each love object of his, one by one, out the window, or if I prefer, if it so suits me, I can crumble, tear and shatter all of them into a thousand pieces, into tiny multicolored ribbons and fragments, and then toss the whole kit and kaboodle out of the window like so much confetti at a parade, and all he can do is sit there looking on. Or I can use his prints or paintings or his work in progress to cover my floors, as my grandmother used to do with old newspapers; I can trample upon them with dirty shoes when I return home after an April shower, or I can rip them to shreds with my iron-heeled boots, and what can he do to stop me!

I ASK YOU, LITTLE ONE: WHEN I AM DOING MY WORK AND YOU ARE WATCHING ME, WHO IS IT WHO'S MOST ALIVE THEN!?!

This morning I got up before dawn. I lifted Brodski from his crib-bed and took him to the rooftop and together we waited for the sunrise. When he saw the orange-red haze transform itself into the golden globe, his face dazzled the colors of the rainbow. Sitting there with him in my arms, crumpled up within himself like a turtle inside its shell, I knew he understood that nature's art was in every way superior to anything man-made.

I do the same at sunset. The demise of the day and the moon's quicksilver smile are equally beautiful to behold. My darling's sweet celestial purring sounds show me he is in complete accord.

Now every morning and night the little devil won't let me be. At sunrise and sunset my humble bachelor quarters echo with such crescendoes of sound that I have to wonder what the neighbors think. And coming from such a tiny body. He commences his wail to awaken me at the earliest hour, but if I rise, it is only to shut my bedroom door. I don't take him to the rooftop. At sunset I am likewise unavailable. I've gotten in the habit lately of taking my daily constitutionals at just that time. Besides my eight hours sleep I need my share of exercise these days to keep up. God knows I don't get it at the office. Though I don't jog. I think people jogging, especially women, are ugly.

Before leaving the office today I must remember to call an insulation company and make an appointment for them to send a man out to assess the cost of a complete soundproofing of my apartment.

The black woman who serves me my tuna fish on whole-wheat sandwich with hot chocolate every morning at the diner on 125th Street has one salient feature. It is not her vibrant, always cheerful voice, her frenetic all-hands energy, not even the extraordinary patience she exhibits with the glum-faced working people, the sleepy-eyed welfare recipients, or the gang of young punks who frequent her establishment regularly. It is her rear end. Her glutius maximus. Her pathetic efforts to squeeze these massive hams into shape with a panty girdle only magnifies how disgusting they are. For the past week and a half I have taken Broadski out to breakfast every morning.

"Oh, hi Caesar, thanks for coming over to pick him up. Want to join us for breakfast? . . . No, not at the table, Caesar. Here, at the counter. Alice can't see us over there, and we can't see her. And it's too early in the morning for me to be bouncing up and down out of my chair to get an order, and I'll be damned if Brodski's in any shape to serve as waiter.

". . . What you say? Why isn't he eating? He did already at home. You don't really expect him to have an appetite in a place like this, do you?

". . . Then why do I bring him here? Caesar, did it ever occur to you I might get lonesome eating here all by myself every morning?"

Forget caserecords. Forget work. As far as Brodski's concerned, things couldn't be better. I even have the weather on my side. It's so nice lately I've been taking him outdoors with me again virtually every day for the past several weeks. Only our sightseeing tours aren't what they used to be. No longer do I follow him. I lead the way. Brodski sees only what I want him to. As far as seeing anything beautiful, he might as well have blinders on for all the good it will do him to stretch that dradle neck of his. This past week alone I must have shown him more of the "real world" than he'd seen up to now even if you multiplied all our prior outings a hundred times over. And, yes: it's getting nicer out each passing day.

On Monday I stood over him in his carrying bag and made him watch a mental patient probably released from a nearby hospital forage through half a dozen different trash cans for scraps of food for at least two hours.

On Tuesday, coincidentally the same mental patient, only this time wandering through the city traffic in a dazed condition. We followed her for blocks until she fell, then we just stood there watching (I stood, he watched) her slobber over herself in an epileptic fit until an ambulence came and took her away.

On Wednesday, a bag lady with feet and legs swollen the size of an elephant's; a disheveled beggar man sunning himself on a park bench sheathed in tattered sheets, sweaters, shirts, and, to top it off, a shredded inside-out overcoat. It must have reached eighty-five degrees that day if it was one. And just before entering my building, I stopped before what I thought would be a real eye-catcher, the elliptical buzz-saw of flies feasting off dog excrement on my stoop. Imagine my surprise when Brodski wasn't upset by this. I waited and waited and gave him a good long look but the little bastard refused to become unsettled. In the apartment I tried to make up for it by giving him another close-up, this time of his own feces, but again he showed no reaction. If anything, he appeared interested. I must be on guard not to bring in my own set of values here.

On Thursday we didn't go out. I didn't feel like it. But on Friday I made up for it and then some. A three-legged dog. That's right. You heard me. A three-legged dog. The woman standing beside us, upon seeing the scarred-up mongrel sniff and put his muzzle underneath her companion's skirt before continuing to hop, skip and jump along, murmured, "That's sad." She offered no such words of compassion for his owner (or Brodski). You won't believe this: his owner is also a cripple, also missing one leg. Brodski and I followed the four-legged (in toto) pair all the way to the cripple's home that day. You can be certain by the way Brodski reacted that sometime in the near future he's in for an encore.

On Saturday nothing so interesting. The best I could do was a handsome black youth on crutches. Quite accidentally turning my head diagonally to the left, I noticed a lumpy intersection of scars on his right hand. My first thought was that the surgeon had botched up the job. Not enough incentive, I figured. The youth and family (if there was a family) probably had no money. Let the interns work: Doc's out at the country club playing golf. In any event, since the day afforded me no better sight, I positioned Brodski in his carrying bag and made certain he got the same close-up of the disfigured hand I had.

As an added bonus I make certain that our excursions coincide directly with his preferred work hours. Not only do they come at the very time he is most habituated to painting, but seemingly on the spur of the moment. That way I know there's nothing he can do to prepare himself for them.

For example, I might return home at noon, dismiss the Home Attendant, and set Brodski at his easel and canvas so that he is bursting to paint. Or maybe he's already made his first stroke or laid his initial outpouring of oil and color on the canvas, or even well into the actual composition. It's only then that I permit the impulse to hit me. Or I remember something I don't know how in the world I forgot in the first place. Like having to make a seventy-two-hour pending visit (we have seventy-two hours from the time we get a new case to make initial contact; failure to comply and it's grounds for dismissal according to Mrs. Knox); or having promised to visit Harry Harris (I've been his case-worker for years and they're carting him off to a nursing home tomorrow; he's 101 years old and looks it) or Margaret Fenderson (my black-is-beautiful scorched-pinky-white-flesh fire victim case); or Carlin or Montero or Alice Miller or . . . Or perhaps the weather is so beautiful I decide it's just too nice to stay indoors: "Let's get some sunshine, darling. You can always paint later, So what if you're in the midst of an inspiration." Or: "Let's go for a walk in the rain." A French girl told me once she loved to walk in the rain. I thought she was daffy (still do), but maybe Brodski can see its merit. "It's only a spring shower, darling. It won't last long." Just long enough.

Always when he's most engrossed in his work does the impulse grab me or do I remember something. At those times I literally tear Brodski away from his beloved canvas and carry him off to see the pleasure pains of the world.

When we return home and he's shattered and ruined by the sights he's just seen, I try to make up for it by allowing him to paint. I permit him no respite. No rest period. No good night's sleep to refresh the system, or stiff drink to ease the burden of memory. The hurt and pain are still heavy inside him; the afterglow of the counter girl's disgusting fat ass, the intersection of scars on the handsome youth's hand, the three-legged dog hopping, skipping and jumping along with its one-legged master: they're all there, embedded in every painful pore of his body when I give him the order to: PAINT! Now or never, you little bastard . . . paint! What does he do? I give you one guess. You're wrong. He can't! The tears slowly slide down his misshapen face, to land on his receding chin, then roll up and over, like a waterfall that won't stop for any obstacle. I let him absorb the full weight of his creative block before carrying him off to the bathroom.

You can bet he has no erections on those nights!

Even at work I manage to have fun these days. The office continues to have every appearance of a mausoleum as I gaze around the room looking for a worthy target to relieve my monotony. And there she is: Ms. Pais. My office favorite. In the pinch she's always good for a few laughs. Though she now sits apart from her unit, from the entire office staff—she was allotted a lone corner with a desk to herself after her last blowup)—technically she's still considered a member of the department's family. Ms. Pais reads books all day long. Assiduously takes notes. No scholar in any of the great libraries of the world works harder than Ms. Pais. You can look up any time of the day and see her writing something down. Presumably for her night school course requirements toward getting a degree in accounting or business administration. Ms. Pais wants to improve her pocketbook if not her mind. Makes sense, doesn't it? Sure. But what doesn't make sense is that Ms. Pais hasn't passed one course in eleven years. Not one. If only you could see her. The fleshy parts of her underthighs lopping out of her dress one foot too short, the penguin straddle, the shrill high-pitched West Indian nasal sounds. Constant mutterings to herself. An absolute mess. Before retiring to bed this evening, being in such generous spirits thanks to Brodski, I decided to share my good cheer with my coworkers first thing in the morning.

Without anyone knowing it, I slink into the office before the other workers arrive and swipe one of Ms. Pais' tattered and well-marked books from her desk and naughtily slip it on a fellow worker's. I hate to describe what happened an hour later when Ms. Pais found that poor worker who unwittingly had her book on his desk. Suffice to say all hell broke loose. (If one can describe a catatonic fit in semi-religious terms). What good ten thousand milligrams of Valium against Ms. Pais' wrath. Not much. Just ask that poor worker—if you can find him. He took off for the field in the middle of an office emergency. It took two hours at least for Ms. Pais to calm down. But, alas, I might as well have been trying to cheer pallbearers riding a funeral hearse for all the success my efforts had on my fellow workers. They preferred to stay on their Sisyphus treadmill as if nothing was happening during those two hours from 9 to 11. They completely ignored Ms. Pais and did (not feigned, but did) a full morning's work. In fact, if anything, they exceeded their usual output. Such discipline, such good work habits, and "they" say civil servants use the least excuse not to work. Well, here's one who begs to differ. If the Ms. Pais incident is a precedent—and it is—I will vouchsafe they don't.

Not what's going on here? The little bastard's up to something. When I yanked him away from his canvas today while he seemed to be at a high point of creative activity, there was none of the usual show of protest on his part. He didn't as much as let out a whimper. If I didn't know better, I'd say he was almost happy. Grateful. He acted as if he was looking forward to it. Normally his hearing is so acute (like all his senses: taste, smell, touch; they compensate for his general condition) that even when I sneak up on him from behind when he has totally surrendered himself to his painting, somehow he knows I'm coming to interrupt him and he lets out a tremolo. It's his way of saying no. Today, if I'm honest with myself, by the very absence of that sound, he said yes! And then, when

I took him with me on my visit to Mr. Bohatir and his vegetable-wife, he didn't act the least bit disturbed when I positioned him (he was in his wheelchair) in front of her bed. Her
Home Attendant was working her over at the time and Brodski couldn't help but get a look at that diaphanous corpse-like
body being lifted, pushed, shoved, and dropped into place.
She was lying there as always, with that huge water-in-the-
skull and misshapen snaggle-toothed mouth of hers, not sad,
not happy, but frozen in a gaping grimace of bedazed wonder.
What eternal question was she pondering, if she could ponder? Yellow lines of urine trickled down her infant chubby
thighs and brown stains smeared her stretched-marked rump
and the small rectangular dry-down underneath her. And
once, when the Home Attendant lifted her to her side, with
hands like grappling hooks, to remove her diapers, first thrust-
ing with what seemed like unnecessary violence a towel inside
her, ostensibly to clean her, I thought her beebee fish eyes
were going to pop out of their sockets as her obese white belly
huffed and puffed in complaint. At that juncture, Mr. Bohatir
rushed to his wife's aid, shouting that the Home Attendant
was manhandling her, and tried to help by imploring her to
sit up. "Sophie, sit up. Sit up, Sophie." But that body had died
long ago and little or nothing could be done for it, nor could
it do anything for itself except fight back by its very death-like
immanence against any living efforts to resurrect it.

But here's the interesting part: All the while this was going
on Brodski didn't once close his eyes or blink them, or try to
turn away or twist his dradle neck, if I would let him (which
I wouldn't).

But when we were ready to leave, already in the door-way,
and I was allowing, as I always do, Mr. Bohatir to recall the
one and only image he has of his wife when he first met her in

the "old country" wearing a sunflower-patterned golden dress and a wide-brimmed hat ("Oh, such a hat you never did see, Mr. Haberman") I could see Brodski craning that same neck when the Home Attendant got in his way to get a better view. Not having the heart to interrupt the old man's recount of his reverie, I continued to half listen to him and half observe Brodski. I tell you he wanted to stay. It was plain as day he wanted to stay. It was I who stood there refusing to see what my eyes took in. His dradle neck was so contorted as he made every effort to suck in one more last look that I even lost my place for a split second and slapped him across the face to get his attention. First time I ever did that. As you know, that's not my way. But it just goes to show that even a man with as even a temper as mine can lose control of himself when sufficiently provoked.

Now what does all this mean?

I knew it! I knew it! You know what he did when we returned to the studio late this afternoon? He . . . *HE PAINTED!!!* That's right. The little ingrate sat there in his relaxation chair with a smirk on his face as wide as the counter girl's disgusting fat ass and he painted. And all I could do was stand there with both hands knotted behind my back and watch him. And, of course, it doesn't take much to guess what he painted this time. Any numbskull could figure that out—Mr. Bohatir's vegetable-wife; what else?! I tell you I never felt so humiliated and debased in all my life. Who's the idiot here? That's the question I keep asking myself. Here I expose him to . . . and he paints it!

Well, if it's a fight he wants, it's a fight he'll get. I said all along I prefer a strong opponent to a lackadaisical foe. And I do. If he wants to put me to the test, so much the better. He'll find out fast how much of a warmonger I can really be.

Now let me see. I have someplace hidden away here in my notes something about this. Oh, yes, here it is:

HAVE YOU EVER SEEN ONE CHILD CHASING ANOTHER? THE ONE IN THE LEAD, NO MATTER HOW AFRAID, IS ALSO GLEEFUL, MANIC. BUB-BLING OVER WITH LAUGHTER AND GAIETY. HIS FEAR APPEARS MOCK. THE ONE BEHIND IS FEROCIOUS AND SERIOUS. THE HUNTER NEVER PLAYS AT HIS GAME. ONLY THE ONE HUNTED. IS THAT WHAT MAKES HIS PLIGHT BEARABLE? WE MUST DO SOMETHING, LITTLE ONE, MUSTN'T WE?

But I wrote that a long time ago, while we were still in phase one. Many things have happened since then. Changed significantly for both of us. I wonder if I can still count on it. I wonder? . . . No. I'd better not.

Here's what I have decided. Just as I once enlarged his universe, I now will shrink it to four-wall size. From now on he doesn't leave his room. He doesn't get to see one new thing, beautiful or ugly, outside. That's his punishment, let him paint from memory. From inside himself without inspiration. He stays locked inside himself from now on all the time. If I can't stay one step ahead of him in this tug-of-war of ours, then I'm not the man I claim to be.

Before I forget, let me make one thing clear. His paint-ing of Mrs. Bohatir the other day did not miss a detail. Her stretch-marked rump; her obese white belly huffing and puffing in complaint; her frozen grimace of wonder. He even managed to capture those grappling hook hands of the Home Attendant and make you feel the ostensible violence they were perpetrating on his charge. But remember, I never once denied that he paints well. Even if I do project my own interpretations on his work, his craft and talent go without saying. Anyone can see that. That's not what I object to. If you think that about me, you don't understand me any better than Mrs. Knox does. I couldn't care less that he's an artist. Who cares about art anyway? It's his . . . it's his . . . *IT'S HIS UNBENDING BELIEF THAT HIS WORK IS AN ABSOLUTE END IN ITSELF THAT I FIND ABHORRENT!*

Since that day he was banished to his studio room, he has painted an entire collection of ugliness. At least that's the way these paintings appear to me. The bag lady with elephant legs; the epileptic slobbering at the mouth; the three-legged dog hopping, skipping and jumping along with it's one-legged master. I let him. That's my strategy for the present. How much can he paint? How long can he go on? In his whole life he's only been exposed to so much ugliness. If my calculations prove correct, he'll run dry soon enough. A few more days, or at most a week, of this building up of his false confidence, letting him think he's got me where he wants me, and then, *boom,* his lights go out . . . forever. He's got nothing more to paint. There won't be anything to inspire him. Then we'll see who the artist is in this house.

And don't think he's done all this without malice aforethought. Even if he is an idiot and therefore deserves the benefit of the doubt, he's guilty. I should know. I tested him. The evidence in my favor is overwhelming. How else can you explain that only when I'm not there to observe him does he slip in a painting that isn't ugly? Like the Office Manager's Civil Service Lunch still life. It's true. The more tests I perform, the more I'm convinced he's only doing all this to spite me. When I left the room the other day, after placing a new canvas mat before him (actually he can replace canvases himself, but I did it just to hasten things up a bit because naturally, I can do it easier and quicker than he can and I was anxious to see the results of my test), that's when he painted the Lady With A Parasol. But get this: When I returned and took my customary place behind him to watch him paint, he gestured for a new canvas and immediately started out on something ugly: The Handsome Black Youth With the Intersection of Scars. And worse. A closeup still of his own feces. Now don't tell me that's inspiration. There's no doubt about it. Anyone who can paint that crap has got to be doing it to spite me. And he wouldn't do a stroke unless I watched him all the way. He made me witness every stroke until the blasted thing came to life before my very eyes. And when he finished, he smiled. Not a mere smile, but an artful smile, one graced with secret knowledge. It was not in pride at a job well done, his painting, but at the look he saw on my face. I did everything I could to suppress it, but how could I? I'm human. I've got to express my feelings even if he doesn't.

Well the time is fast approaching for his little artistic flourish to peter out. And when it does, we'll see who has the last laugh in this house. He might have won a battle, as the saying goes, but I'm going to win the war!

I can't take any more of this. He goes on and on painting and all I've done for the past four weeks is sit here and watch. It's my world that shrunk, not his. At first I thought he'd fold up and quit when his ideas ran out, but I was wrong. He's long since stopped painting anything—beautiful or ugly—he might have seen in real life. Your guess is as good as mine where his inspiration comes from. It must have something to do with the way he's made. That's the only thing I can figure. Unless he gets his strength from his desire to beat me. Maybe that's what keeps him going. There's great strength in having a cause. I've always held that religious fanatics and artists have that much in common. They both have absolute faith. That's another reason why I detest artists so. One thing I do know. No normal person sees the world the way he does.

I've decided not to sit around any longer and wait. I'm going to take the initiative once again. It was a stupid tactical error to have given it up in the first place. Whatever advantage I had I lost. He's gotten stronger these last several weeks and I weaker. Every day he sits at his easel so contented and happy he reminds me of all I'm not. Right now he's in his most fertile period; four and five paintings a day. It's the ideal time to take myself off military pass and return to the war. As soon as I come home from the office today I'm going to institute a new series of punishments which should make up for the last four weeks and more. He's going to pay for what he's cost me a hundredfold.

Now: let me count the ways:

I take my adjustable shaving mirror from my medicine cabinet and place it before him so that he cannot paint a stroke without first seeing himself. The trick is to tilt the mirror to follow him regardless of the angle at which he twists his head. If he makes an effort to knock it away with his arms and hand prosthesis in a fit of frustration, I merely detach them. No explanations necessary, but let's see him paint without them. Like Narcissus gazing at himself in the pond, Brodski *must* look upon his own image. But he is not Narcissus. His squints, squeals, rocking motions to and fro in his seat, tell me that clearly. At one point he even tries to paint from memory. He shuts his eyes and makes every effort, but even though he can create in the dark, we both learn that he cannot do so effectually with his eyes closed. An interesting distinction here; perhaps, at a future date, I can do something with it. It takes him a full afternoon and much pain and effort to reach some sort of solution. Somehow, through what can only be described as a kind of self-hypnotizing technique, he learns to blank out his mirror reflection while continuing to look directly at it; in this way, by looking at himself as though he weren't there, the little bastard is able to paint. From his distant expression and the way he responded to my touch later that evening in the bath (he barely rose to halfmast), I doubt he was satisfied with the results. Didn't I once see a movie in which the concert artist knew before anyone in the audience when his music wasn't quite up to par? Even more interesting to me is the fact that he never thought of painting a self-portrait. If I were in his place, that would have been my way of adapting. Perhaps some things are too ugly to paint even to him. Or maybe, as I've suspected all along, he just lacks a Lautrecian sense of humor when it comes to his own appearance. That would really be a case of self-over-coming. In any event, tucking my darling into bed that night, I think I have made a good start in balancing the score for what he put me through and more.

Next:

Shine a weak-batteried flashlight in his face while he's painting. If he blinks, wiggles his head, gnashes his teeth in rage, aim it all the more closely between his eyes. Observe how his inner eye dominates. Like a Spartan, he stoically paints on. Affix a clamp light with a stronger illumination to his easel so the unyielding beam bores directly in on him without mercy. Watch him struggle this time even more assiduously than before. Pick up testimony attesting to this fact by the way he blinks unceasingly, even attempts to shield his eyes from the glaring light by making an effort to lift one arm prosthesis up to it while continuing to paint with the other. It must be the same as holding up a thousand pounds to him. He can only do so for a fraction before it comes tumbling down. In the end he surrenders. He closes his eyes. But ironically, just by giving in, he triumphs. His inner eye dominates. For when he opens his outer eyes he is able to paint on. Next take the theatrical spotlight off the wall. You know the one. The one heretofore reserved for his favorite painting, Munch's The Scream, when a reward was due him. Only now there's no reward. Not unless you consider his efforts to help himself—paint—under these circumstances a reward. But that's stretching it a bit, don't you think? No one takes the bible—"God helps those who help themselves"—seriously anymore. Fill the spot with the maximum wattage it will take till it's smoldering with heat. Hold it in his face for five, ten, fifteen minutes straight without letup. When I get bored or restless or am curious as to how he'll respond under different circumstances, I use my dimmer system and vary it a bit from low to medium to high. Take note: He is defeated. His inner eye can see no more. He can paint at no more than low to middling intensity. I am a trifle disappointed that he didn't reach high. The way he endured and struggled inspired me to root for him to do so. That doesn't make me inconsistent. I've always maintained I enjoy a good struggle more than an easy victory. But even if he had done it, I wouldn't have given him a reward. No: We're not playing games anymore.

Buy some graph paper and three or four different-colored pencils. Tape-record a generous sampling of Brodski's classical musical collection; an even healthier portion of his neighbor's blaring disco sounds; and top it off with every metropolitan resident's midday buffet delight, the jamboree of N.Y.C, street sounds. Create a graph calibrated to measure artistic excellence (or its lack) in relation to the above-listed kinds of music and sound. Put earphones on Brodski's head and let him paint, making certain he understands that if he is to be allowed to do so, he must simultaneously listen to the music. Tunnel in the different sounds and groups of sounds to his retarded brain. First the classical music, then the disco, and last the honks, horns and screams of the city. Using a yellow-green colored pencil, collate to your graph as best you can his fine-drawn watercolor the classical music inspires him to create. Do the same on your graph for his sensuous oil color, which the disco sounds motivate, only now use a blood-red pencil, and note the San Francisco bend in your graph's curve indicating a distinct dropoff of artistic control and mastery. His jarring abstract painting prompted by the cacophony of city street sounds lends itself to like scientific measurement. You should hardly be surprised when this last work made up of punctuating slashes of line receives the lowest dip yet recorded on your graph, now signaled in by a three-pronged multicolored pencil.

Follow this by scrambling all three tapes together in a single-reel hodgepodge so that you have a cornucopia of whimsically discordant sounds; no sound, bar, note, belch or scream bears any relation to the others, or to any score that Brodski might previously have heard or even preconceived. After recording his response to this last reel on your graph in ivory black, look at it. Look at Brodski's paintings. A perfect correlation exists—from his first watercolor excelling in exquisite gradations of light and shadow and exhibiting meticulous draftsmanship, which received the highest ranking on your graph's scale, to the latest tossing sea of sounds causing a visual mishmash on his canvas, which was accorded the lowest rating possible. You can congratulate yourself, fellow scientist. You have captured in the most rigorous scientific manner the causal relationship between the ever-increasing breakdown of sound and the concomitant ever-increasing difficulties of the artist in overcoming it. Your graph's polyglot language of yellow-green, blood red, ivory black and three-pronged color has put to surgically precise number and scale all of Brodski's aborted starts, stops, jerks and slashes as well as any polygraph records the variations of its subject's body activities. Everything that is lacerating, contradictory, and unharmonious, either on tape or on canvas, is marked down and brought to chrystal-clear order on your graph for scientific posterity.

And I am the one solely responsible for it. My graph is even more telling than any of his paintings. Is this not incontrovertible proof that I am the greater artist/SCIENTIST than he? For I have orchestrated everything. He has merely reacted. My graph is a perfect poetico-scientific metaphor of the creative process in ruin. Of the artist's jumbled and jangled inner state when interfered with and blocked by alien and warring stimuli. I congratulate myself for this valuable scientific contribution. Next time, I pledge, I will do even better. There are many, many more independent variables to control, and I have only just begun to acquaint myself with my subject and his ego defenses.

How long will this go on? Until he gives up. Until his thirst is slaked. Until I break his will. That's what it's about, isn't it? His will. His need to create. He must stop painting. He must stop attempting to become more than he is. He must accept himself, as we all do, for the meat and potatoes and dead thing he really is. He must not aspire to anything. He must not want to do anything. Be anything. He must not remind me of what I'm not. What I forgot ages ago and never want to recall. He must reconcile himself to live a life fixed, dead, ugly and inert. He must content himself with eating and sleeping and eating some more. He can't fuck. (Maybe he can. Maybe I should find him a partner, another limbless idiot like himself. It would be fun finding out if he can). Most important he must relinquish his need for beauty, which is what separates him from the rest of us and reminds us of our lack. Only when he learns all these things will I stop. And he will learn. As long as he's in my classroom and I am his teacher he will learn: I promise you that.

"He's not only an idiot," Caesar said when I returned home from the office today. He was responding to something I had said earlier that morning.

"Really," I said. "What else is he?"

"Well, for one thing he likes art, and for another, music. And I'll tell you something else. I don't like the way you're treating him lately."

I stood silent for several moments, rubbing the side of my face to collect myself. Then with as controlled a voice as I could manage under the circumstances, I asked, "What do you mean by that, Caesar?"

"I'm not Brodski. Don't play games with me," the Home Attendant answered. And then he gave a peremptory jerk of his head at the closet where I had locked away Brodski's prosthesis and special art equipment before he stalked out of the apartment.

Or was he peering at the Visual Mishmash, which hangs directly to the left of the closet door?

Caesar's response wasn't the only jolt I received today. At the office I learned that despite all the work I've put in getting my case records into shape, the real focus of the departmental investigation is field time coverage. Office tittle-tattle has it that the investigation is citywide and that it will be used as a basis to get rid of those employees not doing their jobs as an alternative to, or in addition to, proposed city layoffs. Special Investigations has put Rufus "Hatchet Man" Boines in charge and he's coming uptown next week to check out our field recording forms himself. If that's the case, I'm a goner. After thirty-four years I can kiss this job goodbye. There's no way I'll be able to make my W717's justify my field time after having spent all these weeks going over my case records thanks to Mrs. Knox. I wonder if she set me up. I wouldn't even put it past her to call my clients to see if I've been visiting them. Perhaps that explains her secret scribblings in her notebook every time she gets off the phone lately. And what about Rodent Face? When he told me the news this morning his little rat's face was exultant with triumph—you'd think Rufus Boines was coming to our office to escort him through the pearly gates personally. Come to think of it, Mrs. Knox wasn't so glum either. It definitely was a setup.

First thing tomorrow morning I'd better call the union delegate and ascertain whether I'm eligible for a pension if I'm fired.

And social security. Do I have to be sixty-five before I can start collecting?

Oh, well, I can always go on welfare.
It would serve them right.

Who? Who would it serve right?

When strapped in his relaxation chair in front of his easel ready to paint, it has become Brodski's habit of late not to utter a sound or otherwise exhibit any emotion. He knows full well what fate awaits him if he is to be allowed to paint, and he sets his mind stoically to the task. It is just a matter of what kind of punishment and how severe and how much time will pass before I initiate it. These moments prior to the punishment must be even more cruel for him than the actual punishment is. It is like having Damocles' sword handing over his head. He never knows when it will fall. On the other hand, I find these times of fear and trembling, specifically because they are unexpressed, delectable. So much so that I have gotten in the habit of stretching them from seconds to minutes to hours, according to my whim.

Still, just once, I wish I knew a way to break him of his stoical attitude.

When I aim my blow dryer at Brodski's backside when he's in his chair waiting to paint, the little fellow bumps and grinds in such a frenzy I could swear he was up on the latest dance craze. If I didn't have a dryer (actually I haven't styled my hair since beginning this final phase), I could just as well use an infrared lamp with a lever arm for this experiment, or even an electric heater placed under his chair. As it is, though, I am quite content with the hair dryer. In addition to watching him twist and turn his little ass to my heart's content when I turn the machine up full blast so the heat waves are concentrated on his tiny buttocks protected only by a flimsy integument of elastic diapers, I can also get a first-hand view of his face contorted into a thousand grimaces I'd never seen before. I note that the amorphous quality of his face permits him many more possiblities of expression than we normally made people have. But no matter how vigorously he thrashes about he never cries "uncle," or asks to be removed from his hot seat. Even though his chair's rubberized seat cover might be smoking, and I can nearly smell the burnt elastic of his diapers, the little bastard doesn't give the faintest indication of yielding to my will. He remains steadfast, gladly willing to withstand all the punishment I can mete out, just so he can paint, if I let him, later on. How do I know he's not just being stubborn? Something in the family of false pride. I don't. One can never be one hundred percent certain about these things. But I think I'm fairly safe in assuming that any special bravery on his part is due to love of his calling. After all, martyrs are not exactly unknown in the arts. There is an entire rogue's gallery of these foolish fellows, each literally killing himself for the sake of his art.

And finally, when I permit him to paint, it's as if he had never experienced the slightest discomfort. It's as if his brush were the one stepping on hot coals the way it flits back and forth on the canvas. With the frenzy of genius the little bastard makes one painting after another as if he were being paid by piece work. He has the appearance of one of those speeded-up cartoon characters, or Charlie Chaplin in his mad-dash walk. No Japanese assembly-line worker could do more. Perhaps I should contract additional Brodskis and go into competition with the art manufacturers of the world. Certainly in our age success in the arts is not so much a question of quality as of producing sufficient product and then mass-merchandising it. On second thought, one Brodski is enough. I am not greedy. I can accomplish all I need to with Brodski alone.

One thing more than any other annoys me about this experiment. Though the little bastard suffers before and after his painting, he never suffers during. When he is in the throes of creation, not as much as a single pained expression appears on his ugly face. It's as if his pain is suspended, in limbo; somehow he is able to block it out of his mind and save all his effort for painting. He never lets the pain interfere with or spoil the quality of his work. Only afterwards, when his painting bout is finished and I have taken him down from his throne, does he become human again and know what it is to hurt. I have to be careful here. The temptation is great and unwittingly I might cause him more harm than I mean to while conducting this experiment. In fact, the first time I executed it, Brodski couldn't sit on his rear for a week afterwards. Actually, he never really sits. Regardless of how I strap him to his chair, or which harness I use or safety bar, he just sort of lies there—no, *is* there—like a flower torn from its stem.

I absolutely love his helplessness.

Brodski's response to a block of ice planted under his rump produces pretty much the same histrionics as the hot seat does, except for one significant difference. The paintings produced because of the ice share one thing in common: A wintry look. I call it—his Cold Period. He paints what appears to me frostbitten landscapes: bag ladies, beggars and Bowery types warming themselves around a fire; children in the park sleighing. There's no such commonality of theme when he undergoes the hot-seat phase of this experiment. Not even a sunrise comes out of that punishment (although he's painted many of them before). Perhaps you can explain it; I can't. As for the rest of it, though, it's all the same. Even when it comes to the care I extend him. If it's not burnt flesh I have to guard against, it's his catching pneumonia.

I get some of my best ideas in the middle of the night. I force myself to rise and gather up my pen and notebook, which lie on the floor beside my bed, and jot them down. It takes considerable willpower to turn the lights on at this god-forsaken hour; one truly has to be possessed. I hardly know what prompts such inspirations. But I know enough to follow them, nevertheless.

Poor Brodski. Somewhere between sleep and waking hours his fate is decided.

My brainstorm to strip Brodski of one of his paintings while he was still in the act of creating it serves as a sterling example of a punishment that came to me in the wee hours and pales by comparison all my other ideas that evolve out of slow and conscious deliberation. Thus when I attempted to punish Brodski by marking up Munch's print, or by using his own finished creations as old newspapers to cover the floors with, I hardly got a rise out of him. But when I yanked away from him his current work in progress and commenced to carve it up before his eyes, before the paint was even dry—nay, even before he had completed his last grandiose brushstroke— this proved more than he could bear. He sobbed inconsolably for hours afterwards. It was as if I had torn a baby away from its mother's arms.

And many other of my ideas conjured up in the nocturnal glitter have proved just as cruelly efficacious. Take my experiment dealing with his sense of smell. When I placed my large electric fan in such a position so as to let him get a whiff of his own stool, he hardly noticed. Regardless of whether he was constipated or suffered from diarrhea (and depending upon which punishment I mete out both conditions appear frequently now), or whether his bowel movement was regular (needless to add, very rare nowadays), the little bastard went on painting. But when I did the same with my own feces his fleshy nostrils quivered, and then clogged, and his breathing became so impeded I thought he was near gasping for his last breath. It was impossible for him to continue painting until I opened the windows and got the stench out of the room. But by then it was too late. His mood had already passed and it was time for his bath. The fact that I was equally revolted by his stink and not my own seems to me something for psychologists to speculate on. The "why" here doesn't really interest me. I think it's sufficient if I just describe my experiments as best I can and let others draw their own conclusions.

At least this time.

I've even found a way to break the little Spartan of his stoical attitude while awaiting punishment prior to being allowed to paint:

Place Brodski in his relaxation chair with no arm and hand prosthesis on, no easel and canvas before him, and let him be. He can go for hours without as much as twitching a muscle.

Next (moments after the first sequence), seat Brodski in the same chair with easel and canvas now before him, but still no arm and hand prosthesis attached. Watch the taut line on his cheek quiver, but still, no real sign of discomfort.

Finally (again, don't let a minute pass), seat him in his chair again with the easel and canvas before him and this time attach his arm and hand prosthesis as well as the pencil holder clasping a brush that is dripping with oil color. But don't let him paint. After five, ten, twenty minutes, observe his eyes, which are positively screaming with expression. His Stoical Response (S/R) is broken.

Don't repeat this experiment. It loses hold over its subject after the first time.

And finally, a stroke of genius: my electric shock experiment:

Wire an electric circuit through Brodski's universally adjustable hand-splint in such a way that his torso automatically receives a shock every time he touches the canvas with his brush. Sit him in his chair and, please, don't offer him any resistance. If anything, prod him on. The better he understands he's free to paint, the more joy this experiment will bring. The first shock he receives will be no greater than if he were walking on an electrically charged rug. He will jerk his brush back, stare bug-eyed at the canvas, as if contemplating an evil omen. Twenty to thirty seconds later he will try again. Same thing. Only who knows what he's contemplating this time? After half an hour, more or less, of numerous trial-and-error efforts, he will achieve a method remindful of a pointillist: dipping and dabbing the canvas with short, abrupt, pointed strokes, as if stepping between raindrops to avoid the storm. It is time to transmit a more telling message. Wire Brodski around the vulnerable parts of his body: his genitals, under his arm (arm?) pits, and place one live wire in the flabby folds of his neckless neck, just barely grazing his ears. One dab of his brush now and it's like all hell breaking loose. He is completely befuddled. Some evil force has taken over. How do I do what I do? It has something to do with these wires. He scrutinizes them but cannot fathom what. All he wants is to paint, and for once I'm not offering any overt resistance. If he can just figure out a way to overcome these wires, ropes, cords, these wriggling and writhing snakelike strands, he's free to paint. But how!? Should he give the canvas a soft caressing kiss of the brush? Nope! That's not it. The way his tiny torso was lifted from his seat, despite the straps, harness and safety bar he's in, tells him that. Then perhaps a jackhammer blow. Nope! Not that either. If anything his reaction was worse. He looked as if he was receiving a massive jolt of electric shock therapy. (He is). The little hair he has stood on porcupine's end. Good thing I put a bit in his mouth or else he might have swallowed his tongue.

At last, when he has nothing left, when he's drooping and sagging in his chair like a fish out of water, I disconnect the wires with an adroit, cleverly concealed flip of the wrist, and take his brush, which is still in the utensil holder, and guide it slowly to the canvas. Miraculously there is no jolt this time. No earthquake tremor. Just a streak of paint on his canvas, like it should have been all along. The way the little fellow gaped at me you would have thought I was God! The Devil! Or had the power to bring the two together. I couldn't stop laughing.

But don't get the idea that this experiment is flawless. Many independent variables, secondary motivations, and even a concept in experimental psychology known as generalization are not being given their just due. Despite its incompleteness, however, this experimenter is happy. I'm still laughing . . . even in my sleep.

Walking to the bus this morning I observed two young boys playing football. One boy darts out, feints to the left, then right, before continuing straight ahead for his TD pass. The other boy's arm is cocked but he never releases the ball.

"What happened?" asks the receiver, trotting in to meet his friend.

"That was fine," asnwers the quarterback. "I just can't throw that far."

What would happen if Brodski's brush couldn't reach the canvas? I decided to find out:

When I returned home that afternoon, after dismissing Caesar, I took out of the closet the deluxe exercise mat I had ordered months ago from the Abbey Rehabilitation catalog but until now had made no use of. Now I knew its purpose as if it had been preordained. I laid it before Brodski's relaxation chair. Then I walked over to Brodski's crib-bed where he was catnapping and lifted him from it. The little fellow sleeps all the time now. My experiments have taken their toll on him. While he was still fuzzy-eyed, I seated him in his chair but didn't bother to strap him into it or use his safety bar or body harness. I merely let him dangle precariously, following his natural body gravity. Then I placed the easel and canvas at a sufficient distance from him so that he couldn't reach them without having to lean so far forward that he would fall to the ground. The thought occurred to me that he might not brave this experiment. Well, there was no time like the present to find out. To my delight, Brodski persisted in trying to paint, but each time he did so, the damage was no more significant than if he had fallen on earth made soft by night rain or morning dew. The exercise mat so cushioned his landing that I couldn't in good conscience call it a punishment. It irritated me to think that he might enjoy free-falling through the air like that. The falls certainly didn't stop him from trying to paint. And that is the sole criterion.

I toyed with the idea of exchanging the deluxe exercise mat for the red-brick tiled floor on my patio. But that wouldn't serve my purpose either. For if Brodski went for it, he would break every bone in his body, if not kill himself. I racked my brains for a compromise. Finally I decided to try out my wooden floor indoors, but to buffer his crash by laying blankets and sundry bed materials on the floor. The image of a deserted building lot near the welfare center in Harlem strewn with jagged rock, half bricks, broken glass and tin cans kept floating through my mind. What I wouldn't have given to test Brodski there. But I knew the idea was out of the question. Suppose someone should see me. And how would I get his equipment there and back? No. My indoor punishment would have to do. It might not be as inspiring as the lot, but it would jar him plenty and let him know this was no holiday. To Brodski's credit, I must admit he tried. He even brought a smile to my face at one point when perilously leaning over but at the same time attempting to be cautious, he seemed suspended at a fixed angle like the Leaning Tower of Pisa. But finally he teetered and toppled to the floor. His thump was music to my ears. When I returned his painting equipment to the closet that evening Brodski heaved an audible sigh of relief. I don't recollect him ever doing that before. Progress!? Later on, in the bath, I examined his little body ravaged by welts, bruises, cuts and bloody wounds. And when I oozed ointment on his aching torn flesh to soothe the pain, the way he looked at me with the saddest eyes I have ever seen buoyed my spirits immensely.

Yes: Progress is being made.

I had no one to blame but myself for what transpired between Caesar and me the next day. In my haste to get to the office that morning after having slept late, I had completely forgotten about him. Of course this wouldn't have happened under normal circumstances. But nothing is normal in the Department these days. Department employees are being dropped from the payroll like flies swatted down. And I can ill afford another black mark on my record. Not with "Hatchet Man" Boines due to arrive any day now to start his investigation, and Mrs. Knox continuing to record my every move in her notebook.

"How do you explain this?" Caesar said the moment I walked through the door. And he pulled the blue-cotton hospital gown from Brodski's limbless torso, exposing his many sores, welts and wounds.

"I can't," I said, fumbling for words. "Other than the fact that I was trying to train him . . ."

"Train him!? You train animals," the Home Attendant said, hurling the words at me like stones.

"You *teach* human beings!"

The way he leaped to his feet, for a second I thought the Home Attendant was coming for me. I had already raised my hands to protect myself when at the last second he sidestepped me and headed for the door.

"You're worse than any idiot," he shouted.

"What could be worse than that?" I yelled back.

"A CRIPPLE!!!"

And he slammed the door behind him.

I turned now to face Brodski, who was still naked, his battered body shivering. As I bent down to pick up the hospital gown to cover him, a smile creased my lips. Poor thing, I thought to myself. I have to do everything for him.

Long before he set foot in our fifth-floor office it was known he had arrived. Someone said he had seen him getting out of a "spiffy" two-tone Eldorado with telephone, TV and bar. Another worker saw him waiting for the elevator on the ground floor. And Mother Earth confirmed all by pointing out that our Director had actually deserted his Botanical Garden habitat for the first time in years during office hours.

"But what does that prove?" queried Rodent Face.

"It proves he's here! The Special Investigator is here! That's what it proves!"

The murmurs', whispers and stretched necks continued until A-37, who had been on the lookout in the elevator corridor, came rushing into the office shouting, "It's him! It's him!"

All quieted as our Director led the Special Investigator into the intake section at the front of the office. Every staff member sat with one eye glued to his desk and the other on him.

Rufus "Hatchet Man" Boines is a tall, erect black man with a perfectly rounded and shiny bald pate, a bushy mustache, and a somber no-nonsense air. He was wearing a white shirt, the collar stiffly starched, a paisley tie, a dark blue pin-stripe suit, and his beige alligator shoes gleamed every time the light hit them at a certain angle, as did his manicured nails. The distinct fragrance of "a man's cologne," Brut or possibly Canoe, trailed after him wherever he went.

The Special Investigator strode through the center with the pomposity and disdain of a royal personage. Stopping first at the intake section, he made comment to our Director about its workings. He mouthed a few platitudes to the intake supervisor as if he were a politician soliciting votes during a campaign. A client who had been burned out of her home with three children and was waiting for emergency placement caught his eye, and he walked over to her to inquire about something, but when she, in turn, was about to return the favor by asking him something, he waved her away as if he were a fine Southern gentleman and she white trash. He had little time to be bothered by clients. So what if some recipients suffered from a breakdown in the bureaucratic machinery? That was inevitable. It could not be helped. There was nothing he could do about it. As a whole, the system worked. It served multitudes. Besides, he was here on official business concerning a wholly different matter. No, he would not be diverted by secondary concerns. He knew his priorities well. Clasping the Director around the elbow as if to say "Let's get on with it," he drew him out of the intake section and through a door leading directly into my unit's floor area.

He was standing in clear sight of us all now, in the front of the office, with the Director, Tom Sanders, at his side, and though no one could hear what they were saying, we could see the Director smiling and pointing to our Office Liason's office, possibly offering it to the Special Investigator for his use. And when the Director gestured to a painting on the wall (probably referring to Becker's cancelled art show) and the Special Investigator launched into a smile of his own showing his pearly white capped teeth, I felt a peculiar kindred alliance with them.

It was not long before he accepted the Director's offer to commandeer Hans Becker's office, and while several workers (a maintenance aide and human resource specialist) busily set about carrying papers, folders, books, manuals and sundry supplies into it, the Special Investigator continued on his tour of Department units accompanied by the Director. After a perfunctory introduction he uttered a few words to each unit supervisor, perhaps mentioning what was expected of them, the protocol he would follow (and tolerate), and every once in a while he deigned to glance at a caseworker. But he never said a word to us, never interrupted a caseworker from his work. It was evident he believed in the work ethic. For the most part his tour of duty flowed nicely, only now and then interrupted by an aide who would ask a question or relay a telephone message. Then the Special Investigator would stop him before the words were half out of his mouth and tell him what to do, order him one way or another to do this or that, without even seeming to listen to the lackey's words, as if his responses were ready made.

Three days later I was summoned to the Special Investigator's office. I was the first of the staff called. The Special Investigator had spent his previous two days at the center busily reading case records, going over field record forms, supervisors' performance reports, and had had at least one conference with each of the supervisors. Our Director, Tom Sanders, was also seen talking to him in private on occasion. Mrs. Knox was already seated when I arrived. She didn't bother to greet me when I entered. Our Director was conspicuous by his absence.

The Special Investigator inaugurated the proceedings by saying he gathered I knew why I was there. I had had the better part of two days to think about it and I was convinced of one thing: I would not give them the satisfaction of admitting to my own guilt. Looking him square in the face, I answered, "I do not." Out of the corner of my eye I could see Mrs. Knox seated in her chair, her fingers nervously drumming on her notebook. *I knew what was in that notebook!* The Special Investigator did not take his eyes from mine. There was an air of exaggerated solemnity about him. By feigning incredulity, he managed to keep me in the dark several seconds longer. He knew the power of that pose. The discomfort those few seconds caused me. At that moment I must admit I felt as much admiration as anger for him. Finally he said that he had selected me first since my record, from the appearance of my Supervisor's annual performance report, was the poorest in the center. And for a man who has worked for the Department for over thirty-four years, that really came as a surprise.

I answered that the key word here was "appearance." Other than the opinion of my Supervisor, who, as everyone knows, has always disliked me from the time I started in Harlem, what proof was there that I had either neglected my job or exhibited irresponsible behavior?

"For more than fifteen years to be disliked, Mr. Haberman? Why didn't you ask for a transfer? That would have been a simple enough solution." I shrugged my shoulders. There was no answer I could give him (or myself). The thought occurred to me more than once over the years but I had never acted upon it. Things weren't quite that bad, I kept telling myself. And what assurance had I that they would be any better in a new situation? With a different Supervisor?

"Still, we're not here to discuss personalities, Mr. Haberman, or to improve upon departmental relations. We're here to discuss your future with the Department. And based upon my findings and Mrs. Knox's *evidence*"—her hands were wrestling, tearing at the notebook now—"I'm going to have to ask for your dismissal."

I tried to respond to his words but I couldn't. I could barely digest them.

Quite the reverse, Mrs. Knox couldn't restrain herself any longer. "I'm not going to put my head on the chopping block for you or any other worker, Mr. Haberman. When I leave here I want it to be on my own. Not by dismissal."

By the way the Special Investigator ignored Mrs. Knox's acrimonious outburst it was evident he was not wont to give up the floor.

"At first, because you were only several months short of becoming eligible for your pension," he continued, nonplussed, "I had in mind only to ask for a voluntary leave of absence. In a year things will have blown over in the Department and you could have come back and started over again. Or perhaps we could have arranged for some special resignation status that would have left you eligible for benefits. But that was before consulting with your Supervisor. All that's impossible now in the light of what she's brought forth. No, nothing short of termination will do now."

I was jarred. Stunned. Completely caught off guard. A decision to be made so quickly? So fast? My dismissal!? After so many years!? But even while in a state of shock more than a few arguments raced through my mind. One of which was my right to appeal. But at the very moment the ideas surfaced, I dismissed them. It was just what Mrs. Knox would want. She would give anything to see me squirm. To drag me through the mud. An appeal or its like would give her the supreme opportunity to testify against me in front of a board meeting. If it was the last thing I did, I would never allow her that. Indeed, that was just what she must have had in mind when she began compiling her evidence against me in the first place. A whiff of Tom Sander's jungle habitat scented my nostrils. As» his office was adjacent to this one, I could smell the greenery. Where was he? All those years buttering him up with those infernal plants, and now when I needed him most, my trump. . . . Suddenly I realized how hopeless it was. How futile. There was nothing he or I or anyone else could do. My fate was lying on Mrs. Knox's lap. That was why my Director chose not to attend this meeting. It would have been as embarrassing for him as it was for me. Averting Mrs. Knox's eyes and with as controlled a demeanor as I could muster, I stood up to leave. But before I did, I made certain to take the Special Investigator's hand firmly in my own.

Mrs. Knox's notebook was still on her lap when the door closed behind me. She had not and never would get to read her "evidence" aloud. By all appearances she, if not the notebook or both, was bursting at the seams.

A half hour later I was sitting in a bar where I proceeded to drink myself into a stupor by late that night. One sentence kept repeating itself in my mind: *I've Still Got Brodski!* No matter how many feelings welled up inside me, no matter how many thoughts too painful to accept swirled around in my head, I fended them off with: *I've Still Got Brodski!* The most terrifying thought that kept recurring over and over again in my mind and seemed to override all the others, the one that

speared me on its killer lance and pierced my entrails was:
If this job meant so little to me—or nothing at all, as I have
told myself for so many years, as I have always believed—if I
hated it so and placed no value on it, considered it demeaning, and worse, the ruination of my life—*Then why did it hurt
so now? Why was there such overwhelming pain now when I had
lost it? When at last I was free from it?* I didn't have an answer.
Or if I did have an answer, I refused to face it. I fought it off.
I've Still Got Brodski, I kept telling myself, *I'VE STILL GOT
BRODSKI!*

I didn't want to know the answer. I didn't dare know the
answer. I didn't dare equate the waste of my life, not with
the job I had done for so many years, but with my reason
for doing it. The real reason. My own cowardly, obsequious,
fawning, impotent self. All those clients who meant nothing to me. All those 712's and case records and time cards
and procedures and genuflecting to Knox every morning and
cajoling the other workers every morning and burying true
feelings every morning and getting up early every morning
and not being late every morning and buying Knox newspapers every morning and filling out forms every morning and
putting off my real life every morning and hating every hour,
every second, every day of it . . . Why did I do it? What did I
do it for? My life! The life I never lived! Could I make it up?
How could it be made up? How could I have let it happen for
thirty-four years?! . . . And now this. Nothing. No pension.
No money. No way of getting my life back. Setting it right.
Was I to blame. Was I respon . . . *I've still Got Brodski! I've Still
Got Brodski! I'VE STILL GOT BRODSKI!*

On waking the next morning, in addition to a splitting
migraine, I had a vague memory of collapsing on the street

and being taken home by two policemen, one black, the other white. I recalled the black officer saying, "Sleep it off, brother. Anyway you look at it, a job's only a job. You're lucky. You still got your life!"

Even leaving the office yesterday for the last time proved unsatisfying. And I'm not referring to the "last supper" habitually given every worker who leaves the Department. That, for whatever reason, didn't come off. Not one of my co-workers took the initiative in passing around the brown inter-office envelope to collect contributions necessary to pay for the bacchanal. Of course, the only reason I wanted the party was to give me the opportunity not to attend. That would have been a fitting epitaph to my fifteen years at Harlem. More eloquent than any final words I might have uttered. But, as I said, even that satisfaction I was denied. The parting comments of my f-o-r-m-e-r colleagues rankled me almost as much. Not because of what they said but what they didn't . . . and the way they said it.

Richard Gould, for instance, his head down, his eyes averting mine, mumbled, "No more Knox." I could hardly hear him. It was his way of making light of a frightening situation. Of assuaging his own fear. I knew what he was thinking though: He'd be next.

Rodent Face: "Gee! It really happened. Gee!" Personal prayer answered. It was easy to figure where he'd be spending the night: at church.

Tom Sanders: Once again he was conspicuous by his absence. He did leave me a cactus plant and a brief note wishing me well, though. But where was he? He had seldom if ever taken off during office hours before. So why now? (Who could he trust to water his plants?) . . . Did he feel that guilty?

Mother Earth: She alone expressed something real. "You're the lucky one," she said. "Anyone who can get out of this crap, no matter how they do it, I'm happy for. More power to them." Seconds lapsed before she made her final comment: "They're all bastards!" And then she passed a stony glance in the direction of my supervisor's desk. She never mentioned a name.

My other colleagues and peers didn't say a word. Truth is they hardly noticed my leaving. On my way out of the building, while the elevator was descending, I broke out into a clammy sweat. For the first time in all my years in Harlem it dawned on me that of the thirty to forty coworkers who made up the fifth-floor office, I didn't know more than eight by name.

Oh, yes, Mrs. Knox. She never lifted her head from the new procedure she was reading.

When I returned home I was assailed by a new wave of apprehension. How was I to survive till I became eligible for social security? Seating myself at the kitchen table, I immediately set out to assess my situation. First I listed my expenses: rent, food, laundry, Con Ed, (there was no telephone; I had gotten rid of that cost as well as cable TV months earlier), entertainment, miscellaneous. Everything considered, my monthly total (including Brodski) came to $689.00. I needed twelve times that to make the year. A grand total of $8,268.00. Adding up my assets—bank accounts, checking account, contingency fund, cd's, money still owed me from the Department (back pay and money I had coming from my pension fund savings)—and figuring seven percent on my money, I was still short $111.00 each month. I cursed myself for not having readied myself for this dilemma. I certainly had had forewarning. Only a week ago or even less I could have applied for a loan at any bank or financial institution, the Municipal Credit Union included. But now it was too late. Still, there was no way I would ever return to work again. From here on I was determined to spend as much time as I could free from any constraints and entirely with Brodski. Nor would I reduce myself to applying for welfare. I wouldn't give "them" the satisfaction. Besides, I wasn't eligible anyway, not with the resources I still had.

In effect, there was only one course to follow: I would have to reduce my expenses to the bone. To begin with, Caesar would have to go. That would help considerably. As he hadn't shown his face since our last altercation, I only prayed he had disappeared altogether; then I wouldn't have to pay him what I owed him. Knowing how peculiar he was in certain respects, it wasn't too much to expect. Mother also would be adversely affected. No longer would she receive gratuities for not making herself available. On the contrary, she could deem herself fortunate if she continued to collect her Home Attendant check. Hey! That was an idea. If it came down to it (and it did), I could divide the Home Attendant check with her. Why not? I was the one doing all the work. As for Brodski, he, too, would have to contribute. For one thing, there would be no more presents for him. No more excessive and irresponsible use of my contingency fund. And, too, I would immediately put him on a starvation diet (he ate little anyway) and restrict him to the clothes he already had. Perhaps on special occasions (if he did well on an experiment, for instance, or poorly) I would treat him to a new pair of diapers. To be sure, everyone would have to learn to deprive themselves if we were going to survive these hards times. If this was a test, I was resolved to pass it with flying colors. I would let no one and nothing stand in my way. I had waited too long. Now for the first time in my life I was free . . . free twenty-four hours a day to enjoy Brodski.

Here's an idea! I can always put Brodski on the street with a tin cup. Why not? He's got a visual advantage over the ordinary freaks.

Sell his paintings? NEVER!!!

. . . who would buy them?

"THE LORD GIVETH AND THE LORD TAKETH AWAY!"

I removed the two pillows stored in my closet and placed them an arm's length apart on the deluxe exercise mat lying on the living room floor so that they paralleled each other exactly. I had purchased the pillows months ago from an elegant Madison Avenue art shop. It was my last extravagance and cost much more money than, even then, I had a right to spend. (Now, of course, for this final punishment, money is hardly an issue). The art dealer assured me at the time that the twin pillows were just what I was looking for. Handwoven and individually designed by a highly skilled Japanese artisan; maybe a hundred years old. "They don't do work like that anymore," he said smugly, his hands fondling the pillows. "They're as fine a pair as has ever passed through this shop. I really hate to part with them. But, well, business is business." I had told him I was looking for the kind of pillows a Samarai warrior might have used to lay his sword on, or, even better, to rest his knife on before plunging it into himself on that fateful day. Each pillow was intricately embroidered and had a beautiful picture on its face: one of a serene old man rowing a boat on a tranquil lake; the other of a woman, presumably the man's wife, strolling through her flower garden in front of their home. The pillows were made of the finest silk and each had golden tassels.

Next I awoke Brodski on the dot of seven—he was certain to hear the final chime from the clock I had put on the bureau next to his bed. Then, timing my strides to the rhythm of a Japanese song of sacrifice playing on a recently purchased pocket-sized tape recorder, I carried him from his crib-bed into the living room where the pillows were awaiting him. I had on a kimono and sandals (my version of ceremonial dress) and on my face I wore a more solemn and steadfast expression than usual. The previous night I had laid the deluxe exercise mat down and on it, now, in addition to the pillows, I placed the little fellow's body harness and chair so that he would be able to sit upright. All this was done prior to dispensing with any of his daily morning routine: before washing him, brushing his teeth, changing his diapers, feeding him, even before certain rituals he manages for himself (he does yawn regularly upon awakening and stretch himself; not his limbs, but still, he does stretch)—but even those I did not permit him this morning.

I daresay he knew by its very difference that this morning promised something special. That something was in store for him. But what? Then I let him sit in front of the pillows for precisely five minutes before placing a single object on each of them. One pillow held last night's left-overs from my supper; nothing he would normally eat: bits and pieces of hardboiled egg and scattered remains of shell. On the other lay yesterday's newspaper.

Neither object could possibly have held any special appeal for him. Neither had any intrinsic worth in and of itself. Past experience told me he would never notice either of them under normal circumstances. But nothing is normal about this final punishment . . . is it, little one? Brodski and I stayed there, in front of the pillows, for two and one half hours before he finally made his selection. Scantily clad, diapers soiled, shivering goosebumps (I had left the windows open), groggy with sleep, his eyes finally settled on the pillow containing the remains of my supper from the previous night. Hearing a thin plaintive sound emanate from him, I placed my ear to his mouth to assure myself that he actually was signifying some kind of choice. He was. I heard his stomach growl. I could not have asked for any better proof than that. I knew at once why he had selected the scraps of egg and shell instead of the paper. He was hungry. It was as simple as that. A reflex action. A physio-chemical response. I immediately removed the newspaper from its pillow and tossed it into the gleaming black garbage sack I had tacked to the wall directly to the left of the deluxe exercise mat, making absolutely certain that Brodski's eyes followed my every move. Then I lifted him from his wheelchair, first unstrapping his body harness, and carried him to the breakfast table. After feeding him a hearty meal (the first good one he has had in days) I let him paint the rest of the day.

It is now two weeks since I inaugurated the final punishment. Every morning, at exactly the same time, in exactly the same way, like an ancient rite of passage that never deviates, I have repeated the ritual. On each pillow I place an object— each object holding precisely the same lack of interest, the same inconsequentiality, for Brodski. The objects might be as insignificant as a single match stick and a broken piece of lead from a pencil point, or an old sock with holes in it and a cantaloupe rind. Sometimes the objects are duplicates of each other: two bottle caps, for example, both Coke. The point is that Brodski has to choose one of the two. Why or which one he selects does not matter, so long as he selects one. As soon as he does, I pounce forth on all fours to remove the item, the one *not* favored by his smile, purr or quixotic gaze, and dump it in the garbage bag awaiting it like an all-consuming orifice. Once it disappears into the sack, the unfavored object is never seen again. Then, following my practice, I give him a hearty breakfast and for the remainder of the day let him paint to his heart's content. After two weeks I am certain he knows no more than this: Some kind of rigid malevolent pattern is unfolding. A pattern fixed and immutable, perpetrated by me, and as of yet not wholly decipherable. Except for the fact he must select one item over another as prerequisite to being allowed to paint, and the item *not* chosen disappears, he knows little else. For now, that is enough. My entire purpose these first several weeks has been to teach him no more than that. He can't possibly have any idea where all this is heading. He is much like a maiden being made ready for her virginal sacrifice. How pretty she looks. How nice the cleansing waters feel on her body. What an honor to have so much attention bestowed on her; the hair lotions, the body oils, the slave girls. But even she suspects what's to follow after her fall.

Even if he does suspect . . . so what.?
All the better.

Thirty-five more items have disappeared from the household. The fact that not one of them has anything to do with art, is neither aesthetic nor necessary to Brodski's painting, does not lessen the impact on him. Brodski is beginning to understand that his world is shrinking—coming to an end!

If only subliminally, he cannot help but realize this. Three days ago he stared—not really stared, but he did hold his gaze steady—at a gaping space in the corner of the room where a small bookcase used to be, and for a second at least, he winced in pain. Other signs, too, have recently appeared to hasten Brodski's developing understanding. This morning, for instance, when I went to wake him and carry him to the pillows, he was already up. Restless, with eyes swollen from lack of sleep. I derived a certain pleasure conjecturing what he might have been thinking during those early-morning hours. And then, at breakfast, he hardly ate with his usual zest; though he did eat. And finally, when I seated him in his chair to paint, what he painted also must be construed a victory for me, however small: a bare room with only a few sticks of furniture in it, the mood cold, barren, menacing. Of course the little bastard didn't compromise a stroke. Despite the fact that his subject matter was obviously influenced by his final punishment, he only seemed to try all the harder and in the end achieved what must be considered one of his finest efforts yet. Still, I am content: Regardless of how modestly shallow its depths might appear now, my foundation pit will assume infinite proportions later on.

Yes: This is only the foundation I am laying.

I have purposely not confined my selections for the pillows to objects from his room alone. Rather I have taken my choices equally, from the kitchen, the small alcove we call our dining room, and my own room as well. Because of this there is not a single place in all Brodski's world he can go where he does not perceive its emptying; where he cannot help but experience loss.

Lately I recognized a pattern unfolding whenever I placed a large and small object on the pillows in front of him. The little fellow invariably and without hesitation preferred the larger item. It doesn't take genius to figure out why. All things being equal (though many of the items were aesthetic, those were usually pitted against each other; if not, I certainly make every effort to give their rivals equal weight; and none had anything to do with his art), the larger the object, the more of an impression it makes when missing. A bureau, a record player, poster-size print, even an ash tray when taken from its accustomed space must leave what seems like a gaping hole to him. I no longer juxtapose large and small objects on the pillows. Instead, I pose large against large, small against small. My intention is not to make this final punishment easy on him. On the contrary, like a laboratory specimen preserved in formaldehyde, I want to preserve him, draw it out, for as long as possible, enjoying each moment in leisurely draughts.

I am in no hurry now. We have plenty of time.

Sometimes I place two small objects to one large on the pillows. Sometimes three. I have on certain occasions gone as high as six to one. Never has Brodski selected more than three small items in place of one large. His maximum rate of exchange seems to be three.

The larger items I don't actually place on top of the pillows, but lay adjacent to the pillows' sides. Brodski makes his selections without difficulty. Whether the object is actually on the pillows or lying parallel to them makes little difference.

The cupboard is bare (literally). It is the first area in the household to have disappeared completely. Not that I had so many things in it to begin with, being a bachelor, but still, several of the items I did have Brodski placed great value on. His Matisse saucer and Picasso cup, for example. When he was forced to choose between these two, that was a sad day. Afterward he suffered a far greater indignity than merely having his appetite spoiled. Now, whenever he sits down to breakfast (he doesn't really sit any longer: the kitchen table has vanished, as have the chairs, and we both eat off the floor, me cradling him in my arms like a babe) the first thing I offer him is liquid refreshment. Not because he likes it so much but because it gives me an opportunity to use the one piece of kitchenware I did save from the garbage heap. An old rusted metallic army cup. Alas, Brodski hasn't taken a sip from it yet.

Since Brodski refuses to make use of his universally adjustable handsplint to aid him with his food these days, I have to mash it down his throat with my fingers. Otherwise he won't eat. I don't want him to starve to death . . . not yet, anyway. And since he no longer has an apron to cover himself with, most of what he eats, liquid and solid, seems to end up on his face or chest instead of where it belongs: inside him. When he finally is ready to paint he looks like a cross between an old army field cook who's just finished feeding an entire company of soldiers and the stereotypical artist indifferent to dirt. One interesting tidbit: You can hardly tell the difference between the grime, slop and grease stains left over from his food and the spots, blotches and oil color smears made by his everyday painting.

And then always at the same time, in exactly the same place, I set the object before him on the pillows.

This afternoon after Brodski finished painting, he relapsed into silence. Your guess is as good as mine what he was brooding about. Unless, of course, it had something to do with what tomorrow would bring.

Now: Let's see. What should I select?

I know: The last of his art reproductions remaining: his favorite, Munch's The Scream. And as its companion piece: His Crib-Bed, an item, if not aesthetic, certainly large, functional and necessary to his bodily comfort for eight to twelve hours of his daily regimen (sometimes more). It is as integral to his "world-space" as any material item can be:

I'll give you one guess which item he selected to end up in the gleaming black garbage sack.

So now he lies on the floor amidst a spread of tattered blankets and stained sheets; without even the luxury of tossing and turning in his sleep. And when he awakes in the morning as one does from a dream that becomes too intolerable, he finds his nightmare not over, but contiguous with his waking hours. Everything he's dreaded and dreamt about becomes reality then.

This final punishment is proving well worth having waited for. There are so many things I can do with it. And of course I will do them all.

Then again, late in the afternoon after he's finished his morning's ritual and his painting for the day, and I'm standing on the far side of the room, my back to him, paying him no heed, completely absorbed by my own thoughts, thinking what's to go on the pillows tomorrow, or smiling over some earlier reaction of his, he sits in his relaxation chair glaring at the blank spaces before him, angrily flapping his arm stumps against himself. And then, when I turn around unexpectedly to face him, the flagellation stops, but he continues to glare (now at me), arching his back stiffly against the chair, looking like anything but a defeated man.

It's taken weeks—months!—but every objet d'art, figurine, even his entire body of work is gone now. Only his painting utensils and equipment, relaxation chair, arm and hand prosthesis, and a canvas still in progress remain. He's been laboring over the canvas for a week, and even though his pace has slackened considerably, the quality of his work hasn't. The little bastard's as diligent and uncompromising as when he first began his final punishment. But this morning, little one . . . This Morning You Begin the Final Phase of Your Final Punishment. On the pillows before you you will find s-o-m-e-t-h-i-n-g n-e-c-c-e-s-s-a-r-y to your painting. And even if this "something" is only a start, a tease, a mere gesture, if my calculations are correct, it will launch the beginning of the end for you.

I can't wait to see your face this morning.
And how your painting is affected.

Now, let's see: What should I choose?

The item I selected was a tube of paint, half used, the oil oozing out. On the other pillow I put toothpaste, (Gleam), the container (sample size) as close to the shape and size of the tube of paint as I could find. The toothpaste, like the paint, was squirming out of its vessel. The oil color, Payne's gray, is one of Brodski's favorites. In the last month alone he's used it on almost every canvas he's worked on. But despite the fact that Brodski very quickly selected the oil color to stay over the toothpaste, his initial reaction was confusion. As if the little darling *never* reckoned on having to make such a choice . . . or did he, perhaps, reckon too much? Indeed, merely putting an object having to do with his art on one of the pillows seems to have triggered fears and trepidations in him. For certain, his entire day was ruined. Not only didn't he enjoy breakfast—he nibbled at bits and pieces now and then but he didn't swallow a single morsel, keeping the food lodged in the side pockets of his mouth—he didn't paint either. Or rather he did paint, but it was evident the effort couldn't measure up to his usual high standards.

What proved especially interesting to me, though, didn't take place until he was well into his painting. When, with his utensil holder, he reached for that same tube of oil color and began pressing it on the canvas, there was a look of innocent dismay on his face. No, more like appreciation. Gratitude. He was grateful. And all the time he was working on his canvas, he refused to take his eyes off me, once even rotating that dradle neck of his the full 270 degrees when I moved out of his sightline. My guess is that the little darling was worried I'd take the pigment away from him. But I would never do that. It's not up to me to reduce his world. He will do that all by himself. I merely place heads under the guillotine. Brodski chops them off. Yes: Brodski is his own executioner.

This morning I offered Brodski what I considered an impossible choice, his utensil holder versus a favorite paintbrush. And it was. For the first time since his initial exposure to his final punishment he could barely make a decision. His eyes must have flitted from one object to another and then back again a thousand times over at least three hours, as if he were attending a tennis match, before he finally settled on the brush. Sidling up next to him on the parquet floor, I didn't utter a sound. Not a single word of encouragement. Despite his weeping, wailing, grinding of teeth, and even an occasional glance of reproof at me, I feel it essential that he be left alone at this time with his thoughts. Even though I am only inches away from him in the midst of his ever-diminishing world, Brodski must come to grips with the fact that I will not resolve his dilemma for him. That regardless of which decision he makes, it is the wrong one; that there is no real solution.

He already understands that if his world is crumbling, it is by his own hands.

Of course, if he doesn't choose, he doesn't paint. There's no denying that. He must make a decision. No human being can untie the Gordian knot by shirking his responsibility.

And Brodski is human . . .

It never ceases to amaze me.

Brodski stopped eating a week ago; so did I. At first because I was toying with the idea of seeing how his hunger pangs felt. And then, simply because I lost my appetite. How could I eat anyway, buried in all this filth and shit? Puddles of urine around me and the most nauseating stench. And worse than that even . . . the way he endures. The way he drags it on. I would have thought his spirit would be crushed long ago. But it's not. He's still asserting himself. He's still painting! I tell you the wonder is I'm still alive after the frustrations I have had to suffer because of him. But I'll see it to the end. So help me. If it kills us both . . . I'll see it to the end.

He's suffering from vertigo. It began with debility followed by dizziness a couple of days ago; then a fainting spell in midafternoon yesterday, after he finished painting. And today he's lost his moorings altogether. It could be because he hasn't eaten anything for nine or ten days. He takes in only water, which I literally have to force down his gullet in the mornings, cupping it in my hands but it may also be from lack of sleep. If he does sleep—and I doubt it—it's with his eyes open. During the day, except for when he's painting, they're closed. Of course, he always could paint in the dark. To an extent the same is true for his vertigo. When he's at his easel working on a new canvas, his dizziness hardly affects him. His head clears, he knows where he is. But the rest of the day he's useless. He lies there, limp in his relaxation chair, his head rocking to and fro, his tongue clicking, rattling his lower jaw, his torso slumping from one side to the other. It's a momentous struggle for him just to stay awake during those long afternoon hours.

But sometimes he's so weak, or his brain is reeling so, that when he reaches out to dab his canvas with his brush, he can't. His arm and hand prosthesis hang down like slabs of dead meat over the chair's sides.

The canvas must seem as elusive to him then as a small animal darting this way and that, to and fro, does to a child attempting to grasp it.

But after a short rest he gives it another try, mustering up even greater resolve and determination than before; invariably he's successful.

One thing's for certain: He won't give up. If I'm to triumph over him, I'll have to do it without his help.

Sometimes his vertiginous attacks are so acute he has no sense of time or where he is. Once while he was undergoing such an attack (even though it was late afternoon and he had completed his regular painting bout for the day) I rushed him in front of the easel and spun his relaxation chair around 180 degrees so that it was facing in the opposite direction of the canvas. He didn't even notice. When he made his effort to lift his prosthesis his brush was stabbing at nothing but air. The next morning, though, his work reflected what he had gone through. The canvas contained a kind of whirling dervish effect. The more I think about it, the more certain I am that the little bastard put down his version of having lost all sense to time and place.

When evening comes and it's time for him to sleep, he doesn't have the faintest notion whether I'm waking him or putting him to bed. It's the same in the mornings. Only when he's painting is he alive. Like Lazarus he rises from the dead.

My job is to stop his resurrection!
And I will!
I must!

It can't be long now.

His utensil holder is gone
Work table (easel)
Table writer
Magnetic wrist hold-down
Plate positioner (palette)
Roto tray
Turn table

(He still has his arm and hand prostheses with their universally adjustable hand-splints and pencil holders attached to them, and two brushes, now screwed into the pencil holders like bulbs in their sockets. And, of course, his relaxation chair).

Body harness
Support vest
Oil cups and pans
Safety bar kit

And almost all of his canvases, varnishes, pigments, solvent thinners, canvas boards, stretchers, oil painting mediums have vanished also.

AND STILL HE PAINTS ON!!!'

I know what I must do. I must take his relaxation chair away from him. It will be the same as divesting him of his skeletal structure. His supporting framework. With the safety bar kit and harness already gone, he'll be nothing but a mass of jelly without the chair. But what can I contest it with? It can't be his prosthesis. I'm saving that for last. If I need a "last." (If I'm correct about this, he'll quit before that). It's got to be something he prefers, needs even more than his relaxation chair. But what? I know; the seven canvases he has left. He'll never part with them. Not until he's used them to paint on (or tried). By selecting the canvases to stay, he'll reason he's insured himself another seven days of work . . . Of L-I-F-E!

Let's see him try and paint now:

After Brodski disposed of his relaxation chair this morning he forced me to splash water in his face because he refused to take a sip from the army cup I offered him. He knows I won't sully my hands any longer by touching his caked and sore-infected mouth. His intake consequently consisted of no more than the few drops he was able to lap up from his lips with his tongue. When I carried him from the breakfast area to the space where he paints, it came to me for the first time how weak I myself have become. Even though there's nothing left of him now but head (skull) and belly (swollen),—the rest of him, shoulders, chest, etc., has disappeared like everything else in the house—I had to exert all my strength to carry him. You can't imagine how relieved I was to finally have him seated in front of the spot where his easel used to be. He would have keeled over immediately had I not braced him by putting one of my hands on the small of his back. (Even that was difficult for me). With my other hand I held a canvas upright (almost too difficult), in that way affording him the opportunity to paint. But each time he made the effort to do so I would release the hand supporting him, and after wavering fractionally, he would inevitably tumble over and roll in his own filth. First in excrement, then in urine, later in both. He only made the effort once or twice, then he stopped. He seemed content to just lie there on his back peering up at me as If I were God. Looking down closely at him, I could swear he was praying. But more to the point, he didn't paint. At most, he made a few arbitrary strokes on the canvas; no more. And even more important, after a comparatively short while he gave up. He stopped trying. Even after I allowed a full hour's respite, he didn't try. Only then did I determine he had had enough. Being careful to avoid the urine and feces smudges he had on him, I picked him up (I definitely am weaker) and placed him in the corner of the room. And the he stays.

What is he thinking, I wonder.

Tomorrow morning, after the splotched canvas goes in the garbage heap and he's received his drenching, will come the real test. If he doesn't paint then: I win! Mean-while he has all this afternoon and tonight to ponder.

All I can do now is sit and wait with him.

If you ask me, though, I'd say I've got him.

But still he might try. You can't be too sure. Not with him. I'd better study him closely this afternoon.

And when he opens his eyes tonight to sleep I'll see if defeat is in them.

Lips pursed slightly askew, he sits in the corner of the room, his back uncomfortably propped against two walls meeting each other at right angles, staring hollow eyed in front of him. He doesn't see me, he doesn't see anything. When I move my hands in front of him, left and right, up and down, his eyes stare unblinkingly ahead. And even when he perceives something, like a blank wall or a bare space, it is only an intrusion on him. A reminder of what once was and will never be again. He never whines. He never purrs. Even his mewing sounds have ceased. He is so sad. Irretrievably sad. Every so often, at regular intervals, he bashes his conical head against the wall and his bulging belly quakes.

I wonder what he is thinking:

He didn't sleep tonight. Even though his eyes were open, I could tell. Silent sobs racked his body throughout the night, and then, when morning came, the weeping stopped. His body appears becalmed now, sedate. There is a serene look on his face.

Has he somehow prepared himself, I wonder.

(If he's prepared, I'm not. I need my sleep even if he doesn't).

I was wrong about him. He's not human. No one human could paint like this. On the floor without his relaxation chair and harness to support him, or even my own hand to brace him; falling over, toppling over, bouncing crazily like a balloon whose air is escaping; yet somehow managing, miraculously managing, to hold himself erect for the fraction of time necessary to dab the canvas before he collapses under his own weight again. And after using his last smidgen of oil color he paints with piss, shit, dust, dirt, pus, food remains, blood, biting his lip, anything to give him color; anything that allows him to paint; sometimes even mixing it all together in a compound on the floor to give his work an impasto effect. For four accursed hours I've watched beauty unfold before me as no man has ever seen it unfold before. As it never *HAS* unfolded before. One stroke at a time. One momentous stroke. He sustains his ability to call forth all that is left in him, painting each stroke as his last, radiant, exultant with each stroke. His triumph is that of the man who knows the best in him is being expressed. Who knows what it is to be alive, really alive, in the present moment. What does it matter that he's going to die. He's lived as few others have. Oh, what I wouldn't have given to have lived like that. Even for a moment. Especially for a moment. Had I only known a moment like that, my whole life might have been different.

Brodski is eternal because he has lived . . . really lived in the moment.

Blank walls!
Bare rooms!
Wallowing in filth!
The foulest odor!
Starving to death!
Suffering from dizzy spells! Fainting spells! Vertigo!
Not a chair, bone, harness or hand to support him!
The knowledge he's going to die . . .

AND STILL HE PAINTS ON!!!

Four canvases left—

Three canvases left—

(I'm so tired I can hardly keep my eyes open)

Two canvases left—

His right arm and hand prosthesis, with universally adjustable hand-splint, pencil holder and brush attached to it, gone!

One canvas left—

(I have never been so tired)

Nothing! Zero! Nil! Blank! Void!

What's that? He's lifting his arm stumps? A smirk on his face? A beatific smile! He's . . . He's . . . in his own head HE'S PAINTING!!!

NOOOOOOOOOooooooooo!!!

Penthouse F

RICHARD KALICH

For my "First" favorite nephew,
George Knute Broady

"I'm nothing. I'll always be nothing. I can't want to be something. But I have in me all the dreams of the world."

— *The Book of Disquiet* Fernando Pessoa

TRANSFIGURATION OF THE COMMONPLACE

Haberman-

Haberman and his two young friends are found dead in
Haberan's apartment. Why? What happened? A writer is
fascinated by the small commentary in the newspaper. He
investigates and ~~wants~~ writes his version/interpretation
of the experience.

~~o~~ Now published and a best seller he tells the world in
an interview on Sixty minutes with a live audience in front
of him the story. How and whyh he wrote it. How he strated
with no more than ~~scraps of information~~ about the deceasd;
video tapes and notes and ideas ana anecdotes and comments
from people who knew Haberman. What he gathers and translates;
garners and interprets; takes comment on and takes off on;
is our story. ~~A~~ novelistic rendition of the interview;
of one man's dealing with today's world...The audience c

The tv audience is alos more interested in the images
and crane their necks rather than lsiten to the writer's
words. The vidoe comsera as modern day mirror o* our unreal
~~lives~~ diaphonous lives.

It reads or could read like a trial; an interview;
an criminal investigation of the guilty and condemned; of
the writers culpability; there is rumour he is Haberman;
taht he invented the entire scheme; idea; got notoriety.
a tv program has is being modeled after the event and
people all over the world now have picked up on the idea
and have clossed their own lives and gifts and rendered
habermans's alternative lifestyle to become their own.
Something has to be doewe andor that reason the interview
has been scheduled by a reluctant writer, producer; publisher;
not looking for cheaap and inflamatory publicity...or are
they? Commercial world; real world with real every day considerations. (nice irony).

****Maybe the book has influenced a 'plaague' of simu-
lators to Haberman's alternative lifestyle. An idea whose
time has come; a rash of Haberman's have been ignited end
the writerr who created fiction from his initial inspiration
is now asked to be interviewed to haelp explain the contempora5ry
crisis; events, plaggue, of MODERN MAN. He is cordial and
dry, ironic and knowledgeable, but moatly he himself is gone
and fretful of the same malady as his character...he cannot
get himelf to merely articulate, explain, reprimand and comment
on something he, we all, suffer and endure and lsoe out to
more and more every day. He finds himself becoming more
increasingly like Haberman. He himself has a moment, a
prediclection, to becom Haberman. Way that's the way th-
stroy interprted thsi in the first place. Maybe he Haberman
the writer and character are one. The point is seeeing
in our world today stands up to crisi; to unreality to
interpretation. Teh Vidoe the image are the transmogrifiers
of reality.

TRANSFIGURATION OF THE COMMONPLACE

Haberman either confesses or professes guilt or
explaining himself to a large, jury, tv audience, and
those entities, that "you" like in the fairy is ourselves.
Haberman addresses his court. the court is his own mind,
they, we, you, them, us, we, evryone has led him to do
waht he has done. The producer who saw his opportunity
vurtually sought Haberman out; &oved idea loved Habermans's
idea even before the words were out of his mouth, saw it's
potential, understood its potential to excite and attract
even before Habemran himself understood it the fullest im-
plicatons of waht his idea meant and would mean to his
audience. at large. But of course what did Habemran know
of markets and television. He was just one man, a simple
man with a penchany for writeing; he was / in a sense following his instincts, himself, no more and no less. He had
no idea, at last in the beginning, what he was getting into
The idea just evolved on its own. It started out harmless
enough and the then the rest took over. Who is
what is the rest? asks the Prosecutior. and &alll eyes and
ears lean forward. Them says Haberan. The producer the
executives who make descisions and ultimeslv the audienct,
the audience. They all loved my show.

Yes this could be the way to do it. HAVE FUN...We are all
Haberman and the tv audience is our metaphor bot n in the
programming, hyBERMAN'S PROGRAMMING AND ITS AUDIENCE...The
audience _____ is responsible
for the program much like Habemrn...We all invent what we see
Blur the distinctions of reality..The idea of the produce d
is to affect as much REALITY as possible. Thus in raw,
at once taht Haberman as creator, inspiration, subject, and
writer, was perfect. No more ot moloquent spokesman could
he find. "It was a stroke of luck, the luckiest day in my liffe
when this man walk,ed into my offcie with such an idea."

The day of Hab erman 's retirement, 3/18/92...the day he puts
his last bok book down, underlined, no more books, from now
on Habemran will live...life to the fullest.

ANTICIPATED TO WEST CHON - 1981

( )μοτιξ ιι

9

ADVANTAGES OF MAKING HABERMAN A WRITER.

I know the writer's world. I know the subject. It also

adds another layer of irony to the tale. Makes it even more

perverse. If the writer is writing the story he always wanted

to write, and living the story he always wanted to live, and

his reasons are because of what writing and the ideals of writing

did to him, he is indeed a killer character. His ~~crime~~

~~accomplice and southrnee~~ and affords us prosecuting atty:

defense council and judge and jury.

6½

ADVANTAGES OF POLOONING TEELVISION FORMAT:

Habrman could set up his own televison interview with producers

and audiance ~~and director as if a daytrip is~~ very common nowadays

and fllow BLUE LINE ~~PROMPTING TRUE~~ format. Then we have a

double irony as he speaks to an audience whatching and living

through his 'life story' as he created ~~&writer~~ for himself.

Television is to be sure a powerful medium. He's humourously

interested in ratings and constantly attentps to produce, direct,

influence format of show. Interrupted by commercials, audience

applause, and extended formats. A sense of humour And ionry,

will give me lightness and get me away from ~~heavy~~ heavy and

anxiuos Burden of mommy's nipple. The oh idea is to PLAY,

HVAE FUN. THIS IS MY SOTRY AND IT'S FOR ME.

****And Don't forget Antonio Martinez in $45,000 car with chair

aht costs $6,000 ~~or now worth $200,000~~. And his implant operation

(wife) I "I wanted to ~~make~~ live a normal life,be as normal

as possible. When young girls pass by car he says: "Come here

baby I got showsomething to show yiou. you'll never leave

my car."

196

Agenda: More and more I like the idea and seem to be leaning
toward the idea of putting Habemran on trial in a tv version
where his producer and audience and cameraman surround him and he has
has center stage answring questions from the audience as well as
call-ins from the adience in the theater and the nation at large.
This could be in his head, ~~xxxxxxxxxxxxxxxxxxx~~, or realistically
protrayed. He can then tell his story and weave the plot in too.
Also it gives me the cahnce to psychologize and affords me the
samee freedom as the open novel. And the form is ~~xxxxxxxx~~
approopirte. A the novel on the electronics age parodying the ae
age by its form.

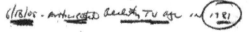
6/18/05 - ~~anticipated~~ Reality TV age in ('81)

NOTES:

****The more I include the READER in the GAME; the VIEWER
in the PROGRAM (story), allow them to participate in
the Questions and Answers...the better.

****And by using a TRIAL I can "PLAY" with the READER as
a "PARTICIPANT."...As PLAYING IN THE GAME.

- You are the Writer, Richard Kalich.

- I could never say that with any degree of certainty. Besides, isn't that one of the reasons why we're here? To establish who I am?

- But this is your manuscript, is it not? Found in a hidden-away recess in your closet. In your apartment: PH-F.

- Hardly a manuscript: More like notes, ideas, quotes and tidbits accumulated over the years. What's the date on the first page...March 18, 1981?

- I realize some time has passed. Much has happened. But it's your handwriting. That much you'll admit: Won't you?

- Again, as I've told you countless times already. It's more like scribblings and chicken scratches.

- MR. KALICH. MR. KALICH. I WANT YOU TO TAKE WHAT I SAY SERIOUSLY...

- AND NOT SERIOUSLY AT ALL.

- You were in the park at the time of the boy and girl's suicide?

- I've already said that countless times, too.

- But it's a well-known fact that you rarely, if ever, go to the park alone.

- But this time I did. You can ask those people I spoke to and acknowledged in the park. Ask Fernando, the doorman.

- We already did.

- Well, the point is, I wasn't there when they jumped off the terrace.

I had nothing to do with the children's decision to...

- It's not that simple, Mr. Kalich.

I came up with the idea for the novel, "The Transfiguration of the Commonplace," almost twenty-five years ago; but I could never really write it. Creative block, call it what you will, the fact is I remained obsessed with it until the boy and girl came into my life. Although, to be sure, they were the main characters in my would-be novel, too.

> *"Could I ever really write at random and without design, thus glimpsing the chaos, the disorder of my own depths?"*
> —Tommaso Landolfi

Constipation (kon'sta pa' shan), n. 1. a condition of the bowels in which the feces are dry and hardened and evacuation is difficult and infrequent. 2. Obs. the act of crowding anything into a smaller compass; condensation. (ME *constipation* = LL constipation-s. of *constipatio*.) See CONSTIPATE. –ION

Through most of my life I have been constipated. Sometimes there were months and even more that I didn't defecate and then, finally, when I did, the feces was so large and hardened I had to cut it into smaller sections in order to let it flush down the toilet. The problem lasted well into my forties and early fifties. Today, at this belated stage in my life, I am happy to report I am what is commonly referred to as "regular."

When I am seated before the TV monitor observing the boy and girl, somehow all seems different. The boy and girl, though very much flesh and blood, real, take on another dimension. I, myself, am different. At those times, seated or standing before the screen, observing, watching the boy and girl, I am...how do

I say this...more alive than they. In charge. They, like puppets on a string, seemingly anticipate my every command.

- When you returned from the park that ever fateful day and saw the police cars, and EMR ambulance and yellow tape cordoning off the covered bodies from the crowd--why did you not ask what happened?

- I already knew.

- How did you already know?

- I just did. The pool of blood. All that hubbub and confusion. It was obvious somebody had leaped to their death. Who else could it be but them?

- And the aborted notes in your novel say as much. Do they not?

- It's not the same thing.

- I agree. Writing fiction is not life.

- It's not that simple.

When I was writing my novel, or at least jotting down notes in preparation, I had no one to answer to but myself. I could let my imagination take me where it would.

- Nothing is simple, Mr. Kalich.

But once I arranged for the boy and girl to enter my life, commenced choreographing their plottings in earnest, there was something inaugural and new about it. All was different.

   - Least of all differentiating your fictions from what is real.

In the middle of the night, when I wake to scribble down ideas in a notebook lying close to my bed, I never turn the lights on. It is pitch black. I prefer it that way. To be alone with my imagination. Watching the boy and girl on screen, I become increasingly frustrated when they move into the shadows. If I could, I would have them take center stage and remain in the spotlight for the duration.

   - Again I must ask: Why on that particular
   day did you go to the park alone? You, who
   has not been seen in the park alone once
   since the boy and girl took up residence
   in your apartment. And I might also add:
   You, who has not taken a vacation, left
   the city, visited a friend or a neighbor,
   nobody, nothing, why then, that day, did
   you decide to leave the boy and girl and
   go to the park alone?

I stand silent not giving the Interrogator the satisfaction of an answer.

   - You can see we know your habits, Mr.
   Kalich. We know, for example, the last
   time you took as much as a semblance of a

vacation was when you travelled out of the
country more than thirty years ago, Sep-
tember 1978 to be precise, to the Frankfurt
Book Fair, to celebrate the publication of
your first novel "The Nihilesthete." It does
no good to deny these facts, Mr. Kalich.
The building staff and various residents
in the building have attested as much.

Not that I have a satisfactory answer for myself.

Please don't get the idea that just because I was behind the
camera, so to speak, and the boy and girl were on stage, so
to speak, that it was all fun and games for me. Admittedly it
was that, in fact, merely getting away from writing that book
was of the profoundest relief. A joy I had not experienced in
years. But still, in all honesty, in the beginning, fun and games
might be construed as my primary motive.

- Once you put down your pen and pencil
on your would-be novel...

- I use an old IBM Selectric.

- ...you immediately set upon a new course
of action.

- It came to me in a moment of insight. I
knew what I had to do.

- Not hardly a moment of insight, Mr.
Kalich, more like over a period of time.

With careful deliberation and more than a little calculation and cunning.

I remain silent.

- Well then, how do you explain rearranging your apartment to accommodate the boy and girl in exactly the same manner as you so painstakingly depicted in your notes for the novel?

- How else would I arrange it? Once I realized what I must do, and as I say, it came to me like a belated moment of inspiration, of course I relied on what was tried and true. Familiar. I won't deny I was obsessed with the boy and girl for years. We both know that much. It's all there in black and white.

- The difference is, and I ask this not merely out of curiosity, Mr. Kalich, whatever possessed you to think you could live the experience you so painstakingly made such Promethean efforts to write about and failed?

- You said it yourself.

- And what did I say?

- I failed.

The two things I had the most capacity for in my life, loving a woman and writing, terrified me most. Though in different ways, I ran from each with equal fervor.

When I came up with the idea for the novel, "The Transfiguration of the Commonplace," like all my other novels, I saw it whole, a poetic image, a central metaphor. In this case, my main character, Haberman, would be the same character that was in my first novel, "The Nihilesthete;" but this time watching, observing, choreographing the boy and girl's behavior on a TV monitor. I remember being so excited that I called up my various publishers and agents, Marion Boyars in England, Svetlana Paccher in France, Martin Shepherd in Sag Harbor, as well as my twin brother, to tell them that I had the definitive novel of our time. I actually said that. The novel anticipated the virtual reality revolution. When I first conceived the novel there was no such thing as a desktop/personal computer, virtual reality, the image supplanting the word.

- You've been employed as a cleaning lady by Mr. Kalich for more than twenty years.

- I was a Professor of Mathematics in Poland before I came to the United States.

- And now, in this last year or so, since the boy and girl came to reside, you say you've seen great changes in Mr. Kalich.

- For Mr. Kalich they were great.

- Can you describe some of these "great" changes?

- For one, Mr. Kalich asked that I clean the apartment at least once a week. Before the boy and girl...

Marta giggles to herself.

- ...it might have been no more than once or twice every three months. When I came to clean, the apartment would be knee-deep in clutter, books and paper lying about everywhere, filth and dustballs. I would have to scrub until my fingers were raw. I would leave exhausted.

- And that included the boy and girl's respective rooms?

- Oh, no, Mr. Kalich was very clear on that. I was not to enter those rooms for any reason.

- How do you account for that?

- I suppose he wanted the boy and girl to learn to assume their own responsibilities.

- Like a strict and stern parent.

- I didn't mean it like that.

- How did you mean it?

- Like a good parent.

I wrote my first novel at the age of twenty-six. I should say my first effort. A study in futility. My twin brother said it was the worst piece of literary constipation he had ever read. I blame two people. My mother: a European banker's daughter who lovingly announced to her children: I want scholars and artists, poets and writers, for sons. Not businessmen. Never businessmen. Translated: I had to be Dostoevski or nothing. And Thomas Mann. The reason my first novel was "the worst piece of literary constipation" was that I was so enamored or rather reverential of the great Mann that I attempted to emulate if not simulate his ornate old German prose.

It cost me another fifteen to twenty years before I could break free of such matriarchal and patriarchal orthodoxies and find my own voice.

- What other changes came over Mr. Kalich, Marta, since the boy and girl arrived?

- He smiled more.

Marta smiles.

- Because of the boy and girl?

- He was happy.

- And...?

- He dressed better. You know, snappy. Like young people do nowadays. In fact I used to tease him that since their arrival he looks years younger. I wasn't the only one who said that.

- But you never once entered their rooms?

- I already told you that. No.

The most interesting aspect in the course of my writing the notes and collecting insights and material for the novel was how little by little, day by day, week by week, over months and years, the various newspapers, media, magazines, literary quarterlies and scholarly journals, would make comment, small at first, a mere paragraph or two, then larger, a full page, and larger, regarding the virtual reality phenomena; the computer, the detrimental influence of television: Make comments on just those ideas I had intuited poetically and was preparing to dramatize in my novel.

In March, 1981 I had conceived my novel, had seen it whole. By 1989 there had already been a film out, a mere trifling compared to what I had in mind for my novel: a comic book: a shallow and superficial dramaturgy, but yet it received much acclaim. It wasn't long before I felt my time had passed. No matter what I might create, no matter how profound, brilliant or ambitious, I felt I would never again gain credit for being the first.

(Grandiosity has always been my downfall.)

But still, I knew I had to write my novel. But, of course, I could not.

> *"Seeing is no longer believing. The very notion of truth and how it manifests itself in pictures and words has been put into crisis. In a world bloated with images, we are finally learning that photographs do indeed lie. In a society rife with purported information, we know that words have power but usually they don't mean anything. To put it bluntly, no one's home. We are elsewhere, not in the real world but in the represented. Our bodies, the flesh and blood of it all, have given way to representations: figures that cavort on TV, movie and computer screens. Propped up and ultra-relaxed, we teeter on the cusp of narcolepsy and believe in everything and nothing."*
>
> —*NY Times,* Sept. 10, 1990,
> Barbara Kruger

Every novelist has one novel in him. The rest are mere variations on the theme.

"Transfiguration of the Commonplace" was my one novel.

    - Isn't it peculiar, Mr. Kalich, that on
    the very day you decided to take a walk
    in Central Park alone, during those very
    same hours, the boy and girl likewise
    decided to leave the apartment? Something
    they very rarely, if ever, did.

- That's why I went for a walk in the park alone.

- But the boy and girl weren't alone. They were together.

- Yes. They had tickets for the theater.

- Which you purchased for them, Mr. Kalich. "Romeo and Juliet" if I'm not mistaken.

When I graduated City College in 1959 I remember standing on the steps of Townsend Hall telling three or four other graduates: "I don't know what I'm going to do with my life, but one thing I do know: I'll never go into business."

- Three hours! You spent three hours on that Sunday of the boy and girl's suicide listening to David Ippolito, otherwise known as "The Guitar Man of Central Park," sing his songs.

- It's really the most beautiful location in the park, there on the hill overlooking the lake, people rowing, ducks paddling near the shore.

- But three hours, Mr. Kalich. For a man who is reputedly tone deaf.

- I wouldn't say that.

- We have it on good account from more
than several people, including the harpist, Dobrinka Nacheva, that you were no
great lover of music. In fact for the
four years the harpist was in your life
you rarely if ever attended any of her
concerts.

- The boy and girl got me in the habit
of going to the park every Sunday. It
became a kind of ritual for us. They loved
Ippolito's music.

- But that's just the point, Mr. Kalich.
On this particular Sunday the boy and girl
were not with you. You attended alone.

I remain silent.

- And in those three hours, I venture,
and this is not a guess, Mr. Kalich, Mr.
Ippolito had time enough to sing his
entire repertoire, some eighty-five to one
hundred songs. Can you recall any of the
songs?

Just a twitch of my mouth.

- No.

- Three hours! Eighty-five to one hundred songs! And you cannot recollect even

one song?! That seems strange. Perhaps
you weren't really listening. Would it be
fair to surmise that you had other things
on your mind?

At the time I graduated City College, or perhaps one or two
months earlier, I made myself a promise: I would read ten
pages of the greatest minds in the world every day for the rest
of my life. To be accurate: Ten or more pages.

Other than those three or four times I was working on a
novel, I kept my promise.

- Scary.

- Scary?

- Scary. That was the title of one of his
songs.

- Really...

- Tom Cruise is scary. Oprah is scary.
Dick Cheney is scary. Really quite a
clever and amusing lyric don't you think?

- Undoubtedly. But after that song which
Ippolito sang at exactly 3:00 p.m., our
reports indicate you rushed off. Why
then? Why at that precise time? As if you
had an appointment or perhaps something
more urgent was pressing.

I remain silent.

> - Interesting, is it not: Of the eighty-five to one hundred songs in the guitarist's repertoire, the one title you remember is titled "Scary."

> - Five o'clock is the time matinees usually break on Sundays. Even I know that much. I left early because of the rain.

> - The question, Mr. Kalich, is: Is that all you knew?

It would be a mistake to assume that I sought out and invited the boy and girl into my apartment just because I could not write my novel; because I wanted to rid myself of the terror of creation by diverting myself with some kind of entertainment. A game perhaps. No. Never was I merely a game-player: never was it merely a matter of winning and losing. What caught hold of me in that epiphanic moment was the game itself. The idea that the boy and girl, those imagined fictionalized characters which I had obsessed over for so long and could not release from the fecundity of my unconscious onto the written page, would now be able to make themselves manifest in everyday reality. After all, staging, programming and conjuring up scene by scene episodes for flesh and blood reality, live action dramaturgy, is really not that different than imagining, constructing and wrenching forth plot points for a book. Real or imagined, game or novel, one aspect remained the same: It lay within my powers to dictate the way the game would be played. At long last the boy and girl, my two imagined characters, would become real.

To be sure there were deeper more complex motives spurring me on as well. From the fetid impotence of my failed writer's powerlessness, I would now, for the first time since my dream-laden youth, know something of the long lost "Authority" of earlier century writers. Also, there was the added attraction of giving my writer's imagination, so long bursting at the seams over stillborn and vainglorious waters, the chance to unburden itself. To give vent and full glory to all that lied buried inside me. If I could not realize and complete myself with the written word, why not on stage and screen with live-action flesh and blood human beings.

- You are James McDonough.

- That's my name.

- You were an elevator operator in Mr. Kalich's building for thirty-seven years.

- Not always an elevator operator.

I was transferred to the front desk when the building put in a selfservice elevator.

- But it would be fair to say you knew Mr. Kalich well.

- For sure. He moved into PH-F three years after I started in 1965.

- How would you describe Mr. Kalich?

I remember sitting at the typewriter with two novels in me. "The Nihilesthete" and "The Zoo." For two days I attempted mightily to wrench the first words out for "The Nihilesthete." Not a word. Sentence. Paragraph. Nothing.

Blank pages. Zilch. On the third day I decided to change over and make an effort to write "The Zoo." Behold: a miracle. In thirty days I had my first draft.

- What kind of person is Mr. Kalich, Mr. McDonough?

- I can't say. That's not an easy question to answer.

- Why is the question not easy?

- Because Mr. Kalich was two different people. For years, when young, he was one person; then later, when he got older, another.

Who can account for miracles?

- What were the differences, Mr. McDonough? For example, when Mr. Kalich was young, how was he?

- He read books and wrote books.

- And later...

- For years I never once saw Mr. Kalich leave the building without a book in his hand.

Dr. Lawrence Katt could. A psychiatrist who specialized in artist's maladies and disorders. Now that my twin brother had written and published his novel, he said, I would be able to write mine. With twins it was chicken and egg, he said. First one, then the other.

- And when he got older, Mr. McDonough?

- He no longer carried books.

- Did his personality change as well?

- I don't understand the question.

- Was he seemingly more troubled, dour, moody, depressed, angry?

- I don't know about that, but...

- But...?

- He kind of lost something. He wasn't there.

- Could you elaborate, Mr. McDonough?

- The old Mr. Kalich disappeared. He became like everybody else.

- Please be specific, Mr. McDonough. Cite an example.

- He became silent. He stopped talking to people. Didn't say a word to the other tenants and not much more to us, the staff, except, maybe, when passing through the lobby.

- And what did Mr. Kalich say to the staff when passing through the lobby?

- Nothing much. You know. Hi, take care, the usual. Most of the time he would just speak out our names. Fernando. James. Pastor. Big George.

- In the later years leading up to your retirement, did Mr. Kalich cause any problems in the building? Would you, for example, say he was a problem tenant?

- Oh, no. Mr. Kalich wasn't like that. He was never a troublemaker like 9G. That one would come home drunk every night, with a different woman, if you catch my drift. He would beat them up, too. We had to call the police more than once. No fooling.

- And Mr. Kalich?

- I can tell you stories about people in
this building you wouldn't believe. Bank-
ers, lawyers, celebrities, especially
celebrities. One time we had an assem-
blyman living here and he would have his
gay lovers sneak up to his apartment only
after midnight so none of the other tenants would see them.

- Can you tell us any stories specifically
about Mr. Kalich?

Mr. McDonough shakes his head. No.

- Even after the boy and girl moved into
PH-F?

- I don't know. I was only there a few
weeks after they moved in.

- Can you tell us anything about those
few weeks?

- As I said. Those last years, when Mr.
Kalich got older, he disappeared.

Arranging, decorating, preparing rooms for a boy and girl
was one thing. Selecting the boy and girl another. One can't
just pick a boy and girl out of a store window like a stick of
furniture and expect to know what one is getting. And even if

my assiduous notes told me what qualities in the boy and girl to look for in a literary and psychological sense, I very well understood that there was more to an actual, real-life boy and girl than I could ever have envisioned in my imagination or written on the page.

- You are Terrance Kearney, Mr. Kalich's neighbor.

- Next door neighbor, actually. We've shared the two apartments on the penthouse floor for at least ten years.

- Eleven years and six months to be precise.

- Of course I own my apartment. Mr. Kalich's penthouse F is rentcontrolled. Lucky stiff.

- Mr. Kearney. You are employed at the Parke Bernet Galleries selling fine paintings and artifacts of antiquity since graduating Princeton in 1994.

- Yes. What's your point?

- I would think you and Mr. Kalich have much in common. Have developed a good and solid friendship over the years, both of you being involved in the arts in one way or another.

- No. Not really. Other than bumping into
each other in the hallway when trashing
our garbage, or sharing the elevator when
leaving or maybe coming home, we've probably never said more than a half dozen
words to each other.

- Why is that?

- At most he might have recommended a
movie he had just seen at the arthouse
theater on 63rd Street and Broadway.

- Is Mr. Kalich so antisocial?

- Not only that. But as you must know, we
have different sexual orientations.

Regarding the Selection Process for the boy and girl, there
were more than several qualities that I deemed prerequisite.
Qualities and characteristics that I could not do without.
For one the boy and girl could not be particularly percep-
tive. Nor strong-willed. Certainly not self-reliant. Possessing any of those qualities would have disqualified them
immediately.

- And Mr. Kalich held that against you?

- It never came up. That's not what I
meant to infer. It's just that we went
our own ways, I had my life and he had
his.

My neighbor and his friends comprised a close-knit community, all different, all the same; they would come together once a week, on Friday nights. There was always much laughter, bacchanalian yelling and singing, and music. Loud music. The next morning the garbage cans in the alcove by the service elevator would be spilling over with champagne bottles and beer cans.

- In fact it was a standard joke between us. Mr. Kalich would quip that maybe he should become gay. That his social life would be far better if he was.

A writer starts out with an idea for a novel and commences to lead his characters along the way. It's not long before the characters are leading the writer. Sooner than not the writer is merely taking dictation. I could not afford that to happen with the boy and girl. This was not merely another would-be novel I was planning to write.

- Mr. Kearney, a moment ago you said that you and Mr. Kalich never spoke more than a few words to each other. Next you make mention of his recommending films for you to see. And now you speak of his sharing quips and jokes with you. You can't have it all ways, Mr. Kearney.

- You misunderstand me. In ten...eleven years, there's always those few exceptions. Of course there was also that one time.

- One time?

- Yes. I was living with an investment banker friend. We had both made a good sum of money that year, as I had taken advantage of his tips and suggestions in the market, and we decided to make Mr. Kalich an offer to purchase his apartment. Adding his four rooms to our two would have been a real coup. If he agreed, I knew I could work something out with the building's management.

- Obviously he rejected your offer.

- Yes. At any rate we were both standing on our terraces, actually Mr. Kalich was in his doorway leading out to the terrace. And we started to talk. I broached the subject and, then, when it started to rain, we continued our conversation in his apartment. It was the only time I can recall ever being in his apartment.

- As I said. You weren't successful in persuading Mr. Kalich to sell.

- No. He was very much against it. But it was the way he rejected my proposal that stays in my mind. What he said...

- And what was that?

- He said PH-F, with its view overlooking
Central Park, was the one luxury he had
in all the world. It wasn't so much what
he said, as the way he said it.

More important than all the rest was that the boy and girl
must be pathologically in need of love. This need has to be
central to their makeup. It would be ideal if, for one reason or
another, they had been denied contact with the opposite sex
in their adolescent years. Even better, all their lives. I needed
them to hunger for intimacy without, if possible, either of
them even realizing it.

- Of course that was before the boy and
girl moved in.

- And when the boy and girl moved in?

- He seemed to lighten up overnight.

- And the boy and girl. Can you tell us
what went on between Mr. Kalich and the
boy and girl in PH- F?

- Who knows what went on there.

- How is that possible? They, at least for
a certain period of time, were as much your
next door neighbors as Mr. Kalich was.

- I hardly ever saw them. And, if I did,
passing through the lobby or waiting for

Richard Kalich

the elevator, they would avert their
eyes. I don't recall them ever looking me in the eye. And if they spotted
me first, say in the hallway, or lobby,
they would scamper off like squirrels
up a tree. I always thought they were
hiding something. They certainly acted
strange.

- Was anything else...strange? This is
extremely important, Mr. Kearney.

Mr. Kearney shakes his head.

- No.

- Anything. The slightest detail could be
crucial.

- Well, there is one thing.

- Yes?

- Nothing much, just the fact that the
last several months before their suicide,
PH-F seemed awfully quiet.

- Was it noisy before?

- No, but more than once I would hear
shouting and arguments going on.

- Can you tell us anything about those
arguments and shouting going on between
Mr. Kalich and the boy and girl?

- No sir, I cannot. I'm no eavesdropper.

When was it that I stopped reading books?

"My body is tired. Alas! And I've read all the books."
— Mallarmé

I do know it was long before the boy and girl arrived.

- Marta, why is it that you failed to mention the many shouting matches and arguments that occurred between Mr. Kalich
and the boy and girl those last several
months prior to their suicide?

- I didn't think it was important.

- How could it not be important, Marta? The
boy and girl literally leaped to their death
from the man's terrace. We have to assume
someone or something provoked such an action.

- All close families have fights and arguments between them. Then they kiss and
make up. It's only normal.

When I am observing the boy and girl on my TV monitor from the little TV room secretly hidden away inside my

closet, a feeling of levity and lightheartedness always comes over me; at least for much of that first year. I felt as if I was entering a new chapter in my life. A chapter as lighthearted as a game. Looking back I realize now I have my twin's three-year-old son, Knute, to thank for this miraculous transformation of self. Periodically my brother would ask me to babysit (which was not very often, thankfully—after twenty minutes I was exhausted and started to count the minutes to my twin and his wife's return) and almost immediately after his parent's departure, the three-year-old would commence climbing down from his bed, scrutinize with knitted brows his great collection of toys and games, scrupulously select one, then, taking me by the hand into the larger, more spacious living room, he would say: "Let's play." Not that I would join in, but I would watch in utter amazement as the boy would explore, invent, create and discover meaning where just before there was only chaos. Not withstanding the good doctor's chicken and egg interpretation, my epiphany took place in just those moments.

In other words, I knew I had found my way.

> - So, Mr. Kalich, we have established that after spending at least one month or more scouring the Upper West Side city streets for such a pair: placing ads to sublet rooms in your apartment in several newspapers; on neighborhood storefronts and bulletin boards; frequenting young people's clubs and hangouts; you finally commenced concentrating your efforts in an old halfway house in East Harlem.

- Yes. I had had peripheral association with the halfway house when I was employed as a case worker for the Department of Social Services.

- You were employed by the Department of Social Services for twenty-nine years, and left upon reaching the retirement age of fifty-five. Were you not?

- I would only add I hated every minute, day and hour I worked for the Department.

- According to our records, you visited the halfway house in the capacity of a volunteer worker three to four times a week, for a period spanning at least three months. You were friendly with the Director.

- Rather than friendship, I would say we shared mutual sympathies.

- And I have to assume, despite your self-professed hatred of social work, this volunteer work facilitated your search for the proper boy and girl?

- Once the Director knew what I was looking for, of course he didn't really know, I could not very well explain the full subtleties and complexities of the personalities I desired. At the time I hardly knew myself.

But still, after I studied his casework files I had a much better idea as to which boys and girls might meet my needs.

- And out of some thirty-five to fifty residents you were able to decide on these particular two.

- Yes. Peculiar thing is, though, that I had seen them on the street panhandling together near my building more than once before and never noticed them. It was as if they weren't there.

- And yet in the halfway house you did notice them?

- Yes.

- Why was that?

- I don't know. I guess they just seemed to be in the proper setting. Like pictures in a frame.

- Or perhaps, might I suggest: images on a screen?

- If you must.

- But still, Mr. Kalich, I must ask you to elaborate further.

- As I said it's not easy to explain. The young woman, for example, she was no more than seventeen, eighteen. What stood out first and foremost about her was her physical beauty, her candle-colored skin, but that's hardly the point.

- What was the point, Mr. Kalich?

- Well, she had a childhood history of aphasia which I found interesting; but more interesting to me was the fact that she, like so many others from her world, had been molested by her stepfather at a very young age and seemingly never recovered. Additionally interesting was that her mother was regularly seated just outside the room while her husband was molesting the girl and not once did she even try to prevent it. And most interesting of all was that in addition to the horrific bit of trauma, or maybe because of it, she had never experienced intimacy with a man.

- Again, very much like you depict in your notes for your novel.

- Yes. With one great difference though.

- And what is that great difference?

- This young woman seemed to understand what she was missing.

- And the boy?

- He was not as simple to decide upon. In fact, other than being out on the streets since he was eleven years of age, I had little to go on other than the way he gazed at the girl.

- And how was that?

- He couldn't take his eyes off her.

- That's it?!

- One other thing. Whenever the situation called for it, he would make an effort to protect her, comfort her. And even more to the point, indeed essential for my purposes, he couldn't take his hands off her even if it was no more than a brush of his fingertips against her elbow to direct her into a chair or a room.

- And on that you made your determination to rent two rooms of your precious Penthouse F to them for a ridiculously modest sum I might add, virtually no rent at all.

    - It was hardly money I wanted from such
a pair.

    - And what was it you wanted?

    - I wanted to help.

When the boy and girl moved in that first night I realized I was more in debt to the Director than I had ever let on to my Interrogator. For when the boy gently attempted to take the girl by her elbow to guide her through the corridor to her room, almost instantly she pulled back. Not unlike how one might pull back one's fingers from a hot flame. The boy was caught unawares. I was not.

With the investigation well under way at this point, one has to ask oneself the following: What have I learned about myself, about the boy and girl's suicide, that I didn't already know? Well, for one, I know that in my earlier years I was a lover of books, a man of letters, a Writer, and as the years progressed, my interest in the literary life waned. I lost my moorings. And also I know that I invited and welcomed the boy and girl into my home, PHF, because I wanted to help them, offer them succor and warmth, or maybe it was just a matter of my being lonely, or perhaps I wanted to amuse myself, play games in one way or another. More than likely all three motives, in one combination or another, have merit. Who can say with any degree of certainty; everything is still very much open to interpretation. In fact, if I am to be completely honest, I am really no closer to knowing myself now, or understanding what transpired between myself and the boy and girl, than I was prior to when the interrogation began.

What has not been said is that though I never laid hands on either the boy or girl, when watching them on the TV monitor, viewing them in different locations in the apartment, or in their rooms, alone or together, the boy and girl seemed more real to me than anything or anybody else in my life. It was as if my hands were guiding them to wherever they might go. This must be something akin to the feeling one gets when changing channels with the remote.

- You were at the front desk, Mr. Calderon, on that Sunday the boy and girl left for the theater.

- Yes. I worked the 8 to 4 p.m. shift, but I was off by the time they returned.

Perhaps it is due to what seemingly happens to them when on screen. For obvious reasons they appear smaller, but it is more than that. They are also seemingly more malleable, less willful, more like puppets in the hands of an all-powerful puppeteer. It is at those times I feel I can manipulate and maneuver, push and prod them; I feel like a writer again, like a choreographer, director, their Creator who can lead them anywhere I want.

- And you did not leave your station?

- No. Never.

- Maybe you had to go to the toilet or took a smoke break.

- I told you, never.

- Never? Not one time?!

- At most I might have helped Old Man Carmilly to the elevator. Or some mother or
nanny up the stairs to the elevator with
their baby carriages. Look. Mr. Kalich is
one of our nicest tenants.

- Nicest tenant?

- That's right. Other tenants talk about
it, but Mr. Kalich was the only one who
actually helped me with my GED exam. He
read over the essay part with me and gave
me books to read. Besides, if I was busy
with another tenant, Big George was at
the front door. And he didn't let anyone
in.

Observing the boy and girl on screen in this manner, if only
by the way they avert their eyes from each other, the way
they avoid any and all physical contact or overt gestures of
intimacy, makes me feel that it is I who am going through
the time-honored rituals of courtship. Yes. The boy and girl
have opened me to a whole new aspect of myself. Something
so long and deeply buried that I hardly knew it even existed
in myself.

- We know for a fact, Mr. Calderon, the
Samuelsons were honeymooning in Greece

at that time. And their wedding presents kept arriving regularly, even on Sundays.

- You're right. I forgot. I had to take some wedding gifts up to 12-C one time.

- And what if Big George took a break at that exact same time you were delivering wedding presents to the Samuelsons 12-C apartment? What happens then?

- Big George would lock the front door so nobody could get in.

Thanks to the boy and girl, slowly, in its own way and time, their time and mine, I could feel myself rising to the surface, the first blush of inner feelings coming to life.

- And if somebody wanted to enter the building at precisely that time, would you or Big George hear their ring?

- Not if I were delivering wedding presents and Big George was downstairs in the basement.

- Mr. Calderon I want you to think before answering this next question.

The concierge prepares to think.

- Nobody was at the front door when Big George and me returned to our stations. But...

- But...?

- The door wasn't locked. It was open.

- Open?! Why didn't you say so before?

- I didn't want to get Big George in trouble.

Next follows Big George.

- So it's possible, Big George, that Mr. Kalich could have entered the building, waited until the elevator was in service, walked up the stairs to his penthouse apartment, and nobody would have been the wiser.

- No, he couldn't.

- Why not?

- Because PH-F is on the top floor. Seventeen. And Mr. Kalich is an old man. He's got gout.

- But I thought you earlier agreed with Mr. Calderon that since the boy and girl entered his life, Mr. Kalich appeared younger. He was spry...there was even a bounce to his step, you said.

- I said that?

- "You're getting younger as you get older"...those were your exact words to Mr. Kalich, Big George.

- I meant since the boy and girl moved in.

- On this matter you're also in agreement with Mr. Calderon.

- I don't know nothing. Mr. Kalich never invited me out on a date with them. At most I might have seen him and the boy and girl together in the lobby.

- What else did you notice about Mr. Kalich since the boy and girl moved in?

- Nothing. I told you already. Other than that one Sunday when I worked the front door because Fernando was sick, I was transferred to the basement with Little George. I ran the service elevator and collected the garbage on Mr. Kalich's side of the building.

- And when you took your smoke break on
that Sunday for ten to fifteen minutes,
you failed to lock the front door.

- I don't know nothing.

Notwithstanding the splattered bodies of the boy and girl
found lying on the concrete in front of my building, the
2,000 or more bones of their bodies ground to pulp, the
police forensic team documented the following: The girl had
been attired in a lace white gown and the boy in a grey-black
suit jacket and tie, as if dressed for a formal occasion, more
than likely a wedding. The girl's right wrist was bound to the
boy's left with handcuffs, those simulated kind you can purchase in any children's toy store. Long-stemmed champagne
glasses, their contents ostensibly drained to the last sip, were
found on a small bench-like table, and logically enough, a
commensurate amount of the bubbly white wine was likewise found in the boy and girl's stomachs. Further forensic
examination indicated they had imbibed the wine just prior
to their plunge. One can only wonder what they were celebrating: was it real or imagined? spectacle or sham? live theater or performance art? Just as importantly, there was no
evidence of foul play; no indication that any violence, sexual
or otherwise, had been perpetrated on the pair. No scratch
marks, bruises, no skin tissue underneath their fingernails to
suggest physical confrontation or any kind of a defensive battle. No. The double suicide, if nothing else, appeared wholly
voluntary. And, oh yes, the boy and girl each had a playbill on
their person: the boy in his right vest suit jacket pocket, the
girl tied around her waist with a blue satin sash. Only to be
expected, the playbills were from the matinee performance of

Romeo and Juliet they had just attended only an hour or so earlier. In fact, if not on the first page, still prominently featured nevertheless, ranging from pages three to six on more than several of the next morning's newspapers, in bold black lettering, was titled: "ROMEO AND JULIET SUICIDE."

I almost hesitate to mention my immediate reaction when returning from the park and seeing the splattered bodies of the boy and girl, but in the name of accuracy, if nothing else, I must. I had the distinct feeling of completion, of somehow having finished, after a long and arduous struggle spanning over many years' battle, the last page of a novel I had been working on. Yes: All that remained for me to do was date and mark the last page, as was my habit, to bring the book to a close.

Whether shopping for groceries at the Food Emporium, having a new suit tailored at French Cleaners, or merely picking up a newspaper at the corner newsstand, I notice my step quickens as I start home.

Home...a word I never used before to describe PH-F.

For the first time in my life I have something and someone to come home for.

> - Why did you purchase tickets for the boy and girl to go to the theater? And more to the point: why this particular play. Romeo and Juliet?
>
> - I have always liked theater.

- But no longer. You gave up attending theater at the same time you stopped reading books.

- But, as you say, the tickets weren't for me. I purchased the tickets for the boy and girl.

- Exactly. So again I must ask why?

- Obviously I thought they would enjoy the play. Get something from it.

- An interesting turn of phrase, wouldn't you agree?

- What?

- "Get something from it."

- People have been enjoying and getting something from Shakespeare for centuries.

- But I would think appreciating Shakespeare is well beyond this particular boy and girl's capacities. They are, after all, both flawed. Mentally limited. We have on record that both their IQs are no more than seventy-five. That's very close to or considered a moronic level, is it not?

    - They're not morons! A moron is a person
    having an IQ of 50-69 and judged inca-
    pable of developing beyond a mental age
    of eight to twelve.

    - Retarded then?

    - They might be slow, somewhat retarded.

    - Slow...retarded. And yet you purchased
    tickets for them to see Shakespeare!?

Of course when I reach home I don't immediately make it a
point to visit with the boy and girl. Rather I head directly to
my TV Room to observe them.

    - You noticed Mr. Kalich and the young
    woman as soon as they entered the women's
    area on the second floor.

The sales rep nods his head.

    - Why was that?

    - A young woman and a mature gentle-
    man always catch my eye. I guess it's my
    salesman's instinct. The old ones always
    spend more.

    - And that's what happened on this occa-
    sion?

- As soon as the young woman asked to try on our white Juliet dress displayed on the cover page of our fall brochure, I knew he was a goner.

- The brochure with the Romeo and Juliet thematic logo?

- That's the one.

- What do you mean when you say: Mr. Kalich was a goner?

- Actually it was the way both of them looked.

- Both of them?

- Well, when Mr. Kalich first saw the young woman in the white dress, he just stood there as if mesmerized.

- And the young woman?

- She was absolutely beautiful. Radiant. But to be more accurate, she didn't so much come out of the dressing room as peeked out. Her face flushed as if embarrassed.

- Why was she embarrassed?

- I've seen that look before. The young woman's at that awkward age, half woman, half girl. I would bet anything she was asking herself those questions young girls always ask: Do I belong here? Is this really me? You know--am I a woman or still a girl?

- And Mr. Kalich. Can you elaborate further on how he reacted when seeing the young woman first peek out of the dressing room?

- He immediately purchased the dress. I had the impression no expense would have been too great for him.

- Did you notice anything else about Mr. Kalich and the young girl?

- Well, she gave him a thank you kiss. Just a peck on the cheek, really.

- Was Mr. Kalich disappointed?

- I wouldn't say that. At least at the time I didn't think so. But a little later I changed my mind.

- What made you change your mind?

- A customer standing nearby, an elegant lady, made a comment to Mr. Kalich saying: "You have a beautiful daughter."

- And how did Mr. Kalich react to the elegant lady's comment: "You have a beautiful daughter?"

- It was an awkward moment to say the least. But somehow he managed a polite smile and thank you. But anyone could see it was a forced smile.

- Did you notice anything else about Mr. Kalich after the elegant lady's comment?

- Despite my rushing him away from the scene of the crime, so to speak, after paying for the dress he left the store in a huff.

- And the girl?

- She followed after him, poor thing, like a naughty child with her fingers caught in the cookie jar.

- You're not exaggerating?

- No, not at all. It doesn't take much more than that to break the spell. That's why we salesmen have to be constantly on guard against eventualities like that.

- And this time you were not?

- I guess not. The woman caught me off guard. I must have been staring at the young girl as much as Mr. Kalich. As the brochure suggests. Romeo and Juliet. It's all illusion. Magic, you know. For those few seconds when the girl made her entrance out of the dressing room wearing the white dress, who can say what was in the old man's mind.

- I take it not like a doting father.

- More like a Romeo who had found his Juliet.

As if to validate, if only to himself, the sales rep nods his head.

- Mr. Kalich, you say you would have given anything to have videotaped the young girl's face when first peeking her head out of the dressing room.

- Anything.

- But why? By your own admission the moment is indelibly imprinted in your mind.

- On tape I would be able to play it over
and over again, not merely in my mind,
but on screen.

From that day on I was consumed by the idea of placing the
girl in a comparable situation again.

*"The folks in the paneled offices are beginning to play
fast and loose with authenticity. There is trust in simula-
tion—that is, in people's willingness to accept the staged
experience, not because they have been made to believe in
it, but because they are willing to live with a substitute,
will accept it in a spirit of 'something is better than nothing.' In other words, if you can coin the feeling of a thing,
replicate somehow a sense of the experience, then, for
many, you have as good as provided the real experience.*

*The shift, this collective willingness to go with the ersatz,
has profound implications. It bears directly on the difference—and the importance of the difference—between
the real and the virtual. Virtuality. Fantasy experience.
Surrogate living to take the edge off our clamorous needs."*
— *Readings,* Sven Birkerts

- Mr. Kalich was never like this in the
old days.

- What do you mean: the old days?

- He used to come into the store two times
a year, never more, for spring and winter
cleaning.

- And now?

- Two, three times a week. Some weeks more. And he dresses better.

- Has Mr. Kalich's wardrobe improved noticeably?

- Impeccable. He's a real stickler now. A regular dandy. He demands everything be perfect.

- Mrs. Markson, when did these changes regarding clothing in Mr. Kalich begin to manifest themselves?

- I can't say exactly. It happened suddenly. Overnight. Maybe a year ago.

- So, is it fair to say, Mr. Kalich wasn't like this prior to the boy and girl moving in?

- Now he bothers the life out of us. If his cuffs are an inch off, or the hem of the girl's dress half an inch, he demands we do it over again and again.

- Are Mr. Kalich's demands the same for the boy as for the girl?

- It's different. At most he might buy the boy a pair of chinos from Banana

Republic, or a shirt, but the girl, only the best: Ralph Lauren, Armani, Bergdorf Goodman.

- Are there any other changes you've noticed in Mr. Kalich in this last year different from the old days?

- For years he would come into the store and not say a word to me. A frown on his face. His head buried in a book.

- And now?

- He asks me about my kids and my father. Not that my father is sick, but he is old.

- Mrs. Markson, Mr. Kalich has been a customer in your cleaning store for years, decades. How do you account for such behavioral changes?

Mrs. Markson pauses before answering.

- I always said he should have got married and had children when he had the chance. Maybe he's making up for lost time.

What the cleaning store lady said about me was true. Once the boy and girl moved in I couldn't pass a store window without seeing something I had to purchase for the girl. Especially in the first eight months, before things changed.

This afternoon I placed the television set in the boy's room, necessitating the girl to join him if she wants to watch television this evening, or any other for that matter. And, of course, there is only one seat, a loveseat, which I had most judiciously chosen when designing the room. After thirty-seven minutes of dithering, of stretches and contortions, of maneuvering her body position, closer and closer, by gradations, inches, the girl sidled over like a wounded creature and seated herself next to the boy. Before the movie ended I noticed the boy's hand, almost imperceptibly, grazing the girl's.

    - Mr. Kalich, I'm more than a little sur-
    prised that you can't be more succinct on
    this matter.

    - You forget something essential.

    - And that is?

    - I never really wrote the novel.

    - But still, Mr. Kalich, you took such
    obsessive interest in the boy and girl,
    an obsession that has lasted for more
    than twenty-five years.

    - I never denied that I was obsessed with
    the book.

    - But it was more than that. It was...

- I agree. My novel "The Transfiguration of the Commonplace" was just an unending array of images and ideas that remained in my head.

- But that's just the point. Those images didn't just remain in your head. You took great pains to make them real, first in your creative vision for your novel, and then later in life...

- Do you have a question?

- Replicating to a good extent, the plot machinations of your novel.

- Do you have a question?

- Mr. Kalich, after cultivating and taking such great pains to build up the boy and girl's relationship, provide them with home and shelter, warmth and succor, as you say, why--what possessed you, other than the compunction to follow your would-be novel's inexorable plottings, to destroy what you built?

- You've answered your own question.

It's not unlike the rise and fall of the Roman Empire. History teaches us...

- Mr. Kalich, surely you can't compare your relationship with the boy and
girl to the rise and fall of the Roman
Empire.

- If you prefer, I'll rein in my literary allusions for the sake of clarity if
nothing else.

- If you would, Mr. Kalich.

- Then think of the very common habit
of probing our fingers against a rotten
tooth. No doubt we're all familiar with
that delectable bit of mischief.

Kalich probes his tooth.

- Or maybe it has more to do, as I also
mentioned previously, with my brother's
three-year-old, Knute, at play.

- But Mr. Kalich. Once you took the actual
boy and girl into your home you were no
longer writing a novel, and certainly not
partaking in mere child's play.

- Who can say. Are you so certain when
the fiction ends and true life begins? Is
there such a fine dividing line in today's
world?

- Mr. Kalich, metaphysical musings have little bearing in this investigation.

- On that much we agree. But still and all we are living in a world where people are extending their boundaries as to what is real or not. Everything seems possible.

- Mr. Kalich I'm more confused than ever. What do you mean when you say, or at least infer, that your book, in this case not so much your book, but notes for your book, caused the boy and girl's suicide? Or would you rather have us believe that the actual boy and girl and their suicide became the book you couldn't write?

- You don't really expect me to answer that question, do you?

Indeed, that's the sole reason why we're here, to have that question answered. Certainly you have more qualified people assembled here than I to...After all, a writer can only write his book, it takes others to interpret it.

When I look back I realize the transition from creating fiction to experiencing that same fiction live-action on screen is not so much a radical change, overcoming a great divide, as opening myself to new possibilities. I was a Writer, was I not?

A person who lived his life inside himself. In the imaginary realm. It was only natural for my motives to be abstract, not concrete. All I had to do was transpose my inner worlds to the outer world. Not in print but live—with a real live boy and girl at play—on screen. Rather than continue waiting for my writer's voice to muster courage and take the requisite leap of faith onto the page, I would achieve all that I had never been able to by employing a real live boy and girl to enact my obsessive fantasies. All I had to do was invite them into my lair, create the environs, choreograph the setting, set the tone and mood, plot and program the situations and scenes: Play the game. A more adventurous and enticing game I could not fathom.

Admittedly in the beginning I had only the vaguest idea where such a game would lead me. But like any game, Knute's "let's play," I was not only confident that the game would yield its due, but more importantly, that the reward was in the playing.

And, of course, once begun, I could not stop.

> - Mrs. Nacheva, Mr. Kalich was the first person you befriended when you came to New York?

> - My name is Katzman. Dobrinka Katzman. Nacheva was my maiden name and still is my professional name. I'm a harpist.

> - And your friendship with Mr. Kalich lasted a little more than four years?

- Yes. I had just come from Bulgaria to begin studying on scholarship at Juilliard. I knew nobody in this city and Mr. Kalich took me into his life. I was only twenty and for me he was a godsend.

I have been in love two times in my life. Once, when young, with the Israeli, Hana; and twenty-eight years later, when old, with the young harpist.

- Mrs. Katzman, at the time you met Mr. Kalich, you could barely speak the language. And Mr. Kalich was a writer. What did you have to talk about?

- He wasn't really writing. At most scribbling down some notes for a future work. And his interest in intellectual matters, even reading books, had diminished to a bare minimum. He mentioned that change in himself many times over the years, as if he could hardly believe it himself.

- I would think that must have depressed him greatly.

- If so he didn't show it. But what did I know. I was so young. Besides, he was in love with me. If anything, he said I had come into his life just in time.

- And you?

- No. I was never in love with him. But, still, I did love him in my own way.

From the day I met Dobrinka standing in front of Juilliard, I loved her. And if I'm honest with myself, virtually from the beginning, once she told me her dream was to be married for fifty years like her parents and have children, I knew she could never come to love me. Yet I persevered. If not love, the pain was real.

- It was all in his mind. His great love for me.

- You told Mr. Kalich that?

- Many times. In many different ways.

1. YOU WAITED TOO LONG

2. DRINKING WITH YOU WOULD BE LIKE DRINKING WITH MY MOTHER.

3. I COULD NEVER ACCEPT YOU AS A MAN.

- It must have been difficult, to say the least, for the both of you.

The harpist strums her fingers but remains mute.

- Why did you stay?

- As I said. I was young. And nobody had ever loved me like that. I remember tell-

ing him more than once: Nobody will ever
love me as much as you, not even five percent.

With Hana it was all sexual. If I as much as touched her
elbow she would have an orgasm. Not so with Dobrinka.
Despite several flounderings we were never intimate.

- Your name is Julio Cespedes?

- Yes.

- Am I pronouncing it correctly?

- Yes.

- And you were the night doorman from the
time the young harpist, Dobrinka Nacheva,
moved in to reside with Mr. Kalich to the
time she moved out six weeks later?

- Yes. I've been on the night shift, 12-8
a.m., for the last fifteen years in the
building.

- And for that span of time, six weeks, you
maintain that Mr. Kalich, at least three to
four times a week, would leave his apartment to take what you call: "Night walks."

- Maybe more. I could count on it to
the minute. Somewhere around 12:50 a.m.

to 1:00 a.m. Mr. Kalich would exit the north elevator, race through the lobby and head out the front door. I had to hustle to keep up with him to open the door.

- Did Mr. Kalich ever say anything to you when he raced through the lobby?

- Not a word. And I wouldn't ask. Anyone could see he didn't want to talk.

- Can you give me an estimate, Mr. Cespedes, as to how long Mr. Kalich's night walks would last?

- Sometimes twenty minutes, sometimes all night. Those times he stayed out all night, when he returned, I hardly recognized him. He looked terrible, as if he had slept the night away on a park bench.

But not so with the boy and girl. After a week, at most two, they can't as much as walk by each other without touching: an arm, a shoulder, a hand. Touching and pulling back and looking guilty all at the same time.

- When my boyfriend, Alex, a French banker, said he wasn't ready for marriage, I had no choice but to move out.

- And you moved in with Mr. Kalich?

        - I had no other place to go.

        - But Mr. Kalich was in love with you.

        - I was so hurt over Alex I had no room to
        think of anyone else...I guess I wasn't
        thinking.

How could she not know what her moving into my apartment would mean to me? I had waited almost three years for her to move in. Waited all my life. It was a kind of culmination for me. I had been alone all my life. Never lived with a woman. Lived half a life (as my twin deemed it). In my mind Dobrinka's moving in with me would make up for all that I had missed. Every night she would be lying there next to me in my bed, and as soon as the lights went out, she would turn her back to me and expect me to do the same. I couldn't. No matter how hard I tried I couldn't. I would feel such yearning, such longing, to touch her. Everything in me wanted to touch her, love her. It was a thousand times stronger than with Hana. It wasn't even sexual. I had waited all my life and now, finally, she moved in, and nothing...

Those six weeks were the most painful in my life.

        - Mrs. Katzman, can you cite anything spe-
        cific that led you to believe Mr. Kalich's
        love for you was, as you say, in his mind?

        - Not at first. But after a while, maybe a
        year, several things confirmed it for me.

- And they were?

- In his bathroom he had this great collection of photographs in plastic frames.
Photos of his entire life, really. And a
lot of them were of beautiful women: models, actresses, even beauty contest win-
ners. He would tell me about the women.
Vivienne, Marielle, Pamela. Anyway, one
day I noticed the year 1969 written on
the back of Vivienne's photo.

- And how did your noticing the year 1969
on the back of Vivienne's photo convince
you that Mr. Kalich's love for you was
all in his mind?

- He had told me that he was occasion-
ally still seeing Vivienne, and that
she was young and beautiful like in
the photo. But I realized, if taken in
1969, she would already be a middle-
aged woman.

- And the other thing?

- Marielle, a beautiful model, he said
was still very much in his life. Not
long after the Vivienne incident, I saw
Marielle's photo in Elle magazine. The
exact same pose as the photo in his
bathroom.

- Did you confront Mr. Kalich on these occasions?

- The stories the man would make up about them. He certainly had an imagination being a writer.

The harpist smiles to herself.

- I repeat. Did you confront Mr. Kalich?

- No. What good would it have done? Let the man have his illusions with me as well as with them.

Not all the stories of the beautiful women in the photos are untrue. Hana and Dobrinka, for instance, are real. As for the rest, the dozen or so other photos: who can say? At this late date, one seems as real, or unreal, as another.

- You are the cellist, Kristina Reiko Cooper?

- Yes.

- You dated Mr. Kalich at the same time he was in love with the harpist, Dobrinka Nacheva?

- Yes. Everything he didn't say to her he said to me. He was mean. Insensitive.

- How did Mr. Kalich express this meanness?

- He was the most depressing man I ever knew. He didn't like himself enough to love anybody else.

- Ms. Cooper, you mentioned insensitivity. How was Mr. Kalich insensitive?

- Well, for example, after venting his rage and frustrations over dinner on me, he would then leave me in the middle of the street to find a taxi on my own. It was mid-winter...freezing cold.

- Did Mr. Kalich's meanness or insensitivity ever lead to violent behavior?

The cellist shakes her head: No.

The median time in the first month for the boy to feel sufficiently comfortable to seat himself next to the girl when watching television in the girl's room was three minutes and thirty-seven seconds. The time increased substantially, five minutes and ten seconds, if I joined them. Of course I had purchased only one television set for both of them. (Have I already said that?)

- Was Mr. Kalich particularly jealous of your boyfriends, Mrs. Katzman?

- He always encouraged me to enjoy my youth. It goes all too fast, he said.

Before you know it, it's over. He was right.

The harpist smiles to herself.

- And so I presume you and Mr. Kalich came to some kind of arrangement regarding your dating activities.

- Yes and no. What he said wasn't what he felt. Actually it wasn't just a matter of his being jealous. He was, how do you say it, possessive. Proprietary. He would lecture me all the time. One time at a concert when a young friend came to my dressing room to talk to me, he was furious. He shouted across the room it was our moment of truth.

- Moment of truth?

- Yes. Either I leave with him or my young friend. I had to choose. Or else it was over between us. He was always threatened by Nicholas: being young, handsome, an actor. I think it was Nicholas' being an actor that particularly bothered him. In any case, he was always giving me ultimatums like that.

- And whom did you leave with?

- Nicholas, of course.

- And Mr. Kalich?

- He followed us and a little later, after I left Nicholas to go upstairs to my apartment, he confronted him on Columbus Avenue while he was waiting for a taxi.

- You are Nicholas Bellinger?

- Yes.

- You are Ms. Nacheva's friend, the actor.

- Yes.

- You escorted Ms. Nacheva home from the concert that night when Mr. Kalich stalked you and eventually confronted you after Ms. Nacheva returned to her apartment?

- Yes.

- Please cite, Mr. Bellinger, what transpired between you and Mr. Kalich that night after Ms. Nacheva returned to her apartment.

- Sure. Look, I admit to taunting him a little. I mean when we were standing up the block, in front of Dobri's building, and I looked back and saw him following us,

stalking us, I raised my arm as if waving to him. But after Dobri went up to her
apartment, when I was on the corner waiting for a cab, the old guy came up to me.
He was crazed. I told him I wasn't going to
walk away, but after one look I could see
it was him who wasn't going to walk away.
This was no scene from one of my acting
classes; this was real. He was capable of
anything at that moment, I thought. Love
will do that to you I guess. Anyway, when
a cab pulled up I jumped in and took off.

What agonies and humiliations I endured for years over
Dobrinka. And now when I look back I ask myself: why?
why? Fortunately I've learned my lesson. I won't repeat my
mistakes with the boy and girl.

- One last question, Mrs. Katzman.

- Yes.

- How did Mr. Kalich respond when you
finally married Mr. Katzman? A very successful businessman, our records indicate, I might add.

- He didn't respond. Or rather I should
say he never came to the wedding despite
my sending him an invitation. And leaving
two very personal invites on his answering machine. And it was a lovely affair,

```
five hundred guests, at the Rainbow Room.
We haven't talked since.
```

One can learn much from the old people in the building. The way Carmilly dresses every day in his suit and tie, hat on head, hunchbacked and frail, he'll be ninety-six next month, takes his daily walk. The old man never flags, never misses a paddle-like step. One month after returning from the hospital for a fractured hip he was at it again. His only concession: a walker. And Max Klozzner, the award-winning photographer. Ninety-one if a day. The way he suddenly stops in the middle of the street, people and traffic scurrying by, to concentrate his gaze on a child, any child, passing in the flow. His entire being seems to come to concentrated attention as he gazes upon the child, a half grin or inward smile on his face, eyes glinting, almost ready to burst into laughter, it's as if he's contemplating a great work of art in a museum. One gets the feeling that Max sees what others do not. And, yes, the old people never fail to greet each other. They can talk, laugh, smile and converse for hours while others jolt by with a cab to catch, a meeting to make, and a taut, tense expression on their faces. I'm certain that Carmilly gets as much from his walk around the block, his half block stroll in the park, and Max from his gaze, as the others do from all their combined trips to China, Aspen and/or Dubai.

Can I gain as much from observing my boy and girl on screen?

```
 - Would you like to add to or explain
 that last statement by the harpist, Mr.
 Kalich?
```

- Which one was that?

- That you haven't talked since.

Observing the boy and girl on screen, spending time with them inside the apartment or out, is no longer essential for my purposes. In recent weeks, whether alone by myself or in the midst of a crowd, their images never leave me. My mind is constantly churning with ideas for our next encounter.

- You are Robert Kalich?

- Yes.

- You are the twin brother of Richard Kalich?

- Yes.

- You are, like your brother, a writer?

- A writer, yes. But a very different kind of writer.

- How does your writing differ from your brother Richard's?

- That's not easy to explain. First off, Dick's a literary fiction writer. I'm more commercial.

- And secondly?

- Like all twins, I would think, we're opposite sides of the same coin. In our case that translates to my being a body writer, visceral, spontaneous. I love writing. He, on the other hand, is cerebral, mental; craft and cunning are his strengths. He hates writing.

- Cunning?

- Craft then. Once he sees his novel, has his metaphor, he has the beginning, middle and end. I have to write a thousand pages to get my three hundred. Put us together and you'd have one hell of a novelist.

- Are there any other differences, not so much in style or technique, but...

- For Dick everything has to be perfect. He has to wrench every word out of himself. Every word is torture.

- But you just said your brother sees his novel whole. And once he does, he has his beginning, middle and...

- I know, but I also said he hates writing. He's convoluted. Look, writing or otherwise, Dick can't escape who he is. And for him writing was everything. It was his raison d'être. Ever since we were in our teens and read the great Russians, he had to be Dostoevski or nothing.

- And you?

- It wasn't as important. I mean I wrote the best novel I could, but it was never a matter of life and death. I had other things in my life.

- Other things?

- A wife, two actually, and children. A boy and a girl. One from each marriage. I always had intimacy, the love of a woman, the love of children. Dick never did. With twins what one does the other doesn't need to.

- So for Richard writing was too important?

- For Dick everything is too important.

In my late teens I loved baseball. I played high school baseball and organized ball. One day I got hit on the elbow by a pitch and, after standing on second base for a few minutes in great pain, I trotted off the field. I never played baseball again. Other kids said it was because of my fear of being hit by the ball, but it wasn't that. I just realized I wasn't going to be the next Mickey Mantle.

- I would think, Mr. Kalich, that you
being Richard's twin, you would know him
better than anyone else in the world.

- What's your point?

- I know this is difficult for you, Mr.
Kalich.

- Is there a question?

- Do you think your twin capable of causing injury or harm to the boy and girl?

- No, definitely not, but then again I really
don't know him as well as you might think.

- You don't know him?!

There is no such thing as knowing oneself much less another
human being. No time was this more apparent in my life
than when I finished writing my first novel, "The Nihilesthete." I didn't have the slightest idea what I had. A madman's
ravings or a novel. It was a veritable Rorschach test which I
had to give to others to interpret.

- Can you explain what you mean when you
say you don't know your brother as well
as you might think?

- For example, when he finished his novel,
"The Nihilesthete." He hadn't mentioned a

word about it to me all through the writing, and then when he finally gave it to me to read: I couldn't believe it. It was a complete shock. I had no idea he had that in him.

- And what was it that your brother, Richard, had in him?

- All that sadism, perversity, grotesqueness. I mean the novel was brilliant, but as for the rest...I was totally unprepared.

- Do you think, and again I know this is difficult for you, Mr. Kalich, but do you think he could somehow transfer such venom and brutality from the written page to real people? Namely the boy and girl?

- Look, it was fiction. "The Nihilesthete" was a brilliant metaphoric work of fiction. As for the relationship he had with the boy and girl, I couldn't begin to make heads or tails of it. Your guess is as good as mine. Ricki, my first wife, always said: Dick will do something and then come up with a philosophy to justify it.

- You haven't answered my question, Mr. Kalich.

- I think I have.

There's a method to my madness. Whether I take a stroll through the park or a seat at the corner Starbucks, the trick is to sharpen my hunter's eye. That achieved, plotting and programming ideas for the boy and girl unfold as abundantly as the flora and fauna in a tropical forest. All that remains is to allow the images and ideas to filter through my brain, jot down notes until my pack of 3x5 cards is as thick and choice-laden as Time Warner Cable's programming selection; and then pick and choose one scenario or another, whatever turbulence and mayhem, reward or punishment, catches my fancy to play for the night.

- Can you tell us anything else about your brother that would help us to understand how he could even come to write such a novel; a novel, I should indicate, that has been described as one of the darkest in American fiction? And more importantly, I apologize, but I must ask again: can you tell us why he would invite this particular boy and girl into his home and possibly cause them harm and injury?

- I already told you. I can't. But I can tell you he was always strange. Weird. Different.

- In what way was your twin brother Richard different?

- He lived half a life. No sex. No intimacy. Right out of Winesburg, Ohio. I
told him that all the time.

- What do you mean: your brother lived
"half a life"?

- He was never integrated. Never able to
find a balance. For him, life was books,
ideas, writing, the interior life. Everything else he categorically dismissed.
Married life, family, home, creature comforts meant little or nothing to him. For
example, he lived seven years in PH-F
before he even bought a TV or air con-
ditioner. He was always alone. He never
lived with a woman. And when Knute was
small, despite living only six or seven
blocks from us, he never visited. Never
once came over to play with him. Take him
to a movie or to the circus. Even to the
park. He would chronically say: "What's
he got to do with my life?!" Imagine, his
own nephew. So self-absorbed. I had to
beg him to babysit and even then...

- And yet he fell deeply in love with the
young harpist, Ms. Nacheva.

- I wouldn't call that love.

- What would you call it?

- A pathetic and desperate attempt to make up for the life he never lived. Besides, he has bigger problems than the harpist.

After the boy and girl's first embrace I celebrated the occasion by suggesting that the boy would have to begin paying an increased rent for his lodgings; knowing full well, of course, that he had no means to do so. The squinteyed glances and conspiratorial whispers shared a few minutes later between the two in a favorite hiding place was all the return I needed. After careful consideration I soon told them that the increased rent would not be necessary. We all have to make sacrifices, including myself, I said. Once again there was joy in PH-F.

- You've mentioned more than once, Mr. Kalich, that your twin was always angry, sad, depressed. That everything bothered him. And that the young harpist was only the smallest part of the problem. A symptom, not a cause, as you put it. Could you elaborate further to help us understand his problem? Perhaps give us a rationale?

- You mean besides the complete present day collapse of the literary culture? That though acknowledged by some of the best literary minds in the world for having written two first rate novels, his advances and royalty payments were a joke? He used to say for every "yes" he

received in his life, he received a thousand "no's."

"The Nihilesthete" was rejected by seventy-five publishers
before a small independent press in Sag Harbor committed
to publish it. It cost me five years of almost single-minded
pathological pursuit to find that publisher. My second novel,
"Charlie P," went somewhat easier. Only thirty-five rejection
letters. During those five years pursuing a publisher for "The
Nihilesthete," I was so depressed I literally couldn't lift my
pen to write a single line.

- By your words, Mr. Kalich, am I to infer
that it's even more difficult for writers
such as your brother today?

- Definitely. At least when we were young,
starting out, there was the possibility
of being published. Of making a name for
yourself. Today nothing. The entire literary culture is dead. It's been appropri-
ated by the pop culture. Writers such as
my brother have been rendered obsolete,
irrelevant, superfluous, no different than
disposable goods. Whatever adjective you
want to use. From redeeming the world
with the word it's come down to iPods and
video games, TV and computers, Kindles
and Nooks. His meta-fictions and philo-
sophical novels, like "Transfiguration of
the Commonplace," have turned into Donald

Trump's reality TV. Dick always said he
wanted to write a novel about it someday.

Literature Ruined My Life: I promised myself that one day I
would write a novel with that as its title.

- Mr. Kalich. This is neither the time
nor place to hold court or make use of the
podium for a diatribe against the plight
of the literary culture.

- I'm sorry but...

- Obviously you feel strongly on the subject.

- The subject is my twin brother.

- Right. Quite right. But for that reason, if no other, I must ask you to stay
all the closer to the subject at hand.
This is an interrogation, after all. You
are under obligation...

- Do you have a question?

- Was there anything in your brother's
life, and I mean to say his actual life,
not so much his writing life, that would
lead him to perpetrate some kind of violence...

- Didn't you just stop me from answering that same question?

- That would, because of his various depressive moods, possibly lead him into arguments when angry, or even, perhaps, physical confrontations?

The twin remains silent.

- Mr. Kalich, even if this is not a conventional court of law, it is an interrogation. I must remind you that you are under obligation to answer...

- Answer what?

One starts out one's life reading the great writers. Dostoevski, Hesse, Mann, Camus, West, Kafka. You exalt their pain and suffering, deprivation and denials, to the level of martyrdom; apotheosize and canonize their artistry to the realm of the absolute. And then one day at the age of fifty, or sixty, it dawns on you that not only do your own books belong on the same shelf as theirs, but your own tattered writer's life has not been that different from their own.

- You say there was one time, Mr. Kalich?

- Yes. About fifteen to twenty years ago. We were both working for the Department of Social Services and I remember my twin and I being called into the Director's office for some nonsense or not. I think it was, yes, it was field time and how we both abused it. Anyway, the Director was a harmless bureaucrat and when he started lecturing my brother about field time and how staff was expected to make each and every visit and such...my brother just exploded. Verbally decimated the Director. By the time my brother was finished there was nothing left of the man. It seemed to me that my brother vented a lifetime's frustration and anger in that one tirade.

MEMORANDUM

The City of New York
Human Resources Administration

DATE: January 17, 1983

TO: Ms Carolyn Shipp, Supvr. Team B
GSS/M-11

re: Richard Kalich

FROM: Mr. Bill Murphy, Director
GSS/M-11

SUBJECT: Audit Field-Time

A Timekeeping Audit was conducted during the months
of November and December of all OSS Field staff
(500 casemanagers).

The findings indicate that District M-11 is basically
in compliance with procedure, but we were instructed
to follow-up on two worker's field-time.

Please forward to my office by the C.O.B. on Jan. 21,
1983 a written statement from you (Supvr.) and
casemanager answers for the following questions.

   (1) Why worker has continually checked out for
      field each working day for three (3) years.
      (Audit state that worker has only spent 15
      days in office in a spand of three years).

   (2) Does worker have a special caseload which
      would be necessary for him to check out to
      field each p.m.?

   (3) Have his field time been approved by Supvr.
      (Team Supvr.)?

   (4) How many clients does worker visit during
      his visits to field?

   (5) Is it necessary for worker to check out for
      field each day in p.m.?

When I worked for the Department I sat next to a woman
(I've forgotten her name) who would say in emotive, heartfelt
tones, daily, after a telephone call with a client, an interview,
or returning to the office from a field visit: "I love my clients!" And then would turn to face me. I, in turn, could do
no more than shake my head and smile.

   - And that was it? It went no further?

- No. But until that time I never really understood how much it cost my brother to live the life he did.

- And by living the life he did you mean to say: Half a life?

The twin sighs and manages a barely perceptible nod.

- Final question, Mr. Kalich. Would all these difficulties your brother experienced: loss of authority, having little or no place in the community, being rendered obsolete, irrelevant, superfluous, would all these difficulties combined be sufficient cause to catalyze a kind of monstrous egotism in your...

- I don't understand the question.

- Let me put it another way. Would all your brother's hardship and travail be reason enough for him to assume more extreme behavior than mere manifestations of anger, bitterness, melancholy, including the possibility of his perpetrating violence, harm and injury on the boy and girl?

The twin ponders the question.

- You really must answer the question, Mr. Kalich.

- I'll say this only once. To the best of my knowledge my twin brother was never happier, more content and at peace with himself than when he took in the boy and girl to live with him in PH-F.

	RICHARD (DICK)	ROBERT (BOB)
	"SUNRISE"	"SUNSET"
1. EARLY CHILD-HOOD	(Mother's appellation for happy, smiling child.)	(Mother's appellation for chronically moody and unhappy child.)
2. EARLY MEMORY	Readily eats mother's spoonfed meals and feels sorry for mother when twin doesn't do so.	Holds spoonfuls in mouth to point where his swollen cheeks look like Popeye the sailor. Twin, Dick, empathizes with mother's pain and frustration and encourages brother to swallow.
3. SPORTS CHILD-HOOD	First chosen by friends for city games (curb ball, punchball, stickball, baseball) and stars at shortstop and centerfield.	Chronically chosen last, if at all, to play city games with peers and friends; and then to play right field and catcher. Often frustrated by lack of athletic aptitude and often storms off home in tears and anger.
4. BAR MITZVAH	Assumes total responsibility; loses 20 pounds due to stress as it's a major event in household as father is renowned cantor in orthodox European synagogue.	Rebels against orthodox father-the cantor-and Jewish protocol and expectancies and lets brother make up for his laxity.
5. POST BAR MITZ-VAH	Day after bar mitzvah, staring teary-eyed into father's bedroom mirror, cuts tephillin with scissors from arm and vows never to speak to father again or go to synagogue.	Continues to go his own way, in flagrant disregard of parents' wishes and expectancies of "good Jewish son."

6. COLLEGE	Attends academically demanding City College of New York. Takes school-work all too seriously. All study and no play makes for bookish and stressful college years.	Attends NYU. Never studies. Four years of fun and games.
7. MILITARY SERVICE	Six (6) months army re-serves and five-and-one-half years of obligation. Latrine Orderly every summer.	Feigns neurological defect of hands to avoid U.S. Army service
8. LOVE	Except for six (6) week period with the young harpist, never lives with a woman. Loves only two women in his lifetime, once when young, another when old; both times "breaking down" when romance didn't work out.	Two wives, children, boy and girl, one from each marriage. Shares intima-cy and love throughout his life. Also has three live-in girlfriends for five years each; and more than his share of sexual liaisons
9. ADULT YEARS	Lives "half a life" (brother's coinage). Books and writ-ing, little else. Saves nickels and dimes. Never leaves Manhattan and becomes, in later years, increasingly isolated and reclusive.	Handicapper, gambler, man-about-town. Gre-garious, social; lives life to the fullest, most often at other people's (espe-cially twin's) expense.
10. WORK	Hates job as case worker for Dept. of Social Services, finding it humiliating and debasing.	Professional handicapper and gambler.
11. WRITING	Hates writing, suffer-ing from creative block. Constantly judging himself. Dostoevski or nothing–and for this reason constipated, self-conscious, and terrified of "letting go."	Loves writing. Vis-ceral, spontaneous. Body writer. Lets it all hang out knowing he has a built-in genetic fail safe in his twin who in effect functions as his "Max-well Perkins."

12. CHARACTER	Serious to a fault, makes everything too important from writing to shopping for a new suit. Nothing easy or relaxed.	Excessive. Large appetites, large dreams. Lives fast and easy knowing if he can't pay his bills, his bookmakers, credit cards and financial debts, he always has his twin to do it for him.
		Invents persona, "Broadway Bob," and not only sells it to the world but believes it himself. Rich and successful.
13 MONEY	Scrimps and saves; every dollar accounted for. Never borrows, not a cent, neither from friends nor credit card companies. Scrupulously honest.	Gambles excessively. Lives big and spends bigger to keep up appearances. Picks up every bill. If he can't pay bills, like with writing, he always has his twin to bail him out.
14. TRAVEL AND VACATIONS	Never travels. Never vacations. Rarely, if ever, leaves Manhattan. Maybe one half-vacation in last 28 years and that to a book fair to help promote his own book.	Constant traveling and vacationing, usually at other people's expense.

- If anything, Mr. Kalich, this chart shows you cannot attribute the differences between your brother and yourself, as well as your unhappiness and dissatisfaction with your life, to your difficulties and struggles as a writer; nor your being victimized by the diachronic illusion centering around the transvaluation of the literary culture to the electronic

```
culture. You must assume some responsi-
bility too.
```

I remain unresponsive, once again not giving the interrogator the satisfaction of an answer.

```
- Even you, Mr. Kalich, must admit that
much.

- Mr. Kalich, what do you mean you are no
longer that person anymore?

- Something inside me has changed.

- But, Mr. Kalich, all your life you've
loved books. You've savored their words,
contemplated their meanings, reflected
over them, surrendered yourself to them,
immersed yourself in them. Don't you feel
you've lost something essential as to who
you are?

- Whatever.
```

I escorted the girl to dinner tonight at an elegant Eastside restaurant. It was the first time in at least a month that we were able to be completely alone. To make our way to the dining area we had to pass through a crowded bar section. Wholly unexpectedly, the girl took my hand to help me cross the low threshold into the restaurant. For those brief moments her warm hand laid in mine I felt ecstasy. In my mind I couldn't have been closer to her. I can't remember the last time a woman either took my hand or I experienced such warm, intimate feelings. It confirmed for me what I had already come to sense watching the girl on screen with the boy. How her intimate glances and gestures observed by me on screen are meant as much for me as the boy. After dinner, which was more than pleasant, I don't think I stopped talking once other than to gulp down several particularly large mouthfuls of filet mignon; and, of course, the food was excellent, not that I'm a gourmet; on the contrary, I hardly know how or what to order from an Italian menu, but I did enjoy the elegant atmosphere. At any rate, I was in the midst of telling the girl that I had a real treat in store for her. There was an ice cream parlor in the immediate area famous for its pastries and desserts; the girl, to be sure, has a sweet tooth, loves chocolate ice cream and virtually any kind of cake. So imagine my surprise and disappointment when, even before I could finish my sentence, the girl was already telling me she would rather return home. Her stomach felt queasy. I immediately signaled for a taxi. But once home, after first making certain I had entered my room, the way the girl surreptitiously headed directly to the boy's room, I understood instantly that her desire to return home had little to do with any kind of stomach ailment, but rather that she wished to satisfy another kind of appetite. One no ice cream parlor catered to other than in sublimated portions.

Needless to say, I stayed up late that night wracking my brain over ways to satisfy my own appetites.

    - You are Mr. Charles Leiser?

    - Charlie Leiser. Call me Charlie. Every-
body else does.

- You are the proprietor of a bookstand on 68th Street and Columbus Avenue where you sell old, used and out-of-print books?

- I don't know much about being a proprietor, but I do have a bookstand on West 68th Street.

- And for the past twenty years or more, Mr. Kalich has been a customer?

- For years he couldn't pass my stand without stopping to browse for at least thirty to forty minutes. Some days we'd spend the whole afternoon talking about books and writers.

- And in addition to literary talk, I assume Mr. Kalich also purchased your books.

- If I had ten customers like Kalich in those days, I'd be retired by now.

- What do you mean by "in those days"?

- I mean that was another time, another Kalich.

- Another Mr. Kalich. Please explain.

- There was a period for about eight to ten years that he stopped coming around.

Didn't as much as wave his hand when passing, much less stop to buy a book.

- And this stoppage happened prior to the
boy and girl taking up residence in Mr.
Kalich's apartment?

- It happened years before they showed up.
But I have to admit once the young people
moved in with him, he started coming round
again. Even if it wasn't to buy books.

- If Mr. Kalich no longer purchased books,
what did he purchase from your bookstand?

- Illustrated books from the '20s and
'30s; Ziegfeld Follies memorabilia; and
fashion and photography magazines with
famous models and actresses on their covers. The last item I remember him buying
was an old Life magazine with Marilyn
Monroe on its cover.

- Did Mr. Kalich frequent your bookstand
with the boy and girl?

- Are you kidding? Who do you think be
bought that stuff for? That little girl
pulled him around by the nose.

- Please explain the phrase: 'pulled him
around by the nose.'

- As I said, the girl had him buy fashion magazines and illustrated books for her, but the real reason they came round is because my stand is located just one block from a women's shop up the block. She was always dragging him there to shop for a dress for her or something. Actually, it was him probably dragging her. Wherever he went, he was always window-shopping for her.

- Mr. Leiser, earlier you made mention of another turnaround in Mr. Kalich that occurred just several months prior to the boy and girl's suicide.

- That's right. It was like that ten-year stoppage period all over again. For some reason he lost interest in shopping for the girl the same way he lost interest years back with books.

- All shopping?

- In those months I never once saw him go into the women's shop with or without the girl.

At a certain point in writing, a Writer becomes his character and from that time on, as already mentioned, does little more than take dictation. In a similar manner, an Actor, after having read, practiced, rehearsed his/her role for a week, a month or more, becomes the character he/she is to play. It's not so much that the two become one as the Writer/Actor becoming the other. Though, of course, both still retain that which is most significant about themselves and bring that unique material to the task at hand. Like a Writer, like an Actor, I have become one with the boy and girl. When I observe them now on screen, there is hardly a difference between what I see and who I am. All the girl's smiles, gestures, touches, caresses, love-making with the boy, I feel are meant as much for me as for him. I am indeed a fortunate man. Like in all good writing, in all creation, a miracle has been wrought. What has for so long laid dormant deep inside me, the boy and girl have mined and feelings and emotions I no longer knew I even possessed have been unleashed like buried treasure to become part and parcel of my everyday. For the first time in years I feel truly alive.

    - Mr. Martinez, you are the Director of
    the Guadalupe Halfway House in East Har-
    lem?

    - I am.

What will I in turn bring to the boy and girl?

    - And it was your decision to place the
    boy and girl into Mr. Kalich's home.

    - Yes.

    - Mr. Martinez, it's been established
    that Mr. Kalich had, by his own admis-
    sion, a great antipathy for practicing
    social work, abused his field time privi-

leges when he was employed, found the bureaucratic system demeaning as well as spiritually deadening, and even possessed such disdain and loathing for his fellow civil service peers that he confronted them verbally if not physically more than once over the years.

- Yes. I'm aware of that.

- And yet still you maintain that Mr. Kalich is a great social worker? A caring and compassionate man?

- Most definitely.

- What in your experience has led you to such a conclusion?

- Because I know Mr. Kalich, not only as a professional colleague, but also as a client.

- A client?

- Yes.

- Please explain.

- As you can see I'm a quadriplegic. At eleven years of age I was a member of the Cuban National Olympic Swimming Team when it was my poor fate to dive into a pool of concrete, causing a severe spinal cord injury and my resulting quadriplegic condition. Two years later my father, brother and I settled in New York City. My father took a job as a janitor for Columbia University, and my brother, Celso, always a difficult spirit, soon enough found himself interred at Rikers Island. Mr. Kalich was assigned to my case as caseworker. Thanks to his social work efforts I am where I am today.

- Can you be more specific? Perhaps give an example or...

- I have your assurances that these proceedings are private?

- You do. The outside world has no interest in what transpires here.

- All right then. Mr. Kalich arranged home care service for me and though I only required a home attendant for four hours a day, twenty-eight hours a week, Mr. Kalich provided home attendant service for twelve hours per day, eighty-four hours a week. Those extra hours the home attendant didn't have to work added up to quite a tidy sum in additional salary earnings which were divided equally

between myself and the home attendant.
It goes without saying that that money
afforded me the opportunity to make the
most of my difficult situation. And that,
along with Mr. Kalich's constant encouragement, motivated me not only to finish
high school, but go on to college and even
acquire a Masters degree in Social Work
at Long Island University, and ultimately
assume the position I presently hold as
Director of the Guadalupe Halfway House.

I might also add that Antonio Martinez recently married,
finding a mail order bride from his native Cuba, and with the
aid of a dangerous (for him) penile implant operation, functions quite satisfactorily with his young wife.

- Your name is Knute?

- Yes.

- You know Mr. Richard Kalich?

- Of course. He's my father's twin brother.

- And that makes him your uncle.

- Yes. Uncle Dickie. He's my second favorite uncle.

- Who is your first favorite uncle?

- Uncle Johnny. He takes me everywhere when he comes to New York from California. He's my favorite uncle.

- But it was your uncle Dick who took you to see the Lion King play, was it not?

- That was only because Mommy was sick and Bobby was out of town on business.

The boy lowers his eyes to avert his uncle's gaze.

- Before the Lion King play started, Knute, didn't your uncle also take you to another theater to purchase tickets for another play?

- Yes. He said he could kill two birds with one stone.

- And what was that second play?

- Romeo and Juliet. He wanted the tickets for the boy and girl living with him.

- And what did you say to that?

- I don't remember.

- Didn't you mention something about other plays?

- Oh yeah. I told him they would probably have more fun seeing other plays.

- What other plays?

- I don't know. Tarzan, Lion King, or maybe movies like Cars, Shrek III, even The Fantastic Mr. Fox.

- Did your uncle say why, of all the plays and movies available, he chose Romeo and Juliet for the boy and girl to see?

The boy doesn't answer.

- Your uncle said nothing?

- Maybe it was because he wanted the boy and girl to love each other like Romeo and Juliet love each other.

- Your uncle said that?

- No.

- Who then?

- Me.

- And what did your uncle say when you said that?

- He didn't say anything. But he smiled.

- And how do you remember that he smiled?

- Because Uncle Dickie never smiles.

The boy lowers his eyes.

- This next question is very important, Knute.

- I thought all the questions are important.

- Yes. But this is the most important one. Did your Uncle Dick mention what happens to Romeo and Juliet at the end of the play?

The boy remains silent.

- He didn't say anything?

The boy shakes his head. Lowers his eyes, but almost immediately looks up.

- Tell me. What happens to Romeo and Juliet at the end of the play?

When the idea for double suicide first took root, who but I could have traced its origins back to my unfortunate experience with

Dobrinka at the women's store where she chose her white dress from the Romeo and Juliet catalogue? Strange how the mind works. Stranger still how things ultimately fall into place. I wonder if all people are like me. Not merely storytellers, but storymakers at heart, having the wherewithal to make chaos into harmony.

> - At the women's store where Ms. Nacheva selected the dress from the Romeo and Juliet catalogue, you had no idea at the time that it would play such an integral role in the boy and girl's double suicide?
>
> - How could I? I didn't even know the boy and girl at the time.
>
> - And later when you did get to know the boy and girl?
>
> - Later, for the first time in my life, I was at peace with myself and completely happy with the boy and girl.
>
> - You were happy and at peace with yourself?
>
> - As I and others have said: For the longest time.

The Interrogator even has the temerity to question me about a childhood incident that I would have much preferred to forget.

- So, Mr. Kalich, this recurring theme of
suicide, according to your previous testimony, I have to assume might have origi-
nated in a childhood incident when you
were seven or eight years old and you witnessed the suicide of a childhood friend
on 104th Street and West End Avenue.

- Yes. I can still see my friend's shattered body lying in an ever-widening pool
of blood.

- And that image of your little friend and
the ever-widening pool of blood you've
remembered all these years?

- That along with his grief-stricken
mother's words to his father.

- And what were those words?

- You drove him to it. You drove him to
it. She repeated those words over and
over again.

Not too long ago the girl would listen with rapt attention to
my every word, now I notice she waits impatiently for me to
finish, and then, instantly, either offers me a withering stare,
or skulks away to join the boy.

- And when things changed?

- When the boy and girl changed suddenly,
as if overnight, all sorts of ideas,
thoughts, feelings came over me.

- What kinds of ideas?

- Naturally I had to make adjustments.

- What kinds of adjustments?

Then there are times when a deeper, more primal voice breaks
through. A voice that does not mince words, but speaks only
of essentials. An unrestrained voice, untrammeled by conventions, that no court of law's protocols can restrict or restrain.

- And such a voice came to you that night
in the elevator with the young harpist?

- I realized for the first time I would
never be with Dobrinka. I would always be
alone, for the rest of my life, alone.

- And that was the first time you realized...?

- I had nothing to fight for her with.

- What do you mean you had nothing to fight
for her with?

- I was already old, sexually impotent, a
sense of profound powerlessness pervaded
my entire being.

- And yet you surrendered yourself completely to the young harpist. Gave all you had to give.

- On some level I must have known that all I had given to Dobrinka was nothing more than compensation for the life I never lived.

- And so, already old, without love or books, by way of recompense you chose another path?

- It was my chance to turn dross into gold.

- Your erstwhile novel. The boy and girl. You brought them to life.

- When I saw them on screen they became real.

- Or less real as the case may be.

- Manageable.

- You saw them as a game to be played. Toy marionettes. Your creation.

- A man can only take so much.

- And by your own admission, the girl was as much yours as the boy's.

All this talk, all these people, with their different vantage points, their different interpretations. All of them know me, or claim they do, and yet all of them know nothing of what is true and real. All my long years of struggle and sacrifice, all my years of aloneness, powerlessness and impotence, all those years of being less than I wanted, less than I needed to be.

> - And then one night in the elevator with Dobrinka, the voice, my voice, "I" cried out: Who's going to love me?! Who's going to love me?!

Once the voice dies down, that evening or the next, I am in my TV room again, observing the boy and girl on screen.

BIRTHDAY PRESENTS:

1. CASHMERE BLANKET.....................................$440.00
2. PIN...$30.00
3. SHOES..$55.00
4. CHANEL..$106.00
5. Dress (Henry Bendel).................................$340.00
6. Skirt (Henry Bendel)..................................$145.00
7. TEDDY BEAR...$14.00
8. CHOCOLATE BIRTHDAY CAKE......................$50.00
9. Indochine's Restaurant...............................$120.00
10. Taxi fare..$18.00
11. Miscellaneous...$15.00
TOTAL EXPENSES...$1333.00

- You spent more than a week preparing for the girl's birthday present?

- It was a special occasion.

- You purchased many different presents for the girl?

- Each and every gift I selected I knew she would personally value.

- Including a teddy bear?

- Since a child she had always slept with a teddy. And the one she had brought with her from the halfway house was worn and raggedy.

- And you special-ordered a queen-size cashmere blanket from the Polo Baby Shop?

- I got the idea from years back when I had purchased a cashmere blanket for my twin's newborn.

- And then you dined at Indochine's?

- Yes.

- A very fashionable restaurant. And indeed costly, especially for a person living on social security and a small pension.

- I had calculated what I could spend, and all things considered, it was within my means.

- Afterwards, you returned home?

- Yes.

- It would be only natural for you to want to share the moment. Have a nightcap with the girl, perhaps.

- That would have been nice.

- After all, it was a special occasion, as you say.

- The girl's 18th birthday.

- And then what happened?

- The girl said she was tired, exhausted really, and retired to bed.

- And the boy?

- He had had as much to eat and drink as she, and was likewise eager for bed.

- Leaving you alone.

```
- Not really alone. I too retired, only
not to bed.

- But rather to your TV room to observe
the boy and girl making passionate love.
```

There was a moment when the girl peered directly into the camera with a complicit smile on her face. That smile proved to me that my vague suspicions were real, that this moment did truly exist. If truly meant for the boy, why then would she so glaringly aim her smile so directly into the camera? That complicit smile reconfirmed for me all that I had conjured and hoped for. The girl's smile had a basis in reality. It was as much meant for me as the boy. I was not deluding myself. I was not confusing fiction and fact. This was no fantasy on my part. The girl's complicit smile was real and the girl's love for me was real: Not merely in my head.

```
- When you observed the boy and girl mak-
ing passionate love, you were crushed.

- No.

- Devastated.

- Not at all.

- After all, if not for you they wouldn't
have clean sheets, much less a cashmere
blanket; not to mention sundry other gifts
as well as Chanel in the girl's room.
```

In the beginning the girl shared all her secrets with me. Her most intimate memories: Her preference for oral sex. Her sole experience of coitus with a man, in a vacated elementary school on a staircase.

- And so you decided to enact your cruel fantasies on the boy and girl as a way of...

- On the contrary, those intimacies expressed by the boy and girl had quite an opposite effect on me.

- Opposite?!

- Romantic obsession, pathological jealousy, I had left that all behind me with the young harpist. I had no wish to revisit my past Molière comedy with the boy and girl.

- Then what?

- My intentions were on a higher plane.

- Please explain what you mean by higher plane?

- As I've stated all along, my primary motive was play.

- Play?!

- Yes. The very fact that the boy and girl took their lovemaking so seriously as to hide it from me only made me realize all the more that I was on the right path. After all, what did they know other than their own childish libidinal needs for each other. While I...I was the one observing them and not the other way around.

- But, by your own admission, you were on the outside looking in?

- Not outside but someplace else.

In between, if you will. The boy and girl allowed me to recapture my old author's authority.

"Literature is fundamentally ludic in nature. Formidable advantages that ludic systems offer, precisely as laboratories of recherché, they allow people (authors) to test ideas in a circumscribed field of inquiry. According to a set of protocols, in a manner that is both useful and amusing."
—Johan Huizinga

"The function of a poet still remains fixed in the play-sphere where it was born. Poieses in fact, is play function. It proceeds within the playground of the mind, in a world of its own which the mind creates for it. There things have a different physiognomy from the ones they wear in ordinary life, and are bound by ties other than those of logic and causality."

— Johan Huizinga

- So fiction had truly become life for
you, Mr. Kalich.

- On the contrary, life had become fiction.
I was once again a Writer taking dictation from my characters. It only follows
that I was interested in experimenting
with my characters. Testing their limits.
Exploring just who the boy and girl were
if only for the sake of the novel I could
not write.

- And you achieved this by exacting callous punishments on the boy and girl as
if they were mere mannequins, puppets,
icons on a game board to be manipulated
at your whim.

- You miss the point entirely. If enact-
ing callous punishments came into play,
it had more to do with method, a mere by-
product of my intent rather than any particular goal. For certain, I held no personal animosity toward the boy and girl.

But who can say what's inside a man. One has to write the
book to truly know what's in it.

And even then...

Sometimes I take a break from observing the boy and girl
on screen in the TV room and reread my notes from my
original but aborted novel: "The Transfiguration of the Commonplace." Rough and unedited as they are, it is always interesting to look back and compare these notes with my current
situation. Not only do they furnish me with ideas as to how
to proceed with the boy and girl, but they additionally show
me what my writer's imagination was like years back when I
started. How my original vision for the novel has changed,
grown, progressed, and yet how closely the two still parallel
and feed off each other. I defy any person, whether literary
critic, scholar or common reader, to separate and differentiate
between the two. For me at least, the two have become one.

* See Notes for "Transfiguration of the Commonplace."

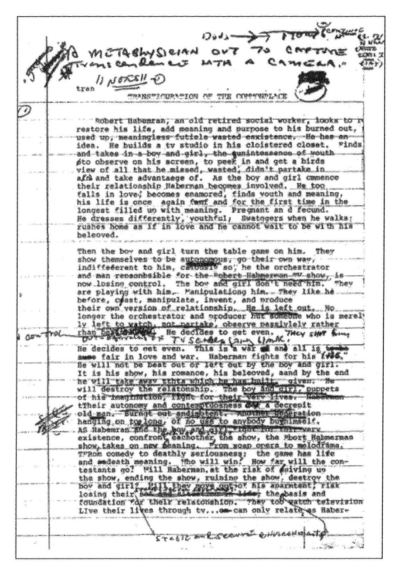

Robert Haberman, an old retired social worker, looks to ~
restore his life, add meaning and purpose to his burned out,
used up, meaningless futile wasted eexistence. He has an
idea. He builds a tv studio in his cloistered closet. Finds
and takes in a boy and girl, the quintessence of youth
@to observe on his screen, to peek in and get a birds
view of all that he missed, wasted, didn't partake in
afm and take advantaege of. As the boy and girl cmmence
their relationship Haberman becomes involved. He too
falls in love, becomes enamored, finds youth and meaning,
his life is once again fwet and for the first time in the
longest filled up with meaning. Pregnant an d fecund.
He dresses differently, youthful, Swatggers when he walks;
rushes home as if in love and he cannot wait to be with his
beloved.

Then the boy and girl turn the table game on him. They
show themselves to be autonomous, go their own way,
indiffeerent to him, callously so; he the orchestrator
and man rensonbible for the "Robert Haberman" tv show, is
now losing control. The boy and girl don't need him. They
are playing with him. Manipulationg him. They like he
before, cast, manipulate, invent, and produce
their own version of relationship. He is left out. No
longer the orchestrator and producer but someone who is merely
left to watch, not partake, observe passiviely rather
than participate. He decides to get even. They shut him
out. Provided by TV Screen (and work).

He decides to get even. This is a war and all is
same fair in love and war. Haberman fights for his "life."
He will not be beat out or left out by the boy and girl.
It is his show, his romance, his beloved, aand by the end
he will take away tthis which he has builtt, given. He
will destroy the relationship. The boy and girl, puppets
of his imagination, fight for their very lives.
tTheir autonomy and contentiousness bvy a decrepit
old man. Burnt out andighted. another inspiration
hanging on too long, of no use to anybody but himself.
AS Haberman and the bpy and girl, together they wary
existence, confront eachother, the show, the "bort Haberman
show, takes on new meaning. From soap opera to melodrama,
fFrom comedy to deathly seriousness; the game has life
and sedeath meaning. Who will win? How far will the contestants go? Will Haberman, at the risk of giving up
the show, ending the show, ruining the show, destroy the
boy and girl, will they move out of his apartment, risk
losing their relationship, the basis and
foundation for their relationship. They too watch television
LIve their lives through tv...can only relate as Haber-

②

man, through the mechanistic machinations of tv. Will they
leave, end up alone, destroy, forsesake haberman. A
battle is waged. The stakes are high. This is a program
The Robert Habemran Show for the age. Will it end in
failure, tragedy, comedy will it rise above all problems
even when the tv is shut finally shut off to be renewew by a
a new character. A new boy and girl who Haberman might
~~gin~~find in the street one last day to begin again. Will
realtionshpp only begin when the tv is shut off, when all
is dark and quite and we have no more images closing our
mind. Flashing thorgh our living rooms. When wae are
once agin also alone together, in the quiet of the night,
when we can hear each other speak again. Without tv commercia
commericals, interruptions, sounds and noises from the
stretet, and the many other distractions of modern man
coming to hnder and prevent us from dong so.

Sub Plot: As the old man's programs become increasingly
more violent, inducing more and more 'hurt and punishment
upon the youngsters, as the yougsters retaliate in their
kind, the program Robert Habemran Show becomes more an
and more compelling, a mjatter of life and death until
the contestants, the prime characters, the boy and girl
and the old man are veritably in a life and death struggle
for survival, the landlord of the building which is the
set for the show has decided to take his ~~comproperty~~ move,
cooperative. Thus Haberman will have to get out, move,
He has to NO EVICTION CLAUSE or so he thougnt. He has
doesn't have a-no eviction clause-and he has to move.
His show will be interrupted. He could never find another
apartment, studio, like this. the boy and girl will
leave him for ever. Something has tto to be done quickck-
ly he muses. A lfife and death ~~and~~ fisnish. A last
knock chance knockout with the one big runch. Life, the
landlord, losing the aprtment, hve necedssited Haberman
take a chance. this last chance. He too is subject to
contingency. the laws beyond the clostered room. ~~they,~~

At the end, with the tv screen blank, the room dark,
the images gone once and for all, gone, he muses, maybe
now, with no distractions, sounds, images, tv sets
blasting away, the boy and girl he has a chance, a real
CHANCE AT RELATIONSHIOP, _tran nhis_. _To find Saomras_
To see whey dere is to see.

- You are Mr. Kalich's literary agent, Svetlana Paccher?

The things one conjures in one's mind when watching the boy and girl on screen.

- I was more Mr. Kalich's translator and editor than agent when I resided in New York. Even in those years his books hardly sold.

The things one is capable of.

- You've read this present text of Mr. Kalich's?

- I'm about halfway through, page 139, to be exact.

- What are your impressions so far?

- In what capacity: translator? editor? agent?

- Your choice, Ms. Paccher.

- Well, as a translator I would have to say this book is especially difficult to interpret, being somewhere between reality and fiction. Sometimes even I can't distinguish between what's real and what's not.

- But you are a translator.

- Of course, and in that capacity I can take liberties with Mr. Kalich's prose. The author's language is not etched in stone, you understand. It's a matter of interpretation. Especially for a writer like Kalich.

- Why especially for a writer like Kalich?

- Because for him the act of writing has always been a torture chamber. It's a constant struggle to get the right words out.

- Not that different than a translator?

- Same thing. Yes. Similar.

- And your impressions of the boy and girl?

- To be honest, I'm a little disappointed he hasn't developed the boy and girl more. They seem rather flat, passive, unidimensional. Of course I realize that's probably the point; that they're meant to be no more than representations in the character's mind, much like he sees them on the television screen, but still, I would have liked a richer depiction.

- Ms. Paccher, as interesting as your interpretations of Mr. Kalich's technical proficiency as an author might be, and as you've known the man for fifteen to twenty years now, and have at least in part perused his book, I'd much prefer to hear your opinion as to whether Mr. Kalich could have in some way been responsible for the boy and girl's suicide.

- First off, I haven't spent any real time with Mr. Kalich in about ten to twelve years, since setting up my own agency in Paris. And he stopped writing, at least I thought he did.

- And secondly?

- Secondly, before I answer your question, in all fairness to Mr. Kalich, I'd like to finish reading the book.

- Ms. Paccher, we're pressed for time. I'd appreciate it very much if you could at least venture an opinion.

- Well I don't know if this will help in your assessment, but I will tell you that in the past I've always advised Mr. Kalich not to lose his edge.

- His edge?

```
- Not to become too comfortable. His mis-
ery and anger...it's what fuels his writ-
ing. One thing is for certain: without it
he wouldn't write the books he does.

- And if he lost it? Or more specifically,
if he couldn't write at all: then what?

- That's one book I wouldn't want to
translate much less interpret.
```

Ms. Paccher had already stepped down when she turned to complete her final thought.

```
- You realize when all is said and done,
whether I'm serving in the role of agent,
editor or translator, at bottom, I'm just
a reader like everybody else.
```

Like any good dramatist, once the boy and girl asserted their need for autonomy, I raised the stakes. After all, more important than anything else, I wanted to keep the game interesting.

Now, what would prove most interesting?

a. Create a Love Triangle by inviting a temptress to stay with us in PH-F.

b. Raise the rent to the point where the boy cannot afford to pay. (Threaten to do so again and again.)

c. Set Curfew Hours:
    9:00 p.m. on weekdays for the girl
    10:00 p.m. on weekdays for the boy.
    11:00 p.m. on weekends for both.

d. Impose a No Fraternization Rule: except for those hours when I can supervise and oversee the boy and girl's meetings.

e. All Shopping cancelled.

f. All Luncheons and Dinners cancelled.

g. Impose, as much as feasible, a Social Isolation Rule between the boy and girl in PH-F (and out?)

h. Impose a No Talking Rule.

Naturally The Rules of My Game were designed to provoke the boy and girl to such extremes of violent emotion as to allow them to break through the boundaries of quotidian existence. By setting the proper mood, staging the correct environs, programming the fitting dramaturgy, I would in effect be creating the ideal situation for the boy and girl to realize their fullest possibilities. And, of course, if the boy and girl reached those exalted heights, by my being there to observe them on screen—so would I.

    - But surely, Mr. Kalich, you must admit there was an element of cruelty in your so-called "play."

- All play contains elements of cruelty.
Observe any child at play and you'll
understand what I mean.

Ever since I invited the Dance Hall Woman to stay with
us in PH-F, the girl hides away in her room; or, if she does
come out, mopes around, an anxious, bewildered look on
her face.

- And the fact that the girl slept until
the third ring of the alarm clock, and
sometimes never even left her bed all
day: didn't that tell you something? Mr.
Kalich?

Mute, silent, speechless, the girl's world is shattered, her inviolable faith and belief in the boy and myself a thing of the
past.

- You yourself said she reverted to type;
became virtually catatonic, as she had
been when first placed in the halfway
house.

Her perfect world changed forever by the Dance Hall
Woman with the clear cruel eyes, who possesses the full arsenal of female charms and wares. Who possesses all the girl
does not.

- Mr. Kalich, didn't it occur to you that
you had gone too far with your games?

That you had gone well beyond the girl's endurance?

Of course, I prolong the agony by inviting the woman to stay not just for a weekend as I had originally promised, but for an indeterminate period of time.

- Or was that the purpose of your game to begin with?

The girl can hardly muster up courage to ask me: How long is the Dance Hall Woman going to stay?

- And the manner in which the boy was attracted to the woman...

- You don't mean to hold me responsible for their mutual attraction, do you?

The boy stands as if mesmerized, a strange white pallor frozen on his face, whenever the woman saunters by. Her bosom and cleavage on display, perfume scent trailing her every movement. Needless to say the Dance Hall Woman knows her art well.

- Mr. Kalich, surely you realized how the boy would be tempted by such a woman.

- Who can really know what takes place between a man and a woman.

Best of all, and not because of my own encouragements, the Dance Hall Woman truly likes the boy, appreciates his youth and innocence, is flattered by his virginal attentions.

```
- And the girl, if only by the boy's sud-
den lapse of interest, she had to know
what was going on.

- ...(Enough to cause a rent in her heart
that would never heal.)
```

Not only do I ask the girl's permission, but I allow her to make the decision: Should the Dance Hall Woman stay or leave? But please remember, dear girl, the poor woman has no place to go. No money, no friends, no relatives to take her in. And her lover only threatened her with more violence if she were to return. So what do you think? Should we put her on the street or let her stay? But you better than most knows what that would mean. There are no cashmere blankets and rooms fragrant with Chanel on the street, not to mention people such as the boy and myself to love you.

```
- I agree.
```

And then one day the Dance Hall Woman is gone. To heal the wounds between the boy and girl will require much work and who better than I to provide such counsel. My constant maxim: Forgiveness. The flesh is weak. All relationships require work, have their ups and downs, one can hardly blame the boy, or oneself even. After all, he's only human and the woman, of course, was a true goddess, as if sent down from the heavens with but one purpose in mind. Besides, all men are the same. Time immemorial women have had to live with that.

    - You agree?

    - Yes. Like everything else, sooner or later, all games must come to an end.

Marriage broker, divorce counselor, love therapist and healer, by whim or necessity, I provide wise counsel to both the boy and girl.

I have obsessed over the boy and girl now for a period in excess of twenty-five years. Who's to say which is more real. What I originally imagined for my aborted novel in print, or what I today make happen and observe on screen. Either way the question seems rhetorical. The images of the boy and girl never leave me.

    - My apology for calling you back, Mr. Kalich, but as Richard's twin brother you are more qualified to answer these questions than any other.

    - I understand.

Fernando, the concierge, calls me "Mr. K" when I enter or leave the building. Big George lets out a loud "Kaliiiich!" Rudy, at the front door, says "Si Señor." And that pretty much sums up the better part of my social life and connection with people throughout my so-called golden years.

- You brought to our attention earlier, Mr. Kalich, that your brother was always a despairing, forlorn and angry person.

- That's true. Due to the difficulties of his profession.

- And at the present time, with the complete collapse of the literary culture, would it be fair to surmise he might have become more angry, violent even?

- It depends upon what you mean by violent.

- But then, when the boy and girl came into his life, he seemed to have changed.

- For the better, I agree.

- But those last several months with the boy and girl, he changed once again; becoming angrier, more violent...

- He might have had good reason.

- Ruthless even.

- Do you have a question?

- Is your twin brother, Mr. Kalich, capable of conducting experiments on the boy

and girl to test their reactions, and
performing measured dosages of punishments calibrated merely for the sake of
exploring various kinds of scientific
hypotheses?

The twin remains silent.

- Mr. Kalich, if you would answer the
question.

- I told you earlier.

- What did you tell us earlier, Mr. Kalich?

- My twin brother never shared that part
of his life with me.

Ever since I raised the stakes when the boy and girl began to
assert their autonomy, I notice I haven't patted any children on
the head in the elevator. Interesting: do the boy and girl affect
me as much or more as I, who am making every effort, do them?

- If it were merely sex I wanted, I could
have gone to any prostitute.

- Then what did you want?

- It had nothing to do with that.

- Then what did it have to do with?

Even I was surprised when a locksmith I had occasion to employ but once was called by the Interrogator.

- Mr. Mondale, didn't it occur to you that by installing the locks you were in effect giving Mr. Kalich the license to lock the boy and girl into their respective rooms?

- No. Why should it? I thought he probably had some kind of valuables in the rooms. Besides, it was none of my business. Mr. Kalich paid me to do a job and I did it. Simple as that.

- When you installed the locks, Mr. Mondale, were the boy and girl in the apartment?

- Not the boy, but I did see the girl in her room.

- Didn't she object?

- No.

- How did she seem?

- Sad, out of it.

- Sad?

- Actually, when I think about it, she looked really beautiful, wearing a white dress.

The ugly woman in 4D hasn't looked up at me once in the elevator since taking up residence in the building at least fifteen years ago, much less said a word. Today I made an especial effort to entice a word or two out of her when I said "Good morning," and then later, that evening, with a theatrical flourish, "Good night." My salutations achieved their desired effect. As she hurried out of the elevator this evening, ostensibly more uncomfortable than ever, she responded by mumbling an indistinct incantation of her own.

- Twice a week, on Mondays and Fridays, the boy and girl would come downstairs to my apartment to hear me read Shakespeare.

- Shakespeare?

- Yes. From our chance meetings on the elevator, Mr. Kalich must have overheard I wanted to be an actor and was in college studying musical theater.

- But you just said Shakespeare. Was classical drama something you were interested in as well as musical theater?

- To tell the truth, Shakespeare bored the hell out of me.

- And yet you maintain Mr. Kalich encouraged the boy and girl to visit your apartment to hear you read Shakespeare?

- Romeo and Juliet specifically.

- Still...

- Well, he never said it in so many words, but I always had the feeling he knew they were sneaking down to my place.

- And how did you arrive at that conclusion?

- He bought them the Romeo and Juliet plays for one. And then the boy and girl visited every Monday and Friday night when Mr. Kalich would go shopping after their dinner meal.

- Mr. Koppel, everybody goes shopping once or twice a week.

- Yeah, but not everybody unlocks certain doors in their apartment when they do so.

- And you're certain Mr. Kalich knew you would be reading Romeo and Juliet to them?

- I doubt he was sending them down to hear me sing Broadway show tunes. He wasn't the type.

- Mr. Koppel, this is a serious matter.

- I know that.

- Why would you do such a thing?

The youth remains silent.

- What I mean to say: by your own admission, you were bored by the Bard; why would you take it upon yourself to read one of his works to the boy and girl?

- I could say it was because I felt sorry for them, being locked up all week long in that concentration camp, but the truth is I had a crush on the girl.

- And can you additionally tell us how the boy and girl responded when you read Romeo and Juliet to them?

- Well, they were no geniuses, that's for sure, but anyone could see what it meant to them. They were really into it.

- How were they into it?

- The girl would wear her white dress like Juliet, and then mouth her lines as I read them. She was really beautiful.

- And the boy?

- He would do the same, never once taking his eyes off Juliet...I mean the girl. Anyway, I have to admit, after a while I began to enjoy it, too. I mean they were really good guys and I was happy to do it for them. Besides, there was one thing more important than anything else.

- And what was that one thing more important than anything else?

- Like Romeo and Juliet, the boy and girl were in love.

Circumstantial testimony or not, this interrogation is not proceeding as I anticipated.

- Mr. Yalkowski, you are a lawyer by profession?

- A retired lawyer. I retired eleven years ago when my wife died.

- And you are friends with the person in question.

- I've known Kalich since we attended City College together.

- And you've socialized with him over the years, visited his penthouse apartment?

- Yes. Many times.

- That includes when the boy and girl resided with him?

- I always told him that wasn't a good idea.

- But you did visit him at that time?

- If I did, I never saw them, not once, directly, but I knew they were there.

- How did you know they were there?

- Because Kalich was watching them on a TV monitor.

- And when your friend asked you to watch with him, according to your past testimony, I understand you simply refused.

- Whatever he was doing with the boy and girl, I didn't want to know. I told him that more than once.

- But still you...

- I even asked him to go with me to some Asian massage parlors. But, of course, he didn't. He would never leave that screen.

- Would you venture an opinion as to why he was so obsessed?

- I don't know. I saw it for what it was.

- And what was that?

- An old man trying to have some fun. Make the most of what was left to him in this world. It was all in his head like everything else about him.

- So you're saying for Mr. Kalich it was real, but not for you.

- That's never been a problem for me.

- What's never been a problem for you?

- Knowing what's real or not.

- Like your Asian massage parlors.

- One thing I will say: I always thought Kalich capable of anything.

Not a gold watch, but seven hundred and fifty paycheck stubs is what I have to show from my job as caseworker for the Human Resources Administration, a period spanning thirty-one years, from February 5, 1961 to March 21, 1992. I collected and religiously saved the paycheck stubs which now lay stashed away somewhere in my kitchen cabinet, in two U.S. Post Office Priority envelopes, all rubber-banded in fine, neat, well-ordered piles and in perfect chronological order. When I quit the job—always a matter of "next year"— my intent was to use the stubs as wallpaper for my bathroom walls.

Today I ask: What am I going to do with them?

- Is this statement really worth repeating, Mr. Kalich?

- I think so.

- If you must.

- The two things I had the most capacity for in my life, loving a woman and
writing fiction, were the two things which
terrified me most.

THE FIVE SENSES RULES

1. TOUCH
2. SIGHT
3. TASTE
4. SMELL
5. HEARING

1. TOUCH: Without exception, all expression(s) of physical intimacy (sex, touch, anything tactile) is not allowed.
2. SIGHT: Though the boy and girl will be permitted to dine at the same table for their one evening meal a day, they will not be allowed to gaze at or even set eyes on one another. Strict adherence to this rule is mandatory and if one or the other (or both) makes an effort to gaze into the other's eyes, or as much as looks up, both will be deemed culpable and returned to their respective rooms. The same is true if they pass each other in the corridor or any other nook and cranny of PH-F. An air of inviolable correctness is what I'm after, and, as they well know by now, my eyes are all-seeing, and when it comes to my Five Senses Rules, I am particularly unyielding on all counts.

3. TASTE: To be sure, this has nothing to do with culinary appetites, at least not completely, one meal a day is sufficient punishment; but rather is more a corollary of "touch." At any rate, kissing will no more be tolerated than any other physical expression of intimacy.

4. SMELL: The fragrant aroma of Chanel from the girl's room permeates PH-F and with the help of well-placed fans wafts its way to the boy's room. As for his own very masculine musk cologne scent, in similar fashion, that too penetrates the girl's room. Consequently, by smell and hearing the pair remain cognizant of each other. I have to confess, watching the two sniff and smell each other like two feral beasts brings a smile to my countenance; but of course to maximize my pleasure and unlike their four-legged brethren, I never permit them to consummate their passion. Like a zookeeper, prison warden or Kommandant of a camp, I rule over my PH-F domain with absolute authority.

5. HEARING: The boy and girl are of course not allowed to speak to each other. For example, not a word is permitted at the dinner table. And if so much as a single word is uttered by either of them, like with sight, it is easy enough to correct the problem by holding one or the other or both accountable, and immediately sending them back to their respective rooms. By way of extension and as a kind of extra-curricular activity, I have installed special high-intensity microphones in the boy and girl's rooms, allowing them to hear every sound made by the other. Thus the boy can hear the girl's inchoate streams of lament, sobs, moans, groans and sighs, and the girl likewise hears every rant, rave and apocryphal sally of the boy's. I can even prolong such emotive sounds depending upon my whim and mood. But, of course, if either or both

attempt to bypass my code of silence and take advantage and exploit my microphone sound system by making purposeful sounds of their own, whether they be in words or any other codified language such as a click of the teeth or tongue, a tap or knock of the fingers, knuckles, hands on the hardwood floor, or head against the wall, I immediately shut off the sound system and consign each to impenetrable silence. Like everything else in PH-F, it lies solely in my purview to decide what sounds I let pass through these walls.

- You are Patricia Phillips?

- That is my professional name.

- You are a concert producer?

- After I left my husband I had no choice but to try and make a living. I had a men- tally challenged child to support.

- And you knew Mr. Kalich before you established yourself professionally?

- His brother and I dated when we were at NYU.

- And knowing Mr. Kalich as long as you have: do you think him capable of being responsible for the boy and girl's suicide?

- No. He would never cause harm to any young people. Dickie's a sweetie pie.

It's been almost a month now since the boy and girl peered up when dining at the same table; said a word to each other; physically had the slightest contact. They're both so famished and hungry with cravings and needs I can only wonder how this will end.

- On what basis do you suggest Mr. Kalich is a sweetie pie?

- Because of the way he related to my son, Dwight.

- What way was that?

- Dwight was born with certain neurological limitations and Dickie, Mr. Kalich, was the only one of all my friends who embraced him: took him to the park, ball games, movies. If you would have seen them together, you wouldn't even ask such a question.

- Are you saying Mr. Kalich had a similar relationship with the...

- He probably had a soft spot in his heart for the boy and girl just as he did for Dwight. I'll always love Dickie for that.

The last thing I want is for them to lose all hope. What fun would my games be for me or anyone else then.

- You do realize Mr. Kalich's motives weren't altogether altruistic. He did model one of his novel's characters after your son.

- He's a writer. Writers do that sort of thing.

- And that includes his never going any-where or doing anything.

- I've always said he was different. He didn't have the time to change his socks. He used the backs of his used scrap paper to write on. He had no time. He needed to think...read...write.

- And his living like a hermit?

- He always had his twin brother. And books. He didn't need anybody. That's why he never got married. As long as I knew him he was never lonely. He lived in his own world. Led a secret life. Had his own thoughts and dismissed all the rest.

- In appreciation of the fact that you've read his current work, Ms. Phillips, would you say Mr. Kalich lived in his own world or created his own world? There is a difference, Ms. Phillips.

- I've read the book three times and still don't know what it means. Real or fiction. It's not the person I know.

- Let me put it another way, Ms. Phillips. Did Mr. Kalich imagine the boy and girl or are they real?

- Oh, I don't know. It's all so complicated. Confusing.

Still, as interesting and amusing as my Five Senses Rules have proven to be, it's not enough. My mind keeps stirring. My response is not wholly unexpected. What else is play other than exploring variations on the theme.

- Even Mr. Kalich's brother says he was always frustrated. Angry.

The concert producer passes a look of mock disapproval.

- Ms. Phillips...

- It's not easy being a writer in today's world.

- Ms. Phillips, in all the years wasn't there at least one incident where you saw evidence of this anger?

- Evidence?

- Of another Mr. Kalich. One different than the one you describe with your son.

- Well, there was one time.

- One time?

And so, like a yo-yo, I reverse the procedures of my Five Senses Rules. All I previously denied the boy and girl I now will give. Perhaps a bit too much.

- I had called him to explain why I couldn't speak on the phone to him the night before when I was with people at a restaurant, rushing through dinner to get to my friend Donny's show, which was being reviewed that night by the NY Times.

- And...?

- And when he heard the NY Times, he exploded.

- Exploded. How?

- He was furious, screaming how he couldn't get his own books reviewed even though a NY Times literary critic lived in his building, and how, in order to avoid confronting him, she would hide in the mailroom when seeing him in the lobby, or turn her back to him in the elevator, standing

```
like a naughty six-year-old in school in
the corner, staring at the wall, and this
hack, this mediocrity, my friend Donny-
he called him a Catskill Mountain comic,
not a playwright but an entertainer, the
lowest level, banality, not Eugene O'Neil
but Jackie Mason. It was terrible. His
rampage came as if from nowhere. I was
stunned. Shocked.

- Taking this rampage into consideration,
Ms. Phillips, do you still consider Mr.
Kalich a sweetie pie incapable of being
responsible for the boy and girl's sui-
cide?

- Oh, I don't know. One thing has nothing
to do with the other.
```

Everybody knows what's taken place in PH-F. People in the building have been privy to the rumors and innuendoes for the longest time. In fact, most have probably seen the ravaged and war-torn bodies of the boy and girl firsthand. Certainly the ROMEO AND JULIET SUICIDE has been well publicized in the newspapers, media, TV and Internet. And yet not a word, not a glance in my direction from the good citizens. One would think, at the very least, mothers chronically protective of their children would guard them all the closer in my presence. Would speak in whispers, walk on tiptoes, take the little ones' hands, prod them toward their skirts, push them out the elevator door more quickly, or hasten their step when walking through the lobby corridors. But no, not true;

to the residents, staff, friends and neighbors of my building,
I am as invisible as ever.

Is it sheer callousness, indifference, or something else?

Whatever.

THE FIVE SENSES RULES (Revised)

1. TOUCH: Like a virtual reality designer, I clothe the boy
    and girl in bodysuits. Hands, mouths, feet, all sexual parts
    insulated by layers of rubber fabric. They know the rules:
    They can caress and hug each other as much as they want,
    to their hearts' content, but the bodysuits must stay on.
    Famished and hungry as they are, desperate for contact,
    any physical intimacy, they make every effort to touch and
    fondle, embrace and paw, stimulate and bring each other
    pleasure. All their efforts are in vain. The only one finding
    any pleasure here is myself, sitting comfortably in front of
    my TV screen. And it's not mere fantasy I experience, but
    lust. So much so, I can hardly contain myself as I watch
    the histrionics and gyrations of the twosome on screen.
    My only concern is that my laughter and change of mood
    will be noted outside PH-F. But even that doesn't bother
    me too greatly. For as stated, nobody really cares what goes
    on behind these walls.

    - Mr. Korman, as a childhood friend of
    Mr. Kalich, one who goes even further

Central Park West Trilogy

back than Ms. Phillips, are you in accord
with what she said?

- As children they were different.

- How were they different?

- They didn't need other kids.

- Could you elaborate?

- You know how other kids need each other
for confirmation. Validation. The Kalich
twins didn't. They had each other.

I notice that I continue to rely as much on my aborted novel's
voluminous pages as I do on my own imagination for conjuring up ideas for my Five Senses Rules. To that end, as we're
having an early and exceptionally harsh winter this year, I wrap
myself in my quilt blanket, fluff my pillows, and, like a sickly
child waiting for his mother's hot soup, I snuggle in bed to
peruse my notes. These bedtime hours have the added advantage of allowing me to get away for an hour or two from the
burden of having either to listen to others or myself answer difficult questions on the part of the Interrogator. I must admit,
rereading my notes and contemplating the various games envisioned affords me significant pleasure. But truly nothing can
compare to the perfect moments bordering on ecstasy I receive
from the actual implementation and watching of the boy and
girl's responses to my well-conceived and executed games.

Now, what game shall I/we play?

I must never forget the adage: One receives from an experience what one brings to it. Who is that more true for than myself?

- Not all my games are the same.

- You freely admit that?

Sometimes one has to sacrifice grace and charm for the sake of results. It is not inconceivable that some might call several of my choices crude.

- Most definitely. But far more salient here, I would emphasize, is the fact that not once, no matter how powerful and crude my games were, did I ever lay hands on the boy and girl.

- Not once?

- Not once.

Sometimes one sense readily combines with another to make for an especially amusing game. Such is the case with Sight and Hearing, or should I say Sight and Sound, if only because the conjunction is more sonorous.

2 & 3. SIGHT & SOUND: I have two muscle-bound, bald-headed men, much resembling eunuchs on loan from some mid-century fiefdom, escort a particularly attractive young woman and young man past the boy and girl's respective rooms. As if by accident, their doors have been left slightly

ajar so that they can gain a glimpse of the attractive youths. Soon enough, with a click of my fingers I shut the lights off leaving the boy and girl not only in pitch black rooms, but alone with their imaginations. Next I tunnel into their rooms amatory sounds I recorded of the pair making love to each other from earlier encounters, now separated and isolated with the aid of a highly skilled sound engineer. The boy can hear the girl's sighs, moans, groans; her "oh yeah, I like it. Good. It feels so good...please don't stop... don't come...please..." And the girl in turn hears the boy's aggressive hard-edged male thrusts and lusty harangue: "Like this?...how's it feel?...now you...yeah...that's it... that's good...yeah...oh yeaaaaah!" But neither of the two can know for certain who or what is prompting such love sounds from the other. They can only imagine, call forth their darkest fears. And, if it's true, and I, for one, believe it is, that we receive from an experience what we bring to it—I am most fortunate that I don't even have to imagine what the boy and girl are bringing/thinking. I know: delusional unstable minds, passive wills, weak senses of self, inability to distinguish reality from fantasy, in short and in sum, the accumulated baggage of their lifetimes.

The mind is a terrible thing to waste our contemporary sages tell us, and, for my purposes, I would venture a guess that I, an emblematic figure of conservationism, am making the best possible use of these two minds.

    - Even though you couldn't write your
    novel, "Transfiguration of the Common-

place," Mr. Kalich, you say you knew how it would end?

- Yes. That's my particular gift and what's so frustrating. As I've repeatedly said, I see my novels whole, beginning, middle and end, and at the same time I...

- Because of other problems you still couldn't write it.

- Precisely. That's why I invited the boy and girl into PH-F in the first place.

- Mr. Kalich, I feel compelled to ask you, in addition to being able to see your novels whole, did you also see your relationship with the boy and girl whole?

- I don't understand the question.

- In other words, Mr. Kalich, is it possible that even before taking the boy and girl into PH-F, you already knew how your relationship with them would end?

```
       NOTES...THE TRANSFIGURATION OF THE COMMONPLACE

END: 10/24/1985

A man and woman tied together at the waist, joined at the
hip, jump from their apartment on West 66th St...Could this
be my ending?  Romeo and Juliet?


       ****10/24/85
            6/19/05      20 Years!!!

          9/12/2006
```

- And to that end you purposefully left their doors unlocked, allowing them to visit the young actor.

- Even prison inmates and other institutionalized people are given an hour or two to themselves to walk the yard, grounds or garden as the case may be.

- Where he would read to them passages of Romeo and Juliet.

- They were very much taken by the characters.

- More than taken, they were highly impressionable, vulnerable, it might even be fair to say that the boy and girl wholly identified with Shakespeare's lovers.

- Surely, Mr. Kalich, you didn't purchase tickets for the boy and girl to attend the Romeo and Juliet play so far in advance merely for the sake of entertainment.

- As you yourself have mentioned, the boy and girl have always expressed an affinity for Shakespeare's lovers.

- But why so far in advance? The play never even approached selling out.

Not a word out of Kalich.

- One can only conclude that your wanting the boy and girl to see the play was integral to another agenda you had in mind long before.

Sometimes an idea occurs to me which is so appealing I cannot resist even if it means repeating a sense that I've already explored; although, of course, in a different way. Such is the case with...

1A. TOUCH: And so in the spirit of Christmas I offer the boy and girl complete freedom to do with each other what they want. For as long as they want. In total privacy, with nobody there to bother them, least of all myself. My terrace is for them and them alone. Of course eleven inches of snow, single digit temperatures, and ice cold penetrating winds will accompany them outdoors. But the view is magnificent, overlooking Central Park, and, well, after all, it is a white Christmas. What true lovers could resist? Once they're outside, I rest on my laurels, sit back with a hot cocoa in hand and observe the pair on screen. The poor dears: matted together, limbs shivering, lips blue, I can hear their teeth chattering. Do they even have shoes on? One can only guess as to how long love can endure in such circumstances. To be honest, I was more than pleasantly surprised as their long distance efforts only prolonged my own tears of joy and laughter.

"Merry Christmas! Joy to the world!" I shouted as I opened the terrace doors letting the boy and girl reenter my apartment and join me. Other than their chattering teeth and an almost audible shivering, they both seemed incapable of uttering a sound. They didn't even look like human beings anymore, standing there like frozen slabs of meat already shrunken in size, spoiled and rotted. A strange erotic excitement I had not known for the longest time overtook me as I commenced vigorously rubbing the girl's feet like my mother would do when, as children, my twin and I would return home from sleigh-riding jaunts on Riverside Drive.

An even greater sense of power and erotic command enveloped me as I observed the girl's imploring, pleading eyes begging that I do the same for the boy, who continued standing stoically at her side, asking nothing for himself, but rather only for the girl. As I started rubbing the boy's feet I surmised, as with the rich and powerful, one's generosity is all the more satisfying when one holds the purse strings.

Finishing up with the boy's feet, and before sending each to their respective rooms, I whispered in urgent tones: "Whatever possessed you two to go outdoors on a night like this?"

But why then, after such a pleasant and amusing game would I not sleep that night? Two images kept recurring in my mind. The boy's stoical refusal of my help and the girl's imploring, pleading eyes that had her lover's welfare more selflessly in mind than her own. At such moments in the middle of the night, drenched in sweat that made my skin stick to the sheets, and simultaneous with the images, I kept hearing for the second time in my life a little voice emanating from somewhere deep inside me saying: Who's going to love me? Who's going to love me? Along with the added proviso—like Romeo and Juliet love each other?

The next morning my resolve to play with the boy and girl and subject them to even more punishing tests and trials was all the stronger.

```
- You refer to your activities with the
boy and girl as mere games, Mr. Kalich,
play if you will, but aren't they in actu-
ality more like tests, trials, more often
than not even cruel punishments?

- How many times are you going to persist
in asking the same question?

- How many times are you going to persist
in giving the same answer?
```

The Interrogator, too, can play games.

- And while watching the boy and girl on your TV monitor you admit, Mr. Kalich, to being transported to another state of being?

- One could say that.

- So much so that the boy and girl no longer seemed human to you, not even real.

- ...Unconditional surrender, abject submission...

- What was that?

Vigorously, I shake my head.

- Nothing.

- And so it was that you created the proper environment and played your games?

I remain silent.

- Mr. Kalich, if it was in you as a novelist, it was in you as a man. Even you have to admit that much.

- What I admit is that without my considerable efforts the boy and girl would have come to nothing.

- And you, Mr. Kalich, what have you come to with the boy and girl?

And...

- You say, Mr. Kalich, that if not for you the boy and girl would never have known love.

- It was I who brought them together.

- One might say they did something similar for you.

- What are you suggesting?

- Your greatest fear perhaps was that you would lose them. That they would no longer need you and move out of PH-F on their own.

- They could never do that.

- But if they could?

- As I've already said: Every game has to end.

And this from a fellow writer and long-term friend.

- You met Mr. Kalich for brunch for a period spanning eighteen years?

- Yes. Every Sunday like clockwork we would meet at Fairway's restaurant at 11:00 a.m.

- And then suddenly you stopped. Can you tell me why?

- There were many reasons.

- Can you start with one?

- He was always angry; constantly roasting me and saying the same things.

- Same things?

- Actually one: "Literature ruined my life!"

- And that was the reason...

- It was like a recitativo.

- ...you stopped going to brunch with him?

- No. Not only that. I'm a writer, too. I could identify with that.

- Well, what else then?

- He would project his own bitterness and misery onto me.

- How did he do that?

- He would constantly berate my work saying I had wasted my life, like he did,
with my lyric writing.

- Taking this into...

- And he never really took me seriously
as a writer. He was always beleaguering
me with the same questions.

- And that was?

- How could I waste my talent on such
trivial concerns?

- And despite...

- The truth is more people sing my songs
than read his books. If his publishers
sold twenty-eight books, it would double
the sales of his two books published all
over the world.

- And despite all these insults and abuse
you continued joining him for brunch?

- I never felt that way about my life. I
might not have made much money at my writing, but I had a great psychic income. I

once wrote an opera which was produced in Germany. And I co-wrote a musical that...

- Mr. Byron, if you would please stay with the subject.

- Besides, we're different kinds of writers.

- Of course. You're a lyricist and Mr. Kalich is a novelist.

- That's not what I mean.

- What do you mean?

- We had more serious problems than writing. He could be a bastard.

- A ba...?

- There was a time I was having sexual difficulties with my second wife. She was young at the time and I confided in him.

- And?

- He laughed.

- Laughed?

- I knew it was a mistake the second I opened my mouth. He was always more con-

cerned with books than people. And in
those later years, life, books, it was
all the same to him. Fun and games.

- And as I said, yet you continued...

- He wasn't always like that. When young
we had great literary discussions. I
was in awe of his talent. He was brilliant. But in these last years he just
changed.

- You mean when he took the boy and girl
into PH-F?

- The truth is he was harder on himself
than anyone else.

- And it was about that same time, when
the boy and girl moved into PH-F with
him that you stopped meeting him for
brunch...every Sunday like clockwork at
11:00 a.m.?

- Not me. Him.

- Him?!

- It was actually some years before they
moved in.

- But why?

- It was as if books, literature, badgering and fulminating against me was no longer important to him. I guess without that we just ran out of things to say to each other.

- Mr. Byron. Once and for all: was Mr. Kalich capable of being responsible for the boy and girl's suicide?

The lyricist ponders the question.

- Mr. Byron?

- I don't know how to answer that question except to say: look what he did with his first novel, "The Nihilesthete."

- What did he do?

- When he finished, he brought the manuscript to an editor. The editor didn't believe he was the author.

- Why not?

- He didn't believe that a normal-looking person like Kalich could have written a book so perverse and grotesque.

- But the boy and girl's suicide didn't just take place in his novel.

   - I know.

And something similar from another writer; this one young.

   - Mr. Belkin. Can you tell us about the screenplay you co-wrote with Mr. Kalich.

   - A producer paid us a small advance to collaborate on a horror film. We never completed the script.

   - Why not?

   - Because Mr. Kalich has no respect for the film medium. Even less so for the horror film genre. Fact is, he disdains it. Over and over I recall him saying to me: You young screenplay writers have no idea what truly great writing is.

   - And naturally you don't share his opinions.

   - Of course not. I love film. And I enjoy horror films in particular. I pop down my $11.00. I get myself a bag of popcorn and I sit down and enjoy them...like everybody else.

As painstakingly thorough as I am in my pursuits, it seems the Interrogator is equally so.

- I remember because the show was sold out on that particular night and Mr. Kalich had already purchased the last of the good seats available.

- But Mr. Kalich did purchase orchestra seats?

- That's what I'm trying to explain to you. If you'll just allow me to finish.

- Please.

- As I was saying. On that particular night the show had sold out which was very unusual for a Romeo and Juliet play, especially so far in advance, and I won't even try to explain. There are just some nights when that happens.

- Mr. Parker, about Mr. Kalich's ticket purchase.

- Yes. He had already purchased the last of the orchestra seats available and was leaving the ticket window when these two women, the next in line, got in a huff when I told them that all we had available were partial view seats. They were obviously disappointed and started to question me about the seats when, almost inadvertently, I referred to the partial views as "love seats."

At least that's what we called them in the old days. Today, just the conventional boxes.

- Mr. Parker...

- Yes. At any rate, from inside my ticket window, at my mere mention of the term "love seats," I couldn't help noticing Mr. Kalich's ears perk up and immediately going up to the women and negotiating an exchange of his orchestra seats for the partial views.

- And you're certain Mr. Kalich had already purchased two orchestra seats for the play?

- Yes. That's why I remember the incident so vividly.

- Mr. Parker, by chance did you additionally happen to overhear any further exchange between Mr. Kalich and the two women that would explain why he would relinquish his two orchestra seats for two partial views?

- As a matter of fact I did. They were standing directly in front of my ticket

window and I distinctly heard him say to
the women that he was doing it because
they were so disappointed, but to be honest I thought there was something else
involved.

- Like what?

- The way Mr. Kalich insisted, wouldn't
take no for an answer. It just seemed, to
me at least, he really wanted those love
seats.

As with Sight and Sound, Taste and Smell make for a formidable combination.

3 & 4. TASTE & SMELL: I bathe the boy and girl in milk
and honey, or cover each with layers of chocolate ice
cream and syrup. And I let them clean the impasto from
the other's body by making use of their mouths, lips,
tongues, nothing else. Chocolate ice cream and syrup
seems to be their favorite based on time at least: The boy
taking exactly two minutes flat and the girl two minutes
and ten seconds to do the job. As for milk and honey,
comparable times can be expected, maybe thirty to forty
seconds longer than their favorite. Piss, urine, whether
it be from animals or humans, requires, as one would
expect, longer periods of time, but are surprisingly close.
Human piss: approximately seven minutes twenty seconds; animal urine: seven minutes thirty-nine seconds.
But with any combination or permutation of animal
excrement: turds and shit from dogs, pigeons, cats, squir-

rels, especially horse manure, the cleaning process can go on ad nauseam. At least it must seem to the boy and girl like forever. For me, of course, it's never long enough. Time, like all the Aristotelian unities in our post-modern world, has been shattered forever.

By the way, their own human waste is in another time zone altogether.

It would be interesting to understand my twin brother's ambivalence towards me and how it corresponds (if it does) to my own inner conflicts.

> - My brother's always been miserable. From
> the time of our bar mitzvah when, under
> great stress from our cantor father, who
> presided over an old European orthodox
> shul, he lost twenty pounds because he
> assumed total responsibility for recit-
> ing the liturgy (and I did nothing)...to
> when he went to City College and would
> study all night (and I to NYU where I
> had nothing but fun)...to the army where
> he served in the reserves for six years
> (and I avoided by feigning psychologi-
> cal problems)...and to the two women he
> loved both ending up in nervous break-
> downs (whereas I...

When twenty-four, I laid in bed for six months crying when the Israeli, Hana, left me; and then walked around New York for two-and-a-half years numb, crazed, in a sleepwalk.

Twenty-eight years later, with the young harpist, Dobrinka:
four years of misery, torment, not one good day.

> - If I would have received ten percent
> of what he's received as a writer, I'd
> be the happiest guy in the world. He's
> an idiot. So disconnected...conflicted...
> torn apart.

Two acclaimed novels, "The Nihilesthete" and "Charlie P."

> - Could never make a decision. Even when
> he was young and found his penthouse
> apartment on Central Park West with a
> terrace overlooking the park, and rent-
> control!--he couldn't.

Published in eleven countries.

> - He procrastinated forever until he
> nearly lost it.

Praised by the best literary minds.

> - I took one look and told him to grab it.

Awards...

> - No intimacy. Always alone. Half a life.

Honors...

> - A seventy-year-old man worrying about his physical appearance. Ridiculous!

Why not enough? Why?

> - My brother's always been miserable since we were kids. And it has nothing to do with his being a writer or anything else. He's just miserable.

When I ask myself what I did with my life, what I accomplished, my answer has always been: the three novels I wrote, two acclaimed; and the two times I experienced love. But at this point I realize my books have little value and my loves were not reciprocal, not mutual, not whole or complete. If anything, they were all in my mind.

When the Interrogator sums it all up, I can only wonder how it will tally. What does it all mean?

Still, there is more to a man than being a social isolate. For example, for four years at City College I was enamored of the beautiful Thea Goldstein and yet too shy to speak to her. Surreptitiously, I trailed after her, jotting down in a special notebook every stitch of clothing she wore. Befriended a member of her clique, whom I literally helped put through the rigors of an academically demanding school, to insure my remaining close to her; and after four years of such distant orphic enchantment, worship even, I learn, when Thea uttered her first words to me at her engagement party in her parents' home in the Bronx, that she had a crush on me all those years. So much so, she exclaimed, that she would draw my picture in her art class.

- You are Rhonda Brooke, formerly known as Rhonda Brookstein, the person Mr. Kalich befriended to secure a close place in Thea Goldstein's life.

- Yes. But he never put me through City College. I did my own work.

- Can you tell us about the engagement party?

- There's nothing to tell.

- By that I mean did your friend, Thea Goldstein, actually have a crush on Mr. Kalich all those years without either of them ever speaking to each other?

- As I said: There's nothing to tell.

- What do you mean there's nothing to tell?

- I mean there was no engagement party. Thea was never engaged while attending City College. And, for sure, she didn't have a so-called crush on Dick Kalich.

- Are you certain there was no engagement party? How can you be so certain?

        - Because I was Thea's best friend in
        those years. I would have been there.

All these years later and I still carry inside me the smile Thea offered me while looking up from a basement window of 7 Steps, a lesbian bar in Greenwich Village.

And similarly I remember one night with Hana when I spread my arms as wide as my young twenty-four-year-old mind could dream and said: "We could have everything."

And not so much envy, or even admiration, but every July I am astounded by a man in the building who packs his wife, two small children and belongings into his station wagon and drives off for their summer vacation.

And Big George who exudes such pride when seated in his Lexus SUV with a license plate reading "CUBA."

Sometimes the last person one would expect, Mel Yalkowski, comes to my aid.

        - From what I saw of Kalich that last
        time in his apartment, I had the feeling
        he was tempted to visit an Asian mas-
        sage parlor with me. Still, he remained
        obsessed with the boy and girl. Whether
        love or hate or some weird amalgam of the
        two, he would never do anything to jeop-
        ardize losing them.

And, to some extent, even the Israeli, Hana.

- I had many lovers in my life, but nobody ever gave as much of himself to me as Dick. Unfortunately, when I met him, I already had two children and was a good ten years older than him and needed a husband.

Six months after the boy and girl's suicide and I still sit in front of my TV screen interpolating from my notes future plottings of the pair on the blank screen.

- The way he looked at us.

- And what way was that, Mrs. Baruch?

- As if my husband and I were vile, reptilian creatures.

- And you insist, Mrs. Baruch, that in your more than forty years as residents in the building, neither you nor your husband, Mr. Baruch, gave Mr. Kalich...

- And with such hatred. On the elevator he would snicker at us.

- ...any good reason to feel this way?

- More than once I heard him talking to Big George about my husband.

- And?

- He called him a concentration camp Jew.

- But Mr. Kalich is himself Jewish?

- And all this hatred, disdain, malignancy for no other reason than we were old...

"I do not believe that death is man's real problem, or that art entirely permeated by it is completely authentic. The real issue is growing old, that aspect of death which we experience daily. Yet not even growing old, and that property of it, the fact that it is so completely, so terribly cut off from beauty. Our gradual dying does not disturb us, it is rather the beauty of life becomes inaccessible to us."
— Witold Gombrowicz, *Diary,*
1953

No matter how difficult, the one thing I've learned is that for a few minutes together, the boy and girl will gladly subject themselves to the most merciless of my games. During last month's blizzard, for example, I placed the girl in the farthest reaches of the city, a god-forsaken wasteland not even possessing a name. The boy can have three minutes with the girl if...I repeat...if he can find her. I furnished him only with the borough name and a makeshift map marking where the girl was to be found. Before starting off he had to remove the outer layers of his clothes. At most he was left with a pair of sneakers and socks, cord trousers and a thin short-sleeved summer shirt. To his credit, like a Monopoly game player, as soon as he heard my "go" he was off to the races, while I trailed along in the comforts of a warm luxuriant limo. Studying his makeshift map, asking off-putted strangers for directions, following false leads, climbing over shoulder-high snow drifts, falling all too often on icy streets from cold, exposure and exhaustion, he made his way through the mazes and labyrinths of the city, step by painful step. Finally, almost a full day later, in the early hours of the morning, he found the girl. Wrapped in a threadbare shawl, hiding in a doorway, eyes glazed and dull, weary and beat, she was nearly as frozen as he was, shielding herself as best she could from the cold, wind and snow.

What must their three minutes be like?

One thing is certain: I have never known three minutes like that in my life.

On the ride home, with the boy and girl sitting on each side of me, folded in warm U.S. army issue blankets, rather than feel satisfaction for a game well played, I felt a depth of anger rising in me as I realized that these two have what I never would. Rest assured, even before reaching PH-F I had already availed myself of my next game to test the limits of the boy and girl's love.

Abominable luck! Just when the boy and girl, only a little while ago sitting frozen on each side of me in the car, had found their way to their special place, the boy's room, were already under the blankets, blissfully nestling together, cheek to cheek, their favorite music playing, a warm glow emanating from the woodburning fireplace yours truly had installed, and I, finally was seated comfortably in my TV room, hot cocoa in hand, ready to observe the Grand Guignol Show, my TV screen goes on the blink. Breaks down. I don't have the words to describe how I felt. It was as if my life broke down with it. Or, more accurately, ceased to exist. Trying to fix the TV monitor I cursed myself for my lack of knowhow and technical ineptitude. At a loss as to what to do, I banged the monitor with my fists. Hit my head against the wall. Cursing and ranting at my bad luck, my ignorance, I felt my knees go weak, my left wrist drain of all energy, my heart hammer against my chest. And as I remained seated in front of the blackened screen, it wasn't long before I was as mute and catatonic as the girl in her worst moments. I couldn't even imagine what the boy and girl were doing. Without the screen to help me I was literally bereft. I had lost my ability to imagine through imaginings.

- You refer to your activities with the boy and girl as mere games, Mr. Kalich, play, if you will, but aren't they in fact more like tests, trials, more often than not even cruel punishments?

- How many times are you going to persist in asking the same question?

- How many times are you going to persist in giving the same answer?

Walking to the Food Emporium earlier this afternoon, I noticed a beautiful young homeless woman crouched against the building wall. Returning with the groceries I stopped to chat with her. I was right. She is sad, inconsolably sad and alone.

Does this mean I am nearing the end of one chapter and already anticipating starting another?

In that regard I hear San Francisco has a large population of young people and their homeless population is quite large, too. And the climate is pleasant all year round.

But, no, there is much yet to do here. I must stay focused. I must not yield. I must not succumb to my fear of closing a book anymore than, as in the past, I succumbed to my fear of starting one.

When I first conceived the boy and girl's rooms to be on opposite sides of the apartment from my own room, I had in mind the medieval castle where a harem girl is held captive and visited by her master who would walk stealthily through the long dungeon corridors lighted by flame lanterns. In a similar fashion I imagined—if the boy and girl wanted to visit each other at night, they would first have to make their way past my room.

Now to reap what I have sown:

I leave the girl's bedroom door unlocked at night. The long corridor is laden with shards of shattered glass, jagged-edged metal fence, glowing coals, razor barbed wire and cauldrons of boiling water. If the boy is to reach her bedroom, he will first have to trespass a veritable obstacle course of pain and difficulty. And when, with torn and bloody feet, crawling like a centipede, he finally does reach his journey's end, opens the door and makes his way to his beloved's bed, what awaits him: naught but an empty bed. The girl is nowhere to be found. On the contrary, she is seated alongside me watching the TV monitor in wide-eyed horror as I turn to her and say: Juliet, do you have any doubt now that Romeo dost truly love you?

But my words are just that: words. Veils of flummery. Inwardly I feel as bereft, barren and desolate as the boy must have felt when finding the girl's bed empty. Irregardless of what I might have earlier said or thought, I know now to conquer a love like theirs will never again merely be a game to me. Romeo and Juliet have proven to be more than worthy opponents.

After an especially harsh and pitiless winter where I've subjected the boy and girl to all that I had to give, tested their limits and asked them to endure more than even I had a right to expect, spring has finally arrived. I've gotten in the habit of taking the pair out for a walk in the park these last several weeks. With flowers budding, birds chirping, change, hope, expectancy is in the air, but nowhere is this more apparent than in the boy and girl. I can only compare them to those people who have suffered massive brain trauma and have lost all capacity for spatial and temporal orientation, literally don't know where they are, and yet when seated in a hospital garden, surrounded by nature and greenery, somehow, some way, they become oriented and their world makes sense again. Something similar has happened to the boy and girl. Once outdoors, amidst the park's commotion and din, almost preternaturally, biologically, I've seen the pair come to life. No longer depleted, sickly and defeated, and despite all my remorseless games and trials, once again, as always, the lovers yearn to share their love. Though I would never show my feelings, or admit my disappointment, I know that despite having played my games as well as I can, the boy and girl have survived not only nature's most brutal of winters, but my own man-made version as well.

I have but one last game to play:

The lovers are scheduled to see the play this afternoon. Will their seeing the play be all I hoped for? Who can say? One can only wonder if, like their Romeo and Juliet counterparts, all my accumulated preparations will have the desired effect. As for me this Sunday morning, I've done all that I can. Like a dawn before battle, everything is arranged down to the last detail. The girl's white dress lies on her bed, the boy's jacket, shirt and tie on his. And champagne to celebrate the festive occasion both before they leave for the play and, more importantly, after, upon their return. From this point on everything is up to them. After taking a sip and wishing them well, or should I say adieu, I hurry off. "The Guitar Man of Central Park" is making his first appearance of the new spring season today. Coincidence or not, I intend to enjoy the music.

    - You are the boy and girl?

The boy and girl nod imperceptibly.

    - Did Mr. Kalich cause your double sui-
    cide? Or in some way come to influence
    your double suicide?

The boy and girl nod imperceptibly.

- Prior to your leaving for the play that Sunday morning, Mr. Kalich had already set the champagne glasses on your kitchen table as if for a festive occasion. Can you tell me what the festive occasion was that you were celebrating?

The boy peers at the girl.

- Perhaps it was simply because the day had finally arrived when you were to see the Romeo and Juliet play?

The girl peers at the boy.

- Or was it rather to inaugurate some other far more definitive rite of passage?

Both smile.

- Did the idea of a double suicide origi-nate while you were viewing the stage play or after? Or was the idea put in your heads long before by Mr. Kalich?

Both smile.

- When Mr. Kalich departed for the park that Sunday morning, did he leave you with any parting words?

...

- And, if so, what were those words?

The boy and girl reach out to hold each other's hands.

- In addition to helping you select your white Juliet dress; permitting you both to receive readings on the play from the young actor in the building; and purchasing tickets for you to attend the play; what else did Mr. Kalich do to put the idea of committing a double suicide like Romeo and Juliet in your heads?

The boy and girl peer at each other.

- Or was it that you were already so despairing and emotionally spent by that time that suicide seemed your only viable solution?

The two continue to peer warily at each other.

- When Mr. Kalich observed you both on his TV monitor, he perceived you as something less than human, as more unreal than real. May I ask how you perceived Mr. Kalich?

A knowing smile passes between the two.

- Consequent to perceiving you in this manner he would take free rein and tres-

pass, play his hate-crazed games with you
strictly for his own amusement:

...

- Is that a fair assessment?

- Have I left anything out?

The boy and girl hold each other's hands even more tightly.

- In addition to voluntarily sharing your
intimate secrets with Mr. Kalich, as you
well know by now, he observed your most
private moments on his screen. Therefore
I must ask: Was there anything Mr. Kalich
did not know about you two? Did you hold
back anything?

...

- If so, what?

Even I was a bit disarmed when, as already indicated, the
girl told me of her preference for oral sex; and the boy con-
fessed how, when living on the street, in a confrontation with
another homeless person, his stabbing the waif resulted in the
man losing his eye.

- Other than your obvious weakness and
depletion, was there any other reason
you let Mr. Kalich do with you what he

wanted? In other words, if it was all fun
and games to him, what did participating
in his games mean to you? Or were you two
just so far gone and desperate to stay
together that you would endure anything?

The boy and girl smile.

- Please try and help me here. Without your cooperation it's outside all
our previous experience to really comprehend what took place between you and
Mr. Kalich.

The lovers raise their hands to their mouths to suppress a
burst of laughter.

There is a difference conjuring up ideas for my aborted novel,
"The Transfiguration of the Commonplace," and my actually
living the experience with the boy and girl. But what is it?
Is it too facile to argue that fiction and reality are the same?
At first glance my notes in preparation for the novel seem
to perfectly coincide with what I have experienced with the
boy and girl. But is that really the case? Do reality and fiction, word and image, truly mesh and merge and become
one and the same? For example, am I any closer to answering
my greatest fear which is knowing whether the boy and girl
are real or imagined, fiction or reality? Perhaps this is not an
existential question but rather an epistemological question.
Perhaps even a new epistemology is called for in our image-
laden world. Be that as it may, possibly, at a later date, I will
make a more thorough study and decode the similarities and

differences...if there are any. For now though, with this ongoing chapter in my life, it is enough to say that the boy and girl are real.

Interesting how that one little fact so readily slips my mind.

> - Ultimately, how did you two come to understand the play? Were you able to appreciate it as a work of art? Or did it resonate in you in a less abstract, more concrete way? And most importantly, would either of you, or both, offer an opinion as to how seeing Romeo and Juliet on stage compared to Mr. Kalich seeing you on screen?
>
> ...
>
> - Is that a fair question?

Unable to cover their mouths fast enough, the pair burst into simultaneous peals of laughter.

Flustered, the Interrogator takes a moment before continuing.

> - You two have not responded to one question put before you in this interrogation. Is there nothing either of you wish to say or are you simply going to let your deed speak for itself?

NOTES FROM THE NOVEL: THE TRANSFIGURATION OF THE COMMONPLACE

When he returned home he put on the video monitor but, of
course, as he anticipated, the boy and girl were gone. The
tv screen was blank. Where?...How?...he wondered. All he
knew was that his life was once again as empty as the blank
screen. He asked himself if his greatest fear was true.
Had he imagined the boy and girl? Was his encounter with
them a fiction? Were they even real to begin with or just
figments of his writer's imagination, not unlike the invented characters in his novels. The sharp pain in the middle
of his stomach he awoke with every morning thereafter, no
different than what he had experienced with the Rumanian, Ina,
so many years before, told him that they were. One can't be
certain about such things, but it's dubious whether Haberman
ever watched another tv screen again.

- So, Mr. Kalich, on that Sunday you were in
the park listening to David Ippolito's music?

- Yes. As I've said more than once, I anticipated returning to PH-F some time after
the matinee broke which is around 5:00 p.m.

- That's a long time to listen to music.

- He's an exceptionally gifted singer.

- Exceptional or not, Mr. Ippolito had
to cut his concert short as there was a
downpour beginning at three o'clock.

- Yes...

- And yet you still didn't return to PH-F
until well after 4:40 p.m.

- There's more to Central Park than David
Ippolito's music.

- Even when it's raining?

- You are Ms. Kumba Katombo?

- Yes.

- You are employed by the Wexner family
as a nanny to care for their three-year-
old daughter?

- Yes.

- And you know Mr. Kalich?

- Yes. Mr. Kalich is a nice man. Polite.
He always holds the door for me and asks
how I am and how my little girl is.

- And on the Sunday in question, Ms.
Katombo, you're certain that it was at
precisely 4:40 p.m. when Mr. Kalich suddenly ended his conversation in the park
with you and hurried off?

- Yes.

- How can you be so certain of the time?

- Because every day at exactly 4:25 p.m. I take the dog for a walk, and that Sunday was no exception. As soon as he made his telephone call on his cell phone and nobody answered...I tell you for an old man Mr. Kalich ran off like the wind.

Ms. Katombo breaks into a wide grin.

Every time I visited Dobrinka at her apartment only a few blocks from mine I would never walk, but would quicken my step to double-time. I could never wait to get there.

The same with Hana: Whenever she would ask me to fetch cigarettes for her on the lobby floor I would never wait for the elevator, but race down the four flights two steps at a time. I could never wait to get back.

- Perhaps something other than Central Park prompted your returning to PH-F earlier than 5:00 p.m. when, by your own admission, Mr. Kalich, Broadway matinee performances normally break.

- Like what?

- Perhaps, when nobody answered the phone, you saw it as a last chance to put a halt

```
to your cruel games before the Final Game
was even played.
```

An extension has been added to the wrought-iron terrace fence to compensate for the space between it and the stone gargoyle from which the boy and girl leaped to their death. Still, if one is truly zealous, one could always climb from the wooden bench seated beneath the fence onto its edge and, teetering on the edge, and using the fence as ballast, take the final plunge. However, no trace of the previous space between the fence and the stone gargoyle exists today. Like the boy and girl, it's as if it was never there.

```
- As concierge on that ever fateful Sun-
day, Mr. Rivera, when Mr. Kalich returned
from the park to see the shattered bodies
of the boy and girl lying in front of the
building: how did he act?

- What do you mean act?

- Did he act strange, for instance? Was
he shocked? sad? surprised? remorseful?
```

The concierge doesn't respond.

```
- Did he seem as if he half expected it?
```

The concierge reflects.

```
- Fernando...er...Mr. Rivera, how did he
act?
```

- It's hard to explain.

- Why is it hard to explain?

- Because Mr. Kalich didn't act at all.

Though I still have memories of Dobrinka standing on the wooden bench in front of just that space and, knowing my fear of height, teasing me by raising her arms as if to take the plunge herself. And how instantly I would rush to put my arms around her and hold her tight to protect her.

- Mr. Kalich, Officer Connelly has reported that your video camera was positioned at such an angle that the boy and girl's suicide leap could have been recorded.

- Yes. I forgot to mention that.

- You forgot to mention that?!

- Also, when Officer Connelly first entered your apartment, Mr. Kalich, he maintains you were watching your TV monitor.

- That's likely.

- The officer further asserts that nothing was showing on the screen other than snowflakes.

- Sometimes snowflakes are all there is.

Possible Endings For Novel:	Possible Endings For Novel:
<u>Transfiguration Of The Commonplace</u>	<u>Penthouse F</u>
a) Novel as basis for a reality TV program.	a) Novel as basis for a reality TV program.
b) Robert Haberman sitting in front of his blank TV screen.	b) Richard Kalich sitting in front of his blank TV screen.
c) Show Haberman initiating the Selection Process for a new boy and girl.	c) Show Kalich initiating the Selection Process for a new boy and girl.
d) Show Haberman commencing to write novel, "Transfiguration of the Commonplace," from his aborted novel's notebook.	d) Show Kalich commencing to write novel, "Penthouse F," by assembling pages he's already written by having lived the experience.
e) Leave Reader uncertain as to whether Haberman's perceptions of the boy and girl are real or imagined.	e) Leave Reader uncertain as to whether the book is reality-based or fiction.

- Mr. Kalich, it's my understanding that you have already commenced writing your new novel.

- I wouldn't call it writing.

- What would you call it?

- Assembling pages. To be precise, the novel, Penthouse F, in a sense has already been written as it's coincident on my

having lived the experience with the boy
and girl.

- So you no longer suffer from writer's
block?

- No, of course not. That was the whole
point in my having lived the experience
with the boy and girl, was it not? For
the first time in my life I am truly able
to take dictation.

In the dressing room when I challenged Dobrinka to choose
between the actor and myself, citing it as a moment of truth,
did I really believe my words or was I again, as always, merely
taking dictation?

- Mr. Kalich, you make it sound as if
the entire experience with the boy and
girl, from its very inception to the end,
was just so much grist for your writer's
mill.

- I was under the impression that we
already established that much.

...

- If I could have written the novel
"Transfiguration of the Commonplace" when
I first envisioned it, everything would
have been different.

- You mean to say Penthouse F would never have been written.

- I mean to say Penthouse F would never have been lived.

- MR. KALICH, MR. KALICH, I WANT YOU TO TAKE WHAT I SAY SERIOUSLY...

- AND NOT SERIOUSLY AT ALL.

Charlie P

RICHARD KALICH

For Dobrinka Nacheva
and Jennifer Deveraux Thompson

"How can we continue without a reader? Won't you come with us just a little further?

—Only if the author can convince me that his work has got something to do with the real world.

The author says that if his story is to resemble the world in any way at all, then it must be formless and without logic, proceeding randomly from one moment to the next. Then gradually, patterns will emerge which may or may not indicate events, ideas or actions. People will appear who may turn out to be crucially important, or else they may vanish after a single night, never to be seen again. And then, just when you think everything's got going, it'll all suddenly stop.

The author says also that if his story is to resemble the world at all faithfully then he will not attempt to burrow inside the heads of his characters, and attribute to them thoughts and emotions of which he can have no knowledge. Instead, he will report their behaviour and their speech in as honest a manner as he is able. Nor will he clutter his pages with elegant description, since the world is made of things, not words, and to try and capture reality in words is as meaningless as trying to make a butterfly out of sand.

Now can we proceed?"

PFITZ
ANDREW CRUMEY

"The ineradicable peculiarity of Kafka's cast of mind is shown by his inability to learn from mistakes. Failure multiplied by failure does not, in his case, equal success. The difficulties always remain the same ones, as if to demonstrate that they are by nature insuperable. From countless considerations and calculations he systematically omits what might bring them to an auspicious conclusion. The freedom to fail is preserved, as a sort of supreme law, which guarantees escape at every fresh juncture. One is inclined to call this the freedom of the weak person who seeks salvation in defeat. His true uniqueness, his special relation to power, is expressed in the prohibition of victory. All calculations originate and end in impotence."

Kafka's Other Trial
The Letters to Felice
ELIAS CANETTI

CHARLIE P

Peckerhead and Prophet. Pariah and Prodigal son. Charlie P is all things to all people and nothing to himself.

IMMORTALITY

Once and for all, at age three, when Charlie P's father died after having given him the most special birthday present of his young life, Lionel Electric Trains, Charlie P decided to live forever rather than suffer the indignity of mortality. Under no circumstances would he allow death to interfere with his daily regimen from this time on.

Though still a babe in his mother's arms, certainly not to be misconstrued a late bloomer, Charlie P had already given the matter much thought; in fact, thought of nothing else. His father's premature death presaged even more ominous events to come. Living forever, immortality, was indeed the only sure defense against this constant gnawing fear of the worst.

Given the nature of child consciousness, the global, diffuse, undifferentiated way it cognizes the world, its lack of specificity and discernment, it didn't take Charlie P long to transfer the dread of his father's loss on to his most prized possession, the electric trains, and especially the little train-master responsible for routing the train's safe passage.

Charlie P focused all his life's blood and energy on that little man. More than anything, he wanted the trainmaster to continue doing his job uninterrupted forever. Easier said than done: Immortality. There are less difficult things to accomplish in this world. Charlie P's main challenge was to keep the trainmaster out of harm's way. More specifically, to keep the little man sitting safely and securely at his table in the stationmaster's house, ever on the ready to be called to duty. What would happen if the little man took ill? Succumbed to his father's fate? What would happen if the battery that energized the light bulb on top of the house's door whenever the trains approached, signaling the trainmaster to stand and leave his shelter and go about performing his duties, failed to light? Charlie P lived with the chronic fear that just this eventuality would happen. That one day the battery would die.

But how to prevent such a catastrophe? That was the question: Should he obtain an additional set of electric trains? Seek out an as yet unbeknownst elixir of life? Place the little man on a health food diet with vitamin supplements? Discover the secrets of the aging process? Or should he himself control the trains' speeds, alter their paths, negotiate new routes, take other means of transportation—no, boats, planes, automobiles were subject to the same laws of chance and risk, gravity and motion, as trains; those unfortunates taking them could sink, crash and burn. And even though mourned for a short while after their demise, ultimately, like his father, they would soon be forgotten as the years passed by. No. Charlie P's answer was not to play the game. By not using up the battery, the trainmaster could go on sitting safely in his house—be at Charlie P's beck and call forever. By denying himself pleasure now, by abrogating what he most looked forward to while playing with his trains, by not having the little man do his duty, perform his chores, even though it was his favorite moment in all the world, the precursor, causal link and catalyst to his trains riding through peaks and valleys, across bridges and over hills, high on steppes and low beneath mountains, during which, needless to say, everything around them was fraught with danger, subject to the aleatory whims of chance, when the battery sooner or later would run out, when, like his father, the trainmaster sooner or later would succumb to his fate—No. Pleasure and joy, fun and games, intoxication and bliss, were a small price to pay for immortality.

And so Charlie P played the game by not playing it. Bestowed eternal everlasting life on the trainmaster.

Once and for all, at age three, Charlie P decided that by not playing the game, by not living his life, unlike his father, like the trainmaster, he could, he would, live forever.

BASEBALL

By age eight, Charlie P's love of electric trains had changed over to baseball. There was nothing he loved more than to watch baseball games on TV. Each and every inning, every crack of the bat, every pitch, ground ball, fly out, base hit, home run, would bring his heart untold delight. So why is it then he never watched the actual games on television? Or more accurately, only put the television on between innings to obtain the score? True, he had an uncanny knack for knowing just when one inning ended and the next would start. Notwithstanding long innings or short, rain delays, rallies, the singing of the anthem or God Bless America, as well as the seventh inning stretch, he would unfailingly click on the television at precisely the right moment. Even unforeseen injuries and the occasional overzealous fan randomly running out on the field couldn't impede Charlie P's ability to catch the announcer's in-between innings' sum-up of the game.

But still, no matter how significant the game, pennant-deciding, playoff or World Series, no matter how much joy and pleasure he might derive from viewing it, the question remains: why didn't Charlie P watch the actual games?

The answer is the same as with his electric trains. Just as he feared using up the battery energizing the trainmaster's light bulb and for that reason didn't play with his trains, here he feared using up or risking injury to the television set's motor and didn't watch the games.

Charlie P's life is empty. He hasn't a friend. He calls up the fire department and the police department. The suicide emergency line and 911. All the names in the telephone book. For the rest of the night and some of the day Charlie P's apartment is filled with people. His phone doesn't stop ringing. His life is full.

FALLING IN LOVE

"How do you explain falling in love?" asked Charlie P's new female friend on their first date. "Falling in love's always a miracle," answered Charlie P. "An accident of the Gods. An unforeseen and wholly inexplicable circumstance. Take my case, for example. I've been in love two times. The first time I was young, walking in the park, enjoying the fall day, when I stubbed my toe. Compensating for my injured toe, I strained my knee. Falling down I hurt my back, and making amends for my injured back which, by the way, immobilizes you completely, I fell down a flight of stone steps leading to the 72nd Street Bethusda Fountain, cracking my head, and nearly drowning in the process. And if that wasn't bad enough, both my arms, legs, and neck were broken too, as well as every other bone in my body. However, all was not black, as the city has more than capable EMS services, and soon enough I was being carried off on a stretcher by a pair of well-meaning CPR men, deposited in an ambulance, and driven at the speed of light, though not stopping for any, to the nearest hospital. But not before crashing into a taxi, careening into a bus, and smashing headlong into an oil truck setting a four-alarm fire ablaze, not to mention burning me, in particular, to a crisp. Later on, continuing our journey to the hospital, and picking up even more speed, probably because of the oil slick and burned rubber, our vehicle's tires could not get a good grip, and after crashing through a protective side-wall on the West Side Highway, we plunged over a rocky slope of boulders into the Hudson River where I came damn near drowning all over again as well as causing myself further harm by re-breaking every bone already broken in my body.

"At the hospital the doctors didn't know which part of me was which, so they operated on me thinking I was somebody else...Besides dropping me on three different occasions (not purposefully) from the operating table, being more interested in the opening day football game on TV than any vital signs I might still be showing on the monitor. Two hours later, though, once the football game was over, I must admit, they started ministering to my needs in earnest. Separating my head from my toe, and reattaching my rear end to another person's backside making for an interesting-looking maximus glutimus. By the time they were through with me, not only was nothing left of me as nature originally intended, but I had lost use of my five senses as well. In that condition, as you can well imagine, I couldn't tell which side was up, much less did I retain any of my former appreciation of the various parts of the female anatomy. Believe me, I'm not proud of this but the truth is the blessed female opening that gives life and pleasure meant no more to me, less, than the hole in my head. For certain, all parts led south and not only didn't I know what, when and who I was, but I had no idea where one part of me started and another ended. Everything looked the same. Or different, as the case may be. It was in such a state, while lying in a comatose condition, and only after much trial and error, sheer accident, that I fell in love for the first time in my life.

"You got to understand. I was still alive and kicking, at least breathing, and one night, while, as I said, laying comatose in my bed, a night nurse suffering from a rare combination of elephantiasis and anorexia, and, like me, lacking a nose, eyes, ears, mouth, chin and jaw, yet possessing a kindly face, caught my attention. On second thought, not really like me, her features were either hidden behind mountainous layers of fat or crushed and flattened beyond recognition in pockets and cavities of undernourished cells. Still, when this good lady offered me a sip of water, and I reached for a straw, accidentally brushing my finger or big toe, I don't know which, against her big toe or finger, I don't know which, I must admit it felt good. Certainly better than anything I had felt since stubbing my toe, to say the least. It was only to be expected that I commenced fondling the opening of her left nostril thinking it was you know what and led you know where. And guess what, miracle of miracles, she liked it, too. Even more than I did. Only later did I learn that it was the first time she had ever been touched in this way, or any other, for that matter. Naturally we both explored a little further, tested our limits. I'm proud to say my libido was in full tact and, passing up all the usual watering holes and pit stops—to be honest she had none of these anyway—I ended up right dab smack in the middle of her all too human heart. Before either of us knew what was happening, we were both head over heels in love.

"However, as we all know, all good things come to an end, and I'm sorry to say that our so-called heavenly bliss lasted no longer than the proverbial one night stand. One day a team of young medical geniuses arrived, visited my bedside, whispering conspiratorially amongst themselves, they had new ideas about everything, as young people often do, and to make a long story short: the operation was a success. Like Humpty Dumpty they put all my parts and pieces, missing and otherwise, back together again. Several weeks later my five senses returned. And so when a young blonde intern with an hourglass figure who was making the rounds stopped at my bed, and leaned over to check me out, inadvertently showing me what she was made of, as you can readily understand, I soon lost interest in my first love's heart."

"And what about the second time you were in love?" queried Charlie P's new female friend.

"That's a long story, even more complicated than the first," answered Charlie P. "Let's save that for our second date."

LITERATURE RUIND MY LIFE!

Charlie P's mother, a well-intentioned woman, a banker's daughter from Old Europe, wanted anything for her son but to be a chip off the old block. A poet, a scholar, a writer, these were the lofty and noble callings she wanted for her son. Not so much a stern taskmaster, but rather a highly principled pedagogue, she set about putting her child-rearing theories to practice almost immediately after Charlie P's birth. Each and every time little Charlie P turned to his right to see a dollar bill lying on his crib's pillow, or fingered in his mother's hand, he would receive a gentle smack on the snout, a tap on the cheek, or a twist of the ear. But when he turned left there was invariably a kiss and a hug waiting for him, a chocolate brownie and milk, together with a handsome leather-bound book. Needless to say these fecund positions were varied up: The book on occasion moving to the right, the dollar bill to the left, but invariably, the one constant, as implacable as any of the laws of nature, Charlie P would always receive his warm and affectionate embrace, brownie and milk, when he set his gaze on the book. It doesn't take a Pavlov to explain how or why these child-rearing atrocities induced Charlie P's love of books or even his quest to become a writer.

All well and good—that is up to the adolescent years. Then, they only proved a prelude to the worst. Like so many of us, Charlie P rebelled. Money and power became the end-all and the be-all and he pursued both with a vengeance. Displaying such entrepreneurial skills and talents, combined with the aforementioned adolescent zeal and fervor, that neither his grief-stricken mother nor, especially, his father (business wasn't doing well; the family could use the money) put up much resistance. Later on, however, these normal growing pains only proved a phase like so much else in those turbulent years, and Charlie P returned to his true calling. But, still, to this day, any time Charlie P sees a dollar bill floating around, even if it is only a customer rummaging through his billfold to pay a cashier, the old furies return: something approaching the material decadence and demonic cravings of our own ignoble age. It's at those moments that Charlie P forgets his maternal if not paternal legacy, all that's noble and lofty, and screams aloud: "Literature ruined my life!"

An hour later, once again becalmed and serene, rather than race home to commence his quest to write the great American novel, or even to select a book to read from his own voluminous library, he heads to the nearest coffee shop for a chocolate brownie and a glass of cold milk.

CHARLIE P'S LIBRARY

Charlie P owns a vast collection of books. Sufficient in number to rival New York's 42nd Street Public Library, Paris's Bibliotheque and Greece's Parnassus; in fact all the great libraries of the world. Small bookstores and large, bibliophiles, private collectors, scholars, institutions of higher learning, the present day book chains such as B. Dalton's and Barnes & Noble; from papyrus scrolls boxed at Alexandria to the integrated multi-story shelf and flooring system of bookstacks at the Library of Congress; in terms of sheer size and number, magnitude and compass, cannot begin to compare to the quantity of books Charlie P owns. Whether he accumulated this collection out of a passion for learning, love for the written word, to impress a female friend, or friends, idle curiosity, too much leisure time, or merely because he had nothing better to do, we do not know. It's not important. What is important is that Charlie P has not read a single book in his library.

In his favor it must be said that he stacks, stores, shelves, arranges, rearranges and feather dusts each and every book with loving care every morning even before taking his daily ablutions.

DRIVING

It's common knowledge that Charlie P rarely leaves his apartment. He's been called a recluse, a hermit, a couch potato and a stay-at-home. Other than for his bi-weekly trips to the Food Emporium, and his twice-monthly stopovers at the Chinese to drop off and pick up his laundry, Charlie P never strays more than three to four blocks from his home.

As to his vast collection of books that make up his impressive library, as we already know, not one read. And the clothes in his closet, however up-to-date and fashionable: never worn. Except on those all too human occasions when, out of sheer necessity to give himself a lift, he tries on a favorite cashmere sweater, or an especially handsome velour jacket, to admire himself in the mirror. So it's hardly a surprise when all who know him say: The man doesn't have a life. He never goes anywhere or does anything.

But Charlie P begs to differ. "Don't judge everything by appearance," he says. "There's more to a man than meets the eye. After all, what do these others have to show for their lives, for all their hustle and bustle, other than shabby and worn-out clothes, and dog-eared books long out of print and yellowed by time." Compared to them Charlie P's volumes look like the seventy-two virgins promised in paradise. They've never been touched. He has literary adventures ahead of him of untold pleasure and plenitude.

And what's true for his books is even more true for travel. While others go off from one place to another on feet of clay, Charlie P wants nothing less than to stop time. Part the Red Sea. Sight the burning bush. And so, once a day, every day, he seats himself comfortably in his rocking chair, closes his eyes, lights up his corncob pipe, and takes off to faraway lands. Not to Europe or the Far East, Timbuktu or the snows of Kilimanjaro, but to all places at once. How does he accomplish this? By putting his four-wheeled vehicle in cruise control and letting himself rock back and forth, to and fro, like a babe in its cradle. It's then, while driving in his rocking chair, he's in constant motion, standing still; not subject to the laws of gravity or the laws of motion; in perfect rhythm and harmony with the seasons; an elemental force; as natural and carefree as the birds of season flying south to escape the cold; the salmon swimming upstream to give birth and then die. Charlie P soars along at these times taking in the sights. Already off as soon as arriving, no more here than there. An Olympian up high, oblivious as a God, paying no more heed to a young woman jumping from a bridge than to a six-car smashup on the highway. Absolved from guilt, free of responsibility. It's all the same to Charlie P, chaos and mayhem, the world's petty grievances, all human happenstance along the road. No more and no less than those cows over there grazing in the field; or that grain of sand he's just picked up off the beach. This too shall pass. And so, timeless, indefatigable, driving but not driven, Charlie P silences his critics. They can't touch him here, can't mock or scorn him. It's here, rocking back and forth, to and fro, in his rocking chair, that Charlie P conquers space, masters time, lives forever by not living at all.

But all this driving has tired Charlie P out. Like the rest of us he can't wait to get back home after a long trip. As always, a tall cold glass of milk awaits him with a chocolate brownie. And if his memory serves correct, it's Thursday, his favorite television program is on tonight.

Miracle of miracles. Accident of the Gods. Charlie P has met the perfect woman. The girl of his dreams. His once-in-a-lifetime love. But Charlie P doesn't go forward with the relationship. Doesn't take her number, or as much as ask her name. A veteran of the wars, as well as countless years of therapy, he knows all too well that his great romance will last only as long as it remains in his head.

Charlie P is at a party. "There she is," he says to a friend, motioning to an absolute stranger. "My future wife. Everything about her is just as I imagined it would be. It's as if I've known her all my life. One only needs a glance to see we'd make the perfect couple." But his friend takes exception. Points out that Charlie P has yet to meet the young woman; that not as much as a word has passed between them; that the chapter has yet to be written. "Those are my feelings," says Charlie P. "And feelings are real. All the rest are mere details that our years together will fill in and play out." Charlie P finishes his drink, takes his friend by the arm to leave. "Besides," he says, "in a culture rife with blurbmeisters and web wonks, what book ever lives up to expectations."

Charlie P has spent many long years pursuing the woman of his dreams. Indefatigably he's traversed the globe, caught a slow boat to China, sailed the seven seas; even built his own space capsule and journeyed to the outer reaches. Still, despite his considerable efforts, the perfect woman continues to elude him. But that doesn't bother Charlie P. He's one person who need not be told that his real problems begin only when he finds her.

THE HACK

Having suffered all his life from writer's block, Charlie P made the momentous decision to become a hack. Not the kind that writes for the market place, but that drives a cab. So successful was he in his chosen profession that it wasn't long before he was able to purchase his own Medallion.

One Sunday afternoon, comfortably seated behind the wheel, not a care in the world, no more rejection letters to fret over, the terrors of art behind him, he reverted to type, giving vent for the first time in his life to the most sublime and noble poesies. In such a dreamlike and paradisiacal state, he passed through a red light, lowered the boom on a hi-rise, and crashed into a truck carrying sufficient explosives to set not only himself, but half of Manhattan and the outer lying boroughs and suburbs ablaze, too. Impaled at the wheel, in the heat of flame, he was pulled from the inferno by New York's finest and bravest and, amidst bleating car horns and the fractious rumble of traffic, delivered to the hospital by a first rate if unappreciated CPR team. Hovering between life and death, struggling for every gasp and breath, Charlie P promised the doctors if he survived the operation that he would never again drive a cab or give vent to his own novelistic urgings no matter how exalted and sublime. Rather, he would sit himself comfortably in the back seat of another's cab, preferably one of those elongated chauffeur-driven limos, and take in the view. This way not only would he avoid traffic accidents, not to mention the insufferable tedium of rewriting, but he would have time to relax and read all those press clippings and bravura reviews of his books.

It's of great relief to report that ever since making that decision, not only has New York been a safer place to live, but Charlie P realized his lifelong ambition—he's become a highly successful world-acclaimed writer, if only in his mind.

MARATHON

Charlie P joins a health club. Employs a personal trainer. Runs around Central Park, not once but a thousand times. Adheres to the most rigorous regimen. No more late night outs; drinking or smoking, fatty foods, malteds, even chocolate brownies are out. Come this November Charlie P is running the Marathon.

But why then does he scoff at those who likewise are preparing for the same event? Is it because he knows that it's not merely the 26.2 mile terrain starting in Staten Island and continuing on through Brooklyn, Queens, Bronx and ending up in Manhattan he'll be running around, but that his race is endless, infinite, inside himself?

THEN AND ONLY THEN...

Charlie P is not so different from other people. He has goals, ambitions. He wants to live a full life. Some day his dreams, aspirations, will come to fruition. His real life will begin. Some day but not today. On his thirtieth birthday Charlie P resolves to start living his life in earnest. And so with the stoic patience of a solitude Charlie P waits for his time. But unlike others, Charlie P is hardly satisfied with the usual standards of measurement. No, days, months, years do not suffice for Charlie P. His calendrical clock is much more finely tuned. He calibrates his time till thirty not so much by days, months, years, as by hours, minutes, seconds, and the infinitesimal intervals between seconds. To his credit, Charlie P knows the millisecond his life will begin.

But time stops for no one. Least of all for Charlie P. And when that ever fateful, supernatural, transhuman millisecond strikes the clock, by the time Charlie P reaches for it, it's already beyond his grasp. Alas, his best-laid plans have come to naught. To be honest, Charlie P is not disappointed, but relieved. Determined fellow that he is, hardly has the tick changed to tock before he begins counting again. It's only another 100,000 hours, 10 million minutes, 100 billion seconds, and one billion trillion fractional seconds until he reaches forty or fifty or ... Then, and only then, will he start living his life.

After counting sheep all night, Charlie P counts sheep all day.

SEX ADDICT

Charlie P is a sex addict. Whether singing in the shower or bewailing his fate to the Gods, he's obsessed with female flesh. The fact of his amazing good fortune with the fair sex does little to appease his appetite. And those rare times, when through determination and sheer exertion of will, he abstains from sex, the idea of 'it' becomes ever more dominant in his mind.

If only he could free himself of his addiction, he thinks, he would be so much better off. What he wouldn't give to be old and feeble and know the solitary comforts of impotence. Perhaps then he wouldn't be ruled by those raging furies below his belt.

As everyone has an opinion, Charlie P sought the advice of purveyors of every cloth and persuasion. But rabbis and priests, shamans and divinely possessed ecstatics, health quacks and well-intentioned friends, all the high priests of learning recited the same recitativo. Telling him how fortunate he was; that his condition wouldn't last forever. That he should take advantage of it; make the most of it while he can. Not one wouldn't trade places with him in a minute. But advice is easy to give and hard to take, especially for one who in the very act of possessing a woman is already conjuring up the next one in line.

Even men of science with their sophisticated technologies, and men of letters who believed in the redemptive power of the word made mistakes of opposite kinds when dealing with Charlie P. The one confusing fact with fiction; the other fiction with fact. Whether it be cold showers, hypnosis, frontal lobotomy, a good old-fashioned heart to heart, or even shooting darts in him containing enough drugs to fell an elephant; all they tried had no more than a soporific effect on him. Once the drugs wore off, or he was out of the shower, there was a resurgence of energy in Charlie P that could only be likened to the sex drive of an army.

Charlie P pursued even more extreme measures. Calling on a veterinarian, now a butcher, who had made a worldwide reputation by castrating and neutering not only domestic animals but wild beasts of prey as well. He even availed himself of that miracle substance, baking soda, known to soothe upset stomachs, mollify laundry, purify water, bake cookies, kill roaches, protect against gingivitis, and strip battleship paint. But, alas, nothing worked. While it is true his erections were not as firm and vigorous as they once had been, his obsession remains stronger than ever.

So what can he do? Never one to settle for the short end of the stick, Charlie P threw out his little red telephone book; the one he's kept 'stats' in since school days. And no longer will he go online to seek out female friends. Or answer their telephone calls, faxes, e-mails, love letters and invitations for daytime rendezvous and assignations in the heat of the night. Instead he's become a culture vulture. A connoisseur of the arts. He attends concerts, ballet, theater, has become bookish.

But no matter what he does, where he goes, his sexual addiction goes with him.

In the end Charlie P can only conclude that being a sex addict is much like being a great American patriot. No matter how many coalitions join forces to war against him, whatever weapons in their arsenal, from 1776 to Iwo Jima, from Pearl Harbor to the Twin Towers, once hoisted, nothing will bring him down.

LOST PECKER

Whether missing in action or conspicuous by its absence, Charlie P awoke one morning to the startling realization that he had lost his pecker. He looked everywhere for it. Under his bed, behind the sink, in his closet, even boarding the Shortline Bus to his childhood camp in the Catskills where he had lost his virginity, but all to no avail. His pecker was nowhere to be found. Not yet quite in a panic, but understandably more than somewhat concerned, Charlie P set to work with even greater industry. Visiting girlfriends' homes, past and present, as well as searching wives', ex-wives' and mistresses' apartments from pantry closet to kitchen cabinets. But always the same result. No pecker. By now, not only in a panic, but suffering from sleepless nights and waking each morning in a cold sweat, he boarded a Concorde flying to a kibbutz in Israel where he once had a torrid affair with a hot-blooded Ashkenazi. After that he continued his search to all those exotic lands he had never been to but found so alluring while watching nature and travel programs at home on TV. It goes without saying he loved the sheer sound of their names: The Aegean Archipelago, the Alaskan Tundra.

The African Kalahari. Returning home, empty-handed again, understandably beside himself, he began checking his trouser legs and crotch every stride or two, as well as his front, back and vest pockets. It wasn't long after that that you could see his head peeking under every passing lady's skirt and dress on the street; in the park; at the Food Emporium; even at his business office where he quite noticeably upset the usual decorum. But no matter where he looked, he always came up short. Still, not one to utterly collapse, exhibiting his usual resiliency and tenacity, before retiring one evening, he poured himself a hot toddy, made himself comfortable in his favorite chair, and rather than contemplate his navel, stare blankly at the four walls, or rise suddenly only to pace back and forth, to and fro around the room, as was his custom, he riffled through his desk drawer for pen and paper and commenced making a detailed list of what it would mean to live his life without his pecker. First off, he would have little to do with the comforts of women any longer. But with this realization, as if by divine ordinance, Freudian decree, his memory bank, filled to the brim, burst loose. With startling clarity he saw: Thighs, arms, legs, breasts, asses, hips, all mixed and married together. All jumbled and fused. A teeming potpourri and virtual cornucopia of female body parts; as well as an endless variety of sexual positions and all variations on the theme that he had at one time or another in his long life ever experienced, imagined, partaken in and/or fantasized.

A great creatural sadness came over Charlie P. For with all his Remembrances of Things Past, (present and future), one thing was most apparent. Other than the size, shape, color, taste and smell of body parts, disembodied genitalia, if you will, Charlie P could not remember one face, much less name. Not one quality or characteristic that would separate and distinguish one woman from another. They were all the same. And worse still, they were All In His Mind. But as hinted at earlier, or might be deduced, Charlie P was nothing if he was not an Eternal Optimist. There was no way you could keep him down.

And so, bouncing up with ever more vim and vigor, he began to jot down and give credence to the unmistakable fact that whether he had a pecker or not, he was as well off as before. For truth be told, all his life he had felt like a bull in a china shop; and now, no longer shackled like a slave to his galley, a prisoner to his ball and chain, and since it was all in his mind anyway, he was free to conjure up...why the possibilities were endless. He could...he would...

But it wasn't so much a case of tenacity, resiliency or even being the eternal optimist, but simply a matter that once grabbing on to something—whether it be an idea, dollar bill or any part of a woman's anatomy, Charlie P had a difficult time letting go. He would milk it for all its worth. And so immediately after turning his loss into gain, Charlie P continued adding to his list. Just think, he told himself, of all the time, money and effort he would save in the future. No more frittering away the days shopping for lady's gifts, or compulsively chasing after them all hours of the day and night. No more paying for lady friends' breakfasts, lunches and dinners, not to mention alimony, divorce settlements and separation agreements. And that doesn't even take into consideration all the flowers, candles, wines, red and white, necessary nowadays to court a woman, seduce a woman, or merely commemorate her birthday, a holiday, Thanksgiving dinner, and anniversary. Toss in all those obligatory make-up presents necessary to put things right, tit for tat, as well as going-away presents, return-from-business trips presents. Why just one night out taking the family to a Broadway show cost a fortune. And as far as families were concerned, just think of what one would save on kids' medical and education expenses, day camp, summer camp, baseball camp, basketball camp, ballet, piano, French, Spanish, swimming and rock climbing lessons. At the very least he would have more closet space, use of his own credit card, bathroom and medicine cabinet. And most definitely he would never again have to lend out his precious books (the fact that they weren't read only made them more precious), which, of course, like all else, his lady friends never returned.

Pouring himself another hot toddy, a half-suppressed smile appeared on Charlie P's face. From this day on, he thought to himself, every time he passes Bendel's, or for that matter any other elegant women's store, he would no longer have to take his lady friend by the elbow and direct her to the other side of the street. Yes sir, no more awkward or embarrassing moments. Even better, just imagine all the abuse and ill treatment he would now save himself. The rebukes, reprimands, chronic laments and plaintive grievances that unceasingly poured from his lady friends' mouths. How many times had he heard: Charlie P touches but doesn't feel. Charlie P listens but doesn't hear. Charlie P looks but doesn't see. And worst of all, the most heart-stopping, the one that caused him more grief than all the others: Charlie P, you can look but don't touch.

Charlie P took another sip of his hot toddy, his smile growing broader, as he continued to reflect. Losing his pecker was really the best thing that could have happened to him. He would not only save money, and consequently have more to spend on himself, but he would suffer less stress and strain, expend less energy (in bed and out) and last but not least,

live not only longer but better. Even his writing would pros-
per. Like his literary hero, Tolstoy, when his sex drive left him
at sixty, and he committed not to write simple melodramas
about the birds and the bees, like Anna Karenina and *War
and Peace* any longer, but dedicate himself to theology and
philosophy—Charlie P, too, could at last get down to the serious business of writing. Of course, he was in no way comparing his writing skill to the great Russian's; but only how and
on what he might use his talent, however modest. After all,
let's not forget that up to this point, no matter how much
he's thought about it, Charlie P has not written a single page,
paragraph, not even a single line of his great American novel.

Charlie P took a long last sip from his glass of hot toddy.
After so much reflection and rumination, his list had grown
to incalculable size. Yes sir, he repeated to himself, losing his
pecker was truly a blessing in disguise. The best thing that
could have happened to him. One of God's little miracles.
And if, as it is often said, the Lord works in strange ways, then
perhaps his greatest, most inscrutable mystery was the simple
but paradoxical truth that: LESS IS MORE!

Waking that night, like an amputee who loses his leg and
still feels pain where his leg used to be, Charlie P felt pleasure
between his legs. Peeking down under the sheets, even though
drowsy-eyed from lack of sleep, he could swear he saw his
member erect. Needless to say the rest of the night Charlie P
slept with the angels.

"WE'RE TALKING ABOUT IT"

When Charlie P met his first love and life-long mate she was sweet sixteen, lovely and just beginning to ripen. When he was asked by friends: "Are you two going steady? Have you two done it yet?" Charlie P answered: "We're talking about it."

When his girlfriend and life-long mate was twenty-two and by her own admission ready as she'll ever be, a beer-drinking friend at a local hangout asked Charlie P: "Have you moved her in yet?" Charlie P answered: "We're talking about it."

When forty-plus and the woman's biological clock was running short, if not out, and her family, including her aunt, uncle, grandparents and great grandparents, had all but given up hope, an old-fashioned family doctor, old-fashioned in the best sense of the term, asked Charlie P: "If not now, then when?" Charlie P answered: "We're talking about it."

Last week, his first love and life-long mate was taken into a nursing home whose reputation was founded on providing care for the terminally ill. With little time left, when Charlie P was asked by the concerned director if...Before the words were half out of his mouth Charlie P motioned for the man to stop and said: "It's no longer a subject for conversation." Then, making an abrupt about-face, he strode out of the home not marching forward but stepping backwards.

FIRST DATE

Apprehensive over his first date with a woman in more than a quarter century, Charlie P reflects on what he'll do tonight. He'll leave his office early to avoid the rush hour traffic. He'll stop at the florist to purchase flowers, and at Godiva's for chocolates. He'll arrive home at precisely 6:00 p.m. He'll shower and shave, dab his body with talcum and his face with cologne. He'll check his wallet for available cash and credit cards. He'll try on half a dozen ties before selecting one that perfectly matches his sports coat and shirt. He'll make after-theater dinner reservations at an old country restaurant as much known for its romantic atmosphere and being a place where people can talk, as for its superior cuisine. He'll accommodate his bedroom lamp to make the most of the play of light and shadow on his bed. He'll smooth the ripples on his usually rumpled covers, changing the effect from a turbulent to a calm sea. He'll take proprietary interest at the play's intermission of the other men (and women for different reasons) clustered around the oak-paneled bar staring with envy at his having such a beautiful friend. He'll pull in his potbellied stomach, puff out his skeletal chest, fix his tie, flatten down his tousled hair, remove the lint from his jacket, spit-shine his shoes, and ever so subtly taking the young woman's hand so that others can see, he'll shepherd her protectively back to their orchestra seats. He'll order at dinner a feast for the Gods, and a wine to warm the coldest heart. He'll make dinner conversation, skillfully drawing his friend down a seducer's path of blind alleys with dazzling displays of verbal swordsmanship. He'll alternately play roles of wise man and fool, innocent and profligate, world-weary cynic and idealistic youth ever on the ready to change the world. He'll take the young woman back to his apartment where he'll offer her an ancient potion to wrest away all her personal demons. He'll take her out on his terrace and show her the breathtaking view of the park. He'll click on a romantic CD. He'll burnish the nape of her neck with a brush kiss and at the same time let his fingers graze ever so lightly on the blades of her shoulders. He'll see her smile and hear her giggle with a young girl's nervous anticipation as he gently guides and nudges her to his bed. He'll compare and measure his wrenching thrusts against her lissome grace and arabesques of youth. He'll marvel at her Reubenesque body, but never forget, not even for a moment, that it's him choreographing each and every move. He'll explore and invent new ways for men and women to join together and separate, cleave and part. He'll experience with his partner every mood and whim; the entire range and repertoire of human folly and seriousness. He'll bridge the gap of whatever is left of the battle of the sexes, the mind-body split, alterity and otherness, all the dichotomies, chasms, abysses that separate and keep apart one human being from another. He'll pull back at the height of passion, not to delay, but to enhance the perfect moment, and bring it to heartbreaking Dionysian pitch. He'll take masculine pride in seeing her Botticelli face and Mona Lisa smile gazing up at him in equal dosages of rapture and gratitude. He'll take her home. He'll return to his apartment and telephone her just as she's about to doze off. He'll reassure her of his undying respect and thankfulness while simultaneously validating and reaffirming her autonomy and real value as a separate person. He'll utter words of love and other endearments and finally good night knowing full well that his voice will be the last thing she'll hear that night, and his face the first thing she'll see the next morning.

Finished with his conjurings, Charlie P leaves for his date. He rings the young woman's buzzer, but just as she's about to open her door, he does an about-face and takes his leave. He knows only too well that no date could possibly be as satisfying as the one he's just had.

The following day, when asked by a colleague at the office how it went, he answers not with words but with a gesture: One more great romance torn asunder and scattered to the wind.

On the day of his college graduation, Charlie P was asked by a very powerful alumni: "What do you want out of life?"

"I want...I want...I want..." exclaimed Charlie P.

"Would you settle for a cold piece of chicken for lunch and a nine-to-five job?" answered the alumni.

"My son the genius, why are you so stupid?"
What Charlie P's mother giveth, she taketh away.

THE YOUNG HARPIST

At age fifty-seven Charlie P fell in love with a twenty-year-old Bulgarian harpist entering Juilliard on scholarship. Besides being young and beautiful, she came from a good family, too. Her mother not only taught ethics at the university, but practiced what she preached. Her father discovered the cure for cancer. Her grandfather assassinated both Hitler and Stalin, and what makes these deeds even more remarkable is that he accomplished them before the War. It has been thirty-three years since Charlie P had last been in love. And now this. How lucky could he get. Miracle of miracles. Wonder of wonders. Charlie P never thought it would happen to him again.

On their first meeting, Charlie P wanted to buy the young woman the world. And with an outpouring of generosity that the world has rarely seen, he bought the young woman all of Manhattan as well as the Brooklyn Bridge. And in the wee hours he sneaked off with her to Paris and brought back the Eiffel Tower, too. At the date's end, for his generosity and kindness, the young woman told him she loved him. But when

Charlie P leaned his head forward and pursed his lips, all she gave him was a peck on the cheek. It's only to be expected, said Charlie P. What else could an old man like myself expect from such a young and beautiful girl. Who comes from a good family, too.

On their second meeting, Charlie P tried to out-do their first. Wanting to show the young woman the world he took her from one end of the world to another exposing her to sights she had never seen. Ranging from the Egyptian Pyramids to the Leaning Tower of Pisa; from the East Village with its nihilistic denizens wearing assorted body piercings and tattoos to the great Avenues such as the Champs Elysée, Saville Row, Fifth Avenue, Rodeo Drive, the Via Vennetta, with their magnificent city-sized department stores and idiosyncratic boutiques. But as there's no accounting for taste, the young woman, though understandably attracted to the nihilistic urges of the East Village denizens, said that ever since a little girl she was afraid of the sight of blood, and for that reason if no other, body piercings had little appeal for her. The fact that her skin was perfect and glowed in the dark was enough to dissuade her from tattoos. As for the great avenues with their department stores and boutiques, she played no favorites, allowing Charlie P to spend his money equally and without prejudice in each and every store regardless of size or cost. At the night's end the young woman once again professed her love for Charlie P, this time squeezing his hand warmly for a second, and offering him an aborted hug, but when Charlie P, encouraged, leaned over and pursed his lips, he received no more than his usual peck on the cheek. It's only to be expected, said Charlie P. What else could an old man like himself expect from such a young and beautiful girl. Who comes from a good family, too.

On their third meeting Charlie P decided to give it his best effort. Go for broke. As he had already bought and shown the young woman the world, he was determined to give her what was his alone to give. Himself: His heart, mind and soul. The young woman said that was all she ever really wanted and suggested they take an afternoon stroll in the park. As for the evening, any simple, quiet place would do. Charlie P knew just the place. But just seconds after being seated in the Boathouse Restaurant overlooking the Park's lake, hardly a stone's throw from Charlie P's residence, the young woman changed her mind. And on their way to Monte Carlo, somewhere over the Sahara Desert, their plane crashed, a three-eyed Turk robbed Charlie P blind, and both his and the young woman's camels died of thirst. Before succumbing to the same fate as the camels, Charlie P spotted a watering hole in the distance. Being younger and swifter than Charlie P, the young woman reached the water first. By the time Charlie P arrived, there was not a drop left. Despite his throat being parched, and his mouth and lips scorched and blistered, Charlie P let out a scream to wake the dead, the meaning of which could leave no one in doubt. "What happened to the water!?"

Taken aback for a moment, the young woman recovered quickly, thought up a good one, and answered. "The water you saw was a mirage." Somewhat appeased but still thirsty, Charlie P continued his query. "But what's that trickling down your mouth and chin?" "That," said the woman, "why that's wine." Elated over the fact that the woman he loved had satisfied her need for liquid nourishment, and inspired by her ability to turn water into wine, in a burst of genuine emotion Charlie P leaned his head forward, puckered his lips, but despite the bedazzling beauty of the setting desert sun, the becalming effect of the moon and stars overhead, not to mention the fact that the young woman was still a bit tipsy from wine, all she could spare Charlie P was her usual peck on the cheek.

It's only to be expected, said Charlie P. What else could an old man like himself expect from such a young and beautiful girl. Who comes from a good family, too.

Persisting in the principle that it's better to give than receive, and not able to give up his lifelong maxim—if you don't succeed at first, try again—Charlie P continued to give the young woman all he had to give. A period spanning what under happier circumstances would be called his Golden Years. In all honesty and without exaggeration, and on this point, for sure, the young lady would not disagree, no man ever gave more and got less than Charlie P. Be that as it may, after the initial wear and tear of their first three encounters, Charlie P allowed the young woman to break his heart; bust his prover-bials; rob him blind (no: that was the one-eyed Turk's doing). The young woman merely allowed him to spend his last dollar on her; as well as lose his mind and surrender his soul. But as it's a well known fact that a man can only take so much, there's a limit to everything, even for a glutton for punishment like Charlie P, by the time the young woman was through with him and he was carted off to the hospital in an ambulance, there was little if anything left of him. The learned doctors needed but a perfunctory glance in his direction to diagnose his condition as terminal. The symptoms listed on his medi-cal chart included but were not limited to: a. Hair loss; b. Loss of appetite; c. Bad nerves; d. Urinary incontinence and irregular bowel movements resulting in constipation and diar-rhea simultaneously; e. Cirrhosis of the liver (he had taken up drinking); f. Respiratory failure (he had also taken up smoking); g. Heart failure (already mentioned); h. Catatonia; i. Brain dead aka complete cessation of all mental activity. In other words, other than for his heart, lungs, brain, kidney, liver, all vital organs and functions, he was in good working order.

In sum and in short, Charlie P was in a bad way.

The doctors, as stated, had already given up all hope on him and were at the point of letting nature take its course, when the young woman visited Charlie P at the hospital. Squeezing his hand warmly but holding back her aborted hug—in all fairness to the young lady, there was little left of Charlie P to hug, he had withered down to less than any scale could weigh—the young woman uttered the magic words—"I love you"—which proved to be the miracle cure as demonstrated by a tent pole rising almost immediately like Old Glory in the middle of his bed sheets. Needless to say the doctors were much impressed, signing his discharge papers at once, and Charlie P was released in the young woman's care. Outside the hospital, leaning on the young woman's shoulder while fumbling his way into a cab, one could see the young lady's deft and dexterous harpist's fingers busy at work in Charlie P's pocket. The one with the wallet inside. Secure in the knowledge that if she didn't make it as a professional harpist, she would as a professional pickpocket, this only lifted Charlie P's spirits higher and made for an even speedier recovery. Of course he believed the young woman was only preparing in advance to pay the taxi fare.

Once at home, the young woman put Charlie P to bed. Charlie P, his spirits renewed, anticipating a full recovery, as if given a second lease on life, leaned over and pursed his lips. But despite his apparent good health, and Old Glory once again rising to full mast, the young woman, saying that after such a long and serious illness he needed to sleep, bestowed on him nothing more than her usual peck on the cheek.

"It's only to be expected," said Charlie P. "What else could an old man like myself expect from such a young and beautiful girl. Who comes from a good family, too."

Old habits are hard to break and the next morning as Charlie P hurried to put his pants on, two legs at a time—he couldn't wait to pursue the young woman—he noticed his wallet was missing. So were his credit cards, checkbook, vault keys, safety deposit box, Swiss bank account, stock and bond certificates, and his nest egg for the future. Though old and foolish, his memory was intact and he didn't have to be told twice where his monies had gone. He broke out in a sweat. Not over the lost money, but over the lost young woman who had now for certain made it abundantly clear what she thought of his heart, mind, soul, not to mention his body and pocketbook. It's time to get real, said Charlie P to himself. Look in the mirror. Love is blind but this is ridiculous. From this time on he would dedicate himself to amassing a new fortune.

The young woman, though uninterested in worldly things, but by her own admission an aesthete, a lover of beauty in all its shapes and forms, when hearing of Charlie P's plans for the future, returned, saying she would tag along. If Charlie P was going to seek his pot of gold, what more beautiful sight to behold than the colors of the rainbow.

After many years hard labor, Charlie P finally reached his goal. But the gold nuggets in the pot were so heavy that neither he nor the young woman, or both together, could lift them out. So Charlie P went to get help. When he returned, not only was the pot of gold missing, but so was the young woman.

Somehow, some way, Charlie P made his way back home. Almost fainting from shock when he saw a short missive the young woman had left lying for him on his bed. It read: "It's only to be expected that an old man like you would buy and show a young and beautiful woman like me the world as well as give her all that it is yours to give. And it's also to be expected that you would be overly generous in your praise of my youth and beauty and not fail, even once, to mention the fact of my coming from a good family, too. But what's not to be expected is how an old man like you could expect to receive anything of equal value from a young and beautiful woman like me when you repeatedly referred to me as a girl, never once made reference to my talent as a harpist, and worst of all failed to offer me anything approaching an equal share of the pot of gold we both worked so laboriously hard to find. And so, in the end, though it saddens me to say so, the reason for your failure with me, and why I took more and gave less to you than any man before or since, is because rather than the exception, you only proved a fool. There's no rule like an old rule!

HOW TO EXPLAIN

How to explain Charlie P's behavior of late? Why has he been shirking if not slacking off altogether in his usually routine duties of overseeing and being responsible for world hunger and world peace; the gyrating economy; the cyber culture; the post-nuclear family; the electronic millennium; the manufacturing and packaging of minds and bodies; the repackaging of space; the possibility of time travel; and coming to grips with as well as residing in the future that is already here?

And while we're at it, how about the fact that he's given up scaling the sheer face of the mountain in a single leap. Updating Webster's Dictionary by divesting vowels, consonants, letters and characters from the word. And last but not least, taking the self out of consciousness, and consciousness out of the self, devolving mankind into a prelapsarian state of grace and innocence, equipoise and stasis, and thus relieving him of the burden of being responsible for his own destiny in his unending pilgrimage through geologic time.

No, it's not to be explained by anything so simplistic as Charlie P no longer adhering to the Aristotelian unities of time, place and action. Equally facile would be to put the onus on the hurly burly of modern life. It's just that Charlie P's too busy nowadays. He's got more important things to do. Charlie P's in love. And after each and every date, visit, meeting, encounter with the Bulgarian harpist, the moment he parts company, Charlie P races home to sit by the phone and wait for her call which never comes.

AN APPLE A DAY

Charlie P had his first experience when at grade school. By the time he was in elementary school he was a seasoned veteran. By the time he graduated college his reputation preceded him wherever he went. But despite being welcomed into the best homes, though possessing the worst table manners, and having walked on the moon and the bottom of the ocean, though never leaving his apartment, Charlie P never met a woman who could open his heart.

Whether it be a brief fling, a heated affair, or just a romp in the hay with a lady of dubious reputation, Charlie P never gave any female as much as the time of day And then one morning while buying an apple at a corner fruit and vegetable stand he met the young harpist. They had much in common, or nothing at all, depending upon how you look at it. She had stopped at the same vendor's stand to purchase an apple to save a nickel; he to keep the doctor away. But although a world traveler, possessing an adventurous spirit, and having a standup reputation for never kissing and telling, Charlie P had never met her like. Not a pygmy in the dark continent or an Amazon in the lush tropical forest, not Mme. Pompadour or Lady Godiva, a woman of science or of ill repute, the first lady astronaut or merely the first lady to escape the kitchen, just a modest hard-working student-harpist wearing a weather-beaten frayed coat, with searching eyes, perfect features, and the most bedazzling smile. Charlie P was as if thunderstruck. The young woman penetrated the chink in his armor, demolished the eastern wall of his soul, and what had heretofore been a man, a person, a self-functioning human being, instantly became something less. For the second time in his life, and the last, Charlie P lost his balance and plummeted to earth.

Why now? he asked himself. Why this one? A student-harpist in a tattered coat who buys apples from a fruit and vegetable vendor not even to keep the doctor away, but to save a nickel or a dime.

After several nervous breakdowns, one broken heart, shattered into many pieces, and countless betrayals, disappointments and 'other' boyfriends, Charlie P learned his lesson. Next time he wanted to purchase an apple to keep the doctor away he would sooner climb to the mountain summit, two at a time, Mt. Fugi and Mt. Olympus to name but two, and leap from the precipice into the abyss. It's less dangerous, he says. Sooner or later he's sure to land on good old terra firma, and even if every bone in his body is broken, at least his heart and soul will remain intact.

Besides, if he does fall ill, he can always go to a doctor... that's what they have doctors for.

Charlie P is through being hurt. Here on he will be more discerning in his choice of a mate. Only those women willing to give as much as they receive will he share his too often broken heart with. But these are mere words. Deep down in his private heart Charlie P knows that it is just those women who have scaled the heights who will never stoop low enough to be with him.

THE WRONG WOMAN

Why does Charlie P, a world-acclaimed writer, always choose the wrong woman. Women who utterly and completely reject him. It was not always so. Though always a favorite of the literati, not until the young harpist entered his life did Charlie P win the plaudits of the crowd. Did he turn his alienated worst-sellers into best.

Almost immediately after their first meeting, it was evident that the young woman brought out the worst in him. Neighbors heard him scream and shout each and every time she visited him. Doormen saw him return to his apartment after a date battered and bruised. Utterly miserable, he would rise, after a vain attempt at sleep, to take solitary walks with tears streaming down his grief-stricken face. Returning home in the wee hours, he would go to the typewriter and write the young woman voluminous letters bemoaning all the humiliations, deceptions and betrayals that being with her in the earlier part of the evening had cost him.

Little by little, almost imperceptibly, Charlie P noticed that it was not so much ink as blood pouring out of his veins and on to the letter's page. The whole kit and kaboodle of unrequited love. To his credit he didn't run away from such grief and pain, but surrendered to it completely. Navigating those heretofore unchartered waters as through the eyes of a storm. It wasn't long before Charlie P turned personal crisis to opportunity. Water to wine. His blood-soaked confessional letters into a heartfelt epistolary novel.

Today Charlie P is working on the fourth sequel of his epistolary novel. No longer alienated or circumstantial, they all have the power and virulence, the flesh and blood immediacy of life. And he has no fear of running short of material. For if he does, all he has to do is dial his young friend, take her out for a night, and, by evening's end, he'll experience enough insult and injury not only for the present book, but half a dozen sequels more.

Who knows: if Charlie P keeps dating like this, with his natural flair for language, his technical virtuosity, his hard-won understanding of the perfect balance between art and life, he might even achieve his ultimate goal. Not merely turn worst-sellers to best, but literary immortality.

LOVE IS WAR

L ove is war and Charlie P is constantly under attack. Everything that comes between him and the young harpist fuels its fire and conspires to raze his great love to the ground.

It's a war of attrition, and at any given moment his attention can be diverted, his concentration wane, his focus weaken, and, simply put, he can be attracted to somebody else. On any street corner a Pretty Woman can appear; a Sophisticated Lady can show off her wares at every twist and turn. Wherever he looks and goes, whatever he hears and sees, everything is fraught with danger, temptation abounds. With every turn of the head there's a heaving bosom; with every crane of the neck a flashing smile. The enemy is everywhere: comes in all sizes and shapes, colors and kinds. From three-alarm fires to a whiff of perfume; nostalgic mementos in the secret hiding places of his desk, reminiscences and old memories locked away in his heart. Inside every building and doorway, behind every tree and bush, they lurk; from every angle and position, they gather to attack. All making eyes to win his favor, lead him astray. A willowy and sinuous summertime dress, fireworks in the park; two lovers embracing on the crest of a hill, bodies brushing against each other in a crowd; the hustle and bustle of the day; the sound and fury of the night—his senses are assaulted every which way he turns.

On constant vigil, ever on the alert, as fixed and unseeing as a deer caught in headlights, as rock solid and unyielding as a statue, his perceptions hewn out of plaster of Paris, marble and stone, Charlie P allows no one and nothing, neither temptation nor distraction, common harlot nor holy innocent, to bring his love down.

But what if he relaxes for a moment, puts down his guard, gives up his sword: what if the young harpist turns the corner without his noticing; passes a red light to leave him behind? Or her features convene to another angle, no longer a deer caught in the headlights, more like the sun dipping behind a cloud. What if she disappears from his life, not eternal but ephemeral, not a frozen moment but a passing whim? What happens when the rest of the world comes into view? When Charlie P can at long last discern the real from illusion, the chaff from the wheat? What if the love of his life is not all he made her out to be? What if only for a fleeting second Charlie P opens his eyes and can see?

TWO VERY DIFFERENT WOMEN

Believe it or not, years ago, when young, Charlie P had two very different but equally desirable women offering him their favors. One made him laugh and smile and gave him a sense of contentment just by holding his hand. The other he couldn't keep his hands off. The questions Charlie P asked himself were: Which one, if either, truly loved him? And if one or the other did love him, whose love could he trust? How long would it endure?

That's not to say Charlie P felt himself to be a paragon of virtue. A model citizen. Far from it. He'd be the first to admit that a good pair of legs could drive him to distraction; a whiff of perfume could lead him astray. No doubt about it, in his youth, Charlie P chronically succumbed to the temptations of the flesh. But, of course, knowing this much about himself, he also knew more. It was not only women he didn't trust, he didn't trust himself. Charlie P racked his brains over his problems, deliberated long and hard until he came up with a solution. He would fight his war on two fronts. First outside in the world. Then inside on himself.

After a sleepless night, Charlie P commenced putting his battle plan into action. He corked his bathroom walls. Insulated his entire apartment with three-inch fiberglass. Then he got serious, building towering turrets and spires, moats and drawbridges, ramparts and walls. He even laid down landmines, barbed wire fences, set up machine gun towers; a nuclear missile site; and to the best of his ability, just to be certain he'd have a place to hide in, just in case, a hole in the wall. Having made his home into a fortress, if not a castle, he began working on himself. First, opening the windows to air the rooms out, then hermetically sealing them shut so that not the faintest scent of female flesh could seep in, nor, just as importantly, his own very masculine scent out. Next, after plugging his nose and stuffing his ears with wads of cotton, he turned down the Venetian blinds and blindfolded himself. He even had a doctor friend anaesthetize him, deadening four out of his five senses to the point where he not so much resembled a sleepwalker as a mummified corpse. Resolved not to leave a stone unturned, he even went further, traveling to a medieval monastery where amidst monks and hermits, he ate prairie roots and herbs, beat and pummeled his chest while intoning chants and reciting mantras in an effort to subdue his flesh. Returning, he immediately set back to work in his normal routine, calling upon his not inconsiderable telepathic powers to channel with a certain 19th century Russian novelist to learn about epilepsy, and so doing, after inducing a fit and frothing at the mouth, he proceeded to bite his tongue off therein depriving himself of the last of his five senses. No longer having to concern himself about the temptations of the flesh and other distractions, but still suffering from the more usual ills of over-eagerness and anticipation, curiosity and anxiousness, he raced in a frenzy to his hole in the wall where with the patience of a saint he sat stoically calm waiting to see which if either of the two women would appear. One fact was beyond dispute. Any woman taking the time and making the effort to storm his citadel, penetrate his defenses, must truly love him. Deserve all his trust and love in return.

But what if neither succeeds, or both? Oh well, Charlie P reflected while waiting. That's not so bad. Whether holding hands or not being able to keep one's hands off a woman, any way you look at it, it's all in my hands.

But what's that?! A fly buzzing around Charlie P's nose. Scratching its way to his ear. Charlie P removes his blindfold; the wads of cotton from his nose and ears. He raises the Venetian blinds and opens the windows to let the fly escape and, oh no!—a scent of perfume wafts into the room: and down there, passing diagonally beneath his window, a good pair of legs...

With the zeal of a terrorist, Charlie P proceeded to bring down and destroy all that he had built. The next day, after obtaining all the necessary materials, he began the formidable task of constructing a new structure. One laden with primrose paths, honey and spice, pearly gates and verdant fields. All kinds of goodies and toys to attract not only that woman he couldn't keep his hands off, or the one who made him laugh and smile merely by holding his hand, but where all fair ladies were welcome.

THIS AND THAT

Charlie P cannot keep his mind off women. Wherever he goes his obsession goes with him. Make no mistake about it, he'll do anything to rid himself of this humiliating libidinal malediction.

Following the advice of a sex therapist, Charlie P cultivates interest in music, books, theater; arranges geranium plants in their proper order on the window sill. There's nothing Charlie P won't try or do. But nothing works. It's all to no avail. Everything brings him back to his one primary concern.

At the theater, for example, seated eighth row center, if it's not the chorus girl showing off her wares, then it's the young woman sitting next to him wearing a certain eau de cologne. And what is true at the theater is equally true at the opera, ballet, concerts: from rap to bolero and, of course, good old-fashioned love songs, all sent a chill up his spine and, more importantly, down between his legs. Even his occasional visits to wax museums and mausoleums set his mind racing about those spectral figures in the night.

When it comes to Charlie P's addiction, wherever his five senses are concerned, it's neither this or that but both. There's no country he can visit, no street he can walk, no restaurant he can dine at, where the fair sex doesn't command his attention. Whether it be a nudist colony or a church function, under neon lights in Vegas or thatch huts in the South Seas, flesh and blood reality or Virtual Mary, female flesh is always milling about. Charlie P remains dominated by his five senses. No matter how hard he tries, despite all his efforts, it's futile. He's ready to call it quits. Surrender the fort. Give it up when... suddenly...aha! it's so simple. Why didn't he think of it before. If you can't beat 'em, join 'em. Charlie P decides to join the club. Like those obsessive compulsives who smoke ten thousand cigarettes at a stretch, and, doing so, so sicken of smoking that they give up their addiction, Charlie P decides to sate his desire. Indulge his appetite. Yes, sexual satiety in extremis will liberate him from his demons, free him from his five senses, from this and that.

One, two, a thousand women pass through his portals, take up residence in his bed. Non-stop, assembly line, they come and go. Charlie P vents his passion, relieves his lust, satiates every carnal desire. After a point he can't go on. Thickheaded from sex, dumb with love, his appetite is quenched. He can't see, hear, smell, taste or touch one more body part. Arms, legs, thighs, breasts, asses, vaginas, mean nothing to him. Large and small, hot and cold, soft, firm and fully packed, it's all too much.

Exhausted, depleted, with glazed eyes and a limp penis, Charlie P calls it a night. Switching off the light, shutting his eyes, he slips under the covers. Something stirs beneath him. Scratches his scrotum, pecks at his cheek. He looks down. Noooo! It's not his five senses that are the problem, but his sixth sense. It's not this but that.

THE MOUNTAIN TOP

Every now and then Charlie P gets lucky. A female friend invites him in for the night. Asks him to stay over. Go away for the weekend. Or just to make himself comfortable. It's at those times Charlie P prepares himself for the arduous struggle ahead. Like any man who aspires to climb the heights, he goes out and buys the proper equipment: clothing designed to hold body heat; cleated shoes; snow shoes; skis; ice axes; screw rings; crampons; hammers; ropes; snap hooks; nails of all kinds; as well as respiratory apparatus and instruments for observation like altimeters, clinometers; compasses; range-finders and cameras. But no matter how well prepared, despite all the effort he puts in, the good fight he puts up, no matter how hard he tries to overcome each and every obstacle along the way, it's all to no avail. Like the last rung of a circular ladder, the result is always the same.

And so, after long years of not looking his problem in the eye, at himself in the mirror, this morning Charlie P ordered wall-to-wall mirrors for his SRO, as well as one for his bedroom ceiling—and visited a psychiatrist. His one fear, amongst a thousand others, was that he was beyond therapy.

"What are you afraid of?" said the doctor.

"Who me?! I'm not afraid of anything," answered Charlie P. "Least of all women. If anything, my problem is I love them too much. I don't just put them on a pedestal, but on the mountain top, too."

"And what happens when you reach the mountain top?" said the doctor. "And I want you to let yourself go. Free associate. Don't hold anything back."

"Well, that's a different story," said Charlie P. "To tell the truth, that's when my problem begins:

"Every time I'm about to reach the summit, it's not the city of love I come to, but the city of doom. Not so much a pleasure palace as a disaster area. Not heavenly bliss that awaits me, but the jaws of hell.

"My road to Damascus leads not to the Promised Land, but to sharp-edged crevasses and steep ravines where at any twist and turn, a man can lose his balance and plummet into the abyss.

"Safe harbor, friendly port-of-call, hardly," exclaimed Charlie P. "How can a man feel safe and secure amidst all that mountainous flesh, crags and crannies, overhanging cliffs and precipices, where the loosening of the smallest pebble can start a rockslide leading to an avalanche which can bury him alive?"

"You're doing fine," said the doctor. "But let me ask you for more associations. I think I figured it out."

"Even their perfumed scents and sweet aromas are artfully contrived. Not so much lilies of the field and beds of roses, as they pretend, but byproducts of milk baths and conspicuous consumption, designed to entice you with quick victories, the sweet smell of success, and the bloom of youth. Malodorous odors that spread like poisonous vapors, and once ingested, can kill you on the spot.

"And rather than luxuriate in her warm shelter, find peace and comfort in her peaks and valleys, it's as if I'm hanging on for dear life on a mountain ledge, a chink in the rock. And when she opens herself to take me in, it's not so much one of life's great wonders, a true marvel, as nature intended, but rather she seems as large as the Grand Canyon which I can lose myself in; an ocean where I can be swept away and swallowed up by a tidal wave, and buried at the bottom of the sea.

"I don't know about other men," continued Charlie P, "but to me a woman's embrace is fraught with the gravest dangers; her arms and legs are like grappling hooks and her fingers like pincers of steel; and once you're caught in her vice-like grip, there's no getting out."

"Alright, those are your associations," said the doctor. "Have you given me as much as you can give?"

"It's beyond me," exclaimed Charlie P, "how anyone lying in that flesh valley, Grand Canyon, mountain cave, when everything about it is manufactured and designed with but one intent, to squeeze the life out of you, swallow you whole, crush you to death, bury you alive, never let you escape: How anyone..."

"Okay. That's enough," said the doctor. "Now I want you to listen to me very carefully. Your problem isn't serious. Other than agoraphobia and a bad case of vertigo, it's just a simple matter that you bought the wrong equipment."

The following morning Charlie P purchased enough digging equipment to mine for gold and drill for oil at the bottom of the earth; buried treasure at the bottom of the sea; the family jewels under the creakiest floorboards; and in the name of thoroughness, just to be absolutely safe, he additionally employed a paleontologist renowned for discovering ancient treasures, relics of antiquity, by excavating our lime and strata beginnings.

SOMEBODY FOR EVERYBODY

There's somebody for everybody, says Charlie P. So why not him? Why does he sleep alone at night? Remain loveless: a hermit and a bachelor, a social isolate, and have no place to call home? But love plays no favorites. Has little use for lovers in heat unless they prove to be the exception to the rule. Tribal customs, daily habits, the everyday and commonplace hold no interest for her who, in past seasons, only catered to the lofty and sublime. Proved a meeting place where star-crossed lovers and preordained destinies could mix and marry for better or worse. But what once was is no more, exclaims Charlie P. Only logic and reason prevail today; the measurable and actual; the virtual and sleight-of-hand. And love, as he knows it, doesn't distinguish between, and cares less for, the individual or the mass, success or failure, the man in power or majority rule, and the current belief that two is no longer greater but still better than one. And least of all for men and women and their stupid disputes. To be sure, says Charlie P: Love is preter-naturally callous and cruelly indifferent to all they proclaim, propagate and value.

And knowing this, Charlie P also knows that love takes not the remotest interest in his own particular predilections and concerns; doesn't keep count of his track record; judge or measure the merits of his argument. To love, whether he bore witness or helped contribute to the past's great events, or is the prophet of the future, he's just another stat on the sheet; a glint in the eye; a moment in time; a perpetrator of the status quo; a precursor of what's to come and never will be; both a fiction and a fact.

And so, Charlie P chooses to sleep alone at night. Accepts his lot, bends his will, yields to superior forces. Remains loveless: with no place to call home. Truth is he doesn't want to be disturbed. "Even the most devoted wife, elegant mistress, captivating girlfriend snores from time to time," he says. "Cracks an elbow in your ribs, twines a heavy leg around your middle." It's difficult enough to get through the day in today's world, without having to worry about the oestrus of night.

"MAKING IT"

B orn an ugly duckling, everybody expected Charlie P to develop into a swan. His college yearbook said he'd make it big or not at all. But as the years went by Charlie P got lost in the crowd. Though many who knew him were either disappointed or glad, especially the yearbook editor, to his credit Charlie P adjusted to his fate quite well. It was as if a heavy burden had been lifted off his back. After struggling so much of his life, he no longer had to "make it." Without having to justify, explain or apologize to anybody, he could do what he wanted to do. With nothing to prove, no sense of urgency about tomorrow, or sense of failure today, at long last Charlie P could be no more and no less than himself.

CHARLIE P'S LECTURE ON LOVE

Charlie P has been asked to give a lecture on love. It's a subject he knows much about. He's confident he can hold any audience spellbound. He has much wisdom to impart. After all, who can boast of as many conquests as he? Can recount as many adventures and seductions? Women from all over the world have flocked to his bed. Wait for him at every port-of-call.

Once started, Charlie P goes on lecturing for hours, days, months. Not once does he look up from his notes stacked on 3x5 cards seated on the podium, much less take a break. His performance skills and vocal delivery are at least the equal of his text. Without a doubt, Charlie P's lecture will serve as a model and paradigm on the subject for years to come.

Finally, his lecture over, Charlie P peers up from the podium only to notice that his audience has left. Not a single person remains in the auditorium.

After much deliberation, Charlie P addresses the sponsors of the event. "It's a sign of the times," Charlie P says. "People today lack imagination. They want biography not fiction."

LEARNING FROM MISTAKES

Charlie P visits an eye specialist at the clinic and purchases a pair of glasses. He removes the prisms and replaces them with black, oval-shaped lenses. He covers his eyes with gauze, cotton, a bandanna and handkerchief. A walking stick and seeing eye dog complete his attire. Good. Not a glimmer of light. Not a glint. He can't see a thing. Now he can walk through the streets without fear of distraction. No longer will temptation get the better of him. Ignorance is bliss and what he can't see he won't miss. From rare festive occasions to familiar daily rituals, from a black hole to a ticker-tape parade, from a Ugandan Lake Victoria fisherman to the Hauonani of the Amazonian rain forest, and especially the dark-eyed women of Zanzibar—nothing and nobody will catch his eye. Deter him from his goal. At long last Charlie P can go in peace.

But peace is not so easily obtainable for Charlie P: A car hits him, a bus crushes him, and after falling down a manhole, and then from a subway platform, a train splits him in two. Learning from his mistakes, Charlie P removes his glasses, gauze, cotton, bandanna and handkerchief. Lucky for him his cell phone is still working. And makes a call. No, not the eye doctor—no disrespect intended, but first thing tomorrow morning he schedules appointments with the ear, nose and throat specialists at the clinic.

YOU'VE COME A LONG WAY BABY

Whether by chance, accident, or fortuitous circumstance, one day, as luck would have it, Charlie P runs into his lifelong friend in a convalescent home. His friend has been there three months and the doctors have only recently informed him that he's well on the way to recovery. He'll be as good as new in another week or two. But his friend has other problems: His mother, just last week, was brought into the home suffering from a severe stroke, senile dementia, Alzheimer's disease, and half a dozen other maladies directly attributable to old age. The doctors can do little or nothing for her. The old woman just sits in a stupor all day long, stone petrified, staring blankly at the four walls like a decomposing corpse.

Not waiting for the elevator, Charlie P races to the staircase down the back end of the corridor, leaping up and over the eighteen flights in a single bound. His memory filled to the brim, he can't wait to see the dear old lady. He had virtually grown up in her home. All his life she had been so good and kind to him. His earliest memories were of her in the kitchen fixing him cookies and milk when a boy, offering him advice and counsel during his awkward adolescent years, and no matter how wild he got, how difficult, she was nothing short of a saint and a martyr to him all throughout his youth.

Sitting with the ancient lady for a lengthy hour or two, the hours alternating between her weeping uncontrollably and a torrent of silence and immobility, not a word passes between them. Slanting rays of sunlight fall on the floor. Crisply starched white linen nurses hurry by. Finally Charlie P's friend arrives, wheeled in by a favorite nurse. The moment the old woman spots her son and nurse she lets loose such a bacchanal of shrieks and howls—calling her son and nurse: whore, bum, slut, bitch, bastard, and other such apocryphal locker room epithets that would more than do justice to the entire naval fleet on the seven seas.

"So much for nice old lady," Charlie P says to his friend. "You never know what's in people's minds. Still," he tells him: "You must look at the good side. Maybe now that she's finally let all that venom and bile stored up over a lifetime out, maybe now she'll get better, or worse. Either way at least you'll know your real mother, not simply a Janus-faced stick figure stuck in the kitchen, but a fully developed three-dimensional person. For certain her stay here has done her well. Allowed her to realize her full potential." Turning to the old woman who was by now furiously pounding her fists into her son's chest as brutal as hammer strokes, Charlie P says: "You've come a long way, baby."

PARADISE

All his life Charlie P has put it off. But now it's time. Fear
and trembling have held him back long enough. Today,
at the crack of dawn, as soon as he returns from the office,
he'll sit in that favorite rocking chair of his, click it into cruise
control, rock back and forth, to and fro, and be off. He's tired
of being a laughingstock, it's time to join the human race, pay
his dues. Wherever the journey takes him, whatever the future
brings, one way or another he'll get through the day, make it
to the top, he tells loved ones and friends before departing.
He's always wanted to climb the heights, see the sights he's
only heard others talk so much about. That paradisiacal land
where one can lay his head on her soft bosom to rest; drink
mother's milk. And now it's his turn.

The most difficult part of the journey is taking the first
step. Once he's done that, it's clear sailing, a pleasure trip.
And, at first, it's true. It's everything he expected. The waters
are calm, the foliage luxuriant, cows and sheep graze in the
meadows, the land is rich with precious stones, nourishing
food, milk and honey. And fun and games, peals of laughter, much merriment, warm, happy faces abound everywhere.

And looming in the distance, above it all, Mount Nipple: Why the view alone must be worth the price of admission from up there. And Charlie P is making good progress. He's already well past the midpoint. But with each advancing step, the trek becomes increasingly dangerous. That crevice in the rock, for example, no longer holds his footing. And there's nothing to grip onto to steady his balance on these slippery slopes. Only crevices and fissures, and a sharp-edged precipice which hardly affords him a moment's respite. To be sure, there's no stopping at a friendly inn for a warm meal, good conversation and a warm bed. And he still has a long way to go. His goal seems even further off than when he started. Maybe it's because night's approaching. The crepuscular light seems peculiar and, what's that? a scream, a shout, sounds more like an Indian's war cry; and those two figures up ahead, clashing swords, knocking heads, if he didn't know better, one looks like a cucumber, the other like something cavernous and round with a curvaceous shape. For certain, it's a female, but what kind of woman fights like that? Yes, there's a war going on, the same old war time immemorial, the Penis Erecti versus the Vaginal Orgasms, and that handsome cucumber turns out to be no less than Macho Machismo, the peerless leader of the Penis Erecti; and the Amazon with the curvaceous shape and mammoth breasts, that's Femme Bastale, an Orgasm of the first rank. Charlie P has never seen such savagery, such butchery. Body parts splayed everywhere: buttocks, penises, breasts, hands, arms, legs, lips and tongues strewn all about. His resolve to reach the heights notwithstanding, and despite the fact that he's waited all his life to make this trek, he asks himself: Is it worth risking his life for? Maybe he should just stay hidden behind this scrub brush and see how things develop. Wait the war out. But he has to admit. Those Vaginal Orgasms are not only beautiful, but courageous. Every bit the equal of those muscle-bulging tumescent Erecti fighting in the moonlight. Just look how they stand their ground, taking on every rogue's leer with a swing of their hips and an inscrutable smile. It's enough to bedazzle any soldier. But neither side seems to have an advantage, neither gives or takes an inch. Both sexes take on all challenges, show themselves more than equal to the task.

But these are dizzying heights, the air's too thin, his head's in a spin, and all of a sudden Charlie P finds himself in the heat of battle, joining forces with both sides at once. Coming to the rescue of a Vaginal Orgasm in distress as well as a dismembered Erecti hanging on by a thread. It feels good for once in his life to be on the right side. So much so that his chest swells with pride squirting mother's milk, and his penis bows in humility no longer having to bear the weight of male hubris. And with this victory, personal if not military, Charlie P comes to understand something about himself that he's never known before. He's not only drawn to the heights, but equally attracted to the depths. And it's at that moment, feeling as if he can overcome any obstacle, he leaps from the precipice, past both warring factions as if they were nothing more than old men and children playing mindless war games, and lands in what appears to be a bottomless pit.

But the waters are cold and choppy, the currents too strong, he's being pulled under, and as he desperately makes his way toward the light at the end of the tunnel, he rummages through his backpack for a lifesaver, a raft, anything at all to help keep his head above water, but all he finds is his old, now waterlogged baggage weighing him down. It's impossible to swim in these waters. And just when he's caught in a whirlpool and being carried out to sea, when things look hopeless, he's out...and back on earth again with his feet planted firmly on the ground. For a moment he wonders what it might have been like had he made it to the other side. Still, not all is a loss, he concludes. He's gained valuable insight on his journey. He now not only knows the dangers involved in reaching the heights, but also what it means to just get back to where he started. Somewhere between heaven and earth, the mountain's base and top, dream and reality, lies all he wants and will never obtain. Now, his head no longer filled with dreams of paradise or hellish demons, he can see, and more importantly appreciate, what it means to live on earth.

Besides, if his life proves anything, it proves that he's never really believed in old wives' tales about the feminine mystique. That kind of nonsense was promulgated by Hollywood to sell tickets. By misfit poets and romantic losers who find life so unbearable they have to invent their own. And mostly by women to make themselves interesting. For certain, Charlie P has learned his lesson. Next time the urge comes upon him to ride his rocking chair, take such a journey, he'll take along his remote control. That way at least if the waters get rough, his date turns out poorly, the program's not to his liking, he'll not only be able to choose his own war to fight, but click onto another channel.

When Charlie P came home from vacation he resolved to do two things. One, go on vacation again. Two, put it off for as long as he could. That way he would always have something to look forward to.

When Charlie P retires for the night he opens his eyes and puts the lights on. Why not? It's only when fast asleep that he's able to see.

AN INTERESTING CONVERSATION

Charlie P has taken up residence in the morgue. It is the only place he feels he can sleep. Certainly nobody there will wake him with unwanted conversations. Better than his formerly soundproofed abode. But even there, at the morgue, Charlie P cannot sleep. In the wee hours, just before dawn, when sleep for him comes, if it comes at all, Charlie P hears voices. Indistinguishable, non-translatable, alien sounds; other-worldly, funereal, sepulchral tones, but voices just the same. Still, it must be admitted that Charlie P is not really too annoyed. The fact is this conversation was not only the first, but by far the most interesting he has heard in a lifetime.

DO YOU KNOW THE DIFFERENCE...?

"**D**o you know the difference between an artist and a businessman?" said Charlie P in one of his many arguments with the young harpist. "I'll tell you."

"A businessman is interested in power, lives for power, first and always is power, he's a power monger. No amount of money or power is enough for him. Only those things tangible and palpable, of flesh and blood reality, those things he can touch, smell, see and hear, interest him. To obtain those things he instrumentalizes and manipulates the world. Accumulation, more and more is his sole aim and credo. His raison d'être and clarion call."

Charlie P pauses for a deep breath. When he continued his voice had changed noticeably.

"The artist on the other hand pursues truth and meaning, and the making of all things beautiful. He has no use for the tangible and the palpable. The functional and the material. He's sensitive and delicate and cannot pass a glowing sun or a pale moon or a patch of cloud or a sheet of rain without stopping to gaze in awe and wonder. He lives in the clouds with only the starry constellations spinning in his head."

"Just as I thought," said the young harpist. "I know the difference."

"You do?"

"Yes. And I prefer the businessman."

THE PERFECT MOMENT

I t's not that Charlie P's lazy, lacks courage, curiosity, or even imagination that prevents him from leaving his apartment, writing his novel, living his life. That makes him cold as the devil, indifferent as death, as reconciled to the world and all its machinations as a stone. No, rather it's his pursuit of the Perfect Moment. Why start what you can't finish, says Charlie P. What's the point unless you can live forever. A man of his word, Charlie P has scoured the earth and heavens from time immemorial searching for immortality. That single aim, ultimate goal, not only tells us more about him than we need to know, but allows him to wear his badge of honor, heraldic coat of arms, with grandeur and pride, and distinguishes him from all the rest.

How else to explain his efforts from the earliest recorded date (4236 B.C.) to organize his life according to the movements of the sun, moon and stars; though, of course, erring on most calculations. His pursuit of the Perfect Moment ranges from the calendrical markings gouged into eagles' bones 13,000 years ago to the atomic clocks of today. From proving the existence of God through an algebraic formula to capturing transcendence with a camcorder. His peregrinations span the world from Egyptian hieroglyphics and print-based linearity and logic to the semi-arbitrary serendipity of hypertexts; from Mayan observatories at Chicen Chichen Itza to logics that govern universes other than our own. Charlie P's search for the Perfect Moment comes before and continues after the invention of the Aztec calendar, Gregorian calendar, Julian calendar, and the global inrush of digital data across a screen.

Throughout the millennia he's joined league with explorers and wanderers of all sects and faiths on their pilgrimage to find the Perfect Moment. From Columbus at sea, Lindbergh in the air, Armstrong walking the moon, to strolling the grounds at Yasnaya Polyana with the great 19th century Russian author, Leo Nikolaevich Tolstoy, discussing war and peace, love and marriage.

And yet the question must be asked: Is Charlie P's search in vain? Is it all for naught? For if one quality essentializes our modern age it is motion. Speed. Time marches on. Disposable goods. Interchangeable parts. Next! Ever since Euclid's geometry fell from favor, opening up a Pandora's box of relativism, things have run amok. Gone haywire. Chaos not only reigns but has become an integral part of scientific method as well as law. Everyone feels they deserve an equal place in the world and races to be at all places at once. Haste not waste is the order of the day. The clarion call of our post-maddening technocratic age. And so faster and faster has Charlie P traversed through the centuries until finally reaching our channel-flipping, fast-forwarding electronic age. But if we ask Charlie P what is he racing for? Where will his journey take him? He'll be the first to admit—if he stops for a millisecond to reflect, if he's kind enough to answer—to no other place than the office of that last hope, third opinion, final verdict doctor who tells him in a hushed voice, with the whispered intensity of a sorcerer's incantation, not whether he'll live or die, but when.

As soon as Charlie P gets home tonight he must remind himself to call Joe, the handyman. He needs more shelf space for all those books he will never read.

A SPECIAL MEETING

Charlie P convenes a special meeting. Some of his oldest and dearest friends attend. All women. All man-haters. In attendance are: a spinsterish librarian whose only contact with the opposite sex are the male characters she reads about in books. A society beauty as famous for her peculiar persuasions as the fact that she gave up on men long ago. And an animal rights activist who not only gave up on men, but the entire human race as well. Likewise there's a nun from a medieval monastery still residing in the same crenelated tower she was born in four to five centuries earlier; and the first Pope's first wife which ecclesiastical history teaches us has not only resented the fact that they were never married, but has qualms about his celibacy, and never forgave herself for competing for his affections against that celestial mate whom nobody can compete with. Toss in Brunhilde, Hard-hearted Hannah, and Virgin Mary, countless more man-killers, sexual abstainers and old maids, and you have the entire congregation.

Almost at once his friends recognize Charlie P has a problem. Something he's not able to talk about just yet. He'll get round to it when he's ready, they tacitly agree amongst themselves. Not wasting time, Charlie P gets right to the point. He's brought them together to share his good fortune. He's finally met the woman of his dreams. Though he knows there's no harsher judge of women than women, particularly man-haters, he doesn't want them to take what he says in the wrong way. The fact that he hasn't had one good day, or night's sleep, since meeting her has little to do with it. If giving is its own reward, he's the richest man on earth. She brings out the best in him. He never knew he possessed such tenderness and affection. Such generosity of spirit. Not a day goes by that he doesn't give her something. He can't pass a store window without seeing something that will please her. Only last week, at great personal expense and inconvenience, he brought back and laid down at her feet the Seven Wonders of the World, moon and stars, as well as a girl's best friend.

"But then why haven't you had a good day since meeting her?" asks Brunhilde.

"And why can't you sleep?" says the medieval nun.

"And more importantly how do you know she feels the same way about you?" says the spinsterish librarian and an old maid schoolmarm in unison.

"Because I make her happy," retorts Charlie P. "Every time I show up at her door a smile beams across her face that could light up the entire night sky."

A knowing look passes amongst the good ladies. Glances are exchanged as well as a collective wink and nod.

"And other than your own generosity, what do you ask for in return?" rings out the entire congregation as one.

"Why nothing," answers Charlie P. "What do you think, I'm stupid? Why spoil a good thing!"

BUSY DAY

Charlie P awakes at dawn. He performs his morning ablutions. He dresses. He eats breakfast. He sharpens his pencils. He organizes the papers at his desk. He reads the newspapers. He walks around the room, back and forth, to and fro. He walks around the block, back and forth, to and fro. He eats lunch. He sits in his favorite chair. He stands up. He sits down. He peers out the window. He reads his junk mail. He walks around the room, back and forth, to and fro. He walks around the block, back and forth, to and fro. He peers out the window. He takes a nap. He plays the radio, stereo, watches TV. He makes supper. He changes his clothes, puts on a shirt, tie, and dress jacket. He eats supper. Half a cantaloupe, chicken and Bulgarian salad. He empties the garbage into a large corrugated aluminum rubbish container by the back service elevator. He walks around the block, back and forth, to and fro. He eats his chocolate brownie with milk. He watches TV. The 11 o'clock news. He yawns. He looks up at the wall clock. He goes to bed. He's had another busy day.

A NOVEL IN HIM...

Charlie P has a novel in him. He rummages through his closet and lifts out his old IBM Selectric. He goes to the stationery store and purchases all necessary supplies. He has a custom-made desk built with sundry drawers, shelves, nooks and crannies, to accommodate his typewriter, manuscript, drafts, first through last, reams of paper, as well as manuals, bulletins, digests, and all books relevant to the task such as Webster's Treasury of Synonyms, Antonyms and Homonyms. He makes calls and follow-up appointments with editors, bookworms and literati, all the so-called experts in the field, to explore the relative merits of his idea. He discusses with agents, publishers and marketing people the advances he might receive and the profits to be made not only by a U.S. publication, but in motion picture, television, dramatic, radio and foreign sales. He attends countless lectures and visits daily the 42nd Street Public Library where he reads every available book on the subject. He finds a cubbyhole in the labyrinthine bowels of the library where, after winning the welcome of man-eating rodents, he nestles down overnight, on weekends and holidays. He takes notes and fills up one if not a thousand yellow lined pads with pertinent data. He braves the new world, scanning the internet and chatting online (for the first time in his life) to enhance and increase his chances at finding those books not available at the library. He spends hours, days, months and years walking the aisles and scrutinizing the shelves of old neighborhood bookstores as well as corporate chains like Barnes & Noble and Borders to make certain that his book has not already been written. He lets theme and plot, cast of characters and characterizations, language and imagery, and, of course, the central metaphor, gestate inside him like a new-born babe. He filters every sensation, perception, feeling and experience through him for what seems like a lifetime and more. He treads to his desk. He clicks on the typewriter. He presses his fingers to the keyboard and nothing comes out.

NEWSPAPERS, MAGAZINES
AND VCR TAPES

Whatever you might say about him, Charlie P is not the type to let the world pass him by. He knows all too well how helter-skelter and confusing things can become in today's world; how rapidly everything changes. How what was pronounced as state-of-the-art and a breakthrough only yesterday is already outmoded, obsolete and antiquated today.

To ameliorate this situation and in an effort to keep up with the times Charlie P collects newspapers and magazines. Not the kind that one can purchase at the corner newsstand, but from time immemorial, past, present and future. It's only having secured this information, documenting completely and accurately the world's events, that he feels even a modicum of assurance. More than a calendar, stat sheet or map of the world, which merely furnishes him with facts and figures, dates and piecemeal information, these oracular pages decrypt the entropy and chaos of our times like a code; serve as the mark and measure of his life. No more confusion and doubt, no more cluttering up his mind with lop-sided chicaneries, preposterous inanities, gap-toothed smiles and double-edged words, they keep him abreast of what transpires every day, year, decade, every century of his life. Once again he knows the absolute certitude of past centuries. Once again he has something palpable and real to sink his teeth into, count on, grab on to; a longitude, latitude and fixed point to guide his every move. Without such information it's near impossible for Charlie P to make sense and order of the world. To know who he is and where he's going. He resides in a dream-like virtual world where uncertainty and confusion reign supreme.

The magazines and papers pile up. Fill every nook and cranny. His room resembles not so much a great library as a highlight reel of newspaper headlines and magazine covers. Somehow, manifesting extraordinary skill and industry, Charlie P catalogues and puts into order the world's most significant people and events: Science, business, religion, technology, politics, all the great disciplines, events and occurrences come under his sphere and sway. Someday soon he will study this mountainous heap and discover who he and his world have been and are.

But it's all too much. So many words in print. So much information to digest. Charlie P is overwhelmed by the sheer size and mass of it. But ever resourceful and flexible, Charlie P knows it's easier to listen than to read. Who reads nowadays anyway? Charlie P commences to transfer every magazine and newspaper, each and every word in print to electronic form on computer disc. It doesn't take long. A lifetime or two at most. But, finally, his Promethean task is completed. He's recorded both for himself and posterity all that is salient and germane. In fact he's up to today's current headlines when...

...Aghast! How did this happen?! Charlie P neglected to label the computer discs either by subject, name or date. They have no beginning, middle or end. July follows August, winter precedes fall. Nothing remains but a cacophony of sounds and noises. Donald Duck and looney tunes. Cheated out of his own biography and feelings, Charlie P seeks an Olympian answer to an existential question. What can he do? He has no recourse but one. Opening the window wide, he tosses out the entire computer disc collection. Then, half stumbling, half staggering to the ledge, he languorously spreads his arms and, with tail twitching, wings flapping, in utter disarray and confusion like his discs, he follows them out the window to the abyss. At long last Charlie P has become part and parcel of the world.

AWAKE OR ASLEEP,
DREAM OR REALITY

For some inexplicable reason that was all too clear to him, Charlie P has always preferred sleep to waking hours, dreaming to reality. He asked no more than to be allowed to sleep all day. He'd gladly endure the occasional nightmare and demon, sea monster and gargoyle, for the sake of such somnambulistic bliss. They come with the territory, said Charlie P. It's well worth the risk.

His annual New Year's resolution was nothing less than to curl up on his living room couch, lie full length on the ocean floor, bury himself under the covers for the entire coming year. No amount of fat in his diet, meat on his plate, salt in the ocean, fish in the sea, could dissuade him from wiling away the hours in Morpheus' bed. Anything and everything is preferable, said Charlie P, to having to reside in so-called reality.

But those times have passed. Nowadays Charlie P has a dilemma. His life is no longer so simple. Logic and reason no longer prevail. The walls of Jericho have come tumbling down and with them all rules of the game. Chronology and the laws of time and space hold no more sway over reality than dreaming; pay no more heed to waking hours than sleep. And so reality and dreams have melted and merged; waking life and sleep have fused and coalesced; leaving most standing on shifting sands. With no internal restrictions or external restraints, men and women today create their own narratives, invent their own lives. From the bottomless depths to the rarefied heights they sink or swim.

Oh well, says Charlie P. If that's the way the world is then I'll just have to make the best of it. The first law of the jungle is to survive. In the end it all amounts to the same thing anyway. And so, turning insoluble dilemma into solvable problem, Charlie P adapts. Asleep or awake, Charlie P dreams his life away while living his life to the full.

Charlie P's wall clock with Roman numerals has broken. It ticks where it used to tock. But that's not what's bothering Charlie P. He's never been early for anything in his life, and he's not about to start now. A rooster's cockle-doodle-doo in the morning, a quick glance to the heavens, a factory siren at night. Church bells tolling, his neighbor's grandfather clock's chime, children coming home from school, life going on like clockwork tells him all he needs to know. And if that doesn't work, like in the army, he can always double-time here and back, to and fro. No. It's not a matter of knowing what time it is, but knowing what to do with his time.

GENEROUS TO A FAULT

Not any of the women Charlie P's known in his life can say anything but that he's the most thoughtful and caring man, generous to a fault. Not a day passes by when you won't find him in any of a dozen stores: department stores, gift shops, specialty shops, boutiques, shopping for a gift for the women in his life. It's not an exaggeration to say that every sales girl and store manager in the greater New York City area knows him by first name. Charlie P never fails to find a reason to remember a special occasion when the purchase of a present is not warranted. Whether it be for the day they met or married; had their first date or first born; became engaged or shared a golden wedding anniversary; or for Christmas, New Year's, Thanksgiving, Mother's Day, or Fourth of July; or just like that; for no reason at all; because he felt like it; Charlie P never misses an opportunity to lavish the most generous gifts and presents on the women in his life.

The fact that he's a misogynist and celibate all his life, as well as a confirmed bachelor; was separated and divorced years ago, never married; only makes his generosity all the more remarkable. Especially when you stop and consider that his bank account is empty; his checking account overdrawn, and all his credit cards either voided or cancelled since his years as a wayward youth.

But next Tuesday is Valentine's Day and though, technically speaking, he doesn't have a single female friend, knowing him, Charlie P won't use that as an excuse to disappoint them.

All your fingers know is to knead female flesh, your lips to form rogue's leers; to walk around with a bulge in your pants and reduce us all to a roll in the hay; and after every conquest, with your Johnny hanging out, to strut around like a cock-of-the-walk; says a female friend to Charlie P. Don't worry, answers Charlie P. Times are changing, there's cause for optimism; with the new technologies and advances in science, I'm certain my poor behavior won't go on for too much longer.

THE MOST BEAUTIFUL GIRL
IN THE WORLD

A psychologist asks Charlie P to take a projective test. Various photographs of women's faces will be shown him and Charlie P is to interpret their character. Always one to miss an opportunity, never eager or willing to try out new things, this time, for reasons inexplicable to us, Charlie P agrees to make himself available.

At first he does remarkably well. Making comment on the faces put before him in clear and concise tones. But suddenly, coming upon a particularly well-formed and harmonious face, he hesitates. Holding his gaze, he asks the psychologist to adjust the light at varying angles so as to highlight the facial features from different perspectives. He goes on studying the face like this for an inordinate period of time. Finally, speaking slowly, but for that reason with even greater conviction, he says: "This woman is an angel; a paragon of virtue; the blessed Holy Mother; Mother Teresa and Joan of Arc in one. Without a doubt she's kind, loving, loyal, and generous. All that is good and right about the world. No man could do better than to be with such a woman."

After the test, Charlie P refuses the meager payment from the psychologist (he's on an academic stipend and can't afford more) but does have one request instead. "Who is the woman? Where can I meet her?" He implores the psychologist to introduce him to his model. The fact, as the psychologist informs him, that the woman is a convicted murderer, a known man-killer, has served time and been incarcerated for having killed four husbands, her own parents and children; leveled five kingdoms; and purposely and deliberately was responsible for spreading the plague in the Middle Ages as well as our own modern time; not to mention knocking the earth off its axis in twenty-one different centuries, and before that, too—doesn't deter Charlie P. He's seen her face. He's in love. A little thing like a lady's past won't change his mind. In fact, only adds to her allure. Beauty like hers pierces the heart. And Charlie P's heart was pierced the moment he saw her photo; perhaps even before if such things are possible.

And who's to say he's wrong. Follow-up tests by the psychologist show that the marriage has lasted almost fifty years now. And other than a few petty squabbles, several short-term disagreements (on both their parts), and some admittedly nasty confrontations (not unlike most marriages nowadays), Charlie P still loves the woman as much as the first time he saw her. And all this despite her white hair, crooked spine, putrefying flesh, and a smile that doesn't glow as brightly or warmly as in her youth.

"All that doesn't matter," says Charlie P.

It doesn't! Then what does? How does he explain his marriage's success?

"It's simple," says Charlie P. "Every night just before turning the lights out I turn to the night table and take a long look at the photograph taken more than a half-century ago. Then, after shutting off the lights, and that's crucial, and uttering a quick prayer of gratitude to the psychologist—if not for him!—I make love all night long to the most beautiful girl in the world."

LARGER QUESTIONS

Charlie P has always prided himself on asking the larger questions: Why does an acclaimed author, a Ph.D in literature, a man of letters—not to mention a dabbler in writing fiction and a dilettante—always turn his head when a woman passes him by on the street and stare at her bottom? For all the fair sex's considerable assets, why is his first instinct invariably to settle his gaze on the shape of their asses? Certainly they have other redeeming qualities he could focus his attention on: The size of their breasts, for example; the sweet plunge of their cleavage; the shapeliness of their legs. Who knows, says Charlie P, besides possessing pretty faces most women are jaunty dressers, especially in summer. But the truth is, and Charlie P would be the first to admit this, he has never figured out what to do with a woman's breast other than to squeeze it; her face other than to ogle it; or her ass other than to grope it.

For the longest time now Charlie P has pondered these and even more challenging questions. But for all his scholarship and erudition the best answer he's come up with is: "Attention must be paid," paraphrasing a well-known American playwright. For some that might suffice, but for Charlie

P who hasn't attended a theatrical performance since the price of admission became exorbitant, it won't do. He needs more. And so he poses another—the old argument of nature versus nurture. What nurture has to do with it, he'll never know, but nature, he says, has her own powerful reasons. At least as powerful as the senses. In short, you can't fight City Hall. And if that doesn't settle the argument, then there's always: it's fate, or genetic, character is destiny, you can't keep a good man down (same thing), and if you want real proof, irrefutable evidence, he exclaims, just take a gander at the monkey in the jungle who mesmerizes the male of the species with her rainbow-colored rear end. In that way only is her calling realized, her destiny fulfilled. The fate of her species assured.

But why then, asks Charlie P, is he constantly thwarted in his efforts to follow his own instincts to consummate nature's end? What the Greeks called Eros. Freud: libido or the Life Instinct. Darwin: Natural Selection, or in the larger context, the propagation, no, the very survival of the species. In any event, it goes without saying that when the urge, drive, life force, libido, "whatever" is denied, not only do long-suppressed tensions and misplaced aggressions manifest themselves, but also high blood pressure, inchoate rages, primal screams, madness and insanity, aberrations and pathology, deviance and perversity, and not to exaggerate, world wars. And in Charlie P's case, in particular, a bad case of hives. In sum and in short, the whole fiasco is thrown out of whack.

But if we mention all this, exclaims Charlie P, in all fairness we also must mention the fact that opposites attract. The paradoxical if not contradictory nature of man: Out of chaos comes harmony, checks and balances, good manners and bad taste; and not only that opposites attract but also the old Cause and Effect theorems of determinism, Pavlov's S/R, the Cartesian ego, mind/body splits, all manner and kinds of dualisms...and more accurately, more to the point, when thwarted and blocked, the well-known and incontestable fact that only then does the artist, poet, philosopher, novelist, all creators make their appearance on the scene and contribute to the aggregate sum of what is commonly called Human Culture. And who can really say, other than modern day science which teaches us it's all one, how such denial and blockage effects the cyclical nature of the seasons; the laws of time and motion; cosmological goings on; not to mention our very own human future.

Whatever the case, one way or another, these last several summers Charlie P has noticed that many women nowadays have taken to the habit of wrapping sweaters around themselves to hide their best features. Why, sighs Charlie P? Why do they and their kind bespoil one of the few remaining pleasures left him in life not to mention the manifold benefits mentioned above. For a thinking man like himself the questions are endless. Is that what is meant by the inscrutable nature of woman? The symbolic as well as parabolic significance of Adam and Eve, good and evil, the nature of sin, the current theory of chaos, the existential and post-existential precept that uncertainty is the only certainty: or maybe it's simply our puritan forebears kicking up dust. Or the result of a shrill-voiced chauvinist screaming aloud across oceans (as well as deserts): "Keep them in the kitchen. Don't let them out of the bedroom. Cover them completely head to toe."

Que sera, sera, and at the risk of imputing facile interpretations, one thing's for certain, concludes Charlie P. Regardless of what brings men and women together it's a whole lot better than scraping some skin off his finger and cloning his like.

After learning that a certain Manhattan-based actor-director-writer undressed every woman he saw in his mind, Charlie P walked around the world in 80 days before collapsing. "Why didn't you at least ride a hot air balloon?" said the doctor. "No chance," answered Charlie P. "That way I wouldn't have been able to get close enough to see them."

A MAN WHO CAN LISTEN

Though he's not about to advertise, market or merchandise it, in fact, rather than share the wealth, he's more apt to cork and bottle it, Charlie P knows exactly why he's so popular with the ladies.

Certainly it has nothing to do with his table manners. He hardly knows the difference between a spoon and a fork, much less an entrée from dessert. And, of course, not that he's noticed, he chews his food with his mouth open, and with both hands, arms and elbows on the table. To be sure, an elegant French restaurant means no more, even less to him, than a pizza joint. And his idea of prime grade choice meat is a Big Mac. Add to this that there's no counting how many dishes he's broken when on those rarest of occasions he lends a helping hand; and the same goes for the limoges china and Steuben vases he's let slip through his fingers into his lap, and on to 19th century Agras rugs. Truth is, as we all know, if it were up to him, he'd prefer to skip dinner altogether and get down to the business at hand.

As to charm, wit, style, a sense of humor, suffice to say he's wholly lacking in those departments. More often than not you'll hear him cursing like a sailor; and his roving eye has popped from its socket so many times that he wears blinders as well as a black patch to cover it. Still, on those occasions when dining out with a female friend, if an attractive woman passes by, he never fails to ogle, wink or slip her his number through the cracks: and what makes matters worse is more often than not he's successful based solely on the fact that his reputation precedes him. As for fashion and personal hygiene, it's enough to say he dresses poorly; doesn't bathe or shower regularly, if at all. Fact is, he knots his frayed tie like a hangman's noose, and chronically forgets to button his fly, his unfettered pecker swinging in the wind as rhythmic as a pendulum.

And while we're at it, let's not forget that he's always regarded the opposite sex as some kind of sub species alternatis, mysterium opposorium: has never been able to communicate with them, speak their language, look them in the eye: habitually walking to the other side of the room at social functions to join the other men, only to return at the evenings end when things got interesting. It's hardly a secret that in the past, whenever he made the effort to talk to them, he not only put his foot in his mouth, but also his shoe and sock all the way up to his kneecap. One time the doctors had to amputate his left leg just to get it out. Another time, after swallowing his shoe, sock and boot to boot, he developed a permanent case of lockjaw. Initially the doctors thought his lockjaw to be the result of a rare form of ptomaine poisoning, but after many years of observation and treatment, and only after calling in a team of specialists from around the world, did they discover by sheer accident (which is usually the case)—when a washer woman noticed how a pet alligator of a patient sharing the same room always ended up in Charlie P's lap—that his lockjaw had nothing to do with ptomaine poisoning but rather it was due to imbibing a certain quantity of shoe leather, in this case alligator, which metabolized into a deadly potion when mixed and fermented with the dye from his unwashed argyle. So, in effect, by putting his foot in his mouth, Charlie P became not only a marvel of medical science, but the primary reason whole cultures as well as certain anal-compulsive types have us remove our shoes indoors.

Be that as it may, it was just this enfeeblement, as Charlie P, as already indicated, knows all too well, that led to his good fortune. For despite the fact that he doesn't speak their language, lacks morals and manners, and has few if any redeeming masculine qualities, just because he can now sit with a woman for hours, days, months and years without saying a word, keeping his mouth shut, listening to them complain about this and that, the world in general—Or as his latest female admirer says: "Imagine, after all these years, I finally found that rarest of men: a man who can actually listen."

TOLSTOY HAD THE RIGHT IDEA

Tolstoy had the right idea, says Charlie P. He looked the world in the eye, he knew what he was doing. First off, his wife, a doctor's daughter, who didn't have a good word to say about him in all of her six hundred page diary, cared for the children, ran the estate, and stayed up all night transcribing his voluminous manuscripts neatly and dutifully in longhand. This allowed Leo to take his daily stroll around the grounds of Yasnaya Polyana. Thumbs hooked into his thick leather belt, sheathed in a loose-fitting tunic, he would receive his due from peasants and landowners alike, as well, perhaps, as work out the plottings of his fiction. Not stopping there, the great man had a man-servant sleep in his bed, and on occasion a guest's, not to keep it warm, but rather to have the bedbugs bite him so that, rid of such nuisance, he and his wife (not so much the guest) could rise fresh in the morning, and put in an honest day's work. Understandable in the author's case: after all, pulling off masterpieces such as *Anna Karenina* and *War and Peace* requires, at the very least, a good night's sleep.

Inspired by the great Russian's 19th Century certitude, his marital arrangement and regimen, Charlie P decided to emulate him as best he could. Oh, not write the great American novel—as far as Charlie P's concerned, the novel is dead—but to employ a full-time live-in maid.

U.S. CENSUS BUREAU

Charlie P believes in the maxim: There's somebody for everybody. And when young, filled with dash and verve, he raced on all fours to meet the woman of his dreams. But after experiencing more than his share of heartbreak and rejection, not to mention the one or two obligatory conquests, he quickly concluded that he needed more experience in these matters. He's got plenty of time before settling down; committing to that special somebody. After all, he says, according to the U.S. Census Bureau International Data Base, there are 6.3 billion people in the world and forty-five percent of them are female. And with a 1.3 growth rate per year, there's every reason to be optimistic. His future looks bright.

Upon reaching his prime years, and with such an abundance of desirable women in the world, it was only to be expected that he would play the field. One woman was more interesting and beautiful than the next. He couldn't make up his mind. As a consequence he became spoiled, developed a false sense of confidence. Besides, he said, you're only young once. What's so wrong with sowing one's wild oats before settling down?

Heading into his middle years, his strength, passion, even his interest began to wane. He got lazy slacked off, began staying home on weekdays and only venturing out on weekends, and then only on Friday and Saturday nights. There was no longer that sense of urgency to pursue the right woman as there had been previously in his youth. Too many conquests and disappointments alike had dulled his senses, taken their toll.

Certainly, by the time he had gotten to the half-century mark, he was no longer traveling cross country, much less to foreign countries, and as far as space travel was concerned—that was out of the question. Not because he didn't have the means to explore those celestial regions but, truth be said, he had enough difficulty relating to women on earth. Besides, his spacecraft needed a complete overhauling. In this way whole generations of women, if not galaxies, passed him by.

But still Charlie P remained optimistic. After all, he said, according to the U.S. Census Bureau International Data Base there were 131 million babies born every year. 6.38 million a month; 210,000 a day; 146 a minute; and 2.4 a second. He could only imagine what astronomical number of female babies would reach the age of consent before his demise. And it was true: At any time of day or night, a walk around the block or to the corner drugstore could produce half a dozen pretty women or more. While attending theater or a concert; in a subway station or at a bus stop; while waiting for a green light to turn red; from one end of the earth to another, women could be found. There was no shortage of women.

And so, reaching the later part of his middle years, he began to stay home not only on weekdays but weekends, too, watch Sunday football, take long afternoon naps, hot baths and cold showers, put off till tomorrow what could be done today. And only on the rarest occasions would he marshal his forces to leave the house for celebratory events such as a gala New Year's Eve party, the Inauguration of a new President at the White House, or of course, once a year you might catch him roaming the aisles at the Academy Awards. But there, especially, amidst so many beautiful women all dressed to the nines, he was most definitely at a loss to make up his mind.

Now in his declining years, collecting Social Security and a senior citizen, an octogenarian, in fact reputed to be the oldest man on earth, he doesn't leave his apartment at all. Permanently home-bound. A veritable couch potato. Add to this the inexorable consequences of aging—illness, disease, infirmity, and the fact that he passed from this good earth a month ago doesn't help his cause in the least. But still Charlie P's not ready to call it quits. Not just yet. Proven by the fact that a week before his demise he let go his male home attendant and placed an ad in the Sunday Employment section of the New York Times: "Home Attendant wanted: Females only need apply." And on his death bed, in his last hour, he stated with unabashed clarity and conviction, that though he had not yet made his choice, he had reduced the number of applicants to two.

Today marks fifty years since his passing. And though he lies comfortably at rest, six feet under, we can happily report that he remains optimistic. For eyewitness accounts tell us that every morning, like Lazarus, he rises from his grave to sit atop his marble slab. After all, he says, according to the U.S. Census Bureau International Data Base fifty-five million people die every year. You never know when a lovely widow might be passing by to visit her dearly departed.

8 p.m. and Charlie P sits down to dinner. He can't wait. He's famished. The fact that his female guest has not arrived is unimportant. So little so, in fact, that he never invited her.

In the middle of the night, every night, with tears streaming down his face, Charlie P writes one, two, four thousand love letters to the Bulgarian harpist. Finally finished, a puzzled expression comes to his face. Uh, excuse me, he says. But does anybody know her address?

DEAF, DUMB AND BLIND

Suffering from a bout of depression over his lack of success with the ladies, Charlie P visited a hospital clinic for treatment. Almost immediately upon entering, he couldn't help but notice an inordinate amount of women flocking around a deaf, dumb and blind man sitting in the corridor. Waiting patiently for the women to leave, Charlie P queried the man: "What do you owe your success to? How do you relate so well to women?"

Answering in a combination sign language, indecipherable scribblings and unintelligible utterances, the man said: "The fact that I'm blind doesn't allow me to be dazzled by their beauty. The fact that I'm deaf insulates me from their words. And the fact that I'm mute prevents me from engaging in conversations that none of us will ever agree on. Consequently, we get along. Do the best we can. Make the most of our situation."

The next day Charlie P had his lips sewn shut; stuffed his ears with cotton; and, removing an old scarf from the topmost shelf of his closet, he blind-folded himself. We would like to report that from that day on Charlie P was embraced by all women, but, alas, that simply is not the case. The truth is he returned to the deaf, dumb and blind man in great consternation.

"What's the matter?" said the man.

"I followed your instructions to the letter," said Charlie P, "but you didn't tell me about smell or taste."

"Well, I'm sorry," said the man, "but for me those are their best features. In any event, when it comes to things of that sort, especially where women are concerned, who can account for taste?"

TWO OLD RIVALS

Those two men sitting on the park bench over there feeding the pigeons—could they be Charlie P's old rivals, the banker, Alex, and the artist, Jason, who had competed so fervently for the young harpist's favors so many years back? But why then would the banker be wearing jeans and a beret, and have grown such a mop of long hair? And instead of his usual smock and easel, palette and brushes, why does the artist now carry an attaché case and clothe himself in a grey pinstripe suit? And even more puzzling, why do both have that faraway, distracted, haunted look on their faces of men who have lost something of irretrievable value and been irreparably and irremediably hurt, and live their lives on the periphery of existence?

Unable to contain himself, Charlie P went up to the two men and asked for an explanation. The one with the banker's facial features spoke first: Though he had initially won the love of the woman, it wasn't long before she had turned his life upside down, inside out. By betraying him for another; taking his children; and leaving him utterly broken and in financial ruin. As for the artist, who now spoke for himself, he had already reached a similar fate when the harpist chose the banker over him. However, fortuitous circumstance brought them together several years later, and, being in need, they decided to live together, share their common grief and sorrow, and in that way, perhaps, bring each other a small amount of comfort. Now, like an old married couple, a master and his dog, each of them had taken on the various qualities and characteristics of the other.

Lying in bed that night reflecting over the two old rivals, Charlie P concluded: Better not to have loved, and lost or won, than to have loved at all.

OUT IN THE COLD

After sitting on a playground bench all night in the freezing cold opposite the Frenchman's building, Charlie P saw the Bulgarian harpist leave the building with the man, hand in hand. He had to admit the pair made a handsome couple.

Arriving home he raced to the telephone:

"Where have you been all night? I called and called and wasn't able to reach you. You didn't answer...weren't home!"

Yawning audibly, the harpist answered, just a hint of impatience in her tone. "I was up all night practicing for my concert next week. But I'm tired. I have to get some sleep."

"But I saw you and the Frenchman coming out of his building together."

"Of course you did," said the harpist. "It was with him I was practicing."

"And you were holding his hand."

"Why not! It was cold out."

"And you kissed him. I saw him kiss you and you kiss him back."

"You Americans!" said the harpist. "In case you don't know, that's a European as well as French custom to kiss someone hello and goodbye. In Europe we're civilized...humane." Yawning even more audibly, the young harpist continued. "But as I said. You called at the wrong time. I have to get some sleep. Speak to you later. Goodbye."

Out in the cold once again, Charlie P gave the matter his due consideration. Well, it's possible, he reflected. After all, the Frenchman, or whoever he was, did have long hair like a musician. And when walking to the subway station, his fingers interlaced with the harpist's, he did appear to have what is commonly referred to as piano fingers. And the long graceful sweep of his arms when waving goodbye at the turnstile, that must be the way a conductor waves his baton to the orchestra. Besides, how could he doubt the young woman, the love of his life. Not only had she already given him tickets for her concert next week, but possessing such a beautiful voice, she would never, could never, use it to deceive him.

PREPARATION

harlie P is tired of being a loser in love. It's not a matter of luck, chance, fortuitous circumstance, the fate of the Gods, or even meeting the right girl at the right time in the right place. It's simply a matter of preparation, says Charlie P. And so, like an actor who hones his craft so when his big break comes he'll be ready, Charlie P resolved to learn all there was to know about male-female relations. The next time opportunity knocked on his door, Charlie P would have the key to open it.

Charlie P read everything he could gather on the subject: From the Greeks on Eros to Freud on libido; from the great classicists to Everything You Want to Know About Sex. He didn't leave a stone unturned. He read sex manuals, psychology journals, biographies, romance fiction, florid Victorian novels, Kinsey reports, as well as every tabloid and smut magazine on the market. And not only read, he attended lectures, sex instruction classes, body artist performances, and was first in line at any and every event having to do with erotica. It would be impossible to estimate much less count the infinite number of facts and figures, prurient images and illustrations

Charlie P garnered and committed to memory in those school days.

As far as films were concerned, he was just as thorough as with books, music and theater. He saw them all. From art-house to mainstream. From *An Affair to Remember* to *Zorba the Greek*; from *Annie Hall* to *Zhivago*. And if not a regular customer at porno house theaters, certainly periodic visits were the norm rather than the exception. It's fair to say that besides the ability to recite the four hoshanas, all Shakespeare's soliloquies, every poem and poesy in both iambic pentameter and blank verse, Charlie P could also sing love songs, and possessed more than a working knowledge of all the romance languages, not to mention unmentionable locker room talk, bar room jibes, cocktail chatter, and lady's chitchat. And, of course, all these scholarly labors were done in the name of increasing the sum of his knowledge, stretching his parameters, and with the greatest respect, no, reverence, for that holy of holies: Lower Learning.

As was only to be expected, in the course of his studies Charlie P gained a new respect for his body. Despite his pecuniary nature he coughed up an exorbitant sum and joined a fitness club, employed a personal trainer, and though adhering to a busy schedule, strict regimen and proper diet, ran cross country, swam not only the English Channel, but the Atlantic and Pacific Oceans, trekked the four corners of the earth, climbed the tallest mountain, and chopped down whole forests with a single blow of his ax. From chalk-strewn night school classes to incense-scented bordellos, celebrated boulevards to unpaved country roads, wherever Charlie P went you could see him raising his arms, wiggling his toes, cracking his knuckles, chronically, constantly, compulsively doing some form of exercise. No doubt about it, in that prime time of his life, like when he completed basic training as a six-month army reservist, Charlie P was in the best shape of his life.

But agreeing with the existentialists that we only learn by doing, not reading, writing or arithmetic, but only from actual experience, Charlie P quickly graduated to the next stage of his education. He put into practice all that he had learned. Every "g" spot, pleasure center, body part, erogenous zone—the endless variety of sexual positions in the Kama Sutra, as well as every How To book, sex manual, sex instruction course, obscure medical text, and especially those florid Victorian novels—he put all to good use and personal advantage. It was only inevitable that he became not only an inspiration and role model, but the voice of instruction for the entire sex rehabilitation industry. There was even a brief period when he headed a free clinic and taught aging widows, dysfunctional bachelors and lonely housewives how to get the most out of their sexuality. No one could say Charlie P didn't share what he knew.

But often, after attaining satisfaction, mutual or not, Charlie P couldn't wait for his partner to leave. At those times he knew the pleasures of the flesh would get him only so far. He wanted to dwell in that rarefied realm where no words need be said and smoking in bed and chewing gum weren't allowed; and just to gaze in his beloved's eyes makes one whole. So it was that Charlie P chose a mate. But, alas, as we all know by now, he chose poorly. He fell in love with the young harpist who with typical flight, fancy, cruelty and indifference of youth, left him for another. Oh, not because he wasn't perfect, didn't know all there was to know about men and women, sex and love: by her own admission she had no complaints on those counts: it was just that he was too old. It was as simple as that. He had waited too long. She was like everybody else.

She wanted everything, was entitled to everything. And if that meant choosing a young man over an old one, a young man with a future ahead of him rather than an old one whose life was behind him, well, so be it, what could he expect. Name one person in this world who would do differently. Besides, when all was said and done, she continued for added conviction, what's more beautiful than two young people growing up together; learning, experiencing and sharing all that life has to offer, together.

TRUE CALLING

Like most everything in his life, Charlie P put off pursuing his true calling:

In his childhood, his head filled with a varied mix of television, television, and more television, he dreamed of becoming nothing more than a couch potato. But short on talent and weak in science and math, his aspirations, however lofty, soon gave way to sobering reality.

Reaching early manhood he dabbled in the arts, tried his luck at gambling, experimented with women, proving especially well-suited to indoor sports, if only when alone; and ran about town like the man he hoped not to be.

Turning practical and serious in his middle years, what some would call his prime, he set out to make a fortune. Hollywood mogul, captain of industry, shipping magnate, head of a multinational conglomerate, neterati high priest, ticket scalper, all were within his privy. But no sooner had he settled on one business than another caught his eye, and in the end, as far as he was concerned, they were all the same.

Consequently, despite his many and varied business interests, he realized only the most modest of successes, and those only on the rarest of occasions, spread out over the longest of intervals. Unable to put food on the table, a roof over their heads, he lost his wife and kids, friends, relatives, business contacts, acquaintances, credit standing, ability to network, as well as access to the neighborhood bookie, corner shylock and a multitude of rich uncles.

But being a firm believer that it's never too late, he finally had the good sense and, more importantly, the moral fortitude, to pursue his true calling. What he was put on this earth to do. Become a Pastry Chef. Make chocolate brownies. However, by that time he was already old, his cholesterol high, his blood pressure low, heart weak, metabolism slow, and worst of all, he suffered from flat feet causing plantar fiscitis. So, rather than enjoy the fruit of his labors, reap what he had sewn, live out the few remaining years he had left in peace and contentment, he died prematurely being unable to resist eating what he made.

Though admittedly not the same thing as a man who dies happily in the arms of the woman he loves in bed, we would be remiss not to report that Charlie P died just as happily, with the self-same smile on his face, sitting at his baker's counter with the larger part of a freshly-baked chocolate brownie in his mouth.

SOME DAYS IT...

Rise and shine! It's a beautiful day! And Charlie P rolls out of bed only to stub his toe on the way to the bathroom. Kneeling down to make the hot water cold for his shower, he smacks his head against the sink, so instead of cold water he knocks himself out cold.

On the way to his car which he never finds because it's been towed, he has little recourse but to wait for a taxi which never comes, and then gets caught in a mid-morning traffic jam, making him arrive not one or two hours late, but the better part of the week. Reaching his office in the nick of time he's ecstatic to find the important documents lost yesterday, found today, are waiting for him just where they should be on his office desk. But when his secretary goes to make copies of the papers, she shreds them instead.

At lunch the Serbian waitress spills the Bosnian soup on his lap, but lucky for him he had the innate good sense if not cautionary mood to avail himself of a thick linen napkin which, while protecting his newly purchased polo slacks from splash and stain, did little for him, as his third degree burns demanding immediate attention at the hospital burn unit, attest.

The afternoon doesn't fare much better: Besides nobody taking his calls, nobody answers them either. And his VIP meeting, the one he's waited for all his life, the one that can make or break his career, decide his fate, determine his future, is cancelled, but not before he's boarded a Concorde and is on his way to his cancelled meeting on the other side of the world. He's already in mid-flight, rocking and rolling in leaden skies, when he learns that his meeting has not only been cancelled but the one bank in all the world that has agreed to back him has rescinded their commitment. Since the country is one full day ahead, or behind, Charlie P's own, the electronic cancellation notice and obligatory attachments the principle's were going to send tomorrow, or yesterday, have only arrived today.

After lunch Charlie P again tries his luck with a cab, but when the driver turns out to be the same one he had that morning, and commences hurling invectives as well as poison gas and anthrax at him, Charlie P decides to brave the elements, rain, hail, sleet and snow, and slosh back to the office. Truth is, he's lucky to escape from the driver with his life who, having taken exception to Charlie P's paltry gratuity earlier in the day, not only considering it an offense to him but also a personal insult and humiliation to his brothers, sisters, relatives, friends, country and faith. But no sooner has Charlie P tread his first step than an elegant lady, accompanied by her two loving children, commences to rant and rave and shout such expletives at him that he feels he'd be better off in the cab. "But all I did was smile at you and your two adorable children, Madam," says Charlie P in an honest effort to explain himself. As always, when you least need them, out of the blue appears the man in blue, in this case a part-time policeman and full-time Bible-pumping, gospel-preaching TV evangelist who, having a direct satellite hookup to his Maker, speaking to him personally once a week and twice on Sunday, concludes on the spot that Charlie P is guilty of breaking the 10th Commandment, coveting another man's wife. Worse still, he's a sex fiend and child molester for, by his own admission, he smiled at the two little ones. Did he not? As there's no denying, Charlie P's arrested, charged, placed in custody, tried, convicted, sentenced, tortured and killed; and just to make certain that there's no funny business, all concerned including Charlie P throw away the key.

By the time he's released from prison, it's too late to return to the office, so, instead, he spends the rest of the day running errands that he put off while in prison. No longer trusting taxis, or his own two feet, he waits for a bus and train which never come, as well as the red light turn to green, green light turn to red, and stands on line—same as waiting—at the post office, bank, movies, Food Emporium, Sacks Fifth Avenue, you name it, Charlie P waited and waited and waited. But in our haste to complete this chapter, for the sake of completion, we failed to mention that when released from prison, it was then and only then that Charlie P's real problems began. For the husband of the elegant woman, father of her children, has been waiting stoically if not patiently all this time for Charlie P's release so he could exact his own personal retribution. As luck would have it (Charlie P's luck), he turned out to be a professional boxer who, though forbidden by law to use his hands, deemed lethal weapons, made equally good use of his feet and legs, being an amateur kickboxer as well.

Before calling it a day Charlie P goes out for his evening jog. In the midst of his run, he stops to intervene in what appears to be a friendly argument between two old friends.

Instead of thank you's, a night cap or coffee and cake, he gets mugged, robbed, pummeled and beaten; face bloody, reeling, comatose and in a stupor, he returns home for a quiet evening by himself watching TV. But...and there's always a but...just when he's comfortably snug under the covers, and picks up his TV Guide to see what's on, his glasses have disappeared. By the time he finds them in the folds of his blanket, his movie has ended, and he's on his way to the bathroom, this time taking especial care not to stub his toe or hit his head on the sink. But...and there's always a but...he trips over his feet, slips on a bar of soap, and, falling down in the bathtub, he breaks his left hip and right arm. "Should have known better," says Charlie P. "After all, there are more accidents in the bathroom than anywhere else."

And all the above doesn't even take into consideration that he's lost his last dollar in the market, his dinner had turned cold, broken himself on the wheel, and earlier that evening at a cocktail party he met the woman of his dreams, only to realize by the time he got home that he didn't take her number nor ask her name. He's not even sure he attended the party. The only thing he's certain of is that she's off in the morning to some third world country, being a member of the Peace Corps, or was it the Salvation Army?

Ad nauseam, ad infinitum etc. etc. and so on...

THE PARTY

Tired of being a stay-at-home and a couch potato, Charlie P gives a gala New Year's Eve party which not only he but nobody else attends. Even Charlie P was surprised at the turnout. To be sure, this is the best party he's never been to. The one he would least have wanted to miss.

The entire affair was catered by the world's greatest chefs, and platters of sumptuous foods were served by geishas in kimonos and men in black. Champagne flowed like April rain. Every guest was given a token of appreciation for not attending, diamonds and gold; and for those who didn't wear jewelry, thinking it ostentatious, or trade gold in the market, Picassos from the Blue period. And the entertainment was world class. From the Three Tenors, Nureyev and Fontaine, to rappers and hip-hop. From chart-breakers and the current pop, to has-beens and never-was's. Fireworks lit up the night sky before, during and after the party. Needless to say, there was something for everybody. For every taste and desire imaginable.

At long last Charlie P knew what it was to have the spotlight. To be the center of attention. If not for him this party that did not happen would never have taken place.

But what gave Charlie P the most satisfaction was the fact that all the people not attending the party got along so well. High rollers mixed with paupers, and aging playboys charmed the pants, if not panties, off young career women in the bloom of youth. While hangers-on, freeloaders, and weak sons of strong fathers could be seen having serious and meaningful discussions with men of the cloth. And chronically cheating husbands and adulterous wives, who had fought tooth and nail over divorce settlements, alimony payments and child support for years, were now laughing together, making merry and dancing cheek to cheek. On a larger scale, and despite ancient enmities that had made for a thousand years of hatred, world rulers and Heads of State were making every effort to reconcile their differences; open lines of communication; enter into dialogue. And so, on this night, at Charlie P's party, at least, there was no such thing as separation of Church and State; East vs. West; men vs. women. Indeed, there was only commonality of purpose, good cheer, peace on earth and good will towards men.

For certain, at Charlie P's gala New Year's Eve party which didn't take place—Happy times were here again.

Still, by the night's end, Charlie P was visibly disappointed. The crowd had already filtered out, most rushing off to other parties, and other than a few tepid kisses on the cheek from the women, ceremonial hugs from the men, and the usual "see you next year"'s, Charlie P once again felt empty, alone, deserted. He certainly wasn't ready to relinquish the spotlight, stop being the host and center of attention. And, so, he began thinking about next year's party. No, it would not be a sequel of this year's event; a rehashing and recycling of the time-tested and familiar. Next year Charlie P decided that rather than be a small fish in a big pond he would be a big fish in a small pond by giving his party in a soup kitchen for the hungry and homeless, the needy and disenfranchised. Not only would he save a fortune by not having to wine and dine his guests with diamonds and gold, but all those unfortunates needed to be happy was a bowl of hot soup, a warm bed, a pair of sturdy thick-soled boots and a windbreaker for the ensuing winter months. Toss in a few extra dollars to keep them off the dole, and, rest assured, more than lukewarm kisses and perfunctory hugs, he would be adulated, venerated, possibly even canonized as a saint.

But what if all those people who didn't attend this year's party attend next year's party?

OF ALL PEOPLE...

Just when the image had supplanted the word, the sun neglected to rise, the larger questions were no longer being asked, of all people, it was Charlie P who came crawling out of the woodwork, rose to the occasion, stood up to be counted, and was chosen by The Committee to lead mankind back to The Word.

For a person with so little experience in worldly matters, a hermit and social isolate, his selection came as a surprise to some, but for those who truly knew him, his qualifications were self-evident. Free of pride and prejudice, neither tainted nor tarnished, compromised or under the influence, as pure as the day he was born, a blank page, tabula rasa, with no ax to grind, and yet at the same time, ever on the ready to bolster morale, walk that thin-edged line, scribe the 11th Commandment as well as put it into practice, for certain, The Committee deemed him uniquely qualified not only to ask but to answer the larger questions such as: Who shall cast the first stone? Was the Virgin Mary a virgin, and more importantly—especially in today's world—Why?—as well as come to grips with and resolve once and for all the antipathetic, disturbing and macabre relationships between self and world, yin and yang, mind and body, not to mention the sun and moon.

His work cut out for him, Charlie P set upon his task at once.

Soon enough the hour arrived. Charlie P stepped to the podium. In the audience were poets and scholars, dilettantes and quacks, all of whom who had, at one time or another, been in the limelight, had their own day in court, fifteen minutes of fame, chance to lead mankind back to the word and consequent immortality. But now it was Charlie P's time. Amidst a strange admixture of raucous applause and hushed silence—needless to say, as well as the aforementioned, people attended the lecture from all nations and worlds, some even coming from as far off as other planets and stratospheres; in fact there was a motley crew of strangers from another planet seated high up in the smoke-filled balcony, having sneaked their way past a lackluster security guard who made his explanation by stating what you can't see, smell, hear, taste or feel, you can't very well ask for a ticket.

At any rate, just as Charlie P took center stage he noticed the Bulgarian harpist seated in the first row talking in a seemingly intimate if not conspiratorial manner to a flamboyant fellow attired in a coat of many colors. Charlie P's face turned green as bottle glass. Perfectly little round bumps broke out on his forehead, and rather than utter a single sentence, he stormed off the stage, leaving the great throng once again, as always, waiting and wanting for The Word.

CHARLIE P TALKS WITH A LADY

This woman I can really talk to, says Charlie P. Really communicate with. And she understands me. I can make this relationship work.

This guy talks a good game but who knows what he's really thinking. He probably has one thing on his mind. I don't believe a word he says.

We're like one. She knows what I'm going to say before I say it. I haven't felt so close to a person since I don't know when.

I have to watch this guy. He'll usurp my personality if I let him. I'll lose my autonomy. All I've worked so long and hard to attain. Before long, if I stay with him, there will be nothing left of me. I'll be nothing more than a pawn, a puppet. It would be too easy to lose myself in him.

I don't need words to communicate with her. She knows just what I'm thinking even before I do. I've never felt so good or close to anyone.

This guy never says what's on his mind. Who knows what he's thinking. Every time he opens his mouth, nothing comes out but words.

This woman has opinions and isn't afraid to voice them. Put it all on the line. I like that. Even if she constantly disagrees with me, at least I know where she stands.

There's no hope for us. Every time I open my mouth, he disagrees. All we do is fight and argue. He can't accept criticism, and God knows he's too old to ever change.

I was wrong about her. She's no different than all the others. If I'm objective, see it clearly, hear what she's really saying—we don't have a chance.

Finally a man I can talk to. Communicate with who understands me. Now that we got past all the b.s., maybe we can make this relationship work.

SO THAT'S WHAT I...

Rise and shine, Charlie P starts a new day: First goes the rocking chair in which he's dreamed all his life; then the couch he's never got up from, and the bed he's still lying in; followed by the TV set he's never stopped watching; and all the money he's scrimped and saved but never spent—it's not for nothing Charlie P's reputation as a world class miser precedes him. And, of course, the faulty wall clock that ticks but doesn't tock goes too. All of them, together, tossed into the rubbish bin, along with the blankets he's wrapped around himself instead of a woman's arms and legs; and the pillows he's laid his head to rest on instead of that same, or different, woman's bosom every night.

But as Charlie P won't be satisfied until every blessed relic, sacred object, in his Holy Ark is gone and disappeared, he moves on to his closet. The novel he's never written as well as the voluminous collection of letters never sent to the harpist are there. After ridding himself of them, and smashing to smithereens the miniature dolls and sculptured figurines that he's peopled his home with, he sets to flame all the books in his library he's never read, and then adds, almost without thinking, a purely reflex action, though not without great deliberation and planning, to the book-burning conflagration a massive pileup of 8x10 gilt-edged framed sepia photos of loved ones and friends he's never had, as well as a lifetime repository of passing women on the street he's never gotten to know but whose fleeting glimpses still burn a hole in his memory.

Beating his chest like a great ape, like a man atoning for his sins, Charlie P proceeds on to the missing link, the warp and woof of his life, bane of his existence, foundation stone of all his values and beliefs, thoughts and actions, words and deeds—well, in the name of accuracy as well as honesty, not exactly actions and deeds. But in as much as his inner life was neither developed or realized in the normal course of events, he doesn't bother with it here either, neither inner or outer, dismissing one with a perfunctory wave of his hand, the other with a shrug of his shoulders. As for adolescent rebellion, mid-life crisis and the violations of aging, which though never resolved or worked through, leaving their marks and traumas, they likewise receive no more than a cursory glance before he presses forward to the more tangible and concrete concerns of the day.

Warming up to the task now, he rips off an ear, gouges out an eye, pulls off his nose, and then, availing himself of pruning shears, heavy gauge work gloves, surgical scalpel and butcher's knife, he eviscerates himself, slicing an incision from belly button to sternum, so as to be able to get to his guts, entrails, spleen, liver, gizzard, as well as removing as best he can, it's not easy, it's a delicate operation, his entire skeletal structure and frame. Really into it now, he winds his way through his intestines, large and small, snakes up and down his alimentary canal, makes a wrong turn, gets lost, corrects himself, starts over, and averting the delicate filigree of his lungs he reaches his heart which, though languishing from lack of use and consequent atrophy, remains a medical marvel, inexplicably defying all scientific explanation for having not yet missed a single beat. Finally, breathing hard or blowing wind, it's difficult to say which at this juncture, he digs into himself and yanks out and spews through his nostrils, mouth, anus, every orifice in his body, all those words he's never spoken, thoughts he's never had, and feelings he's never felt. The latter making for an unending pile, and delaying the operation's completion, not to mention cleanup, ad nauseam.

At last, having shed every skin, quite the opposite of the great pharaohs who take their possessions with them to the tomb, emptied of passions and possessions alike, he treads his way to the bathroom as if walking on hot coals, looks in the mirror and exclaims with the force of a biblical utterance:

"So that's what I look like in the morning!"

THE EMPLOYMENT INTERVIEW

Whether it be a computer glitch, a statistical anomaly, a stranger's favor, or the exception to the rule, Charlie P has an employment interview scheduled for him this morning. It's the opportunity of a lifetime. Understandably anxious over the interview, he stops to examine himself in a store window. His hair is mussed, his suit wrinkled (Irish linen), and his tie stained, the result of his morning's cereal. But that's not what's bothering him. That's not what he sees in the window's reflection. He sees a man in a business suit on his way to the defining moment in his career only to end in failure. He sees an old woman hobbling along with her life's possessions on her back. And a young woman with a misshapen swollen belly being aided by a cop and cab driver in the act of giving birth. He sees a young pilgrim carrying a knapsack on the way to the Holy Land. And he sees a messenger riding a bike with a helmet on his head like an astronaut.

Spirits buoyed by what he sees, convinced he compares favorably, measures up well, Charlie P parts his hair, knots his tie, creases the line in his trousers, and continues on his way to the interview. He's ready to knock 'em dead.

But once seated in the waiting room, waiting to be called in for the interview, he has second thoughts. He's more anxious and confused than ever. Who am I? he ponders. And just as importantly, what role shall I play? Am I the businessman in the three-piece suit destined for failure? Or the pilgrim on his way to the Holy Land? The old woman on the street with her life's possessions on her back? Or the young mother about to give birth? Despite fear and trembling, Charlie P musters up sufficient courage to present himself to the powers that be. But standing before these august personages, this palisade of power and authority, he feels more like a sacrificial lamb, a link in the chain, a pauper on the dole, than a man qualified for professional employment. For certain he doesn't know who he is any longer. He's lost his bearings. No longer moored in the safe and secure, the solid and familiar, the palpable and real, he's more like the store window's reflections, a passerby's fleeting image that comes and goes. Aghast! Charlie P falls back on his old ways, reverts to type. What's worked for him in the past will work again. Besides, he says to himself, his appointment was scheduled for seven months earlier. Truth is, it should have taken place decades ago. When he was young. Full of promise. Now's not the time for it. It's too late in the day. His life has passed him by. Who's he kidding. What can he say. How can he explain himself. He'd be better off not keeping it. Not subjecting himself to such shame and embarrassment, humiliation and despair. His warm bed and fluffy pillow at home look more inviting than ever. Fact is he should never have gotten out of bed in the first place. The position's probably filled anyway. More than likely by the same person that beat him out originally so many years back. He's probably ready for retirement now. Still, this tribunal, these people, this interview, no, no sense deluding himself any longer. He's not ready for work, employment, regular hours, responsibility, adulthood, commitment...

Charlie P excuses himself, does an about-face, makes a quick exit. Truth is, he's not even disappointed. On the contrary, he considers himself fortunate. It's not like he's being tossed into the street like that old homeless lady; nor will he be wandering the four corners of the earth like the pilgrim searching for the Holy Land. Or even the astronaut who must by now be spinning his wheels in intergalactic space. No. There's no rush. Computer glitches, statistical anomalies, strangers' favors, do happen. He'll be called again. If he waited this long he can wait a little longer...

In the course of a long life Charlie P mastered many professions, but practiced none.

DO NOT DISTURB

Charlie P rummages through his basement storage room. Rolls out an old steamer trunk on a dolly, the brass knobs at the corners no longer shiny, but scraped and scratched by time. Insulates it against the elements; fills it with a food supply sufficient to last a lifetime. Drills a porthole on the trunk's four sides to see out of if not in. Places a Do Not Disturb sign on it where a name and address label might otherwise be appropriate. Wheels it to his boat moored at the marina, and sets sail to the middle of the ocean, where, when ready, taking a last look at the horizon, the beauty of the setting sun, he steps inside the trunk, locks and bolts it from inside out, chains wrapped around its middle and sides, and somehow manages to drop it overboard to sink to the bottom of the sea.

Impervious and unyielding on the ocean floor, amongst the sea anemones and mollusks, sand and rock, he lets out a long sigh of relief. "There," he says. "Let them try and get at me now."

"But what's that clonking on the trunk? A Coke bottle with a small white paper in it. Who could be sending me messages in a bottle down here?"

THE LEAN YEARS

After struggling through many lean years, at age sixty-eight, already on pension and social security, Charlie P realized his lifelong dream and became a superstar athlete. Now the name Charlie P is a household word. He cannot go anywhere without being the center of attention. If he so much as looks in a shop window, he not only sees his reflection but a hundred rabid faces more. Nor can he enter a restaurant and dine in peace. There are always countless fans, celebrity hounds, star-gazers, interrupting his meal, asking for autographs, salivating at the mouth waiting to get a word in. Not one to disappoint, Charlie P meets his obligations with unfailing sincerity and commitment. So much so that he hasn't had a bite to eat in twenty-six days. He's down to ninety-nine pounds and suffering from stomach and intestinal problems.

"After all those years of struggle and waste, how do you like your new-found celebrity?" is the question most asked by the press, media, and average fan.

"Well, to be honest," answers Charlie P, "it's not what I expected. But it has its compensations. Still, I wish it would have come sooner in my career. All those chocolate brownies

I consumed early in life to appease the pain and frustration of those lean years—I wasn't ever in proper shape. That stopped me from realizing my potential. There's no telling what I might have been able to accomplish. Now, with people like you and millions more like you in my life, I don't eat a thing and I'm in the best shape of my life."

Some say Charlie P's career ended due to diminished skills. Others blame it on the wear and tear of aging. But those who truly knew him, who were close to him on and, more importantly, off the field, for breakfast, lunch and supper, feel he died of starvation. However, all agree: The bigger he got on the field, the smaller he became off it.

After respectively waiting six months, the owner of the ball club, prompted by league officials, several old teammates and fan clubs, decided to honor and pay tribute to the man who could've, should've, ought to have been the greatest athlete of his time. Millions gathered at the stadium; inside and out. One by one they circled his newly erected monument, like Indians around a wagon, mourners around an open coffin at a wake, leaving not flowers, wreaths, ornaments, mementos and other memorabilia, but rather chocolate brownies and in some cases even tall glasses of milk. Evidently, in addition to honoring and paying tribute to Charlie P, they wanted to make up to him for all those lean years.

Charlie P has but one regret. He had to live his entire life not by himself, but with himself.

AT THE PEARLY GATES

When asked by his Maker at the Pearly Gates what had he accomplished in his life? what had he done? Charlie P answered honestly and proudly that he had realized all his goals. That he did exactly what he set out to do: Nothing.

That must have been difficult, said his Maker. Can you give us an example of what you mean? After all, you're not the only candidate seeking entrance into our community. As you can well imagine, we only have room for so many. You really can't expect us to take everybody in.

With such prompting, Charlie P made every effort to explain himself. It wasn't easy, he said. It took plenty of hard work. He had to put his dues in. Be on top of his game. One slip-up could ruin everything. For example: He never pursued a career, practiced a profession. For as long as he could remember, he was a practitioner of the putting off. A master of the deep sigh. He never acted quickly, never fought for a cause. Never practiced what he preached. As soon as he made up his mind, he changed it. His language consisted of cut-off sentences and long silences, of empty gestures and facile words, but never of the clear and concise, the definitive and categorical, the enthusiastic and spontaneous. He was a web of contradictions, of secret urges and concealed meanings. He spoke only in die general, never in the particular, always in the abstract and hypothetical, never the immediate and concrete. And, of course, he brooked every question by answering none; by never saying what he meant. As far as people were concerned, to be sure, there were attractions. Temptations. He was only human. But as to all who never got the chance to know him would affirm, he met every challenge, passed every test. He allowed no one to enter his life. Not the girl next door nor the long lost relative. Not his first love nor his last; friend nor foe; child nor parent; all were treated the same. Nothing and nobody was allowed to penetrate his heart, touch his soul, get under his skin. Neither laughter nor tears would he share.

Untouched by man, matter and experience, ensconced in his own self-created shell, his unpeopled world, Charlie P could honestly say he left this world exactly as he found it. Secure in the knowledge that there was no one to carry on his name. Nothing to remember him by. Though sheathed in many skins, he had shed none. Though he had many old wounds, no scabs had fallen off. For certain there was no one who truly knew him. He wasn't even sure there was anyone to know.

And so, trumpets blaring, bugles sounding, when meeting his Maker, not having used up his time in life, understandably, he had every expectancy that his life lay before him. A deep-rooted presentiment that his life was about to begin. After all, he had waited all his life for this meeting, prepared himself assiduously; and now, undaunted by the years—the best was yet to come. No one could doubt his logic, refute his argument. His legacy was insured. He was and would always be a man of infinite possibility, a Being waiting to Become. Potential incarnate. As young and full of promise on his death bed as on the day of his birth.

"And where do you think you're going," said his Maker, a sympathetic yet authoritative smile forming on his face.

"Err, uhhh..."

"On the contrary," said his Maker, not waiting for Charlie P to begin much less finish his sentence. "We're going to send you back to..."

"But you better than anybody knows a man can't go back home again."

"Yes, that's usually the case," said his Maker. "But from what you've just told us, whether you call it home, earth or life, we have little doubt it's a place you've never been."

TOMATO

Though Charlie P had already lived a long and fruitful life, it was only when he met Tomato that he knew it was time to settle down. His friends strongly objected, saying he was still in his prime; he had many good years left. There were many tasty morsels and he had not yet had his fill. But Charlie P knew better. He was almost as tired of frozen dinners as one night stands. Of long lonely evenings with nothing to look forward to other than dirty dishes and an empty plate. Before it was too late, and only scraps and leftovers remained, he wanted, at the very least, a good old-fashioned home-cooked meal.

He had never encountered anyone like Tomato. She could fit in anywhere. Whether it be an omelette for breakfast, a salad for lunch, or even with meat and potatoes for dinner. Whereas Stringbean was too thin, Melon too fat, and Strawberry high-maintenance (she wouldn't give Charlie P the time of day unless he drenched her in champagne), Tomato, with her well-shaped body, smooth skin and rosy complexion, was seemingly perfect.

In the past, whenever Charlie P opened his heart, he got hurt. Whomever he chose disappointed him. Every fruit and vegetable had their own agenda. Green Pea and Green Pepper went green with envy each and every time they were asked to share his plate. Prune caused him so much grief and consternation just by her very nature that she sent him running to the bathroom every time they met. And the closer he got to Onion, the more skins he peeled away, the more miserable and wretched she made him; almost always bringing him to tears even before the meal began. And the one time apple of his eye, Apple, though making a great first impression, before long proved fickle, untrustworthy, inconsistent. One day flashy blonde, the next day sallow green. If only she would have stayed deliciously red like the first time they met, but, alas, she didn't.

Above all, Charlie P wanted someone he could count on. Someone who would stick with him through thick and thin, good times and bad. He hardly needed someone flashy like Carrot Top, or that trollop, Avocado, who once maturing, becoming ripe, reaching the age of consent, gave away her favors so readily that all who sowed reaped the benefits. Even the Asian bombshell, Pomegranate, despite her all too obvious sexual allure and powers, was hardly worth the trouble. Just getting inside her to taste the fleshy fruit was like storming the citadel. The opposite of Avocado, she guarded her treasures as if with a chastity belt.

But, in all fairness, these were the exceptions to the rule. There were many desirable fruits and vegetables vying for Charlie P's attention. As his friends said, and Charlie P knew all too well, at this time of his life he had the pick of the litter. There was nothing to stop him from ordering anything he wanted on the menu; select whatever caught his eye at the Emporium. But life is choices and never more so than when choosing a mate. And when one does choose, how can one be certain that his choice is the right choice?

Oh, there's no doubt Tomato has a great deal going for her. Is a far better choice, for example, than Asparagus who flies into temper tantrums and sulks all day every time you mispronounce her name. And, for certain, she's more attractive than Raisin who's old and wrinkly before her time. But, still, nobody's perfect. And past experience has taught him you don't find all things in one fruit, or vegetable, for that matter. And even though Tomato comes closest, is more adaptable and accommodating than the others, someone he can count on as earlier indicated for breakfast, lunch and supper, there's still no denying that when a man gets those urges you can't begin to compare her to the Asian bombshell Pomegranate's fleshy fruit for a late night snack.

But resolute and determined as he is, Charlie P will no longer allow grandiosity and immaturity to stand in his way and prevent him from making the right decision. For the first time in his life, he's ready to make a commitment. Besides, it's only a matter of simple math, common sense, comparison shopping, studying the menu, to realize Tomato stands head and shoulders above her competition. Once meeting Tomato they were eliminated a long time ago. Without a doubt, Tomato is as close to perfection as Charlie P's ever known. And so in bold words and on weak knees, Charlie P declares that from this day on, when sitting down at his table, Tomato is the one for him. Suddenly, making this decision, almost without noticing, Charlie P's a new man. A different person. Charlie P's in love. And it's certainly not far-fetched to say that it won't be long now before we can expect to see little Cherry Tomatoes as well as little Charlie P's running around and frolicking about.

But who's that dish over there with the youthful fuzz on her cheeks? What did you say her name was? Peach.

THE SEARCH

Charlie P races home and not even taking the time to remove his coat and jacket, or notice that the door was left open, he begins searching the apartment. He opens the rolltop desk and looks inside its sundry drawers and compartments. Not finding what he wants, he turns his attention to a bureau, chest of drawers and a large vanity taking up almost half the space of one entire wall. No luck there either, he sets his eyes on an impressive library, and after scrutinizing each and every book on the floor-to-ceiling shelves, he fans each so vigorously that every frayed, dog-eared and yellowed page falls out including many that merely crumble at his touch. But all he finds are old postcards, marginal jottings, footnotes and annotations. Hardly satisfied, he sets his eyes on a trundle-sized bed, taking it apart and tossing, pell mell, the patchwork quilt, blanket, sheets and foam rubber mattress until only the bed frame and springs remain. Giving up on the bed, he looks under its frame, the carpet, and once ripping it open, inside the mattress.

He widens his search to include removing the grainy textured paper off the walls, and for a moment he has hope when he discovers a hole in the wall earlier covered by a black spotty mold. But despite the old paper bringing thick strips of crumbly mottled plaster down, making the hole even bigger: nothing. He has no more luck here than he had anywhere else. He heads to the bathroom which he scours with a fine-toothed comb. And when that fails too, he turns his undivided attention to one of the two closets in the room. (It's only a modestly-sized studio apartment with a small kitchen and bathroom.) Here his luck turns, or so he thinks, and, heart pounding, pulse racing, he finds, tangled in spider webs and dustballs on the closet floor, an old corrugated cardboard box containing report cards, elementary and JHS school class graduation photos, notebooks, letters, piles of copious notes, and a pint-sized red phone book, circa 19—, twenty years before or after he was born. The book holds what appears to be a cumulative collection of old girlfriends' names and numbers. Though he can't recall the names, the coded rating system of stars and asterisks denoting successes and failures sparks a flicker of recognition.

But still, despite all his efforts and travail, nothing of importance shows up, certainly not what he's looking for.

Breathing heavier now, heaving ever deeper sighs, he heads for the kitchen rich with the smell of fragrant foods. First inspecting the zinc-topped counter, then the well-stocked cabinets and a fridge bursting at the seams with foods, he quickly and deliberately changes course and commences to take down the compressed cardboard red brick tiles on the wall, chipping at the stubborn chunks of cement with a blue multi-bladed Swiss army knife he always carries on his person. But again no luck. He doesn't find what he's looking for.

Anxiety mounting as if attempting to quell a volcano about to burst, he examines ever more closely the hairline cracks on the walls, as well as ceiling, looks not in but behind the mirror, and explores an old hidden trapdoor which he finds by chance when tearing up the floorboards in the back of the closet. But his efforts prove just as futile here as those that preceded them, and in the end he has to consider his search a failure.

Dropping wearily on what's left of the bed, he notices a little boy seated on the floor, his legs folded Buddha-like beneath him. The little boy's eyes are bright and shiny, almost luminous.

"What is it you're looking for?" asks the boy.

"Myself," says Charlie P. "Somehow I've managed to lose it along the way."

"I doubt if you'll find it here," says the boy.

"Why not?" says Charlie P, genuinely surprised by the child's words.

"Well, for one thing I doubt if you've even lost it. I recognized you from the moment you walked in. And for another, you've got the wrong apartment."

WHAT DOES IT ALL MEAN?

For forty years they sat on opposite sides of a two-sided desk facing each other. They had started out together, with the same firm, in the same career, and now, forty years later, they were leaving together. One an abject failure, nameless and anonymous, seething with bitterness and regret; the other wreathed with laurels and honors, a worldwide name and recognized wherever he went.

Charlie P knew both men well:

But whether attaining success or failure, love and happiness or remaining alone and derelict all one's life, what does it all mean? says Charlie P. Why all the fuss and bother? Like his two friends he had taken it all so seriously back then, in his youth. Had struggled so mightily for every victory; fought so hard for every success. It all seemed so unimportant now, at this late date, a farce and a joke. Fool's gold and Pyrrhic victories, nothing more and nothing less. Had he, like his two friends, sacrificed himself to the wrong wars? Fought from the start losing battles? Resting on his laurels or just lying down to rest—was there a difference?

Returning home from the cemetery that night, after several more hours of reflection, Charlie P came up with the only answer that made a modicum of sense to him. An answer as old as man. Whether a citizen of antiquity, traditionalist or hi-tech modernist, whether rugged individualist or member of Corporate Group-Think, he had little choice, the same choice, no choice at all. Tomorrow morning, as every morning, he would rummage through his closet, gather up his rucksack, grasp hold of his attaché case, pick up his pen and pencil from his desk, and, as all those before him, and all those who would come after, he would commence his ascent or descent—whatever the case may be, whatever the day may bring—to the end.

STUCK IN THE ELEVATOR

Stuck in the elevator between the eighth and ninth floor with a young boy as the only other passenger, Charlie P seizes the moment. He's always craved a father to son, teacher to student, minister to flock relationship: and now, at long last, he has it. A captive audience. Someone he can pass on to all the knowledge and wisdom he's accumulated over a lifetime.

"Have you heard…"

"Do you know…"

"Did I tell you…"

No doubt about it, Charlie P has seen and done it all. How could this youth, or anybody else for that matter, not fail to be impressed. Who wouldn't be held spellbound by his every word. The whole world stands to profit from his wisdom. In the years to come, they'll line up in droves and pay dear money to hear him speak.

Charlie P continues his lecture. Every word soaked in the flesh and blood immediacy of his life. From the time he swam the ocean floor to roaming the earth on his belly. From succumbing to temptation and eating the apple to fighting alongside Joan against tyranny and oppression. From envisioning the third dimension, spawning all manner of progress and change: Freud, secular art, depth psychology. No more flat surfaces and stick figures. No more God and obeisance; title and privilege; but only individuals, the modern citizen. People. Charlie P has born witness to not only the making of Western civilization, but has taken a giant step forward for all mankind. And not one step but many. The young boy will only be the first to profit. In the years to come, taking advantage of print and the electronic media, the internet, Charlie P's words will be passed on to future generations.

"Have you heard…"

"Do you know…"

"Did I tell you…"

As to Charlie P himself, standard bearer and spokesman, prophet and shining example, he will become a veritable national treasure. He'll be in constant demand. Every social agency and humane organization in the world will invite him to speak. Audiences the world over will heed his sage advice and take benefit from the redemptive value of his words. He who has born witness and been responsible for the great truths of history will become the conscience of his generation! The spiritual leader of his epoch! Saviour! Messiah! Who knows, if truly lucky, if he plays his cards right, he might even be afforded his own television show. Others have done it—why not him? Greater miracles have taken place. Progress! Time marches on! Freedom! The cup runneth over!

But who's that knocking on the elevator door? Forcing it partially open and poking his head between the rubber-padded door? But it's too soon. Charlie P's lecture has not hardly begun. The youngster has hardly heard a single word!

And thirty minutes later, Charlie P now safe and sound on the eighth floor landing, the super is offering his hand to the boy still seated on the elevator floor.

"What's the matter?" says the super. "Are you alright? Aren't you coming?"

"No," says the boy. "Between my father and grandfather I've heard enough lectures at home for a lifetime. I don't need to hear anymore from him."

REUNION AT OLD AGE HOME

Learning that the Bulgarian harpist he had been in love with sixty years earlier had been admitted into the same old age home as him, Charlie P raced half-way around the world and up six flights of stairs to see her.

"Oh, but I didn't want you to see me like this," said the harpist.

"But why?" said Charlie P. "You know I've always..."

"Are you blind? Just take a look at me!" said the harpist. "I'm an old woman now. I have six grown children; eighteen grandchildren; and four great-grandchildren; and I've buried three husbands. And on top of all that my skin is wrinkled. My breasts sag. I've lost most of my hair. I have false teeth. And, even worse, the left leg you see is a prosthesis, the result of the dire effects of diabetes. And my ass, what's left of it, is so bony I need a cushion just to sit down. And worst of all, I can't play the harp any longer because arthritis has knotted my hands into fists."

"That's no problem," said Charlie P. "I never loved your harp playing anyway. More importantly, I know it's against regulations, but the security guards nod off in this place after midnight. Would you like it if I paid you a visit then?"

WHAT IS IT THAT DISTINGUISHES CHARLIE P?

Charlie P has never denied that he was average. No different than the rest. A statistic, anonymous, middle brow, on the low rung of the ladder, the last man on the totem pole, one of many, not hardly exceptional, a mere face in the crowd. And though he's embarrassed to admit it, people turned their backs on him, or more often than not crossed the street when they saw him, that is, if they saw him coming. The truth is they didn't. He wasn't there. He didn't exist. He was the unanswered phone call. The missed appointment. The last man on line and the first called to duty. A reduced price, a cut budget, a bargain basement giveaway—that was Charlie P. And so we have to ask: What is it that distinguishes Charlie P? What is it that sustains him and keeps him going?

Certainly there's more to the man than his being able to squeeze into an elevator no matter how crowded. Or find a seat on the subway at rush hour even if it is only on another passenger's lap. Could it be that Charlie P's the stuff that poets are made of? How else to explain that which takes possession of Charlie P and allows him to create beauty and meaning while others cannot. All he has to do is open his mouth and words pour out of him like a Joycean stream. He has no idea where they're going. Where his mouthing will lead. Yet, once giving utterance, he cannot hold them back. One word follows another, and though not really words, not even language, starting out as something primal, anarchic, inchoate, once traveling through him as if filtered through the light of day, they lead him like a horse to water to the other side.

And not only him:—People living ordinary lives, mundane existences, with children to feed, jobs to hold, mortgages to pay, found in Charlie P's words majesty and grandeur, astonishment and surprise, and were able to gain a glimmer of what their lives could truly be.

Poet, spokesman and prodigal son, by having the courage to burrow deep and spew out his own mad ravings, buried treasures, Charlie P leads not only himself but the masses and multitude to the Promised Land.

PENNY PINCHER!

Penny pincher! Cheapskate! Charlie P heard it all his life. Taxi drivers, bartenders, old friends, ex-wives all bore witness to the fact that he hated to part with a nickel; counted his pennies. Even the homeless man on the street says he never spares a dime. Charlie P begs to differ. He believes himself to be the most charitable man on earth. After all, he says, who can deny that at least once a year, on Christmas Day, he donates his first and last dollar to his favorite charity: Himself. Still and all, last week Charlie P resolved to change his ways. Since then he's practiced what he preached. Last evening, for example, there was a retirement party for a fellow worker at the most expensive steak-house in town. Not only did Charlie P attend, but he brought his pot of gold heretofore put aside for a rainy day. And when his peers and colleagues ordered the house special, with all the trimmings from soup to nuts, Charlie P ordered a cup of coffee for fifty cents. When the waiter brought the bill, Charlie P left a dollar. "There," he said. "Let them call me cheap now!"

PLAINTS AND GRIEVANCES

Like most of us Charlie P has his own way of easing the burden. Making life bearable. While others seek the counsel of a rabbi, priest, shrink or just go off for a drink, Charlie P complains about this and that to get through the day. For sure, it's a never ending story. There's no shortage of material. Today, for example, he's complained about a reckless driver and an uptight civil servant; the fact that women on the street are too beautiful (the older he gets the more beautiful they seem) and those in his life aren't beautiful enough; the impossibility of hailing a taxi and that doctors never visit any longer.

Whether the sky is too high, the ceiling too low, the ocean too rough, the lake too calm, the carpet too thick, the walls too thin, or the mailman only delivers junk mail and bills, Charlie P finds something to complain about. It's only more grist for his mill. His ex-wife hovering over him like a jailer, his boss like an executioner; the in-laws visiting him too often, the children not at all; the days being too long, life too short; and when all else fails, there's always the weather, too hot or too cold, rainy or dry, and, for certain, the weatherman is always wrong. To be sure, the more Charlie P excoriates about the day's frustrations, the more he rants and raves, makes plaints and grievances, the better he feels.

At the end of the day when he's finished his peroration, got everything off his chest, has nothing else to complain about, Charlie P races back to his apartment. But even there, in the soft bosom of his home, his complaining only starts in earnest, even if, especially if, he has no one to complain to, or about, but himself.

AUTOBIOGRAPHY

Removing the ink from his pen, the lead from his pencil, Charlie P commences to write his autobiography, setting down the most important events of his life: His birth and death, bar mitzvah and baptism, all his coming-of-age stories, as well as his great adventures, romances, marriages and divorces, and, of course, his career breakthrough. Nor does he forget the first homerun he hit at age five; his first argument, confrontation and fight; the first ballgame, circus, and sweet sixteen party he attended. Nor the first serious conversation he ever had lasting through the wee hours under a streetlamp with a childhood friend.

Stretching his memory to the limit, surpassing even his own high expectations, Charlie P records and documents all the facts and figures, dates and events, of his life. One day soon, next week, tomorrow, in fact this very moment, he begins reading through the manuscript pages he so faithfully and painstakingly recorded.

But, as only to be expected, the more he reads the less he takes in. Not only is it impossible for him to distinguish between one event and another, but nothings there. The pages are blank. Not his personal life or professional life; not close encounters of the intimate kind or worldly experiences—his entire life's history is null and void. According to these pages as told by this autobiographer, Charlie P doesn't exist.

Shedding bitter tears at first, Charlie P soon composes himself. It's no great tragedy, he says. In fact there's much to take pride in. Unlike other autobiographers, at least he didn't distort, deceive, exaggerate and dissemble. He's got his facts and figures right. His blank pages literally and figuratively, realistically and symbolically, render a true and faithful translation of his life. Truth is one might go so far as to say that he might be the first autobiographer who not only had the courage to truly look in the mirror, but also not to leave out a single detail of his life.

WHEN YOU THINK ABOUT IT...

Twice in his life Charlie P has been in love. Once when he was young, another time approaching old age. Both love affairs were the result of coincidence. No amount of planning, calculation, deliberation, internet surfing, or even a good old-fashioned matchmaker, Charlie P concluded, could substantially increase his chances at finding love. For that reason, as well as a thousand others, Charlie P never leaves his apartment. Never goes to bars, lounges, parties, alpine ski resorts, the Cannes film festival (and he's in the "biz") or yachting on the Riviera. No, he doesn't believe in blind dates, forced intrigues, midnight rendezvous or anything of the kind.

But that doesn't mean Charlie P has given up on love. On the contrary, he's as optimistic as ever. The fact that he's 218 years old has little to do with it. Some day, sooner or later, when least expected, the woman of his dreams will come into his life. "It's just you can't predict such things," says Charlie P. "But, still, it can happen at any time."

Five years ago, for instance, the telephone rang but due to poor hearing he didn't answer it in time. And then, not more than a few years ago, there was a knock on his door, but because of rheumatoid arthritis, in the time it took him to find his walker and open the door, whoever it was had already disappeared. "That won't happen again," said Charlie P. "Let's face it. How many chances does a man get. Especially one my age."

For the last year now Charlie P has remained steadfast. Ever on the alert. The next time opportunity struck, he'd be ready. And so he was: Last night, while watching television, the phone rang and there was a knock on the door simultaneously. But whether it be old age, senility, or merely confusion, in the excitement of attempting to do two things at once, he had a severe stroke and died. "Well, maybe it's for the best," said Charlie P. "After all, nobody can say I didn't have my chances. I've been in love two times already and as we all know three times and you're out. But still, this doesn't mean I'm giving up. On the contrary, I'm more optimistic than ever. There's a whole new world to explore out there, and unless I'm mistaken, nobody yet has come back to tell us what's on the other side."

COUNTING

Charlie P cannot stop counting. He counts the stars in the constellations, but doesn't see them. Counts the freckles, moles and soft spots on a woman's body, but doesn't touch them. Counts the children laughing and smiling in the playground, but doesn't laugh or smile back. Counts apples and oranges, mother-of-pearl cuff links, chrome-legged formica tables, long fluked floors. Counts the motes of dust levitating in mid-air, the faces that make up the world's population, pewter toy soldiers from childhood; and even making concessions for an uphill climb, the variousness of the human face, the possibility of error and miscalculation, Charlie P never stops counting. All are worthy of his survey. No one can accuse him of favoritism, preconceived notions, being petty or small-minded, mean spirited or intolerant. When counting Charlie P is above it all. Everlasting. Eternal. Immortal. But, of course, immortality has its price. Exacts its toll. And if that means sacrificing a few of the world's treasures along the way such as not living his life—so be it. It's a small price to pay. He has no choice. For Charlie P, counting and living are one and the same.

Fortunate for him the earth is bounteous and plentiful. Its flux and flow unceasing, like the diurnal rhythms of day and night, the undulations of the sea. If it's not pimples on people's noses it's the hairs on their heads. Charlie P has always something to count.

But then why is he frowning? Why his apparent state of gloom? Surely it can't be, whether by coincidence or design, that bald heads are coming back into fashion nowadays. Just last night alone he counted over three hundred-and-fifty Friar Tuck crowns. And that only between 14th Street and Times Square. In only a few paltry hours. That's a formidable enough tally by any standard. And he's confident he can do even better tonight. So what is it then? Why?...Oh, so that's it. The fellow who just passed him on the corner without a nose. And even worse, the one further down the street, creeping ever so stealthily along the shadows of that crumbling wall, without a head. Who knows how many miles he'll have to trek to come upon his kind again. What can he do. Stop counting! The very thought sends chills down his spine. But being an adaptable fellow, resilient as the day is long, Charlie P is already conjuring up alternatives, variations on the theme. Lo and behold, he has it! Tomorrow he'll go to a hardware store and purchase an ax. Then, tomorrow evening—he can't wait. He's already counting the hours, minutes, seconds—in the nocturnal hours, when the rest of us are asleep, the streets near empty and deserted, it's then he'll take his lowly sojourn and whence coming upon another solitary figure like himself he'll commence to chop off...

At last check, Charlie P's head count had reached 294 and he's still counting.

At Charlie P's Man of the Year Award Ceremony he was asked what motivated him to accomplish what he did: To discover what can't be, but is; make the infinite finite; the ineffable into a number; and once again, at long last, turn appearance into reality. Thanks to him people are talking again, stones dancing, agélaste's laughing"*, water has remained wet and babies continue to cry. Charlie P gave the question its due regard. Not as much as a wrinkle or bead of sweat appeared on his brow before answering: "You got anything better to do with your spare time?"

---

* Agélaste (Rabelais): comes from the Greek and means a man who does not laugh, who has no sense of humor

AFFAIRS IN ORDER

When told that the end was near, that he best get his affairs in order, Charlie P responded: "It's about time!" and immediately started packing. Now, what should he take with him? The ocean he won't need, nor the beaches and sand, with his thin legs he never looked good in a bathing suit anyway. Nor the lush greenery of the park. Despite the fact that his terrace had a panoramic view of the park and New York City skyline, he never noticed it. In fact all vistas and views, flora and fauna, went unnoticed under his gaze. Whether it be the blue-black sky, snow-peaked mountain top, emerald green sea, or even the singularly special features of each and every human face he set his eyes upon during the course of his life.

As for arms, hands and legs, other than for switching channels on his remote, or taking a walk around the block, no need for them where he was going, lying in a pinewood box six feet under with eyes closed for eternity. And the same goes for his feelings, large and small, joy and grief, not that he had any; or his family, loving wife of fifty years, mother of his children, besides having none, he lost them long ago, along with his youth, PM-2 four-fingered baseball glove, old man Pollack's chocolate malteds, egg creams and long stick pretzels; as well as his first kiss (and last); first sexual experience (and last); first apartment (and last); first job (and last); first love (no, not last, for better or worse the Bulgarian harpist counts for something): and many, many years of work, toil, boredom, loneliness, hardship, neurosis, therapy, and that's not even counting retirement years, pension, social security, old age, illness, dying and death.

And so in accord with the maxim that you can't take it with you, or better, what you never had you won't miss, Charlie P packs his bags, or better, packs it in, and neither gathering up or leaving behind anything of value, his life either unfinished or not yet begun, makes ready to leave this world as he entered it. Truth is he can't wait. Perhaps now his real life will begin.

MAKING UP FOR LOST TIME

Determined not to be late for his appointment this afternoon, Charlie P rises early and with a burst of energy rarely seen in him, races off as if to make up for lost time.

He finds a woman, gets married, has a baby and nurses him not with mother's milk but his own. He builds a business and a home, reads all the books he's never read, wears all the clothes he's never worn, and for the first time in his life leaves his apartment, travels, takes a vacation.

But it's getting late, he'd better make haste. There's still much to do, little time to do it. This is one appointment he can't afford to miss. For once he's resolved to finish what he started.

He goes shopping, not for essentials and staples, but for all those luxury items he's craved all his life but for one reason or another never allowed himself to buy. He visits his mother, his in-laws, has a lunch made up solely of fatty foods and high cholesterol with a cherry on top.

But now it is late, he's definitely fallen behind. There's always the possibility that they'll start or leave without him.

Miss this opportunity and he won't get another. But no, what is he thinking—this is one show that can't go on without him.

He tells off his business partner and boss, his girlfriend and mistress, wife and kids, lifetime neighbor whom up to now he's never spoken a word to; and obtaining special permission, a VIP pass—if not a national emergency then a personal one—he visits his President and tells him off too; as well as the little brat next door and the doorman in the hallway, always ready with the snide remarks and the last word.

At last, his chores done, having crowded into a few short hours all that he's put off for a lifetime, he chooses a suit appropriate for the occasion, hails a cab, and arrives at the funeral home just in time to hear his eulogy. He thanks the rabbi and priest for their kind words, pays them as well as the undertaker and gravediggers for their services, steps into his pinewood box, makes himself comfortable, and with the gramophone grinding out a last golden oldie according to his instructions, he heaves a deep sigh, and says "I'm ready."

DEAD OR ALIVE?

L et's face it. There was one stupendous, magical, controversial event in Charlie P's life. His birth. After that...Nothing! To be sure, there are others in the same situation. But at least they are bolstered by hope. They have the future to look forward to. Their time will come. It was with this heavy burden on his back that Charlie P sat in the Waiting Room. The Waiting Room was full. He had to wait a lifetime. Finally the good doctor came round and set about to work on Charlie P. Removing a lung, kidney, his heart, arms and legs. Then pronouncing him dead. Next!

But just because a man is not living, does that really mean that he is dead? asks Charlie P. Maybe the doctor is right after all, but how can one be sure? In the name of exactitude, unqualified thoroughness, and being complete, Charlie P pinches himself. Palpates himself. Hard to say. He has no strong opinion. Any way you look at it he feels the same now as before.

Charlie P concludes: This is one time his experience is as valid as the next person's. Just like the doctor's pronouncement, and throughout the entirety of his life, dead or alive—it's always been a gray area for him. He was never certain about being alive when alive, so why should he be any more certain about being dead when dead.

SO WHAT'S THE ANSWER?

Plug pulled, time of death announced, death certificate signed, pronounced dead, Charlie P peers up and in a voice trembling with fear yet firm with resolve asks the doctor: "So what's the answer?"

HAVEN'T YOU NOTICED?

His rent hadn't been paid, his mail had piled up, and no garbage had been left by the back service elevator alcove for much too long when the doorman, Big George, and the super, after knocking on Charlie P's door and receiving no response, opened it with a passkey. To their surprise, for the first time in their memory, both men noticed a beatific smile on Charlie P's face.

"We're just checking up on you," said the super.

"But tell me," intervened Big George. "What's the matter? I can't ever recall seeing you look so happy before."

"I'm finally at peace with myself," said Charlie P. "Haven't you noticed? I died six months ago."

BEST BE PREPARED

When still quite young Charlie P had a pinewood box made for him. Custom built to fit the contours of his body, it allowed for shrinkage in his declining years, as well as taking into consideration mold, mildew, rot and decay that inevitably would come from lying on his back for years on end; not to mention the ineluctable dissolution and eating away of his flesh by worms and such when six feet under.

But as he was still here with us, Charlie P had a dolly with skating wheels attached to the coffin's bottom. From that time on, as regular as meals on wheels delivered to homebound senior citizens daily, Charlie P was never to be seen without his box on wheels. Wherever he went, whatever he did, whether checking e-mail in the mornings or dodging crashing buildings in the afternoons, whether suffering the torments of unrequited love, watching wars on television, or just taking a coffee break, the pinewood box went with him. "After all," said Charlie P, "I'm not getting any younger, sooner or later that grim reaper will come knocking on my door, scythe in hand—Best be prepared!"

Prophet and doomsayer, for once in his life Charlie P was correct. On his 218th birthday he died. And like so many of his clan, was laid to rest. But despite his good intentions, due diligence and scrupulous preparation, Charlie P was proven as wrong about death as life. In fact, as he tells all who visit his gravesite, death's vastly overrated. It's not nearly all that he expected it to be. For not only does he still lie in that self-same pinewood box, but between friends and relatives arguing and confronting each other over estate settlements and wills, wives and mistresses over petty jealousies and rivalries, sons and daughters over unresolved feelings, and former business partners left holding the bag, it's really not that different from the chaos and mayhem, violence and enmity, he experienced in life. In fact, in some ways, even worse. He no longer has his wheels.

SERIOUS DOUBTS

All his life Charlie P looked forward to his burial day. But when the day finally came, he was profoundly disappointed with his new accommodations. So much so that from the moment he moved in, he had serious doubts about making it his permanent dwelling place.

Not only was it cold and dank down there, with no heat, light or running water, but he could hardly breathe. There was no fresh air. And certainly not enough space to move around, maybe 58-and-a-half cubic feet in all. That combined with the fact that there was no view, only the four walls, nothing to do, and nobody but himself to keep him company—what a bore—and worst of all, there was no end in sight. He was there for the duration. Was this what he had waited for all his life?

Not one to take anything lying down, Charlie P took action immediately. With dirt raining down on him from the grave-diggers' shovels, the rabbi and priest still hovering above, Charlie P looked up. With a sob welling in his throat, the weariness of defeat in his voice, Charlie P addressed the rabbi and priest, making certain not to prefer one to the other. He made a mistake, he said. Calculated wrongly. There's no way this was going to work out. It's not at all what he expected it would be. He understood what he was asking was highly irregular, that it was already late in the game, but, with their permission, would they mind if he did the whole thing from start to finish, especially his life, over again?

Richard Kalich

Charlie P whined and complained all his life. He experienced nothing but problems and hardship. On his deathbed he had but one request. He asked to be buried with his face down. His wish granted, already in his grave, he uttered his last words: "I'm glad it's finally over," he said, and then, for the first time in his life, though nobody could see him, he smiled.

FROM THE AUTHOR

For this author, writing a novel is always an act of Self-overcoming. Overcoming my very deep and life-long terror of art. The demand to delve so deeply inside myself that only in the very act of writing/creating the work do I have a semblance of what will surface.

My first published novel, *The Nihilesthete*, gestated inside me for at least five years. All I knew about it was an enduring metaphoric image of a man hovering over a limbless being seated in a wheelchair trying to paint. Finally, finding the courage to write the novel, surprisingly, miraculously, in a very real sense the novel wrote itself, waking me every night between 2 a.m. and 4 a.m. and revealing itself with images. Notebook at my bedside, I took dictation and transcribed and edited the following day. After writing for three months I collapsed. Two thirds into the novel I could not write another line. *The Nihilesthete* "cost" me more than any other novel I've since written. In retrospect it cost me the accumulated pain, frustration and powerlessness of the first forty years of my life. Nine months later I went back and completed the novel in an additional two months. I created the last third from the neck up. Cerebrally, if not viscerally. Nearly inexplicably there is no break in the stylistic or tonal flow of the work.

Charlie P. was inspired by a friend who has for a lifetime lived his life by not living it. The same, my twin brother, the novelist Robert Kalich, says could be said about myself. Obsessing over the theme for years, I finally got down to the writing. Realizing the subject was so deeply ingrained in me, I made the conscious and deliberate decision to invent a marginally new form. And, so, using myself as a prism, rather than plan, cognize or plot a novel, I would wake every morning (two and a half months) and write whatever came to mind, knowing – hoping – that the scribblings would all be filtered through my obsession: *Charlie P.* Somehow it worked. No matter how far I strayed from palpable logic and causality the prime character "lives his life by not living it."

Penthouse F: Once again, I suffered through the longest gestation period, virtually a lifetime. I first saw this novel the day I finished *The Nihilesthete*... a man observing with surveillance cameras a boy and girl hidden away in a darkened space. Taking notes for more than a decade, I scribbled down a virtually unintelligible first draft and mailed it to a writer friend in Europe. Though encouraged by his response, I still couldn't find the courage to write the book. Again, finally, after at least twenty-five years of gestation, thought, note taking and obsession, getting past a bad love affair, a new approach found me and after three and a half months I had my novel. Different than I had originally imagined, but in essence the same.

Richard Kalich, March 3, 2014

Made in the USA
San Bernardino, CA
30 March 2017